FORGOTTEN KINGDO

· BOOK C

ISABELLA KHALIDI

BOOKS BY ISABELLA KHALIDI
(DARK FANTASY ROMANCE)

FORGOTTEN KINGDOM CHRONICLES
The Snows of Nissa
The Storms of Fury
The Sands of Titans
The Plains of Wrath

UPCOMING RELEASES
Buried Souls
(A Dark Fairy Tale Retelling of Goldilocks and the Three Bears)
To Claim a Silver Curse

BOOKS BY ISABELLA KHALIDI WRITING AS BELLA DURAND (MONSTER ROMANCE)

WICKED CREATURES TALES
Roses for the Damned
Lilies for the Cursed
Poppies for the Hunted
Daisies for the Broken
Tulips for the Chained

Copyright © Isabella Khalidi 2023
2nd edition
Cover Art © Isabella Khalidi 2023

Isabella Khalidi asserts the moral right to be identified as the author of this work.

All rights reserved.
No part of this publication may be reproduced or transmitted in any form or by any means, electronic or mechanical, including photocopying, recording, or any information storage or retrieval system, without prior permission in writing from the author, except for the use of brief quotations in a book review.

This is a work of fiction. Names, places, events and incidents are either the products of the author's imagination or used fictitiously. Any resemblance to actual persons, living or dead, is purely coincidental.

To all the ladies that like their men complex, intense, and loaded with spice.

AUTHOR'S NOTE & CONTENT WARNING

Series contain strong language, explicit sexual scenes, scenes of violence and death. It is intended for mature audiences only.

Dear Reader,

This is a dark book and not a sweet love story. Its characters are flawed and scarred, leading to many questionable and potentially immoral decisions as they fight their way through life. The men are possessive and overbearing, while the women are strong and unashamed; they do not fear to ask for what they desire, nor do they run away from temptation. If you are not a fan of spice, then this is not the book for you. Here, lines are crossed and reason is stretched, where the human touch is an absolute necessity for the functioning of its characters.

For those of you that love an intricate plot that's heavy on the steam, I hope you enjoy this book. Oh, and don't forget to stay well hydrated.

Your truly,
Isabella

KINGDOM OF TYROS

King Fergal Vilkas
Queen Amelie Vilkas
Crown Prince Cian Vilkas
Prince Edan Vilkas
Prince Valen Vilkas
Princess Leila Vilkas

General Cathal Ragnar
Lieutenant Axel Fendergar
Lieutenant Rhun Brayan
Captain Kane Maelys
Spy Master Bror Lovas

Captain Moira
Duna Damaris
Petra Da'Nyla
Lir Killik
Kala Maelys

KINGDOM OF NISSA

King Lucan Raidon
Crown Prince Madir Raidon
Princess Roesia Raidon

General Gavin Broxon

Captain York Boe

Master of Arms
Doran Algernon

Royal Personal Guard
Mikella Corr

Lady in
Waiting Epona

KINGDOM OF BAQAR

King Basel Achaz

Crown Prince Faiz Achaz
Prince Kalad Achaz
Princess Arela Achaz

Captain Borvo Ballaam

Royal Guard Adio Dakaarai
Royal Guard Miraz Ashmul

Head Attendant Sonia

Monk Aarav
Monk Bezu

PROLOGUE

The drums beat a steady staccato rhythm, resonating across the once desolate vast plains now overflowing with both man and beast. Vultures circled above the large mass of moving destruction, biding their time, for there was sure to be an excess of carrion for all to keep them well sated for at least a fortnight.

Standing on top of a hill not too far away, backed up by the shadows of the dense woods, she watched as a solitary figure emerged from the violent horde of clashing leathers and steel, pulling himself up onto an angular grey boulder.

As if summoned, the sun suddenly emerged from the otherwise ebony sky, blazing a trail of magnificent white light to the mortals below, illuminating the armor clad warrior.

Movement ceased, weapons frozen in midair. Not a sound was heard, not a word was uttered. As if the earth itself was holding its breath; as if time itself had stopped.

Like a beacon in the dark, the warrior lifted his obsidian sword, his heavy shield pressed tightly against his powerful body, its ominous insignia burning bright like a brand, reflecting the brilliant light from the sky onto the awaiting throng below.

Jolting, she gasped, realization striking her like a bolt of lightning. As if by reflex, her right arm jerked up and behind her intricately embossed galea, the spear in her hand poised for the attack.

As if on cue, the warrior turned his equally magnificent black and gold crested helmet toward her, his gaze piercing through the tension filled air.

Their eyes locked.

The earth sighed.

And all hell broke loose.

CHAPTER

1

She heard it before she saw it.

The deer was quite loud and non discreet for an animal of its size and caliber, its species well known for their otherwise vigilant and highly alert nature. Duna observed it for a few moments, deciding that the specimen currently grazing the forest floor a few feet in front of her hiding place was most likely a doe, judging by the lack of antlers and the slightly rounded top of its head between its ears.

Slowly pulling an arrow out of her quiver, Duna placed it across the middle of the bow with the bowstring in the arrow's nock. Holding the bow at its center with her left hand, she drew the arrow and bowstring with the other while simultaneously aiming for the unsuspecting deer.

Just as she was about to loose the draw, a sudden snapping of a nearby branch echoed through the silent woods, frightening the nimble doe which then bolted away into the early morning light.

Duna cursed, angry with herself for not seizing the moment when she had the chance. She would have to be quick in capturing a replacement for her lost game if she wanted to get back to the village in time before she set off to work at the local inn.

Her grandmother would already be waiting for her for sure by now, as she always does, silently reprimanding her for, once again, going off into the woods all by herself at the break of dawn.

There have been rumors of bandits in the area for a few weeks back now. Duna, however, was not worried about encountering one, for her village was small and bland, consisting mainly of lowly farmers whose daily wages amounted to almost nothing in comparison to the wealthier villages stationed closer to the capital, Scythia, in her home Kingdom of Tyros.

No, bandits were the furthest thing from her mind as Duna Damaris contemplated on settling on a rabbit or returning to her small cottage and her elderly grandmother without their weekly meat rations.

God, damn it. I'll have to be quick. Maybe she won't notice me gone.

She snorted. *Highly unlikely.*

Sighing, Duna picked up her packed quiver and aging bow, slinging them both back over her tired shoulders. Lost in deep thought she failed to hear the breaking of branches behind her and the increasingly louder shouting coming from the direction of her home.

A moment too late, she registered the commotion just as she was about to emerge from the thick foliage of the forest.

Blazing white and bright orange intermingled with angry red flames, dancing on the rooftops and dried up land surrounding the huts and run down cottages of the villagers. People were screaming, running absentmindedly and erratically in and out of burning buildings, as the fires engulfed not only their humble homes but the fragile lives of their loved ones.

Duna flew as fast as her legs would take her.

Stumbling as she went, barely holding her pounding heart in her seizing chest, she begged the gods of old and new and whoever else might be listening that day to spare the life of her grandmother.

She was Duna's only remaining family, her only safe haven and tether to this miserable world. Her parents had died when she was only three years old, succumbing to a disease of the intestines which even to this day had no known cure. Seeing as she had no siblings and no other living relatives, her already struggling grandmother had taken her in and cared for her since that somber day twenty years ago.

It had been Duna's mission ever since she was able to take care of herself to pay back her grandmother for all the unconditional love and care that she had shown her in those dark and trying times in the only way she knew how - by likewise taking care of the elderly woman, working any and all jobs that would hire her, no matter the wage – hunting in the woods for their meals when even the long tedious hours at work wore her down.

Duna had never complained, never shown a miniscule sign of dissatisfaction or regret for all of the sacrifices that she gladly put forth every day for the last decade.

Her grandmother was a kind woman, a hard working human being. She painstakingly labored the small patch of land around their weathered cottage, growing a trifling amount of vegetables and fruits for their basic needs, selling the nuts and wildflowers she gathered once a fortnight at the market of a nearby town. To say that she gave her strength and hope was an understatement.

So, Duna prayed. With all of her young, naive heart and unstained soul, she prayed.

Little did she know that the gods were absent that day.

Her home was in ashes. The half rotting roof collapsed in, the heavy wooden beams blackened and toppled over each other in a haphazard way. The windows paneless, the glass in a million little shards on the scorched ground below. Dense smoke drifted to the sky above and across the decaying grass, engulfing and suffocating Duna in its toxic fumes.

Coughing violently while hopelessly attempting to inhale oxygen into her burning lungs, she frantically searched the remains for the one person whose face would obliterate all fears running rampant through her panic-stricken mind.

Seconds turned into agonizing minutes, minutes into torturous hours, and yet there was not a single trace of the elderly woman. Could she have escaped the punishing inferno? Perhaps her worrisome grandmother had grown tired of waiting and had finally gone in search of her while she was still out hunting.

A fragile bud of hope bloomed in Duna's chest.

Gods, please, let her be alive.

It is said that hope dies last. That all else in one's life can be irrevocably lost but that hope will always, even then, ultimately prevail.

Duna might have believed that, had she not stumbled upon the scorched remains of a body in their once flourishing vegetable garden. She might have even held on to that feeble belief while she visually examined what little remained of that said body for any clear signs of the person's identity that would console her breaking heart.

She would have continued to naively hope that, against all odds, her grandmother was still alive, surely searching for Duna as Duna was searching for her. Had it not been for the small coin shaped silver pendant hanging from the disfigured neck, she would have spent the rest of her days in perpetual pursuit for the woman.

But, alas, Fate does not follow the rules of the heart. It does not listen to reason or want. It forges its own path, interweaving an infinite amount of variables, each thread accompanied by its own immeasurable number of finalities.

Wheezing like a terminally ill pulmonary patient, her airways restricted by the sudden shock of her discovery, Duna collapsed as if struck onto the hard ground. Closing her eyes, she let the realization of her grim reality set in.

What madness was this? How could a life that was breathing and thriving just mere hours ago suddenly cease to exist?

It should not be possible. Yet, there, just a few feet away from her, her grandmother's lifeless body lay motionless, the evidence of the damning fire clear as day.

Duna opened her eyes, staring up into the clear blue sky, the sun blazing warm and bright as if mocking her in her misery.

A single salty tear fell from her right eye, followed shortly by another one from the left. Soon the increasing pressure of the rapid onslaught of emotions was too much, overwhelming Duna with grief and agony and rage. The flood gates that held her sanity broke, her entire body violently convulsing.

She wanted to die; wanted to close her eyes and remain unmoving until her body turned to stone, until weeds sprouted beneath and around her petrified body and animals started grazing the lands once more.

It was not meant to be, for that treacherous organ in Duna's chest cavity was beating relentlessly, refusing to succumb to such emotional abuse.

Inhaling a lungful of much needed air, she sat up and looked around at her darkening surroundings, becoming acutely aware that nighttime would soon be upon her, and that she not only had no shelter against the cold autumn evening but her grandmother's dead body still lay where she had accidentally stumbled upon it that life altering morning. She could not leave it like that, no matter the barely recognizable state of it.

Duna owed her grandmother that much, at least.

She would have to be quick if she wanted to bury what remained of the body, for the light from the sky was diminishing rapidly and she had no ulterior light source to illuminate the ground while she worked.

Bolting up, Duna ran to the shed that was by some small mercy still intact and found the shovel that she would need to accomplish her task. She worked without pause, digging until the blisters on her hands bled, not registering the pain that laced her straining arms.

Each strike of the shovel was like a strike to her aching heart. Duna would remember those sounds until she drew her last breath in this unforgiving world.

As the last rays of the dying day finally faded and stars replaced the red and orange evening sky, Duna swore an oath to the Waning Moon. Never again would she be helpless, never again would she allow someone she cared about to be hurt.

As the fates would have it, Duna blamed herself for this ultimate tragedy. For if she had not been out hunting that unusually warm autumn morning, she would have been able to detect the fire in time to get her grandmother away from the furious flames to safety.

If she had been at home like she was supposed to have been, her grandmother would have still been alive.

No, Duna could not forgive herself.

She would faithfully carry the memory of that terrible day like a brand across her blackening heart.

CHAPTER 2

Five years later.

"General, it's time."

Cathal stood on his expansive terra cotta tile covered terrace overlooking the blossoming royal gardens, his back turned to the equally grand suite from which his lieutenant general's voice had come from. He didn't particularly care for flowers, but then again no one had asked him for his preference when he moved into the palace all those years ago.

Five long years, to be exact.

He would have much rather preferred to be close to, if not literally on, the actual official training grounds, where countless soldiers from the kingdom's formidable armies vigilantly trained from the break of dawn until the Sun went down over the horizon.

"General."

He sighed. "Yes, I heard you. I will be down shortly, you may leave now." Waiting for the sound of the closing door, Cathal inwardly frowned, not knowing the root of his agitation.

When the door had still not shut, he abruptly spun around, his eyes resting on the Lieutenant who was standing in the open terrace doorway. "What is it, Axel?" he growled. "You are testing my patience. And for fuck's sake, drop the formalities, there is no one here but the two of us."

"Fine." Approaching him with his hands clasped behind his back, the male looked more like a stern father who was about to deal a verbal lashing to his imbecile son than the much younger stoic warrior that he was.

Intimidating at over six and a half feet tall with a broad muscular frame, Axel Fendergar was the epitome of the merciless ever imposing lieutenant that sent their enemies running for their lives.

As he was currently off duty, he was clad in a moonlight blue linen shirt that was casually tucked into crisp black pants and matching black leather lace up boots. His sleeves were rolled up to his elbows, straining over bulging arms, revealing the endless, intricate dark runes that adorned his caramel skin. Thick, grave eyebrows rested on top of piercing blue eyes. High cheekbones and full pink lips resided under a slightly crooked nose. His wavy, dirty blond, shoulder length hair was casually tied back at the nape, a few stray strands loosely hanging out of place, framing his strong, square jaw which was in turn covered in a neatly trimmed full beard.

An old, two inch, ragged edged scar that started just above his brow bone divided his left eyebrow in half, completing the unnervingly massive warrior's rugged appearance.

"Everyone is already at the ball room, *everyone* including the King and your betrothed." Schooling his features, Axel leaned on the heavily decorated stone balustrade, resting on his elbows and forearms, clasping his hands in front of him. "What the hell is wrong with you, Cathal? You are acting like a complete idiot." He sighed. "Are you having second thoughts?"

Cathal froze, holding his breath. Was that what this feeling was? "Absolutely not. You know how much I care about Leila."

"Yes, well, *caring* for her and wanting to marry her are not one and the same. The first does not always lead to the second."

"It is expected." Cathal straightened, lowering his voice, "I will not back down from my duty." He turned to the gardens below, watching an enthusiastic mockingbird hop from one branch to the next, chirping away on the breeze. "Besides, I love her. She is my soulmate. There is no other woman I would rather spend the rest of my days with."

"Soulmate, fated mated, one true love – whatever you want to call it – that is not the point right now."

Cathal was getting frustrated again. He hated that he sounded so angry but there was no helping it, "We have known each other for almost two decades, Axel. Two *decades*. We grew up together. Laughed and cried together when the–"

"Who are you trying to convince, me or you?"

"She knows me, damn it!" he snapped. He needed to end this. Now. "Understands me. There is not a single soul in this kingdom who I trust more with my life–"

"Cathal–"

"Enough!" he barked, fists clenching at his sides. "I am not going to stand here and listen to this crap." Leaving a stern looking Axel on the terrace, Cathal retreated into his somber bedchamber, mentally shaking off the foreboding feeling that kept nagging at him.

What the hell was happening to him? He wanted to crawl out of his own skin.

The last time that he had felt this level of complete and utter helplessness was exactly five years ago to the day, right before the King had ordered him to move into these very same rooms at the request of his youngest child and only daughter, Princess Leila Vilkas.

There is no going back now. You love her. That little fucker, with his idiotic questions, asking him who he was trying to convince.

Checking himself one last time in the unwieldy oval mirror before opening the heavy oak door, Cathal finally emerged from his hiding place and made his way down to the decorated ball room.

He had been purposely avoiding that same grand space for the past few days, going out of his way to find alternative routes, using which would sometimes take him almost double the time than it normally would to reach his chambers on the second floor of the elaborate palace.

He would do anything, just so that he wouldn't have to go near the damned thing.

As it was, Cathal had more than enough obligations to keep him occupied. He was the Commander General of the Tyrossian Royal Army, and at the ripe age of thirty eight he was also the youngest General to ever lead His Majesty's armies in the long, gruesome history of the southern kingdom. He took his role very seriously; the safety of the Crown and the Royal family as well as the people of the Kingdom of Tyros were, after all, his responsibility.

All the reason why no one ever questioned him when he silently stole out before the break of dawn while the rest of the palace was still sound asleep, nor did anyone find it strange when Cathal faithfully returned every night with the Moon hanging high in the midnight sky.

He exhaled a strained breath.

Cathal loathed these gatherings with a passion. Could not see the point of them.

The women were always overdressed in unnecessary layers of silks and satins while simultaneously being borderline obscene in their choice of gowns, as if competing with each other on who could attract the most attention from the disgusting males in attendance. They hid their actual features under a heavy mask of paints and kohl, leaving the observer to wonder what their real faces looked like under all that grime.

The men, on the other hand, always acted ridiculous, making a laughing stock of themselves, filling their already enlarged stomachs with unnecessary amounts of alcohol and foods that were difficult to digest.

He did not understand the appeal of such a lifestyle, not because Cathal did not consume alcohol - which he did, regularly, and not because he could not imagine looking down at himself and not being able to see his cock - which he was extremely fond of.

For Cathal, his body was his shrine. A deadly weapon which he honed from an early age, painstakingly training for hours on end each and every day and night, giving his all every time and expecting the same level of devotion from his men.

It was grueling work. The level of discipline that was required in the life of a Tyrossian warrior was not for the faint hearted. That was why the Kingdom of Tyros had one of the deadliest armies on this side of the Continent. Not because of their numbers, which were rivaled only by the equally formidable armies of the Kingdom of Nissa. No, their strength lay in their stealth and resilience; in their mastery of every possible weapon known to man.

And what weapons we have, indeed.

General Cathal Ragnar did not care for appearances, for they were for the shallow and superficial. He valued strength, integrity, courage. Loyalty. A keen mind that could cut a man quicker than a sharp-edged blade ever could.

All qualities which these pompous asses currently overindulging in sweet, aging wine miserably lacked.

Approaching the large ornate table at the head of the impressive ball room, Cathal noticed that King Fergal Vilkas was indeed displeased. A substantial man in his early sixties, he sat with his back straight, his crown of hammered bronze resting proudly on his head of graying hair, looking out over the gyrating throng of courtiers.

Looking at him now, Cathal realized that he never really took the time to appreciate the craftsmanship that had gone into the legendary headpiece of the King of Tyros.

The crown itself was actually an open circlet surmounted by ten extremely sharp obsidian spikes in the shape of wolf claws. Affixed on the front was an elongated dire wolf head with a pair of matching obsidian gemstones in place of its eyes. Surrounding the menacing insignia were intricately carved ancient runes. It was a masterpiece in its own right.

The King finally noticed him, waving Cathal over to his side. "General Ragnar, I am glad that you could make it to your own betrothal celebrations. And not a moment too soon, I'm afraid, for I was inclined to send my daughter in search of a replacement for you."

Cathal nodded his head ever so slightly, muttering obscenities to himself. "Your Majesty, I was detained at the training grounds."

"Ah, yes, what news do you have on the recent raids?"

"It is the same as always, Your Majesty. The bandits come sweeping in at the break of dawn while people are still in bed or just getting ready for their day, rendering them unprepared and at a risk of being robbed or worse yet, killed." Cathal paused, contemplating whether this was the appropriate time to further the subject. He was already on thin ice here.

Fuck it.

Lowering his voice so that only the King and the select few surrounding them could hear he said, "There has been an increasing number of said robberies in the past month. The raiders are getting more daring, attacking not only at dawn but rather at all times of the day now. A select few are using arson as a means to threaten the already scared villagers, going as far as setting their meager lands and collapsing homes on fire while people still reside in them." He paused, sudden anger overtaking him, "It would seem that our missing culprits have returned."

King Fergal balked, turning red in the face. "You cannot be serious, General. Those men have long been apprehended and hanged for their treacherous crimes."

Cathal refused to back down, "Two of them had escaped, as you well remember. They were never captured."

"I remember no such thing, General." Clenching the solid arms of his great oak chair, his gaze never wavering from the impressive warrior still standing in front of him, Fergal continued, "And seeing as I am the King," he focused on Cathal, "my word is the law."

That arrogant, pretentious, ignorant bastard.

"These are no ordinary attacks," Cathal fumed, inwardly restraining himself. "The raiders are being led by the same two men that had burned the entirety of an impoverished village along with every single one of its inhabitants all those years ago close to our border with Nissa. There was no such second instance before or after that tragic event five years ago. Not a single one. There is no other explanation for the fiery raids that have started up in the north."

"Enough!" Fergal shot up from his chair, ready to combust. Coming within an arms length in front of an outwardly unbothered Cathal he growled, "I will not have talk of such nonsense, General, especially not today when we are celebrating the betrothal of my daughter," he leaned in, "and your future wife."

That fucking prick. "How can I ever forget?" Seething, Cathal turned his head to the side and ignoring the reddening male, finally acknowledged the only person for which he was willing to put up with the insufferable man. "Princess," he smiled, trying with all his might to calm himself, "dance with me."

Princess Leila blushed, her pale skin tinted ever so slightly by that wonderfully pink hue, "I thought you'd never ask, General."

Taking her slender, silk covered arm and tucking it in the crook of his strong, leather clad one, Cathal led them to the center of the overflowing dance floor. They stopped, eyes locked on each other, her delicate fingers intertwining with his rough ones. His large hand went to her petite waist, pulling her close to him.

Leila rested her free hand on his shoulder, lifting her head to look up at the handsome warrior that she had loved ever since she was a young girl.

Slowly moving to the music, bodies barely an inch apart, Cathal leaned in and whispered in her ear, "Leila," he started, "I'm sorry."

He was an ass. She did not deserve him. Or rather, he was not worthy of her. A man could only dream of such a woman, and yet, here she was in his worthless arms.

"You have nothing to be sorry for," she said, resting her soft cheek on his broad chest. "I understand that you have an army to lead, that your soldiers come first," she paused, inhaling his musky scent, "that they will always come first."

If you only knew. Closing his eyes, he rested his chin on top of her head, her soft silver waves caressing his skin, "I do not deserve you." Indeed.

"I am not angry with you, Cathal." She peppered light kisses under his chin, "I know what you are.." along his jaw line, "know what it means to be with a man like you. The sacrifices that one has to make..." moving up to his ear, she whispered, "I do not care. You are worth it. Your love is worth it."

Cathal clenched his jaw, a new wave of guilt washing over him.

Still whispering in his ear she said, "Let me make you feel good, let me take away your worries." Fisting his shirt in her small hands, she pulled him even closer to herself, "I've missed you."

His arms went around her slight waist, his large, calloused hands splaying wide across the small of her back, tightening his hold on her. Ignoring the gawking courtiers and obvious stares from across the room, he leaned in, murmuring, "Princess, do you intend to fuck me tonight?"

Eyes wide, mouth hanging open, Leila instantly became aware of all the people watching them. Heart hammering away, her throat dried up. Her pupils dilated. Liquid heat flooded her core. "Oh, God.."

He chuckled, "No need for formalities. Just Cathal."

He loved to fuck. Loved the smells, the sounds, and the views that accompanied it. Like the one that he was currently seeing, of one particular petite silver haired female choking on his cock.

"That's it sweetheart, you're doing so well."

She moaned, bobbing her head up and down his stone hard shaft, desperately trying to fit it all in her tight mouth.

Cathal watched her on her knees struggling, trying to restrain himself but failing miserably. "My turn." Grabbing Leila by the hair with both hands, he stilled her head and held it firmly in place, "Are you ready, Princess?" Mumbling something incomprehensible while his cock was still in her mouth, he slowly pushed himself in until he felt the back of her throat. "I'll take that as a yes." She moaned again. "Hold on tight, I'm going to fuck your mouth raw now."

That was the only warning that she got before Cathal unleashed himself.

He fucked her hard and long, holding her head while he pumped her mouth full of his cock. Holding on for dear life to his thick thighs, she gagged incessantly, saliva flowing out of the corner of her mouth, tears of ecstasy streaming down her cheeks.

"Such a good princess, choking on the general's cock." She moaned. He increased his tempo, his balls slapping against her chin, savoring the obscene slurping and gagging sounds coming out of her hot mouth. "Fuck, yes," thrust, thrust, thrust, "I'm going to stretch that pretty mouth of yours," thrust, thrust, thrust, "until you're begging me to spray down your throat," thrust, thrust, thrust, "until my cock is imprinted on your brain forever."

He kept pumping, feeling the approaching orgasm until it finally hit him. His balls seized up and with a final thrust, he exploded. Endless streams of hot white cum shot down her throat and around his shaft. He groaned, draining the last drop from his still erect cock.

Slowly pulling himself free, he walked over to the bathroom, returning with a clean washcloth for Leila. "Let me clean you up." Lifting her up into his arms, he gently placed her on the edge of the bed. "Are you alright?" Cleaning her face and neck he finally kissed her, caressing her long silver tresses, "I'm sorry if I was rough with you."

"You weren't, it was perfect." Kissing him back, she lay down on the lavender satin sheets, exhausted. "Come to bed, Cathal. I want to fall asleep in your arms tonight."

Kneeling at the side of the opulent bed, he observed his betrothed as she got under the heavy covers, still naked. Creamy white alabaster skin covered her small frame. Striking grey eyes and a narrow button nose decorated her oval face. High cheekbones and a bee stung pale pink mouth were surrounded by silver straight hair that went down to the small of her back. Long, lean legs with slender thighs that connected to wide hips and a plump ass. A slim waist topped by heavy breasts with large pale pink areolas.

A classic beauty in all it's glory. She was, indeed, a magnificent sight to behold.

You stupid, stupid, piece of shit.

Dressing quickly in only black linen pants, Cathal walked over to the substantial arched windows and looked out at the star filled night sky. He would still have to make rounds of the training grounds before he allowed himself to join his mate in bed. His soldiers should be finishing up their regular evening chores by now, which means–

A sudden jolt to the chest halted Cathal in his thoughts. Leaning his outstretched arms on the window glass, he tried to calm his racing heart. *What is going on?*

As if summoned, that awful feeling of foreboding returned. It would not leave Cathal for the entire night, nor would it leave him later on while he ruthlessly pounded away into the Princess. That same damning emotion would keep him awake all night, making him anxious and rendering him, once again, helpless.

So, when Leila woke the next day, blissfully content and overflowing with emotions for that wonderfully dark man that she loved with all her heart, she was greeted with an empty bed, the sheets undisturbed where Cathal should have lain.

It would seem that while Leila had slept peacefully in that very same bed where she now shed tears of sorrow, the General had put on his leathers and swords, and silently in the dead of night departed for the north, in search of some long overdue answers.

CHAPTER

3

It was pouring outside. Duna was soaked through, her white linen blouse plastered onto her chest, accentuating the modest slopes of her shapely breasts. Her olive green gabardine pants clung snuggly to her thick thighs and full hips, leaving little to the imagination. Her heavy black cloak was rendered useless; her knee high dark leather boots caked with mud. Even the mask that she usually wore while training to stop her from inhaling a lungful of dirt was worthless in these conditions.

Pulling on the unavailing hood covering her head, Duna cursed. Leave it to her to always get the most tedious assignments in the most dreadful of weather.

Glancing over to her right, she saw that her companion wasn't doing much better than her.

Petra Da'Nyla was leaning on a tree, equally drenched through like Duna, cleaning dirt from under her nails with a seven inch, polished hunting knife. Her ginger hair was matted to her forehead, the rest of it hanging freely from under her hood, framing her freckled, ivory face. Clad in head to toe carbon black leathers, a pair of matching daggers on each side of her hips, it was hard to mistake her for a naive damsel accidentally caught out in the cold autumn rain.

Duna analyzed her, questioning the female's sanity. Aside from the four daggers, Petra also had a pair of double edged long swords strapped across her straight back. And there, just peeking out from under the front of her cloak and sheathed across her chest, was a set of four stainless steel throwing knives.

What, in the gods, is wrong with this woman? "Do you think you brought enough weapons?"

Petra looked up from her nails, the intimidating hunting knife frozen in midair. "What? I like to be prepared."

"For what, war?"

Petra shrugged, placing the blade back in it's scabbard. "You never know what we might run into in these woods." She grinned, "Besides, not all of us are blessed with a natural talent for killing."

Ignoring the five foot seven woman, Duna glanced up at the sky. "The rain's stopping. We should get going while it's still light outside. I don't want to be caught in the forest after dark unless it's absolutely necessary."

"Didn't think you were afraid of the dark, little warrior."

She wasn't. She just didn't like to waste her time. Besides, their captain was adamant about this being a quick scouting mission, not a week long stroll in the park.

They were to check the dense woods along the border with the Kingdom of Nissa for any wondering individuals or stray soldiers. Not many people ventured into the forest, and the ones that did were usually lost villagers or young couples searching for a secluded place to have a quick tryst.

"Moira will be waiting for us to report back to her as soon as possible. Let's just get this over with." She needed a hot bath and a set of warm, dry clothes. *And rest. Definitely rest.*

Duna hadn't slept for more than a few measly hours over the last couple of days. Not to mention that she hadn't been actually sleeping during those precious times but had been instead half-awake sitting up, her back leaning against a tree. Her body was begging for a much needed reprieve.

The two women walked side-by-side, wordlessly interacting, never taking their eyes off of their surroundings. They would be heading back soon, anytime now. Just a little more land remained to be searched–

Noises reached them from behind the crowded trees in front. Loud shouting followed by the clear sounds of clashing weapons echoed across the forest floor.

Duna lifted a calloused finger to her dry lips, silently signaling to Petra her plain intent to get closer to the commotion. Crouching low, they approached. Like wraiths in the night they crept between the tree trunks, nimbly weaving through the ancient foliage.

Seven assailants dressed like vagabonds surrounded two men and a young woman. At first glance, it appeared as if the trio were nothing more than ordinary folk. On closer inspection, though, it was clear to Duna that the three individuals currently being tied up on the rain drenched ground were anything but common. Multiple hidden silver blades adorned their compact bodies. Two short, slightly curved steel cutlass swords were strewn across the ground, lost in the skirmish.

The two captured males were lying face down on the ground, their hands tied behind their broad backs. One of them had a nasty head wound, wine red blood slowly leaking down the side of his soiled face, seeping into the cold grass below. The other, larger male, was struggling against his restraints, desperately attempting to get out of them but failing nonetheless. He, too, was covered in dirt and grime, but lacked the blooming head wound of his unfortunate companion.

Duna searched the clearing for the missing woman.

There. Two hideous, raggedy looking men with half of their teeth missing were dragging her along the ground, her hands tied back with thick strands of rope. Pants torn at the knees, her cloak hanging loosely from her shoulders, she was giving her capturers an impressive fight.

Duna cursed to herself, watching with a knot in her stomach as the two men led the fierce female to the edge of the clearing. Clothes disheveled and tarnished, long raven black hair falling out of her intricate braid, she was kicking and screaming at the disgusting bastards.

Locking eyes with Petra, Duna pulled out an arrow from her quiver. Steadily she placed it in the bow's nock and pulled the bowstring back. Aiming for the larger of the two men dragging the feral female away, she breathed in a calming breath.

Now.

As if guided by the gods themselves, the arrow flew across the wide opening, hitting its target directly between his shoulder blades, severing his spinal cord and instantly rendering him dead. Another three men went down at the same time as Petra released her throwing knives with meticulous aim. Shouts rang out, the three remaining assailants desperately scrambling for cover.

Blood pumping in their veins, hearts pounding in their chest, Duna and Petra exploded from the shadows. Swords drawn they charged at the men, incapacitating them while barely breaking a sweat.

Only one remained. That nasty bastard that had his filthy hands all over that unfortunate woman. Duna pointed her sword in his direction, "You're mine."

For a brief moment in time, the man stood there unmoving. Then he started to laugh hysterically, a high pitched cackling sound coming out of his grotesque body. "I'm going to have so much fun with you, you little whore." He spat. "I'm going to cut up that pretty face of yours while your friend over there sucks my cock and then, I'm going to piss all over your battered body."

Grinning widely, Petra stepped aside, giving Duna more space. "I love it when they get so creative."

Duna smirked, finally taking off her hood, her long, braided mane of chocolate brown hair releasing itself from its confinement. Shrugging off the rest of her cloak and soaked mask, she neatly folded them and handed them over to her sister-in-arms.

Cracking her neck, she turned to her opponent, "Let's play."

Rushing at her with his sword raised high, he attacked her with full force. The man was like a battering ram, predictable and cumbersome. His height advantage did him no favors, leaving his midsection wide open for a much shorter Duna to strike at.

Quick as a snake, she ducked her head out of the way just as he was lowering his sword and plunged her blade into the side of his liver.

Blood rushed out, staining his clothing a deep crimson, a heavy copper scent permeating the air. He collapsed on his knees, hand pressed tightly against his side where the worthless liquid drained from his body. His other hand was still clutching his useless sword, as if his soggy brain had still not received the information that he was profusely bleeding out and dying. Finally, after a few brief moments, he crumbled face first in the saturated dirt.

"Well, shit."

Duna spun around, sword poised for the attack.

A tall, dark, devastatingly attractive male stood at arms length, grinning widely as he inspected her, "I think I'm in love."

"That makes two of us, pretty boy," Petra winked at her, helping the bloodied one stand up as he rubbed and soothed his reddened wrists. "Besides, I think a thank you is in order."

"Of course, how could I forget." The dark stranger turned to Duna, bowing slightly at the waist while keeping his eyes locked on hers, "My companions and I are forever indebted to you." He straightened. "Anything that we could do for you, it will be done."

Duna stood rooted to the spot, perusing the male in front of her. He was tall, with strong wide shoulders and a well defined, broad chest that tapered down to narrow hips and thick muscular thighs; she could just imagine what he would look like without all of those unnecessary layers covering that powerful body.

His raven black hair was tied in a loose bun at the nape; his eyes the rare color of blue tourmaline. He had a sharp, angular jaw and high cheekbones that led to a regal nose, and beneath that, a set of full, rose colored lips.

"Like what you see?" he smirked, licking his juicy lips.

The arrogant fucker. "Maybe I do. Is that a problem?"

"Not at all, sweetheart," he stepped closer to Duna, towering over her with his six foot two frame. "Although I must admit," he leaned in, piercing her with those striking eyes, "you are a magnificent sight to behold."

Petra cleared her throat, "Do you have a name, pretty boy?"

"Yes, of course. Madir," he turned to his two companions, gesturing at them as he spoke, "Mikella and," he pointed at the battered man leaning on the disheveled woman, "York. We have been following those men for some days now, you have saved us a lot of unnecessary trouble."

"Why were you following them?"

"They robbed some very important people and so, we had no choice but to go after them," he said.

"Interesting. All this trouble just for a few pieces of gold?" Picking up her last throwing knife, Petra placed it into it's holder. "Tell me Madir, where did you three come from?"

He cleared his throat, hesitating, "Morinya."

The capital city of Nissa. "You are a far way from home." That they were.

"We rarely venture this far down south." He turned to Duna, "Like I said, you have saved us a lot of unnecessary trouble. Although, I can't say that I am sorry to have met you."

"Nice try, *pretty boy*," Duna leaned in, "It's too bad flattery doesn't work on me."

Madir smirked again, his voice dropping low, "But you think I'm pretty."

Bored from this nonsensical conversation, Petra threw Duna's items at her, "For fuck's sake, enough. If that is all, we should be going Duna. Nightfall is just a few hours away, if we hurry we can make it back to camp just in time for evening call. I'm not in the mood to go to bed hungry, again."

Madir tilted his head, narrowing his eyes. "You're from the military."

Placing her mask back in place, Duna ignored the male. She, too, was starving, having consumed their final meal rations just that morning. *I wonder what Cook made for dinner?*

She snorted. She'll eat just about anything at this point, even grimy old boot soles, as long as she had something in her stomach.

Lost in thought, she failed to notice how close Madir was standing to her until he leaned in to whisper in her ear. "Duna," he purred, "if only we had more time, I would gladly repay my debt, many times, over and over again." Squeezing her fingers, his heated tourmaline eyes burned a hole in her unblinking hazel ones.

She sighed. The man was persistent, she'll give him that, and although she was flattered, she also didn't have time for this, "Goodbye, Madir." Pulling her fingers out of his hold, Duna threw her heavy black cloak over herself, clasping it around her neck. Her quiver and bow she strapped across her back, sheathing her sword in it's holster at her hip.

Glancing at the impatient Petra who was already moving towards the direction of their barracks, Duna retreated into the forest shadows, counting down the hours until she would be back in her warm bed again.

Duna woke the next day with her body aching all over. It was as if a carriage had trampled her in her sleep and left her battered in bed.

They had returned during the late evening hours, merely moments before Cook closed down the kitchens. After inhaling some dry bread and cold porridge, she had collapsed naked into bed, not bothering to wash all that dirt off. Her body had been bruised and tired, nothing that a good night's rest hadn't been able to fix.

Throwing on a plain, knee length used night shirt, she walked over to her private bathing chamber, one of the many perks for being in the army for so long. It wasn't large or ostentatious like the captain's was, but it was her little piece of heaven that Duna cherished with all her heart.

A small washing basin stood to the side of the make-shift wall, a medium sized simple mirror hanging above it. To the right of the open tent flap where Duna now stood appraising the area, was a fairly large tub and a little bench where all sorts of body washes and shampoos were lined up. Walking over to them, she picked up a lavender scented one and poured a small amount into the water filled tub.

Just as she was gathering the courage to get into the icy water, Petra rushed in, arms spread wide, cursing as she went, "Duna–" she stopped when she saw her standing naked by the tub, "for fuck's sake, put on some clothes, woman."

"I'm trying to have a bath, as you can see."

"Yes, well, do it clothed. Or better yet, don't bathe at all. The General is here–" she picked up Duna's night shirt, "What in the every loving gods is this? Don't you have anything normal to wear?"

Yanking her favorite sleeping wear from Petra's clutches and throwing it over the bench, Duna immersed herself into the freezing water.

"What are you doing?!" Petra shrieked, clasping her hands on top of her freshly washed ginger hair. "We have to go! The General is here, god damn it! Moira is going to skin you alive if you're late!"

"I don't give a rat's ass about Moira and the General. I am going to take a bath, wash my hair," Duna counted on her fingers as she rambled on, "put on some clean clothes, eat, lie in bed, then eat again, train–"

"You cannot be serious."

"Do you mind? I'm trying to have a calming bath. Besides," teeth chattering, she scrubbed away at her arms, "there are hundreds, if not thousands, of soldiers here at camp, no one is going to notice my absence at the training grounds. Especially not Moira, who is going to be busy kissing up to the General."

"She notices everything, I swear that woman is like a hawk." Petra leaned on the edge of the tub, "Can I wash your hair, at least? You know, to speed up the whole process."

"No," she said.

"Why not? You have such pretty hair."

Duna splashed her. "Get out."

"Fine, but don't say I didn't warn you. You have no idea what the General is like when he's angry." Petra got up, smoothing out her trousers and dusting off nonexistent flint from her shoulders.

"It's a good thing then that I have never met him before, and that I intend to keep it that way."

After the insufferable woman finally left, Duna scrubbed away the dirt and grime from their trip, so much so that her skin was taking on a worrisome crimson hue. She vigilantly cleaned her hair, relishing in the feel of her smooth, silky strands running down her straight back.

After drying up and wrapping her hair in a towel, she emerged from the bathing chamber, rejuvenated and ready to start the day.

She dressed quickly in her sturdy body forming suit, the smooth black leather hugging her delicious curves, accentuating the hollows and dips of her toned body. Her still damp chocolate brown hair she tied up at the top of her crown, braiding it all the way down her back and tying the ends with a thin, burgundy, velvet strap.

Two narrow leather strips crisscrossed over her back and in between the slopes of her modest breasts, holding her favorite pair of throwing knives. Strapped around both of her thick thighs were matching charcoal black holsters with twin seven inch polished daggers sheathed in rich, dark leather scabbards. Black leather gauntlets covered her knuckles and forearms.

She covered her face with a breathable black mask. Hood pulled over her head and cloak hanging down over her backside, only her almond shaped hazel eyes remained visible. Pulling on her matching black, knee high boots, she grabbed her sheathed long sword and exited the tent.

Duna breathed in the crisp morning air. Lungs full of life, heart full of joy, she started toward the training grounds.

Let the games begin.

CHAPTER 4

The military base at the northern border with the Kingdom of Nissa was one of the largest ones that Cathal had ever had the honor of commanding. Housing over ten thousand deadly soldiers and an additional five thousand in the heavy cavalry, it embodied the Tyrossian Kingdom's most formidable army division.

One particular legion consisting of over three thousand warriors was notorious for it's ruthlessly skilled fighters and legendary military victories.

It was at the training grounds of this renowned legion where Cathal currently found himself, observing the many sparring fighters. A large portion of men were doing heavy conditional exercises, while a substantially smaller one was doing advanced technical one-on-one combat skill reinforcement. Not too far away from the former was a secluded clearing with numerous warriors engaged in open sparring, armed with an impressive variety of deadly arsenal.

"Captain," Prince Edan Vilkas spoke, "is it not a little too early in the day for such heavy training?" A warrior in his own right, he was the middle son of King Fergal and the second in line for the Tyrossian throne. Standing at an intimidating height of six foot eight, he towered over the much shorter war veteran.

"Your Highness, it is never too early to hone one's skills. One can never be too prepared, wouldn't you agree, General?" Captain Moira turned to Cathal, who was observing a group of five said fighters as they faced off each other using steel-headed long spears.

"Is this a daily routine or do the soldiers take turns sparring?"

"Usually they rotate every few days, however, there are a select number who are adamant about incorporating the heavy duty sparring into their every day basic training." Moira paused, proudly lifting her chin, "They are our most prized warriors."

Cathal arched an eyebrow, "Then they wouldn't mind if we joined them."

The trio, accompanied by Cathal's two lieutenant generals Axel and Rhun, approached the clearing where a multitude of simultaneous sparring sessions were well under way. They watched as weapons clashed in the early morning sun, bodies bending and flying in an almost ritualistic dance.

"Each individual is tasked with choosing at least one, but not more than three, specific weapons," Moira started, "which they then must master over the course of one year, and not a day longer. They undergo exceptionally grueling training and demanding monthly assessments which they in turn must pass in order to be able to remain in this specific legion."

Axel snorted, "Doesn't seem too challenging, Captain. Most of our commanding officers have that level of skill."

Moira turned to the massive warrior, face stern, "Highly unlikely, Lieutenant. The hours that a single one of these soldiers puts into his training exceeds, by far, the tedious hours that said commanding officers ever spend on the battlefield during their entire careers," she grinned, "combined."

Lieutenant Rhun Brayan chuckled, rubbing his hands together in anticipation, "I believe that is a challenge, Axel. What do you say, Captain?" he turned to the aging woman, "Do you accept?"

"Absolutely." Grinning wide, eyes sparkling with delight, she turned to a dueling couple, "Lir! Show our Lieutenant what it means to be in my legion."

A dark blond, full bearded six foot tall bulky warrior ran to them, his war axe held in one hand, the other flinging his long braid over his shoulder.

"No," Axel started, smirking deviously, "I want that one." He pointed to a much smaller male sparring with a spear.

Captain Moira balked, suddenly apprehensive of the considerable male's request, "If I may suggest another opponent, Lieutenant, one who is mo–"

"Now."

"Very well." Clearing her throat, she approached the black, leather clad hooded figure who's back was turned to them. After a brief exchange of words, she returned, gesturing the impatient lieutenant over to the awaiting warrior, "Your challenge has been accepted. You may start."

Cathal watched as his most trusted commanding officer descended to the open grounds. Picking himself up a spear to match his opponent's, Axel inclined his head to the covered figure, signaling the start of their match.

Faster than the eye could see, the black figure advanced on him. It thrust its sharp spear forward and back impossibly fast, jabbing at him around his neck and face. Axel ducked, straining to keep up with the lithe figure. Jab, duck, jab, on and on they went until the masked figure pushed him almost to the edge of the fighting pit.

Cathal held his breath, mesmerized.

Still on the defensive, his opponent not giving him a chance to throw in his own jab, Axel tried pulling out of the way. The masked figure followed him relentlessly, advancing on him with unwavering force and agility, thrusting and jabbing at every turn.

Lowering to the ground on both legs, upper body bent backwards in an almost impossible horizontal position while using the spear for balance, it lifted its one leg and kicked an unsuspecting Axel directly under the chin, sending his head flying backwards. Using the momentum of the kick, the figure flipped back over itself. Spinning its spear around to it's blunt end, it hit the angry male directly in the gut. He grunted, swearing profusely, his face turning crimson. The figure spun around and with a final move thrust its spear forward, the sharp end of the steel-covered tip pressing moderately into the Lieutenant's neck, right over his pulsing carotid artery.

Axel froze, dropping his weapon to the ground, feeling the light trickles of blood flowing down his neck and over his collarbone.

The masked figure retracted its spear, inclined its head, and without a second glance left the fighting pit.

"Like I said," Moira cleared her throat, addressing the returning lieutenant, "perhaps a different opponent would have been more appropriate."

"Perhaps." Cathal spun around, chuckling under his breath, and ordered the Captain, "Have that soldier come to my tent in an hour's time. I am in need of a good sparring partner."

Finally, a worthy opponent.

He grinned to himself, fiery anticipation burning him from the inside out, as the four seasoned warriors returned to the General's barracks.

CHAPTER

5

Duna stood in front of the large, white, octagonal shaped tent an hour later, waiting to be received by the General himself. After her sparring session with that massive blond warrior, she had returned to her own tent and washed off the dirt from her face and hands.

She had enjoyed the fight with the bulky male, it was perhaps the highlight of her week. All that remained now was to see what this man wanted from her, and she could finally get back to her awaiting duties.

"The General will see you now."

Glancing up at the male standing in front of her, she narrowed her eyes in recognition, "You're that one from the training grounds, the one that I beat today."

He cleared his throat, holding open the tent flaps, "You got lucky, don't get used to it."

"Anything that helps you sleep at night." She winked at him, entering the grand tent. She gasped, spinning around herself as she advanced deeper inside.

Multiple lanterns of all shapes and sizes hung from the ceiling, illuminating the open space in an array of white and yellow dancing lights. Intricately decorated large Persian rugs overlapped each other, covering the ground from the entrance all the way to the other end where another, smaller room seemed to be situated. The bathing chamber, if she had to guess.

A considerable make-shift bed lay to one side, with a pair of white rectangular pillows leaning on the wall behind it. Thick furs of browns and blacks sprawled over the covered mattress, daring Duna to bury herself underneath them.

In front of the bed was a set of four large, earth colored sitting pillows arranged in a neat circle. In the center of said circle was a low wooden table, housing a multitude of fruit and a half empty bottle of whiskey.

As Duna continued her perusal of the space, she forgot all about where she was. The blond warrior nudged her, returning her attention to the present. "What?"

He jabbed his chin forward, silently indicating her to face the front of the tent.

Turning her head, Duna for a moment forgot how to breathe. Standing in front of her, just a few feet away, was the most beautiful man she had ever seen.

Tall at about six foot six, he was clad in head to toe black. Broad shoulders extended into powerfully built arms that weren't overly bulky, the sleeves of his black linen shirt straining ever so slightly over the corded muscles. The collar of his shirt was unbuttoned to under the middle of his sternum, showing off lightly tanned skin and a sculpted chest. A flat abdomen connected to masculine, narrow hips. Thick, strong thighs and calves were tucked into carbon black, knee high leather boots.

Duna blinked, trying to clear away the haze. Hair the color of the darkest night, it was shorter on the sides and longer on top, a few silky straight strands falling leisurely onto his face.

Oh, God.

His face was a canvas of devastating features. Thick dark eyebrows narrowed down to a straight nose. High, chiseled cheekbones and a sharp, angular jaw descended into a wide, square masculine chin. Bow shaped, full lips the color of milk toffee. A neatly trimmed black beard and mustache covered the lower part of his face to the top of his neck. An old, narrow scar cut across his face diagonally, painting a startlingly lethal edge to his breathtaking attributes. Starting at the top of his left cheek, it extended down to the left corner of his mouth. And his eyes – His eyes were the most striking color of green aventurine, rimmed by thick, dark lashes.

The man was like sin personified.

Mouth gaping open, Duna thanked the gods for her mask. *Get it together.*

He stood there with his hands in his pockets, brows slightly furrowed, silently analyzing her. His gaze was unwavering, perusing her from head to toe with his piercing eyes. "You're a woman," he pressed his lips tightly together.

Duna looked down at herself, "It would seem so, yes."

He frowned, looking her over once more.

"Will that be a problem for you, General?"

His eyes snapped to hers, a slight grin slowly spreading across his face, "Not at all…"

"Duna," she said.

"Of course." Turning to the blond warrior, he said, "Lieutenant Fendergar, would you please inform the Prince that we are ready for him to start our lesson."

Axel left, leaving Duna alone with the intimidating male.

Hands in his pockets, he slowly made his way towards her. The man moved like a panther.

Silent. Deadly.

Every move calculated and precise. He circled her, head slightly tilting as his eyes rowed over her cloaked body, "Why do you hide your features?"

Duna cleared her throat, trying to calm her racing heart as he stopped right in front of her. "I am not hiding anything, General. The cloak keeps me warm during my long hours of training. The mask keeps the dirt out of my lungs," she pierced him with her stare, "otherwise I would suffocate from all of the grime that your so-called warriors kick up while fighting me."

He rubbed his strong jaw, "You've got quite a mouth on you."

She smirked, "Wouldn't you like to know?"

Dead silence. The General stood there, not moving, his features frozen in place. He stared at her, eyes wide, unblinking.

For a brief moment in time, Duna was sure that she had seen the last of her sorry days in the army. Maybe in her short, miserable life, as well.

Stupid, stupid, STUPID girl. Why can't you just keep your mouth shut?

Just as she was about to open her said mouth to apologize, the General threw back his head, roaring with laughter.

Duna stood there paralyzed, mouth gaping open for the second time that afternoon. It was a a rich, velvety laugh, transforming the man's already beautiful features into devastatingly stunning ones. His eyes were pressed together, full lips stretched wide open, revealing a full set of white teeth.

It was a hearty laugh, sincere and unfiltered.

Suddenly schooling his features, hands back in his pockets, the General stepped up to her, invading her personal space. Towering over her much smaller five foot five frame, she had to arch her neck back just to be able to look at him.

"Your big mouth will one day get you in a lot of trouble," he leaned down, coming within an inch of her masked face, inspecting it. "Lucky for you, I am a tolerant man." His aventurine eyes locked onto her hazel ones, drinking her in, as he purred, "Take of your mask. I want to see your face."

Mouth drying up, heart hammering away, Duna begged the gods to save her. His masculine scent enveloped her, a rich concoction of spice, leather, and whiskey invading her over stimulated senses. If he leaned in any closer she was going to combust.

"General," her voice lower than she'd like, she cleared her throat, "my face is of no consequence. I am here to train with you and your men, as my captain informed me earlier."

Still leaning in, he stepped forward, a hair's breadth of charged air separating their heated bodies, "Are you questioning a direct order?"

"What? No–"

"Then take it off," he purred in her ear, his voice getting dangerously low, "Don't make me repeat myself, soldier."

Hands shaking at her sides, Duna contemplated on her options.

She did not mind going around without her mask, it wasn't as if she had anything to hide. Her face was plain enough. Heart shaped, it was embellished with large, almond, hazel eyes, a straight, narrow nose, and medium sized plump lips with a defined cupid's bow. Nothing exceptional about it. However, even though her former reason for wearing the face mask was mostly true, it was also not the only one.

The mask hid her identity, making her job much easier when she went on potentially dangerous scouting missions across the border into Nissa. It, also, kept her safe from unwanted attention seeing as Duna was one of only a hundred or so female soldiers in the mostly male populated army. She had had a healthy amount of lovers over the course of the five years since she had enlisted, all males which have seen her face, but even then she had still remained anonymous to the outside world.

True, there was no one else in the tent but her and the General, so her latter reasoning seemed borderline ridiculous. It's not as if she was going to see the man after today's sparring session, so what harm could possibly come from her disclosing her face to him?

Finally deciding, Duna lifted her hands as if to take off her hood and mask. Just as she was about to do so, the tent flaps flew open, revealing two large warriors.

"General Cathal," the giant of a man started, "the Lieutenant has informed me that we are ready for today's lesson. Let us begin."

The General straightened, fiery eyes burning as they bore into Duna, "Yes, let us. Your Highness," he turned to the Prince who was still standing in the open tent flaps, "there is a matter that I must first resolve, you and the Lieutenant may start without us. We will be joining you shortly."

"Very well." And with those final two damning words, Duna was, once again, left alone with the domineering male.

Cathal.

She backed up, eyes locked on him.

Brows furrowed tightly, he grabbed her by the elbows, pulling her towards him. "Where do you think you are going?" he hissed. "I have not dismissed you. We are not leaving this tent until you show me your face," he leaned in, whispering, "What are you hiding, little warrior?"

Gasping for breath, she started shaking all over. *Please, God, don't let him notice.*

She couldn't breathe. Her lungs were pressing against her chest cavity, her heart beating erratically. She had to get away from him.

Duna did not understand why she was having such an extreme reaction to the man. Aside from having a god-like appearance and a voice that could easily seduce any woman into bed, she did not know him at all.

Yanking her elbows out of his punishing hold, she turned around and bolted through the tent flaps toward the training grounds, not daring to turn around lest she catch the General's intense gaze.

She did not see him as his face crumbled, features drawn in confusion, his hands fisting at his sides.

The General had not come after her as Duna had feared he would. The man seemed obsessed with seeing her face.

She sparred with Prince Edan, desperately trying not to kill the royal. She liked her head right where it was, on her shoulders. It was unfortunate that the giant warrior was, to her surprise, quite skilled with a blade. She just wasn't prepared to hang from the palace walls, so she turned down her impressive fighting skills while still retaining her pride and dignity. It went without saying that she was obliged to let the arrogant male win at least once out of the three times that they sparred that afternoon.

"Enough," a deep voice barked from behind her. "Let the real fighting begin."

Duna stood rooted to the spot, refusing to acknowledge the General as he descended to the fighting pit. Lifting her sword in preparation, she signaled to the Prince that they were to go another round.

Edan inclined his head ever so slightly, sword still at his side. "That will be all from me for today, I'm afraid. Duty calls." He turned to Axel, "Lieutenant, lead the way."

Duna couldn't believe her luck. She was, once again, left alone with the brooding male. She cursed profoundly, not caring that Cathal could hear her. "As much as I would like to stand here all day in such lovely company, I'm afraid that I have some business to attend to. If we could hurry this along, it would be greatly appreciated."

The General shook of his cloak, picking up his double-edged polished silver sword, inspecting it, "I'm sure you do, so let us not waste any more time. Choose your weapon."

He had changed into a simple slate-black leather ensemble, not bothering with gauntlets. A set of three heavy, rectangular gold rings with carved insignia adorned his long fingers. Rolling up his sleeves to his elbows, he revealed a multitude of bulging veins that crossed over each other down to his knuckles.

Duna salivated profusely, her throat drying up in a matter of seconds. Closing her eyes, breathing in a steady, calming breath, she tried clearing out her mind as she always did right before a fight.

"Any day now."

"Shut up," she barked.

A loud, boisterous laugh echoed across the clearing. Duna opened her eyes, drinking in the enigmatic man. That was the second time today that she had been witness to such an occasion. How many people had had the honor of hearing this rarity? Not many, she was sure of it. And yet here he was, laughing away in front of her.

"Like I said," he pointed his sword at her, "you have a very, very big mouth on you."

Duna chuckled, picking up a second, matching sword and testing it's weight in her hand. "And like I said, you have no idea just how big." She lunged at Cathal, sword poised in front of her.

He blocked her, raising his own sword and swinging it down on Duna. On and on they went, thrusting, blocking, slicing. They spun circles around each other, swinging their swords, eyes locked in a perpetual dance of defiance. They sliced, feinted, then thrust again. Sweat pouring down their backs, clothes drenched through, neither one of them was willing to back down. It seemed to Duna that they went on for hours like this, her soul singing with joy.

The General was a truly spectacular sight to behold. He moved with preternatural stealth that for a man of his size and stature should not have been possible, and yet, he matched every one of her thrusts, blocked every one of her slices.

Duna was impressed, but she had had enough of this playing around. Feinting to the right, she then suddenly dropped down low on the ground and pulled Cathal's feet from under him. He collapsed backwards, hitting the hard ground. Duna jumped on him, pinning his arms down with her legs spread over his heaving body. Straddling him, she placed the blade of her sword under his chin, pressing it slightly into his moist skin, a horizontal crimson line appearing where she held the blade.

They lay there staring at each other, neither one of them willing to break the charged silence.

A sudden wave of heat crept over Duna, pooling in her lower abdomen, burning her core. Her cheeks flushed, lips swelling as if bee stung. Her throat dried up, making her parched. She swallowed, Cathal watching the movement from under her pulsing body.

"Let me see your face," he begged her, green eyes blazing.

Her sword still held under his chin, she yanked off her hood and mask, finally revealing herself to the fierce warrior.

Looking at her, he blinked a few times, as if trying to focus his eyes. Not a word was spoken between them. They stayed there like that, unmoving and silent, for what felt like forever to Duna. Cathal spread out on the ground, staring up at her face with his mouth parted. Duna straddling him, gripping the hilt of her sword, staring right back with the same intensity.

Not what you expected, is it, General.

Without a word, she got up, sheathed her sword, and walked back to her tent, leaving a sprawled out Cathal laying on the ground.

CHAPTER

6

A week had passed before Duna saw Cathal again. She was making her way to the training pit one day at the break of dawn, hoping to get in at least a couple of hours of solid training before the clearing was overflowing with soldiers, when she spotted the General.

He was magnificent in the early morning sun.

Carbon black riding leathers and matching knee high boots covered his powerful body, and over that, a gold studded, midnight black brigandine with an elongated gold dire wolf insignia embedded in the middle of his chest. Heavily embossed gold leather gauntlets went up to his elbows and over his knuckles, his set of gold rings blazing on his fingers. A long, matching, light leather cloak was thrown over his shoulders, clasped around his thick neck with a gold chain. Sheathed over his back were two double-edged polished steel long swords.

Shadows seemed to radiate from his formidable body, encompassing him like sinister snakes of gloom.

He was lethal. Menacing.

The God of Death incarnate.

Moving with the gait of a predator, Cathal approached an enormous, almost two meter tall, pure ebony stallion. His coat was a shimmering river of radiant midnight; a thick, long straight mane fell over his crest and down the sides of his powerful body. An equally rich tail was swinging in the morning sun. Cathal patted the top of the horse's muzzle, rubbing it gently, murmuring soothing words to the animal.

Duna stood transfixed, head tilted to the side, drinking in the sight of the baffling, brooding male. There was something so contradictory about him, as if two polar opposites were meshed together in a confounding mixture of nonsensical attributes.

She frowned, shaking her head. It was not her place to ponder on the man. He was nothing to her, and she was nothing to him. They had had a brief insignificant encounter the previous week, that was all. Although he was a sight for sore eyes, Duna was certain that she had nothing in common with the seasoned warrior.

She lifted her hood over her freely flowing mane of chocolate hair, checking if her mask was in place–

Her skin tingled, a sudden bolt of electricity shocking her heart. She gasped, hand flying to her stammering chest. Lifting her head, she saw him.

The General was watching her, his eyes burning holes in her face. He stood frozen beside his giant steed, hand poised on the saddle.

Duna refused to back down. She was not going to let this man intimidate her. Staring right back at him, her sword hanging loosely at her side, their eyes locked in a battle of wills.

Her face heated, body going into overdrive. Sweat covered her palms and trickled down her nape, heart beating at a maddening galloping pace.

Cathal frowned, as if irritated that she had the gall to stand in his godly presence.

That makes two of us.

He shook his head, finally turning away, and mounted his war horse. Without another glance at Duna, he cantered away, followed by his two lieutenant generals and a group of four glowering warriors.

She released a strangled breath, her body returning to normal. Spinning on the spot, she entered the training pit.

The Moon was high in the night sky by the time Duna returned to her tent. Stripping off her soiled clothes, she went directly to her bathing chamber, immersing her tired body in cold water. Scrubbing away, she pondered on the General.

What was it about him that kept her so perplexed? Why did she always have such a strong, physical reaction to him whenever she was in his presence?

It wasn't as though Duna had never seen an attractive man before. Sure, not as beautiful as Cathal, but nonetheless. She wasn't a woman who was easily distracted by one's physical appearance, however pleasant it might be.

She valued someone's intellect and charisma more than any chiseled abdominal muscles or bulging biceps. Determination, virtue, devotion. A kind heart and willingness to sacrifice one's own happiness for the better good. Those, she valued.

She finished up her bath, dressing in her warm sleeping gown. Toweling off her hair, she lightly oiled it, combing it through with her fingers and pampering it with the necessary attention. *Bed, here I come.* Climbing under the quilted plain grey covers, she blew out her lantern and finally closed her eyes.

"Get up."

Her hand flew forward before her eyes snapped open. It latched onto the trachea of a thick neck, fingers pressing tightly around the organ, straining it out of oxygen. Her other hand went around and underneath the other's arm, right under the armpit, lifting them up and back onto the mattress. Her knees pressed into their chest, she finally assessed her unwanted visitor.

Dirty blond hair braided back, square jaw, a face covered with a full beard, and a jagged scar across the left eyebrow.

Axel. *Motherfucker.*

"What are you doing here, Lieutenant?" she hissed at him, hand still pressing his trachea. His face was turning an alarming shade of crimson, but Duna didn't care. How dare he come into her tent uninvited. "Do you have a death wish? Hmm?"

Unable to speak, Axel pounded on her suffocating hand, trying to get some reprieve. His other arm was still locked beneath Duna's, rendering it completely useless. After a few deciding moments, she finally released him, pushing off of him and coming to a stand by the side of her bed.

He coughed and wheezed, bent over the covers, color slowly returning to his normal caramel shade, "What, in the ever loving fuck, is the matter with you, woman?"

"I could ask you the same question. Why are you here, in my tent, in the middle of the fucking night?!" she shouted at him, arms flailing at her sides.

"The General has requested to see you," he coughed again, "I am here to escort you to his tent."

Well, shit. "No," she said, crossing her arms over her chest.

"No?" he balked, "What do you mean, no? It wasn't a request. You are to go to the General's tent. Now. That's a direct order from your commanding officer. I will drag you there myself by your miserable legs, if I have to." He crossed his arms, imitating Duna's pose.

"Fine. Let me change. I am not going to him dressed in my nightgown." When he didn't move, she said, "Do you mind? Get out while I change."

He cleared his throat, eyes darting around, suddenly looking like a five year old boy who was caught stealing candy. "I will wait for you outside, don't take too long. The General is not a very patient man."

She dressed quickly in some black leggings and a loose ivory linen blouse, not bothering with her mask. It was nighttime and everyone, except an insubstantial number of guards, was mostly asleep. There was no point in her wearing it, unless she wanted to be labeled as a complete idiot. Throwing her cloak over her shoulders, Duna exited the tent.

They made their way to their desired destination in record time, moving through the barracks in the moonlit dark like two wraiths. Entering the General's tent, they found him sitting at his desk, writing away under the light of three burning lanterns. *Smart man.*

"General," Axel barked, "as requested, I have brought you our little fighter."

Cathal's head snapped up at that, arching a dark eyebrow as he focused his gaze on the Lieutenant.

"Duna, I have brought you Duna," Axel corrected himself.

Placing his quill down onto the heavy oak table, Cathal slowly got up and with his hands in his pockets sauntered over to them, his gaze never wavering from hers.

Duna noticed that he had changed into plain black pants which were tucked into his riding boots and a light grey linen shirt, its top three buttons undone, revealing his chiseled chest underneath.

Brows furrowed together, lips in a straight line, he approached Duna until he stood a foot in front of her. "You're late," his voice lowered, "I don't like to be kept waiting." He stared at her uncovered face, slowly perusing it.

Duna's heart stammered. Stopped. Then started beating erratically.

"Apologies, there was a slight issue that we had to resolve," Axel glanced at Duna, quietly adding, "She attacked me."

"And why would she attack you, Fendergar?"

"He came into my tent while I was in bed, naked," Duna said, crossing her arms.

"What?" eyes snapping to Axel, Cathal hissed, accentuating the T. His jaw clenched hard, eyebrows bunching close together.

"You little liar, you were not naked!" Axel shouted at her, turning to the seething General, "She was not naked, she was in her nightgown. And it was dark, I barely even saw anything. Besides, who sleeps half covered like that? It's ridiculous."

Cathal stepped up to the shouting male, getting close to his face, his eyes wild, blazing infernos, his nostrils flaring wide. "You saw her in her nightgown?" his voice a deadly low, like the calm before a storm.

Axel balked, blinking repeatedly, glancing between Duna and Cathal, while he stuttered, "I–I announced myself before entering, she did not answer me. I presumed that she was awake, seeing as the lights were still on."

Cathal surveyed the male with cold eyes, his face a hair's breadth away, his body seeming to grow in size as he did so. "You presumed wrong," he leaned into his ear, "Do not make the same mistake again."

The blond warrior blanched, all blood leaving his face. Mouth gaping open, he swallowed. "Of course, General. My apologies."

Cathal straightened to his full intimidating height, hands in his pockets, looking Axel over. "Leave us." After the male left, he made his way back to stand in front of Duna. He stood there towering over her, a confounded look on his stunning face, his merciless eyes rolling over her tense body and face. Settling finally on her lips, he approached her ever so slowly, stopping barely an inch in front of her.

His eyes darkened as they locked onto her mouth. His jaw clenched.

She inhaled him, his leather and whiskey scent permeating the charged air around them, invading her senses. Her throat dried up.

She swallowed. He followed the movement, his intense aventurine eyes darting to her glistening hazel ones. They stood frozen, their gazes locked on each other, both breathing heavily, chests heaving.

Duna was first to break the tense silence, "You summoned me."

Nothing, and then, softly, "I did."

When Cathal didn't continue, she frowned, annoyed, "And are you going to tell me the reason for doing so in the middle of the night or am I going to have to beg?"

He smirked deviously, fiery eyes darting to her pink mouth. Leaning into her ear, he purred, "No, little monster, you will know when I want you to beg."

Duna choked, trying miserably to catch her breath. Her mouth hung open in an embarrassingly wide way, saliva pooling at the corners.

Cathal chuckled, lifting a long, callused finger to the underside of her chin, closing her gaping mouth for her, and turning, walked back to his desk. "Get some rest, Duna. We leave in the morning."

The group of six left at dawn the next morning, riding out of the barracks at first light. Cathal on his black stallion, Rhun and another warrior by the name of Kane with their own massive chestnut mares. Not having their own horses, Duna, Petra, and Lir had saddled the ones chosen by their very own Captain Moira, presumably not trusting them to make the appropriate choice and therefore embarrassing her in front of the General.

The previous day, Cathal and his entourage of men had went out to inspect a village that had been raided and destroyed in an ambush by a group of vigilantes.

In a matter of hours, they had apprehended the culprits and sent them heavily guarded under the cover of darkness to the capital city, Scythia, to be persecuted by the King.

Upon returning to Duna's training camp, the General had received word of two more villages close to the border with the Kingdom of Nissa that had fallen under the same misfortune. They agreed to split up. Axel, Prince Edan, and a small number of warriors were to ride out to one of them, while Cathal and his group were tasked in investigating the other remaining village.

Not particularly caring for the scenery, Duna trotted away on her horse, humming to herself a low tune that her grandmother had sung her when she was a young girl. She missed her so much, it hurt Duna whenever she thought of the elderly woman who had died more than five years ago the most tragic of deaths.

Approaching her on the right, Rhun nudged her shoulder with his knuckles, "Not that your singing isn't lovely, but seeing as we are going on a hunt for some bandits, it would be to our advantage if we kept a low profile. Wouldn't want to scare away the bad men, eh?" He winked at her, grinning like he had said the funniest thing.

Duna scrutinized the auburn, short-haired male with hazel eyes, shaking her head at the – once again – giant man. *What do they feed these people?* At six foot five and a lean but stocked build, he stood out with the rest of the substantial males in their entourage.

"You know, Lieutenant," she started, "I believe that the bandits are bound to *see* us first before they actually hear us, what with you four *massive* fellows prancing around in the forest on your four *massive* horses." She flashed him a dazzling smile underneath her mask, trying her best not to roll her eyes at the ridiculously large warrior.

Roaring laughter reached her from behind. Without needing to turn around, Duna knew who it belonged to. She would recognize that heart warming sound anywhere, it was so rare.

Rhun seemed stunned, whether at her comment or the General's show of amusement, she wasn't too sure. He retreated to his original spot in front of the line, only to be replaced by the very man himself who was still laughing away.

Cathal assessed her from the corner of his eye, before finally turning his whole head towards her, "How did you sleep? Any more unexpected visitors during the night?"

Duna arched a defined eyebrow, perplexed by his abrupt question. "Are you worried about me, General?"

He quietly analyzed her features before responding, "Cathal."

She hesitated. "What?"

"My name, it's Cathal. You don't need to address me as General when we are alone."

"But we are not alone," Duna was, once again, completely

dumbfounded.

"To me, we are," his intense gaze bore into her, willing her to comprehend what he was silently imploring her.

She scrunched her brows in confusion, not understanding the underlying implication, seeing as another four people trotted along around them. "I don't understand."

Cathal cocked his head, his eyes bouncing between her two questioning ones, as if contemplating on what to say. Ignoring her inquisitive gaze, he said, "The village is just around the bend, behind that line of trees. Get ready, it will not be a pretty sight."

"Anything in particular that we should be on the lookout for?"

"Fires," he answered sternly, "lots of fires. People burning in them. You are not, under any circumstances, to go running into a blazing home. Do you understand me, soldier?"

"Duna," she repeated his words to him. "My name is Duna. I much prefer to be addressed by my first name than the title soldier."

He looked utterly and truly baffled at her admission.

Sighing, she elaborated, "I have never participated in an actual battle. My five years in the army have been spent training and going on scouting missions for the Captain. I would hardly call that the definition of a soldier," she paused, "I most likely should not be admitting this to you – the General, but I did not have a choice when I joined the military. Nor did I enlist for righteous reasons. My heart was in a dark place when I made the choice to join, it was never meant to become my life."

Cathal contemplated on her words, seeming to mull them over in his head, "Sometimes it is not our motives that matter but what we do with the choices that we make thereafter. It takes a lot of courage to admit to ourselves our own imperfections, to accept them," he turned his face to Duna, regarding her with an unreadable expression. "The strongest individuals are forged in the most trying of times." He gave her a one last indecipherable look, and rode back to his current place at the back of the group.

Duna was left stumped. What an enigmatic man. She couldn't get a clear reading on the General. One moment he was broody and demanding, while the next he was giving such insightful advice that she wondered how old the male actually was.

If she considered his long military experience and legendary status as one of the most revered Generals to have ever led the Tyrossian armies in the long ominous history of the Kingdom, he had to be at least in his late forties. His face and physique, on the other hand, painted a much different picture, where the man appeared to be in his late twenties to early thirties. What puzzled Duna the most were his eyes.

Those magnificent, soul searing green aventurine eyes. Eyes that seemed to have lived through millennia of turmoil and regret. Ones that stripped her of her defenses, leaving her bare and vulnerable.

She did not like to be vulnerable, and yet with Cathal, it seemed as natural as breathing to her. Within a single brief moment during which their gazes collided, he peeled away her layers of apathy and coldness, breaching the walls that she had erected all those many years ago. She did not get the impression that he was a dishonorable human being, that he would exploit her vulnerability for his own personal gain.

The group came to a sudden stop, ceasing Duna's inner musings. What greeted them was a devastation so complete that for a brief moment in time, Duna wasn't sure what it was that lay before them.

Until she recognized the familiar sight of fire singed buildings, the decaying black grass, the ashen turned ground.

They rode through the ruined village, where by some unknown mercy a small number of people could be seen tending to each other. Others were rummaging through the ruins in hopes of reclaiming what little salvageable belongings they could find.

A little girl of no more than eight summers was tending to an elderly woman who was lying with her back on a make-shift bed. Duna dismounted and approached them, her insides turning in an agonizing way, violently threatening to be expelled from her body. "Hello, little one," she spoke to the red haired freckled girl kneeling besides a seemingly unconscious woman. "My name is Duna. How is your companion faring? Where are your parents?"

The girl looked up at her with tear filled eyes, her lips quivering as she spoke to Duna, "I don't have any parents. They died two summers ago from a bloating sickness. My grandmother is the only mother and father that I now have." Turning back to her grandmother, she continued to silently wash her face with some cold pond water. Quietly she whispered, "I can't imagine my life without her in it."

Duna blanched, her stomach knotting up until it turned to impenetrable stone. Her heart hammered frantically, her body shook uncontrollably. Bidding the girl farewell, she quickly fled the scene, desperately trying to gain her composure.

She was going to be sick.

The little girl's words echoed in her head. She was eight, alone, with her grandmother who was lying unconscious, dying as a result of a fire. The parallels were too great, the old wound on her heart too fragile.

Duna bolted to the edge of the ruined village as fast as her legs would take her. Yanking off her mask, she retched into the grass. Her breakfast was soon replaced by bile, burning her throat and insides with an acidic punishment.

Someone was suddenly there then, holding her hair back, grasping it tightly while she expelled the very last remaining drop of agony out of her body, leaving only an empty shell of sorrow and helplessness.

Duna kneeled back, wiping her mouth with the sleeve of her riding leathers. A gentle hand caressed her drenched hair, the sweat slowly beading along her temples, down her face.

"Are you alright?" a deep, velvety smooth voice rumbled softly from behind her, making her turn towards the speaker. Cathal's soft sage eyes burned through her, sorrow coloring his devastating features. "It is a tragedy, what these people went through. Your reaction is expected and completely justified." When she started to turn her face in embarrassment, he caught her chin in between his gloved fingers, turning her pale face back to his, softly speaking, "Please, let me look at you. You do not have to hide yourself from me." He rubbed his thumb along her jaw, caressing the skin of her cheek. His eyes followed the movements, then went to her parted lips, finally settling on her tear filled eyes.

Duna crumbled in his gentle hold, the tears flowing down her cheeks, saturating her skin with salt and moisture. She wheezed, collapsing into his arms, gulping for air while crying hysterically.

Cathal held her like that, his strong arms going around her shaking body, pressing her tightly into his sturdy leather clad chest. He held her like that for what seemed like hours, caressing her head, murmuring soothing words of comfort in her ear.

"We should be getting back," Duna said, wiping her eyes, "the others will be searching for us." She rubbed the moisture from her skin, pulling her hair away from her glum face.

"The others are of no consequence. We will return when you are ready," he searched her worried face, tucking a stray strand of chocolate hair behind her ear, "You have nothing to fear when you are with me, Duna. I will keep you safe." He stroked her blushing cheek with his thumb, hand splayed wide over the nape of her neck.

She sucked in a shaky breath, her heart fluttering away, a thousand wild butterflies growing in it's constricting chambers. His soft eyes were filled with an emotion that she couldn't place. Regret? Sorrow? Dread? Duna wasn't sure. The man was a walking conundrum.

"And who will keep me safe from you?" she whispered back.

His hand froze, lips parting slightly. He blinked a few times, as if struck by her question. Did he realize the effect that his presence had on her whenever he was near? The emotions that waged under her skin, deep in her organs, when he looked at her as if she was the most precious thing in the world?

Duna shook her head. She was being silly. She was over stimulated from her grief, her body decimated from the retching and the hysterical crying.

Cathal had shown her a rare kindness that she had rarely encountered in her short life of twenty eight years. He was being understanding, consoling her in her time of sorrow. It was a humane thing to do when another person was suffering. Her reaction to him was nothing more than her body's acknowledgement of that simple fact. There was no need for her to make something more out of it.

She stood, brushing off her leathers, and placed her mask back on. It was time for them to return, she needed to be alone. "Thank you for your kind words, General. I will not be taking up any more of your valuable time. Please, feel free to return to the rest of the group, I will come in a little while. I just need to gather my bearings together first. I don't want the others seeing me like this."

Cathal stepped towards her, reaching for her arm, "Duna, I–"

"Please," she stepped back, putting more space between their bodies.

He silently nodded, looking her hesitantly over one more time before he turned around and walked back in the direction of where the others were most likely already waiting for them.

Duna breathed out a long, strangled breath. She would wait until she returned to her tent at the training camp before falling apart all over again.

It was late evening by the time the company had returned to the barracks. They were exhausted, emotionally more than physically. Petra and Lir returned their horses to the military stables, giving Duna the chance to withdraw undetected to her own tent. She barged into her bathing chamber, not wanting to waste any time before collapsing into her bed. She would eat in the morning, she had lost her appetite long ago.

As Fate would have it, she would not get the reprieve that she had hoped for. "Finally, they think of us–" Petra balked at the open flaps of the bathing chamber, spinning on her feet when she saw Duna naked. Again. "Oh, come on, woman! Have you ever heard of clothing?"

"And have you ever heard of privacy?" Duna immersed herself in the surprisingly warm water. Or maybe her body was just too cold from the taxing emotions that had exhausted her. "You know, knocking, asking for permission before coming in? It's not that foreign of a concept," she shot Petra a critical look, "Well, to most people at least. You and that lieutenant seem to be unfamiliar with it."

"What lieutenant? Are you seeing someone?" Petra looked shocked.

"What? No, of course not," she rolled her eyes, "Never mind. What do you want?"

Petra regarded her with suspicion, eyes narrowing to thin slits. "The Captain is hosting a soirée tonight in honor of the General and Prince Edan. We are to attend, no exceptions. She was explicit on that last part."

Duna groaned, rubbing her face viciously with the palms of her hands, "I am not in the mood to go gallivanting around some pompous royals. Why bother inviting us, it doesn't make any sense."

Petra shrugged, picking up a lavender scented shampoo bottle, opening it before inhaling some of the aroma, "I believe she said something about representing her legion in a formidable light in front of the General. And you are one of her best warriors, regardless of what you may believe, Duna." Frowning, she picked up another bottle, this one of some essential almond oil that Duna used on her long, straight hair. "What is this crap? Do you actually use all of this? I feel like I walked into a concubine's nest, for fuck's sake."

She threw her towel at the incorrigible woman, "I am not going to any soirée, punishment be damned. Now, get out, I want to be left alone."

"I am sorry, truly I am, but Moira was adamant that everyone be there, even you. She will not take kindly to her direct order being ignored. Besides, you do not have to be there for long, just long enough until she sees that you made an effort. Then when she's boring the General to death, you can escape," Petra clasped her hands together, winked at Duna, and left.

Having no choice but to follow orders, Duna got dressed. She wore a simple olive green button up blouse that flowed freely over her breasts, accentuating the modest mounds and complimenting her healthy, sun kissed face. Her leather trousers she exchanged for body forming charcoal leggings that hugged her succulent curves and demanded attention. Her long, straight hair she left down, letting it air dry as she combed through the tresses. Not bothering with her mask, she pulled on her freshly polished black boots and left for the Captain's barrack.

Moira's tent was much grander than Duna's, but not as grand as the General's, of course. It was a strange mix of colors and furniture that the Captain had collected over her long years of travel and conquests in foreign lands. Large sphinx like statues greeted her at the open tent flaps, while inside was a multitude of colorful sitting pillows thrown haphazardly around the edges of the tent. Officers and soldiers mingled around, some laughing away on said cushions, other's immersed in deep conversations over, no doubt, some political matter.

At the head of the tent was Prince Edan, who was in deep conversation with a young woman with short, copper curls, who Duna recognized to be Kala, the warrior-healer that she had trained with on occasion.

To the left of them sat the General, mulling over a glass of whiskey which he was swirling around in his long fingers. He was lost deep in thought, it would seem, for he didn't register the Captain when she approached him until she lightly tapped him on the shoulder. He looked up at Moira, and that's when he saw her.

Their eyes locked.

Shock waves of intense energy collided into Duna. An onslaught of never ending charged particles exploded across her skin. Her body overheated, her organs starting to shut down in a desperate attempt of self-preservation. It all happened in a matter of seconds, in a solitary moment of time while they held each other's gaze across the room. Then the Captain moved, blocking Cathal's view of her, and Duna could finally breathe again.

I cannot go through this again. It's too much.

She spotted Petra and Lir debating with a group of three men, all dressed in ordinary soldier uniforms. Like a savior in the dark, she went to them, her body demanding a cure for her charged system.

Duna could feel the General watching her throughout the evening, following her every move. His eyes bore into the back of her head like two heated beams of light whenever she conversed with a fellow warrior. Like a lion lying low in the bushes, waiting for the opportune time to strike at it's unsuspecting prey. Except Duna was no one's prey, nor was she helpless.

The crowd grew larger as the night progressed. It seemed as if the whole tent was overflowing with leathers and strange scents. The Captain had acknowledged her multiple times during the night, there was no need for her to remain.

Having had enough of the crowd, Duna bid Petra farewell and exited the tent.

Being too strung up from the evening's celebrations, she walked to the edge of the barracks where a small lake lay secluded by a few rows of old trees. A thick blanket of violet bellflowers bloomed all around the edge of the water, as if drawn to the very life force from which it thrived. She would sometimes come here to clear her mind when she was feeling frustrated. She found that the tantalizing scent of the old pine trees mixed in with the wildflowers and the crystal cool water of the lake was like a balm for her senses.

Approaching the water's edge, Duna looked in. The lake was actually a large pool of bright blue water which now in the moonlit evening sky appeared almost silver. The Moon shimmered across the still water, giving an almost ethereal feel to the place. Duna was aching for a swim in the clear waters. They always helped her mind settle.

Stripping of her clothes and folding them neatly on a nearby rock, she slowly entered the lake, immersing herself until her entire head was submerged. She stayed like that until her lungs started burning, relishing in the sensation that made her feel alive. When she couldn't take the pressure any longer, she emerged, wiping her eyes as to clear away the moisture.

Blinking rapidly, she gasped.

An enormous, black, ominous shadow was looming over the water's edge, it's pair of blazing ruby red eyes locked tight on Duna.

CHAPTER 7

He was irritated and angry. At himself, at his surroundings. He wanted to punch something, and Cathal could not even begin to comprehend the root of such violent impulses which were currently plaguing him.

For the past ten days his emotions have been taking him on a wild rollercoaster ride, sometimes interchanging in a matter of minutes and then back to another wave of irritation and frustration.

Ever since that day, when he had first laid eyes on her.

Duna. That infuriatingly maddening woman.

There were times when he had wanted to strangle her, to wring her little neck for talking back to him. He chuckled to himself, remembering her little outbursts. He was lying to himself; he found her bantering endearing, even seductive. A characteristic which greatly annoyed him in other people, but which he could not get enough of with that walking contradiction of a woman.

She was fierce, lethal. Impossibly fast.

A force to be reckoned with.

Even now, remembering how she had fought Axel and then him, he could not stop being awe inspired. And there were not many things in the world that impressed Cathal. Her skill with the blade had been the first thing that had drawn him to her, even though at that time he was not aware that she was, in fact, a woman.

When she had taken that mask off, his world had crumbled. She was breathtaking. Her features so singularly simple yet when combined together they painted a magnificent canvas of pure feminine beauty. Creamy, slightly sun kissed skin. Large, bright eyes the color of warm honey, surrounded by thick, dark lashes. A symmetric, medium sized straight nose. Lips– Cathal closed his eyes, groaning at the memory.

Those fucking lips.

Lips moderate in size but so plump and defined that he could only imagine what it would feel like kissing them. Licking them. Sinking his teeth into while he sucked them into his own mouth. He had been left speechless in her presence, lying on the ground of that fighting pit like a mute.

Days had passed by without seeing her after that fight. He had needed some time to recuperate, to get his bearings together. He was the General, for fuck's sake, he did not swoon over some woman. Especially, not Duna. He had a mate. A betrothed. *Leila.*

Cathal felt ashamed of himself for the way that he had left her in his bed, without notice and in the middle of the night. He had intended to write to her to explain himself, to make her understand that his abrupt departure had nothing to do with her. It was all him. His need to find answers to his dreaded feelings, to the helplessness that had eaten away at him in those last days at the palace. Something had not been right, and he had needed to find out what that something was.

He searched the celebrations for the little warrior, but she was nowhere to be found. *She was just standing there in that corner with that idiot of a man.*

He clenched his jaw, almost breaking his teeth. Every single man in that room had been stalking Duna with his eyes as soon as she had entered the Captain's tent. Like vultures circled carrion, he had seen how they leered over her. How they had made ridiculous attempts at getting her attention, some going as far as feinting to kiss her hand, which she had quickly pulled away.

Those little boys playing men were no match for her. She would eat them alive and spit them out before repeating the process again. And she would enjoy it, too, like the menacing warrior that she was. Only a real man would ever be enough for a woman like Duna, only a real man would ever be able to satisfy her every need.

Like himself.

He would worship her like she was meant to be worshipped, like the goddess that she was. Even under that heavy cloak and those ridiculous leathers that she wore to training she could not hide her delectable body from him. Curves for days, with thick succulent thighs that Cathal could just imagine gripping while he fucked her into oblivion.

He hissed, his hand straining against the decanter which he was holding on his knee. *Where the fuck is she?*

He had to get it together. He could not allow a purely physical reaction to deter him from his promise to Leila. He would not be that type of man.

Cathal had to be reasonable. He was a healthy, virile male of thirty eight, in a military training camp where men were a majority. It was no surprise that his hormones were raging, it was a natural response to a beautiful female body. And he was not blind, every man could see that Duna was every man's walking wet dream.

I will kill any fucker that even looks at her.

Having had enough of his contradictory feelings for the woman, he downed his whiskey and left the tent. He was acting borderline insane. One moment he was pining over Duna like a hormonal adolescent and the next he was cursing the gods for not making him stay at the palace, with the Princess.

That was another thing that confounded Cathal. He already had a fated mate, as rare as it was for mortals; it should not matter that she was far away, the bond would stick, should grow even stronger when two mates were apart. Yet, he did not feel it as he had prior to this trip. He had never even noticed another woman besides Leila up until Duna had come along. How was it possible that he now lusted after two females?

He frowned, silently reprimanding himself for such an idiotic statement. He did not lust after Duna. She was attractive, yes, but that was all there was to it. His feelings for her were nonexistent, did not breach the standard General-soldier relationship that was normal for all of his officers.

When he returned to the palace he would fuck his brains out with Leila and this stupid issue would be resolved.

She probably left with some prick for the night, anyway.

Cursing colorfully out loud, Cathal walked through the barracks, weaving through the tired soldiers. Duna was a true puzzle to him. Aside from her exquisite beauty, there was a feeling of sadness that followed her around, as if she had lived through some great tragedy that had imprinted itself onto her soul and now shone through her piercing hazel eyes.

He could recognize a tortured soul, for Cathal's was equally tormented. His life had been filled with great injustice and stark devastation that even to this day he could not forget. What could have happened to a young woman of Duna's age to have such a grim outlook on life?

He thought back to that scorched village from earlier on that day, to how she had crumbled in his arms, rivers of tears drenching his leathers. How she had bared her soul to him; had allowed herself to be vulnerable in front of him. Something had changed in him at that moment, while he had been holding her shaking body tightly to his chest. His heart had ached; had felt it crack just a little. Cathal could not stand to witness her so morose and distraught. It seemed to cause him physical pain to do so. If he could only take away her sorrow and place it in his own miserable body.

Lost in his ponderings, Cathal failed to realize that he had come to the edge of some woods bordering the training grounds. He mentally went over some field maps, searching for some hints as to what this forest was. If he remembered correctly there should be a small, secluded lake somewhere in those trees. He should go investigate; he loved to investigate.

It's not like you have anything better to do.

He made his way down to the woods, a feeling of excitement overtaking him. It had been such a long time since he had been able to explore without interruptions. His daily routine and duties as a General left him with little free time, he was always occupied, always–

Cathal stopped dead in his tracks. He inhaled a strangled breath. Leaning on a tree trunk, heart raging, he watched from the shadows as the scene unfolded before him.

Standing by the edge of the lake was Duna, naked. She was breathtaking. Exquisite. The Moon illuminated her resplendent body, drawing Cathal's eyes to every dip and hollow of her exposed figure. The delicate lines of her neck, the modest slopes of her supple breasts, her toned narrow waist, hips that went on for days, a round, mouthwatering ass, thick toned thighs that ended in elongated calves.

He could not stop salivating at the sight of her. It was an image that would forever be imprinted on the insides of his retinas. It would haunt his days and long, despairing nights, until the very day that he drew his last breath in this unjust world.

Cathal watched mesmerized, unmoving, as she immersed herself in the shimmering waters, her straight, silky strands of chocolate hair flowing freely to the middle of her back.

The gods were playing a cruel joke on him. There was no other explanation. Pushing off the trunk, he straightened and exhaled a calming breath. That's when he saw him, hiding in the shadows.

Roc.

His dire wolf was there, staring at Duna as she bathed, unaware of the beast's presence. Cathal had not seen his companion for a few weeks now, having no control of his comings and goings. He was a wild animal, a creature of the night, with his ebony dark fur and ruby red eyes. A massive demonic figure in the ever looming shadows.

Like Cathal, Roc loved solitude. He was not easily impressed. He did not easily trust. The only other person that Roc had allowed to come near him was the Lieutenant, Axel, and even with him Roc was on unpredictable grounds. The fact that he was sitting by the water's edge now was a precedent that even Cathal had never before borne witness to.

The General observed as Duna locked eyes with the animal, going stone still in the dark waters. She slowly backed up, never removing her eyes from Roc. The dire wolf followed her movements, getting up and ever so slowly approaching the place where the water met the ground at the lake's entrance. The place where Duna now stood naked and dripping wet, her gorgeous body glistening in the moonlight.

Cathal's heart hammered away, panic slowly setting in. He had to do something, this was not going to end well. But if he acted impulsively, he could endanger Duna. Roc would not hurt him, but he could not guarantee the same for the little warrior.

The two enigmatic creatures stood staring at each other, as if sizing the other up. Duna took a single miniscule step closer to Roc. He remained standing on all fours, his ruby red eyes promising retribution to anyone who dare approach them.

Then, the strangest thing happened. Roc lowered his front legs to the ground, his head following next, as if in submission.

Cathal stared, eyes wide, mouth gaping open, dumbfounded and shocked at the scene that was unfolding before him. It appeared as if the dire wolf, an alpha himself of the highest rank, was bowing to Duna.

How is this possible.

To the male's utter astonishment, Duna approached the bowing creature, and crouching down in front of him, started softly rubbing his fur covered head all the way to his muzzle. A low, rumbling sound emanated across the lake to where Cathal stood hiding.

He's purring.

"You like that, don't you?" Duna said, laughing at the intimidating beast, scratching him behind the ears with both of her hands, while he plastered himself on the grass like a fluffy puppy.

Cathal was going to have a heart attack. He blanched, suffocating, his heart beating at an immeasurable rate, his blood boiling to dangerous levels. If he could only get into that water and cool down his body, it would all pass.

He didn't get the chance, for Roc suddenly stood up, nuzzled and then licked Duna's cheek, and peacefully retreated into the shadows.

What, in the ever loving fuck, was that.

Cathal stood on the outskirts of Moira's fighting pit, looking on as Duna battled two seasoned warriors that could easily crush her with their arms.

She was a sight to behold. Two cyclone tri-edged spiraling daggers with obsidian sharp blades that spanned almost the whole length of her forearms were spinning and jabbing away at her opponents. He noticed that the two men were strapped up in light chain-mail while Duna fought in only a body forming black leather bodysuit, leaving nothing to the imagination as the fabric hugged her delectable curves, no additional armor covering it.

Even with their height and weight advantages the two men were no match for the fierce warrior. Cathal realized then that the chain-mail was maybe not enough protection for the males, little good it did them against the tempest that was Duna.

Her silky hair was braided today in a thick braid that sprawled the length from the top of her crown to the middle of her back. No cloak today, just her black meshed leather mask. *That stupid mask again.*

Cathal understood why she wore it, he was not a complete imbecile. Her lifestyle of sparring in the dirt almost ten hours a day would leave her lungs blackened and useless if it weren't for that mask. But he still hated it. It blocked his view of her magnificent face.

"Leave us," he barked to the two warriors struggling to keep up with Duna.

Bowing at the waist, the males placed away their weapons and exited the fighting pit. She turned to him, her two daggers lowered at the sides of her mesmerizing body, slowly appraising Cathal from head to toe and back up to his blazing green eyes. "To what do I owe this pleasure, General? Come to play with us mere mortals?"

That mouth. "One of these days, Duna," he paced right up to her small five foot five frame, towering over her in his training leathers, his head tilted so their eyes locked, "I am going to shut that big mouth of yours right up." He lowered his heated eyes to her mask covered mouth, irritated that a piece of cloth was blocking his view.

Duna chuckled, seeming to be quite amused by his statement, "Highly unlikely that you will be going anywhere near my mouth, General." Arching a defined brow, she stared right back at him, her gaze unwavering.

"Who said anything about me going near your mouth, hmm?" Lifting his fingers to her face, he took off her mask. "By the time that I am done with you, little monster, you won't even remember where your mouth is." He licked his lips when he saw her juicy mouth parted just so, imagining that it was her plump lips that he was licking instead.

Her chest heaving, Duna swallowed. Clenching her daggers, she fumed, "I am sure I will find someone willing to help me locate it. After all, what are my fellow comrades for?" she grinned, as if she knew she had hit a nerve with him.

"The fuck you will." Rage consumed him, lowering his face to barely an inch from hers, his temper rising to uncontrollable levels at just the thought of another man touching those lips. Brows furrowed tightly together, eyes wild with anger, he growled, "I will punish every man and woman that touches you, and then I will make you watch as I do it again, over and over, until you finally get it through that pretty little head of yours that I do not tolerate disobedience." Her intoxicating scent of lavender and almonds sent his senses into overdrive.

"It is fortunate, then, that I am not your betrothed," she shot him an icy stare, cooling him down instantly, "for I would hate to have so many lives on my conscience."

Well, fuck me. "My betrothed is of no concern to you, do not speak of her again." He straightened to his full height, stepping back to give himself relief from her suffocating presence. "You are to address her as required, by the title Her Highness, or the Princess Leila. Do not make me punish you. I will not tolerate unruliness."

"Of course, General," Duna curtsied low, mocking him, yanking back her mask from his punishing grip, "I will never make the same mistake again." Placing the mask back on her face, she sheathed her daggers and started to exit the fighting pit.

He stepped in front of her, fists clenching furiously at his sides, voice deadly, "I did not give you permission to leave, soldier. You will do so when I release you from my company."

"With all due respect, *General*," she lifted her furious gaze, staring him down, speaking dangerously low, "I do not give a fuck about your permission. Now, move." Steam seemed to billow out from her ears, her whole body still as stone, like a deadly beast preparing for the kill.

Cathal stood there, not moving, not knowing what to do.

He pushed himself on her, his abdomen coming within a hair's breadth of her chest, intending to grab her arms as a last desperate attempt to make her stay, to not leave him; to make her see just how much she was driving him insane.

In the flash of an eye, the sharp tip of her dagger was pushing into the underside of his chin, it's blade breaking his skin where it made contact.

"Do not touch me, General," she hissed. His head tilted back as she pressed the blade even further into his skin, "for it will be the last thing that you ever do." With those final words, she slowly lowered her dagger, not bothering to return it to it's holster. Bowing low at the waist, she left Cathal, miserable and alone with his conflicting emotions.

He did not know what to do with himself. He wanted to crawl out of his skin; to punch something until his knuckles were broken and bleeding. He paced up and down along the edge of the fighting pit, trying to work off some of the brewing anger.

Everything that he did, it was pointless. His agitation and frustration grew even more, every step that he made like an iron weight on his aching heart. He fumed, cursing loudly and profusely, pulling at his hair which he gripped tightly in his stiff fingers.

Roaring, he threw his sword across the field, impaling it in the heart of a wooden training dummy.

Why couldn't she see how exasperating she was? How her presence brought out the possessive beast in him? Even he, himself, did not know what to make out of if, out of the tornado of emotions that were continuously swirling around in him, growing exponentially in size as the days and nights went by. It was maddening, driving Cathal to the point of total and complete insanity.

He loved Leila, he had no doubt about his feelings for the Princess. He would die for her if it ever came down to a choice between her life and his.

They had met two decades ago when he had been appointed to Leila's personal entourage while she had been only a young girl. They had grown close together, spending all hours of the day side by side, Leila playing in the gardens, horseback riding, going to her lessons, all while the dutiful young Cathal stood vigilantly at her side, being her armor and shield from the outside world.

At some point over the following decade, their relationship had changed, becoming a close friendship that later as she grew more mature evolved into a burning flame of lust and eventually, love. There was never a doubt in Cathal's mind that Leila would be the woman that he would one day marry.

However, something had changed in the last few years. She had become more subdued, more apprehensive, as if she was afraid to speak something that would upset him. She never challenged him anymore, always settling just so that a conflict would not ensue between them.

It drove him crazy, for he did not know how to act around her when she retreated into herself. He had tried talking to her, to extract the cause of such a drastic change, but she had continually informed him that she had always been that way, that it was he who had changed.

Cathal shook his head, trying to clear his dreary thoughts. A small knot of apprehension was slowly growing in his gut, increasing in size as he stood stoic in the fighting pit of the military training camp. It felt as if a thousand little sharp needles were embedding themselves in his mucous membranes.

Why were the fates so cruel?

He should not have met Duna Damaris, should not have inhaled her intoxicating scent. Should not have seen the shattering torment in those breathtaking hazel eyes. It was as if her soul called to him through those glistening glass membranes. He could not escape her, even in his dreams she loomed there uninvited and ever wanted.

What was it about that little cool fireball of a woman that confounded him so? That caused his body to overheat and wreak havoc on his insides. He felt a desperate need to know what she was doing, to witness with his own eyes that she was safe.

Cathal refused to ponder any longer on their relationship. *What relationship? You don't even know her.*

Nodding to himself, he sauntered over to the training dummy, pulling out his impaled sword and inspecting it. Throwing it back and forth between his hands, he contemplated on his ever pressing issue. He would be leaving the military barracks in less than a fortnight. He would have to deal with his growing curiosity for the little she-devil at a later date, preferably never if it the fates were kind to him. The sooner he left the better.

Little did Cathal know that he should be careful what he wished for, for his wish might just come true.

CHAPTER 8

For the next three days, there were no changes to Duna's routine. She woke up every day while the Moon was still in the sky, ate her portion of porridge and bread, and trained all day until the Sun went down over the horizon. There had been a few breaks in between the sparring sessions, mostly to relieve herself and to fill her body with much needed fuel. Petra and Lir had been her dueling partners on those days, having mostly the same daily routine as Duna.

The General had made his appearance on multiple occasions in the fighting pit, mostly observing the fights. There had been a few instances when Duna and him had sparred under the excuse that he was too ruthless for the other warriors and therefore they did not present themselves as worthy adversaries.

She had obliged without a second thought, not because she wanted to indulge his ever changing whims, but because she, too, felt that no other compared to the General as far as combat skills went. There was no challenge when she fought the others, no level of satisfaction when she single-handedly beat them. Cathal was a worthy opponent, one that pushed her to her physical limits and challenged her mental resilience.

So, they sparred for hours, neither one of them willing to call it a draw, pressing the other until their shaking bodies had begged them for a reprieve.

Cathal taunted her, played with her, tried to pull forth any reaction from Duna. She ignored him each time, barely uttering a single word to the male during the entirety of their encounters. She could see that it was driving him insane, her ignorance of his imposing presence. But she would not relent, would not give him the satisfaction of getting a rouse out of her.

He wanted her to be obedient? Fine. She shall be the obedient little soldier that he wanted her to be. She will play into his obnoxious role as the General of the Tyrossian armies, into his obvious need to be addressed with reverence and awe.

Duna wanted to puke just thinking about it. *You shall address her as Her Highness.*

What egos these royals had, even the high standing officers seemed to suffer from an over inflation of the self, the General included. She had pegged him to be different, to not be affected by such senseless standings. As if one's title equated to a human being of higher worth.

How preposterous for someone to even indulge in such a shameful thought, let alone live by it as his life's standard.

It was obvious to Duna that the General thought of her as less. Not good enough. She shook her head, thinking of his last words on the very same fighting pit as the one that she was now standing on. *I will not tolerate unruliness.* She clenched her jaw, her anger already rising up to the challenge.

Returning back to the present, she focused on the General who was standing on the sides, observing a group of four while they sparred with spears. Perfect time for her to retreat. She had had enough of training for today, her bed had her name written all over it.

Reaching her modest tent, she pulled off her dirt covered boots and placed them in front of the tent flaps. They were too dirty for her to walk in with them, and she really was not in the mood to waste her dire time scrubbing away some filthy footwear.

Duna bathed and pampered herself, relishing in the soothing body creams and oils. She loved to treat herself to such little luxuries, feeling that she deserved them after all the effort and energy that she put forth daily training and scouting for the kingdom.

Pulling on a freshly washed light blue nightshirt that went to the middle of her thighs, she drained the remaining water from her hair and wrapped it into a towel, finally leaving the stuffy bathing chamber. She would do her hair tomorrow morning, the important thing was that it was nice and clean.

"Why have you been ignoring me?"

Duna jumped, her hand flying to her chest, clenching the nightshirt over her erratic heart. "What is the matter with you people?" she shouted at the General, "Does no one ever knock anymore?"

Cathal stood in front of her in his leathers, seemingly to have come directly from the training pit. His hair was disheveled, as if he had run his hand through it many times. He was appraising her in her nightgown, eyes hovering on her bare thighs and calves.

As breathtaking as ever, Duna stood entranced by him. It was not only his god like appearance that made her breath catch every time she laid her eyes on him. It was the way he held himself, his confidence and self-worth that radiated from every pore of his body. His nonchalance and coolness that he wore like a second skin. Nothing seemed to able to deter him, to break through his defenses.

He was like a beast; ruthless, menacing. Always poised for the attack.

"I asked you a question, Duna. Answer me," Cathal seethed, his eyes darkening to a deep forest green color. "Do you enjoy making me angry?"

Duna laughed, head thrown back, eyes tearing up from the irony of the whole situation. "Gen–Pardon me," she bowed low at the waist, holding her nightgown to her body so as not to reveal her cleavage to the virile male. "General, I apologize if I have offended you. It was not my intention. I take my position as your and Her Highness's humble servant very seriously. Please, if you could find it in your virtuous hearts to forgive me, I will be forever obliged to you."

"You dare mock me, soldier?" he spat, never increasing his voice, the rage vibrating within his darkened eyes.

"I do no such thing, General. Once again, I am sincerely sorry if I have done anything to cause you discomfort or the feeling of subordination. You are my commanding officer," she inclined her head mockingly, "and I am a nobody. I will accept whatever fitting punishment you deem appropriate for such an error." Lowering her hands, she clenched the edge of her nightshirt, wringing the material so as to calm herself. She would not be intimidated by him, she would not allow anyone to make her feel less worthy just because of her status at birth. "If you would excuse me, I would like to get some rest. Even though not as taxing and demanding as yours most certainly was, I did my best to serve this Kingdom as a true, devoted soldier always should."

Cathal appraised her once more, slowly stalking to her across the space, his hands in his pockets, a slightly bewildered look on his face, "Enough of this nonsense. Why have you been ignoring me, Duna? I demand to know," as if he had not heard a single word that Duna had just said, he strolled right up to her irritated face.

"May I speak plainly?" she said, refusing to back down.

"Has there ever been a time when you didn't?" he arched his thick eyebrow, playing with a strand of her wet hair which had fallen from her towel wrapped head.

Ignoring the male's attempt to addle her, she cleared her throat and started, "I don't appreciate being made a fool of. I don't appreciate being mocked and humiliated just because I was born a commoner. My worth is not determined by my title, or rather, lack of one," breathing in, she continued, "I do not expect kindness nor do I need it. From anyone. I don't need pity. I will always fulfill my duty to this Kingdom and its people," she clenched her fists, lava hot anger boiling her insides, "Do not treat me like an insolent little child just because I have a mind of my own and because I refuse to be trampled on by men and women alike, whatever their standings might be. I may not be a princess or a queen, but I am not a worthless piece of flesh. Furthermore, you do not know me, General. You can not even pretend to understand the life that I have left behind and the one that I have been forced to lead." She lifted her proud chin, eyes boring into Cathal. "To answer your question. I have not been ignoring you. I have only been following your orders, General, to be obedient, respectful, mindful of my place, si—"

"You ignorant, maddening, infuriatingly obnoxious woman," he fumed, arms splayed wide while he rambled on, "You are by far the most irritating person that I have ever had the misfortune of knowing in my entire wretched life!" Cathal grabbed her by the shoulders, eyes begging her to comprehend what his words were failing to convey, "You have done nothing but get under my thick skin, from the very first godforsaken day, and drench the life out of my worthless body. Like a leach you have caught on, sucking my blood dry like a demonic plague, draining it ever so slowly from my organs, replacing it with an addictive substance that is singularly consumed by the intoxicating essence that is you," he released her, backing up, his face crumbling with despair, "You are like a drug, one which you know that you do not need but that you nevertheless inhale because the feeling of it flowing through your veins is the most exquisite sensation that you have ever experienced." He closed his beautiful eyes, cutting off Duna's life source.

Lowering his head, as if admitting defeat, he whispered, "Even though I know that it is not good for me, that it will only cause me irrevocable harm, I have grown addicted to it."

If there ever was a sound for hopelessness and despair, Duna imagined that it would sound something along the lines of the one surrounding the two of them at that very moment. Silence. An absolute consuming lack of sound. As if all the air has been drained from the room, leaving only their two beating hearts and unspoken thoughts.

She could not form words, her tongue was left lying in her oral cavity like a lifeless piece of flesh. She could not begin to comprehend let alone allow herself to misinterpret the General's admission.

What ever could that magnificent man want with a simple commoner like her? To add even more fuel to the fire, he was to marry another woman. It was laughable for Duna to even ponder on the miniscule possibility that the male could even slightly be interested in her. It was just not possible, and so it would do her no good to extrapolate such an absurd notion.

"General, now it is my turn to ask of you, do you mock me? Am I really that worthless in your eyes as to make such a cruel play at my emotions? You are betrothed, to Princess Leila no less. I have understood that quite well the first time that it became known to me. I will not overstep again in regards to your status and ranking. If my word means nothing then please, discharge me for my insolence and be done with it."

Cathal balked, mouth parted, seeming at an equal loss of words as Duna had been mere moments ago.

He did not need to elaborate – she understood perfectly well what he was trying to convey to her in kind language instead of being hurtful and condescending.

"Duna–" he started to say, softly speaking as if trying not to frighten off a wary deer.

"General," Axel barged in, interrupting Cathal's speech, "you have been summoned back to Scythia by the King. He is demanding that we return at once. Prince Edan and Lieutenant Brayan have already left. The dispatch didn't say what all the fuss is about, but I can imagine that it is something of high importance for Fergal to dare to interrupt your military campaign in such an abrupt manner." He turned to Duna then, finally acknowledging the state of her undress in which she was standing in front of the General, "I suggest you get some clothes on, little warrior, it is going to be a cold night." He winked at her, grinning like a madman.

Cathal snatched him up by the collar of his shirt, hissing in his face, "I thought I told you already to never presume anything. Yet, here you are, once again, barging into her tent in the middle of the fucking night. Do you have a death wish, Lieutenant?"

Axel blanched, then reddened, the sudden change in color happening almost instantaneously. He barked at Cathal, "Did you not hear just what I said? You are to leave at once for the palace! There is an issue of the utmost importance which requires your attention!"

Cathal smoldered, still holding the massive warrior by the collar, the weight of his hard grip almost tearing the clothing around his fingers. "The King is the last person that you should be worried about right now, Axel. Do not, ever again, overstep my direct order, do you understand me? This is your last warning." Releasing his hold on the blond man, he continued, "Pack my things and prepare the horses. We leave immediately."

Duna could only stand and listen while the two males stormed at each other, wondering about their relationship. They seemed close, like old companions who have gone through a lot of hardships together.

The Lieutenant left, leaving a pondering Cathal still standing in front of her, his eyes lowered in thought, his fists clenching at his sides. Duna observed him as a colorful array of a thousand different emotions played along the General's stunning features.

He was leaving, and Duna would most likely never see him again. What a cruel, unjust world she was living in. But she knew this was inevitable, that his place was and will always be at the palace, by his betrothed. *Princess Leila.*

Duna had no place in his life, in any shape or form. She was just a soldier in a military camp, one of hundreds of thousands. Who would remember a single grain of salt in an overwhelming wave of the ocean?

Finally finished contemplating, Cathal glanced at her, standing in that short blue nightgown of hers, with her hair still wrapped in a towel on top of her head. An unreadable look was in his eyes, one that Duna thought she had seen many times cross his face when they were in the same vicinity and she had caught him staring at her.

Nodding his head in a single slight inclination, a blank expression on his face, the General turned around and simply walked out of her tent, not once looking back to see if Duna was observing him as he walked away and out of her life.

CHAPTER
9

They rode through the night and the day that ensued, arriving at the palace just before dusk. There was a commotion of some sort, guards were running in every direction, soldiers and servants going in and out of the Throne Room as if being chased by demons.

Cathal entered the grand room without waiting to be announced to the King, eager to find out the basis for this ridiculous display of hysteria. To discover, from its source, the reason for which he had been forced to a swift departure from the military training camp and his little monster.

Duna. That enigma of a woman.

She had crawled into his system like an invisible thief and made herself a home in the fragile cavity of his breakable chest, right beside that conniving beating organ of his that was threatening to implode from the very idea of being away from the female. He had no choice but to admit to himself that there was something more to his never-ending curiosity for her, that it was not just a question of physical attraction.

Cathal did not know what to do with his ever-growing interest. How to proceed.

He was betrothed. To another woman.

To a princess, nonetheless, of a kingdom to whom he had vowed fealty to all those years ago. He did not want to be haste and make a premature decision that could end in disaster. He had to think of Leila, of her feelings for him, of Cathal's feelings for her. It was a complicated mess of multiple factors, where the alteration of a single one could change the entire course of their lives. Of his life, of Leila's. Of Duna's.

It was not fair to either of the women for Cathal to give false hope to. He was not a bastard of that magnitude. He would cut his own throat if it ever came down to intentionally hurting either one of them.

To make matters even worse, he didn't know what make of the fierce woman herself. Duna was a conundrum of contradictory actions and perplexing displays of emotions, one that left Cathal even more baffled each time that he left her presence.

He sensed her attraction to him, there was no denying the obvious physical signs; the dilation of the pupils, the parting of the lips, the fast inhaling of strained air whenever he came near her. The erratic beating of her heart when he touched her.

He could smell it on her, that sweet smell of vanilla mixed with lavender and almond, raging like mighty rivers of wild turbulent waters, freeing themselves into the overly charged air and attacking his senses. They mixed with his own frenzied pheromones, causing an explosion of fireworks in his organs and mind, begging for a release.

What gave him pause was that Cathal did not know how far her attraction for him went, if it were merely a bodily response to his imposing presence, or if there was more to it, a deeper sense of connection.

Duna did not know Cathal, just as he did not know her. She had shown a fierceness and an unrelenting dedication to her craft that he greatly respected. Her devotion and loyalty were admirable, so much so that he had caught himself in awe of the woman, of her relentlessness to surrender until she expended the very last atom of strength from her overtired muscles. And even then, she had not given in to her weariness, to her aching body.

He had seen how she trembled with fatigue on multiple occasions during their many sparring sessions. Had witnessed how her organism had begun to shut down from the onslaught of adrenaline and exhaustion. It was of no consequence to Duna, however; her mind was like an iron fist, gripping the strings of her limbs, controlling them, pushing them to obey her every ruthless command.

Cathal had a need to study her, to dig into her thoughts. To experience her mind. To burrow through her memories and relive them with her. He knew that he could not continue to pretend that Duna was of no importance. That she was just another nameless person in the vast emptiness that was his life.

"General Ragnar," Prince Edan interrupted his wondering mind, "you must come with me, at once. The King has been waiting for you, he is highly agitated that you did not heed his summons earlier."

"Did he say what this was about? Why the sudden haste?" Cathal walked beside the giant of a man, who was the only one of a select number of males in the Kingdom who towered over the already imposing large frame of the General.

"No, he has not said anything to anyone, not even to Cian. It seems as if he is waiting for you to disclose of such information. I imagine that it is highly sensitive since everything is covered under a thick veil of secrecy."

They arrived at the War Room, a large oval open space filled with a long, rectangular mahogany table surrounded by twelve wooden chairs and one slightly grander for the King himself. The royal was already seated in his make-shift throne at the head of the table, his crown of obsidian claws and the dire wolf insignia planted proudly on his graying head.

They took a seat. Prince Cian Vilkas, the eldest son at the age of thirty five and the heir to the mighty throne of the Kingdom of Tyros, was to the right of his father, looking stern as ever. At a much shorter height then his younger brother, Edan, he sat at six foot two, with a full head of curly jet black hair that was cut off just under his chin. In contrast to his massive brother, Cian was a lean build of elongated muscles, forged for the cavalry and the many long hours of training that he did with the javelin while riding his war steed. His piercing grey eyes were always focused and clear, as if they could see right through to the very workings of one's mind.

Prince Edan, a spitting but slightly bulkier image of his eldest brother of two years, seated himself to the left of the King. The General sat next to the Crown Prince, who was having a staring contest with Axel, seemingly irritated with the man. Rhun sat down next to Cathal.

"There has been a raid in one of the neutral territories between our kingdom and the northern Kingdom of Nissa," the King began, addressing the men at the table, whose focus was on the elderly royal. "We received word of a potential humanitarian crisis in that area. I had allowed a small contingency of soldiers to accompany my daughter and her ladies in service to help the people, seeing as for years back she has been heavily involved in the Royal Aid and has gone to many humanitarian missions in the past, as you are all well aware of," Fergal paused, seeming to take a calming breath before continuing. "We sent our best palace guards, our finest men stationed on the grounds, that were trained in combat." He looked directly at Cathal. "It should have been enough," he swallowed, clearly aggravated. "Princess Leila, they have taken her hostage."

A wave of curses and murmurs went around the table as the news sank in. Cathal joined in the former, muttering colorful words under his breath. *Unbelievable. The idiot sent his own daughter to a raided village.*

"Your Majesty, how is it that I was not consulted before sending out soldiers on such a delicate mission? And no less then with the Princess, my betrothed?" he simmered, trying hard not to let his emotions show.

"General, the soldiers had been hand picked by myself and Lord Darcell, my Head Advisor to the King. Surely, you trust our judgment."

"It is not your judgment that I doubt, Your Majesty, but your objectiveness which may impede your ability to choose appropriately for such an important task. This issue could have been avoided all together if you had simply summoned me beforehand."

"How dare you question my decisions, General?!" Fergal shouted, turning crimson in the face as he sat on his make-shift throne, "I am the King!" he pounded on the table, "I do as I see fit, and I saw it fitting to send my daughter with her formidable guards because it is something that she has done on a countless number of occasions prior to this, and not once had there been an issue of such magnitude!"

"You insult me, Your Majesty," Cathal seethed, his temper rising, threatening to explode, "Your General of more than a decade. I have bled for this Kingdom, for Your throne. For Your family." He stood up, the chair scraping along the marble floor. "You will answer me, for I demand it of you." He leaned onto his hands, arms spread wide on the wooden table, his voice deadly low, "Why was I not informed of this humanitarian crisis? Why was I not summoned to the palace at once before you sent the Princess gallivanting unprotected into strange lands?"

"Enough!" the King shouted, bolting upright from his chair, which was pushed back from the table, "Leave us, all of you!"

The men in attendance filed out, troubled gazes darting between Cathal and Fergal, as if they were contemplating if it was wise to leave the King alone in a room with the General of his armies.

"General," the King finally turned his gaze to Cathal, moving to stand in front of him, "I will not tolerate such displays of insubordination from you. Know your place."

Cathal chuckled, straightening to his impressive height, "I will do no such thing, *Fergal*," he stopped in front of the royal, his hands casually placed in his pockets, "for you seem to have forgotten how it is that your ancestors came to sit upon that throne. Whose generosity and show of faith granted you your title." Cathal walked around the King, sauntering towards the make-shift throne, "Do you need a reminder, Fergal? Of whose blood and sacrifice anointed you the power and the privilege to call this once barren land your own?" He pulled the chair back to it's place at the head of the table, making himself comfortable in it as he continued ever so calmly, "I have lived through a hundred deaths and have been reborn in the most excruciating of ways in the span of a millennia as a sacrifice for my choice to come back to this gods forsaken land and to these dejected people until an appropriate ruler could be chosen. One that could be trusted to lead the immoral people of that time in a just and firm hand, unforgiving and ruthless, one that would maintain the laws of the gods and punish all who dared to defy them."

The General pointed a callused finger at the male who stood white as a ghost, stoic, unblinking, "You swore an oath to me when I chose you to be one such faithful servant. *You*, swore an oath, to *me*, Fergal, one of blood. As I, too, had vowed that day to keep these people safe. Do not mistake my tolerance for your ever-growing impudence as a sign of allowance. I, who have left my soul on the Plains of Iphigenia when the War of the Four Kingdoms decimated these lands. Whose blood still taints those same fields now stripped of all life, where not even the breeze dares to blow. Where ghosts of all those fallen warriors haunt the barren plains. You would do well to remember that, Fergal, for just as I have gifted you the throne, I will also be the one to take it all away from you."

The King held his breath, not daring to move, as Cathal approached him, slowly appraising him as he stopped a mere foot away. "You will instruct the princes that they are to accompany me on a search mission for the Princess. I will be taking my men and any other persons that I deem necessary to successfully accomplish such a task. I expect unrelenting support from you and your advisors. I will not stoop to dealing with a group of petty, squabbling old men."

"One prince, please," Fergal begged him, desperation coloring his features, "My eldest must stay in Scythia with me, he is my heir. I will give you Edan, you are already best acquainted with him."

"Fine, Prince Edan will accompany me. Do not deter me any longer." Cathal sprung open the heavy wooden double doors, not bothering to acknowledge the King as he left the War Room. Walking by the warriors awaiting him with the two princes, he shouted at them, "We leave in the morning!"

He lay in bed, the night sky turning from its midnight blue hue to a magnificent ruby red shade, overlapping an equally dazzling array of pinks, oranges, and whites. His thoughts wandered, finally settling on the last time that he had been in this very bed.

The Princess had been the last person to have lain in it, without him, as he had dissolved into the breaking dawn in search of some reprieve from those despairing foreboding emotions that had relentlessly haunted him for the last month or so. How could he have known that it would have been the last time that he would see her, possibly ever again?

He refused to believe the worst of the situation. She was alive, he knew it, felt it in his gut. It was only time before they found her and then he would make things right with her. He would try to work matters out between them, to give their relationship the chance that it deserved.

Maybe it was all in his head, maybe he didn't remember it correctly. Perhaps the stress and pressure of the impending betrothal had caused in him such negative emotions, blowing the whole thing out of proportions. It was possible, after all, that he had imagined the whole thing. He had been pushing himself without pause for the past year, training new recruits and reinforcing their lines, making sure that their artillery was up to date and impeccable– *Duna.* Cathal groaned, rubbing his face with his hands; just the image of her face in his mind sent his heart beating frantically.

It would be a challenge to ignore her lest he saw her again, and it was inevitable that he would for she would be part of the small faction of soldiers that Captain Moira had chosen to accompany the search party to the north.

He would have to stay away from her unless absolutely necessary, there was no other way that he would be able to distance himself from her and their uncertain relations. He had to, for Leila. For his mate.

He got up and changed into his riding gear, not bothering with chain-mail and the like which would only slow him down and get in the way of doing swift reconnaissance where time was of the essence. He put on his throwing knives and double-edged long sword and left.

Rhun was already waiting for Cathal at the stables, where he saw that his war horse Rais was already saddled and prepared for the trip. "Is everything ready? Then let's get going. We will meet up with Captain Moira's team on the border. If everything goes according to plan we should be making a stop for the night later on this evening."

"Prince Edan and Axel have gone ahead to scout the land for any information on the Princess. If we're lucky someone will have heard something about the kidnapping. Oh, and Cathal," Rhun shot him a worried look, "Bror's here."

"What? What is he doing here? He should be on an assignment in Morinya." Cathal shot him a questioning look, already knowing the answer to his question. "You told him about the Princess. Of course, you did. You just can't keep your mouth shut, can you Rhun?"

"He was bound to find out anyway, I just sped up the whole process," he winked at Cathal. "Besides, he is like a brother to you, I don't understand what the trouble is. His contacts will help us in tracking down the Princess."

"The problem, Rhun, isn't that I don't want him here. The problem is that he is supposed to be my eyes and ears in Nissa, where he is meant to be keeping a close eye on the Crown Prince who, as you know, is acting highly suspicious and may even be planning to overthrow his father. He is no good to me here, damn it." Not to mention the fact that Bror was, in fact, a spy and an assassin. But Rhun didn't need to know that.

"Yes, well–" Rhun billowed out his cheeks before quickly releasing the pent up air, "–shit. I hadn't thought about that, I'm sorry. I just figured that you would want all the help to get back your beloved, and there is no one who is better at tracking and getting leads on individuals than Lovas."

Cathal didn't answer, only sat atop Rais, thinking about their next step. Rhun was right, he could use Bror's impeccable skills as a spy to get a lead on Leila. She was most likely being held in some barn by some imbecile thieves who wanted to make quick coin out of the transaction. Except there was no ransom demanded, nothing that the kidnappers wished to trade for the Princess. That was what worried Cathal.

They exited the palace grounds and caught up with the rest of the search party. Kane Maelys, one of his more promising captains and a healer in his own right, greeted them. His lean but tall stature of six feet went perfectly along with his calm demeanor, as if his craft shown through the way that he held himself and the way which he spoke.

"Good to see you again, General. Lieutenant. It's been a while since we last saw each other. Can't say that I'm sorry, but the circumstances are not much to be admired." Kane rode on beside them, filling them in on what they've missed, "Prince Edan and Lieutenant Fendergar have sent word back that they are following a tip in a nearby village. They will join us when they see if and where it leads to. Bror is waiting for us at the gates to Scythia, the guards found him too suspicious to let through so he agreed to just wait for us at the entrance to the city."

"I had no doubts that he would be causing trouble first day back. Why would the guards even think to check him if he was just simply minding his own business? I find that highly unlikely, even for him," Rhun frowned.

"Have you seen the man?" Kane threw Rhun an astonished look, "He looks like a walking nightmare with those almost black eyes of his. Not to mention the two dragon hilted twin katana swords that he always seems to have strapped across his back. He is a walking red flag."

"What do his eyes have to do with anything? That is ridiculous..." They bickered like children. Cathal groaned, letting them go at it. At least the trip will be quieter once they get it out of their system and then he can have some peace.

Reaching the iron gates to the entrance of Scythia, the General barked an order to the guards to let them through. The guards were opening the gates even before the words were out of his mouth.

Kane and Rhun continued bickering, getting on Cathal's nerves. "Enough already!" he barked. "You're like two old hags at each other's throats all the time."

"General–" and a "He started it–" ensued at the same time, followed by a "I did not, it was–" and a "You little shit–"

"For fuck's sake, shut up!" Cathal had had enough. "You are giving me a headache and we haven't even left the god damn city. Perhaps a month on cleaning duty will keep your mouths shut."

"Sorry, General" and an "Apologies, General" followed, igniting the whole damn cycle of childish arguing again. Cathal was going to lose his mind if he had to listen to this every day.

"I see the ladies are at it again, as always," a new voice joined the idle talk. "Can't say I'm surprised though, those women that they always have sucking on their cocks seem to be rubbing off on them. Tell me, oh mighty ones, have they eaten your balls as well?" Bror Lovas flashed a devilish smile, his eyes glittering in the daylight, "For it seems that you have replaced them with cunts."

Cathal roared with laughter, glad to have his friend back by his side. He appraised him now, as he sat on his dark chestnut steed, having a go at his two companions.

The man was, to put it lightly, a menacing sight. Tall as Kane at six feet, he had a slender but defined body, with pale ivory skin and short, dark blue hair that was shaved on the sides and hung loosely over his forehead and back across the crown of his head. His eyes were the darkest shade of brown, so dark that they appeared almost black, as if the pupil had blended in with the brown iris part of his eyes, giving him a frighteningly wraith like appearance. Both of his ears were studded and adorned by multiple silver hoops along the cartilage. A long horizontal scar went across his right cheek, just under his eye.

A walking nightmare, indeed. "Bror," Cathal clapped the man on the back, "tell me you have a lead for us."

"You doubt me, General?" the sinister looking spy put a hand to his chest, feigning feelings of hurt. "My contacts have informed me that a group of five highly suspicious men have been travelling toward Morinya. It would appear that they have a couple of cloaked figures in their company whom they hide day and night, only allowing them breaks to relieve themselves and to eat." Bror grinned at Cathal, highly satisfied with himself, "I believe we have found our Princess, General."

Adrenaline pumping high, heart racing fast, Cathal stormed towards the border with Nissa, Rais flying across the open lands of Tyros.

It was time he got his princess back.

CHAPTER 10

Captain Moira's band of warriors arrived at the designated meeting spot as the Sun was making it's descent over the horizon. Duna, Petra, Lir, and the warrior-healer Kala dismounted from their steeds and left them at the inn's adjoining stables to be groomed and tended to while they went inside and got themselves rooms for the night.

Seeming as the General's party had still not arrived at the place, the group of four made their way to the inn's shared dining room where guests were already occupying most of the tables.

"I'll get us some food and ale, you ladies go find us a table for the night," Lir instructed them before leaving for the bar and relaying orders to the woman pouring drinks to customers.

The trio searched the space for an available table, which was beginning to appear as an impossible task. "Well, then, it would seem that there are no free tables," Petra puffed, pursing her lips in annoyance. "Duna, go threaten someone. That should do the trick."

Duna smacked her across the head, "Hilarious. Why don't you flash someone with your breasts while I'm at it and then we can call it a night?"

"No need to get jealous," Petra winked at her, "You can have my breasts if you let me play with your swords."

"You little–"

"Stop playing around," Kala scolded the two women, who were glaring at each other. "We need a table, and we need one now. I'm not sitting on those filthy steps while eating my food." The three turned to those same steps where a patron was busy vomiting their dinner. "Disgusting," they sang in union. Table it was.

Scouting the room, Duna noticed a generously sized table in the corner where only a pair of middle-aged men were lounging while sipping on their ale. "Ladies, I think I have found us a spot. Follow me." They followed her to the said table, surrounding it on all sides. "Gentlemen," Duna flashed a smoldering smile, "may my friends and I join you for the night? All of the other places seem to be taken, and seeing as there are only two of you, we hoped that you would have room for a few more."

The pair of men looked them over, their eyes roving over their bodies, hovering on their breasts. For the second time that evening, Duna had a feeling of extreme repulsion. Questioning her judgment and hoping that the men would turn them away, she was inwardly disappointed when the larger one with the missing teeth grinned at them before nodding his head to the seat beside him.

Filing in after each other – Kala being the lucky one who got the seat next to the toothless bastard – the women held their breath. If death by stench was possible, Duna would have been long rotting on the table, her nose bleeding and tongue hanging out from desperation. She felt bad for the warrior-healer, who seemed to have it the worst, her face already turning a sickly grey color, her eyes bulging out their sockets from trying so hard to breathe through her nose.

"Where are you lovelies from?" the smaller one, with stale breath and a balding head, asked Duna, getting up and moving over to sit beside her. "Maybe we could get acquainted better," he twirled a silky strand of her chocolate hair around his crooked finger, "have some fun tonight. What do you say?" He leaned into Duna, her level of disgust flying through the roof, "I'll make it worth your while, lass."

Duna cringed, pushing the man away from her face, trying with all her might not to break his nose, "Maybe another time, thank you."

Turning away from him, she didn't notice the blade at her side until the man in question was hissing in her ear, "Try again, lass. I believe you were about to unzip my pants, take out my—"

"Finish that sentence, go on, I dare you to," Lir taunted, his own blade pointed at the filthy bastard's jugular. "I believe you gentlemen were leaving. Do kindly, move along." The heavily inked blond warrior pressed the tip of his seven inch blade further into the male's neck, little beads of red forming on it.

The men quickly got up and left the table, their eyes glued to the massive male who stood appeasing them. "I leave you alone for *one* minute— Trouble, always trouble with you girls." Sighing, Lir shook his head at the three females who were slumped in their seats, heads bowed down in embarrassment.

The barmaid brought them their portions of stew, corn bread, and pie, along with their ales, and placed them down on the table with a loud bang. Having made sure that they won't be needing anything else, she handed them their room keys and went back to the other customers.

"We each get our own rooms!?" Petra squealed, bouncing up and down excitedly on her seat. "How did you do it, Lir Killik? Did you promise her a nice little roll in the sheets later? Oh, I bet she took one look at you and her panties were already soaked through." She grinned at him, eyes twinkling with delight, "Can I get in on the action? You know I don't mind sharing."

"For fuck's sake, Da'Nyla, you need to get laid already." He threw a piece of corn bread at her, which she caught and swallowed in one bite. "Besides, the rooms are meant to be shared. The General will be arriving shortly with his men, they'll be needing lodging for the night as well."

Shit.

Duna's gut clenched up, her stomach doing awkward summersaults as she sat unmoving at the table. She had forgotten all about that man, or well, rather, she had tamed down her daily ponderings on him to a minimum.

Groaning, she ate the rest of her humble dinner and prayed to the gods that she won't have to see Cathal before calling it a night. She desperately hoped that she could avoid him until morning came, at which time she would be forced to be in his stately presence.

Alas, it would not be so, for the doors to the inn opened, and the very man himself sauntered in, sucking all the air out of Duna's lungs.

Why does he have to be so good looking, damn it?

He was even more breathtaking than she remembered him. Remarkable what a few days away could do to a man.

Towering over all but Prince Edan, he was truly an arresting figure to behold. His strong, broad shoulders filled out his leathers as if they were molded on, his sculpted chest pressing against the front where his throwing knives were strapped on. His long cloak hung loosely at his back, barely being held up by a thin gold chain around his thick neck, while a double-edged long sword peeked out from behind his head. Hair the color of the darkest night was disheveled from riding for hours, only accentuating his stunning face.

Duna groaned again – she was in so much trouble. This was not going to end well. She needed to stay away from the General. Needed to remain strong and vigilant whenever he was near, she could not afford to let her guard down around him. He would spin his little thread of seduction until he caught her in his web, and once he devoured her whole, there would be nothing left of her, not even a carcass for others to bury. She would become a shadow of her self, a shell of a being.

Duna knew it to be true, felt it in her bones. Cathal was a man that would take all from her, would demand that she surrender the entirety of her body and soul to him. He wouldn't even have to ask, she would give it to him willingly, and she would beg him to take everything from her. She would become a pathetic, whimpering mess of a woman, like the one that she became whenever he was near her. Whenever he touched her.

Whenever he looked at her with those soulful green eyes.

No, she would not allow herself to become weak and pathetic. It was not in her nature, and she would not stoop so low as to crawl for a man.

"Look who the devils dragged in," Petra nudged Duna with her elbow, "I swear, it should be a sin to walk around looking like that. How is an ordinary man supposed to compete with that? It's just not possible."

"He's not, and us, ordinary women, shouldn't even attempt to dream about a male like that." Kala chuckled, shaking her head as she perused the General from afar, "We all know what kind of women those–" she nodded her head in Cathal's direction, "–kind of men take home. And neither of us here at this table – no, in this entire kingdom, fit that mold. That, my ladies, is why a male like that–" she pointed her fork at him again, "–is betrothed to the Princess. She is exactly the type of woman that was made for a man of that caliber." She went on stuffing her face with more meat pie, nearly choking herself from overstuffing her face with food.

"Careful now," Petra teased her, "we don't want you dying of an obstruction of the airways due to a lack of oxygen because your trachea was blocked by a ridiculous amount of solids."

"Wha'?" Kala mumbled incoherently through a mouth overflowing with food, "I 'm no' s'uffin' ma' fac', I'm jus' 'ung'y."

"And now she speaks gibberish, brilliant. Stop stuffing your fucking face, Kala!" When the woman kept throwing her confused glances, Petra shouted at her, "You look like a gods damn pig that's about to be roasted!" That ought to do it. And it did. Especially when Petra grabbed her forearm, clenching it so tightly that her knuckles turned white. "Who–" she pointed at the burly man that had just entered the inn, "is that? Do we know him? He is magnificent!"

Duna turned to where her friend was pointing a long, callused finger at, and chuckled to herself. Of course Petra would notice Axel, they were like two peas in a pod, it's a wonder that nothing had happened between them in the past.

"That's Lieutenant Fendergar, the General's right hand man and close companion," Lir answered before Duna could say anything. "They were together in the Royal Guard at the palace before moving up in the ranks. Ruthless, that one."

"I'm not talking about that homicidal brute," Petra winced, "I'm talking about that–" she pointed at the other towering giant standing beside the General, "–beautiful male specimen."

"What is wrong with you, do you have amnesia? That's Rhun Brayan, the other Lieutenant General in Cathal Ragnar's army. We went with him not too long ago on a scouting mission." She shrugged in confusion. He shook his head with disapproval. "Can't tell you much about him, he keeps mostly to himself." Lir got up from the table, dusting off bread crumbs from his pants as he did so. "Well, ladies, it's been a pleasure. I'm off to bed."

"Can I come with you?" Petra winked at the blond warrior.

"No."

"Oh, come on! Why not? I can be quiet, no one has to know."

"No shame, that one, I swear.." Lir grumbled under his breath, throwing his long, blond braid over his shoulder, leaving a pouting Petra to pine after him.

The girls were once again alone at the table. Duna inspected the crowded dining room where more and more patrons were filing in, wondering where all of those people would fit.

She felt a slight tingling on her neck, as if someone was watching her. Glancing up to where she suspected the perpetrator to be, she saw a man of about six feet in height, lean but with obvious muscles under his leathers, and a head of copper curls that ended just under his chin. Light stubble in a matching shade adorned his face over his lower jaw and mustache area. A wide array of intricate black runes wound around his neck like a collar, coming together into a menacing snake on his neck, just under his left ear. He was observing her from across the room, a stern look on his face, as if Duna had committed some sort of personal injustice to him.

Seemingly having decided in his mind about something, he made his way towards her.

"Ah, but of course, he has to come along," Kala grimaced as she saw the male walking in their direction, scowling her face into a mask of repulsion. "Hello, brother, whatever brings you here to this humble abode?"

"Cut the crap, Kala, what are you doing here?" the copper curled man spat at her companion, visibly agitated to see her at the same place as him. "You were to stay at the military training camp, working on your skills as a healer. We made a deal, if you remember, that you would not go onto any scouting missions unless the General specifically requested it of you. Those were my conditions for letting you join the army." Crossing his lean arms in front of his chest, he stood scrutinizing the trio.

His eyes, which Duna now saw were a deep green color, a slightly darker shade than Kala's, slid to Duna, lingering on her once again. "Kane Maelys," he extended his substantial hand towards her, introducing himself as he went along, "We went scouting together with the General not too long ago, if you recall."

"Duna Damaris," she shook hands with the warrior, whom she now realized resembled a male version of Kala. The only difference, beside the man's obviously strapping appearance, was the intricate black snake that was inked into his skin, one which Kala did not have.

"Dance with me, Duna," he held onto her hand which they still held in a shake like gesture, tilting his head slightly to the side where the filled dance floor was situated. "I promise I won't bite." He smirked, a small smile threatening to appear at the ends, his teeth a perfect set of whites.

What the hell, I might as well. He's pretty enough.

Kane led them to the center of the floor, where a multitude of couples were already grinding to the loud music. Placing his left hand on her waist, he pulled her towards him, while with his other free one, he lifted hers, masterfully leading them around the gyrating throng.

Duna was impressed. The man knew how to dance. "You're quite good at this, can't say that I'm not surprised. Most men can't seem to hold a beat to save their life."

Kane chuckled, twirling her around in circles, "Good thing that I'm not most men." Winking at her, he threw in another charming smile. "Tell me, Duna, do you find me to your liking?"

Laughing out loud, her head thrown back, she teased the charismatic warrior, "You're different, that's for sure." He threw her a sheepish look. "Alright, yes, you are quite handsome." She laughed some more, so much so that her cheeks hurt from the strain of her muscles being stretched so wide. "But I don't think your sister would approve of us getting together."

"My sister is of no importance," Kane leaned into her ear, lowering his voice, "after all, it's me that you'll be dancing with later on tonight, not her." His grip on her waist tightened, pulling her slightly closer to his taut body.

Duna blushed, then frowned, not knowing what suddenly came over her. Must be the ale that they drank. She knew she should have stopped after the first pint. It wasn't like her to drink alcohol, and the times that she did, she merely sipped it, so as to not overindulge in the blasted liquid. The impending headaches that would otherwise ensue would always be a stark reminder of the fact that she couldn't hold her drink.

Picking up a stray piece of hair from in front of her face, Kane gently tucked it behind her ear. That's when she felt it. The burning sting in the back of her neck. As if someone was focusing a high frequency light beam into her skull, attempting to burrow through to her brain.

She winced, not from physical pain because there was none. But because she didn't like being observed from the shadows, where she couldn't see her opponent, couldn't challenge him back.

Duna kept dancing with Kane, laughing and joking with the warrior, secretly enjoying herself. It had been such a long time since she had felt any type of joy. She relished in the feel of it now, no matter the source of it.

Kane seemed to be kind hearted, with a calm and studious demeanor. His outward appearances reflected on this, his face being made up of soft lines rather than rugged, harsh edges. His eyes were like two pools of moss filled ponds, striking in their color. He was a healer, just like his sister, the snake on his neck a silent ode to his craft.

Duna gasped, a tingling sensation crawling up from her spine to the nape, making her skin vibrate ever so slightly. Just as it had started, it suddenly stopped. Then began anew.

The tiny hairs on her arms stood on end, sending shivers down the length of her whole body, enticing her nerve endings and causing her body to tremble. A shock of warmth followed. Down her body it went, igniting every little starved cell with its fire, causing liquid heat to pool in her lower body, spreading violently to her extremities. Her toes curled, her fingers clenched, involuntarily fisting an unsuspecting Kane's shirt in the process.

She dropped her hands from his body, suddenly aware that she was appearing quite inappropriate. She couldn't stay here anymore, though, as rude as her reaction would seem, she had to leave.

Kane grabbed her wrist, worried about the abrupt change in her demeanor, "Are you alright? We can have a seat if you don't feel well."

Duna shook her head, slowly backing away from the curly haired man, needing to get some fresh oxygen. "I'm alright, I just need to get some air. Thank you for the dance, Kane." Not waiting to hear his reply, she ran for the stairs, her room key already out of her pocket, aimed at the door handle.

Barging into the modest chamber, she grabbed a change of clothes and flew into the bathing room, desperate for some reprieve from the heat that was consuming her body.

Stripping off her leathers and quickly changing into some thin leggings and a plain black top, she splashed cold water onto her face and neck, relishing in the cool sensation that seemed to be lowering her core temperature to a livable one. If she could only keep it that way through the impending days of travel.

Groaning from the foreboding thoughts that overflowed her mind at the notion of being near the General in only a few hours time, she left the bathroom and threw herself onto the medium sized bed.

"Are you enjoying yourself?"

She bolted upright, the voice like a jolt of lighting to her thundering heart.

Cathal sat in a plain grey armchair in the corner of the room, cast in shadows like a demon on the hunt. One leg was crossed over his knee at the ankle, his head leaning against the back of the seat, arms splayed wide on the armrests. His leathers were gone, replaced by a simple black shirt with a wide open collar and matching black linen pants.

The man was indeed sin personified, the very reincarnation of a merciless god. Imposing, menacing, gloomy. Striking in his beauty. He sat utterly still, not a hair moving on his head, as if not breathing at all.

The General surveyed her from head to toe. Ever so slowly, his heated gaze returned to Duna's trembling one, burning a hole in her erected walls, threatening to bring them down into shambles. "Come here," his velvety smooth voice a deadly low, his gaze promising swift retribution should she not obey him.

Shaking, she went to him. One leg in front of the other. Inhale, exhale. Repeat. Like a mantra she repeated these words to herself, praying to the gods to give her strength and resilience so as not to turn into a pitiful mess of emotions and sensations right in front of this stunning man.

Stopping right in front of his wide open legs, she mustered her courage, "What are you doing in my room, General?"

Tilting his head, he reached for her hand and pulled her in between his spread legs, his knees holding her tightly in place. Heat pooled between her thighs. "Were you expecting someone else, perhaps?" he caressed the back of her legs, right behind her knees. "A certain copper haired healer?" He continued stroking her legs, from the back of her knees to the top of her thighs, stopping only a mere inches from the curve of her ass, then back down again. "Do you remember what I had told you before, about letting another man near you?" When she didn't reply, he continued, "Let me remind you. I will kill anyone that dares to touch you. Anyone–"

"Punish, not kill," Duna interrupted, breathing heavily, his soft but firm strokes sending goose bumps up her legs and down her arms.

He grinned, a satisfied, arrogant grin. "So, you do remember. And yet, you dared to disobey me. Do you know what the punishment is for disobedience?" His deft fingers stopped right under the curve of her ass, the pads of them threatening to touch that sensitive area of her pulsing body. "Answer me."

She swallowed, her throat so agonizingly dry, it was almost painful. "No," she croaked, then cleared her throat, "I can only imagine, General." Her heart was hammering away, a violent rhythm overtaking her heaving chest.

Cathal softly caressed the underside of her ass over her thin leggings with the pads of his fingers, back and forth, outwards then back to the center where her crease lay, never pressing on her round mounds of flesh nor going in between her thighs or over the middle of her crease. His gaze bore into her the whole time, memorizing her every reaction to his burning touches.

"Your mind cannot even begin to comprehend how I wish to punish this body of yours, little monster," he purred, eyes perusing her burning body. "The things that I would do to you if circumstances were different." He splayed his fingers wide over her round cheeks, cupping them gloriously with his massive hands.

She gasped, her nipples cresting into round pearls of arousal. Fisting her hands, she tried desperately not to touch him.

As if sensing the tightening of her mounds, Cathal leaned his head in and watching her from hooded eyes, blew on the painful peaks. Hissing, he did it again, and again, turning his attention to the other nipple poking through her thin top. "Fucking hell," he swore. She whimpered. He continued his quest on her lower body. "If we had met at a different time–" he lightly massaged her flesh, squeezing ever so softly now and then, "in a different life–" he increased the pressure in his hold, grabbing handfuls of her ass, "you would already be mine to worship, and I would already be yours to obey."

She moaned then, her self-restraint breaking.

He played with her ass like a man on a mission, where his only goal was to pull despicable sounds out of her malleable body.

His hold was punishing, tightly gripping her while he doughed the flesh, spreading her cheeks agonizingly wide before pushing them back together. His massive hands full of her ripe ass, her moaning like an animal in heat, shamelessly not caring for the noises that were coming out of her mouth.

"So filthy. You like that, don't you?" he chuckled, the bastard, knowing exactly what he was doing to her. "Listen to you," he tsked, "so needy."

His middle fingers moved from under her ass cheeks to in between her thighs, not touching the area that was drenched for this devil of a man, making slow, torturous circles with the pads just where her ass connected to her inner thighs.

Gasping, her hands flew to his shoulders, gripping them in a deadly hold. She shamelessly spread her legs just a little wider, moaning and whimpering when he wouldn't go lower. Her panties were soaked through, there was no possible way that this evil, evil man wasn't aware of it.

"Are you going to be a good girl from now on, Duna?" his fingers inched closer to her drenched core, drawing circles over her pants, "Are you going to let another man touch you?" closer still, but not there yet, "Am I going to have to kill Kane because of your insolence?" He stopped, right at the entrance of her pulsing core, her pants wet from all the slick that was shamelessly streaming out of her.

She clenched his shoulders even tighter, daring him to back down. "I swear to God, Cathal, if you don't move that finger I will fucking murder you."

Stunned, his lips parted ever so slightly. "Say it again," he pleaded with her, "My name, I want to hear it again. Say it," his eyes hiding an emotion that Duna couldn't decipher.

"Cathal," she breathed, her heart racing as she did. She wanted to shout it at the top of her lungs, but, alas, it was not possible. Like a cold wave of awareness, realization hit her.

What was she doing? She should not be doing this. He was betrothed, to a princess none the less. The one who's very life they were trying to save, the very reason for their current mission.

She stepped back from Cathal, giving herself room to breathe.

Reality seemed to hit the General at the same time, his demeanor changing instantly to one of gloom and regret. For what, Duna wasn't sure. Was he regretting touching her? For coming up to her room in the first place? Or did he wish that it had been the Princess that he had been caressing just moments ago, not her. Maybe, just maybe, he was regretting their reality, where they could never be together.

It would seem like a sobering thought, yet Duna had known this all along, she was not naive enough to ever believe that she could have the General for herself. He was a man of high regards, maybe even more revered than the King himself. Whatever could he want from a simpleton like Duna?

She laughed ironically, rubbing her face with the palms of her hands, forcing her body to physically come down to earth, to stop fantasizing about something that could never be.

She was stupid, so unbelievably stupid.

Walking towards her locked door, she turned the latch and held the door wide open. "Good night, General."

She watched as the breathtakingly gorgeous man walked out of her room, not even stopping to give her a second's glance.

CHAPTER
11

The company rode out at first light the next morning, not bothering with breakfast. They wanted to make it into the Kingdom of Nissa before noon, where they were to make camp for a while before continuing on with their journey to Morinya.

Bror, the informer in the group, had received news during the night from one of his scouts that the Princess had been spotted with a band of men entering the capital of Nissa, so that is where they were now headed to.

It was a few days riding out into the northern kingdom, where temperatures would be dropping low as they got closer to the infamous palace of King Lucan. The White City, they called it. It was nestled in between five massive mountains that were said to breach the clouds, with it's sharp snow capped peaks reaching for the heavens.

No mortal had ever seen those obsidian sharp summits, where it was rumored that the gods themselves sat, watching over the unsuspecting humans below.

To reach Morinya, one had to enter through a narrow mountain pass through the snow drenched mountains. The only other way would be to go around the entire icy mountain range which would sometimes take months if the weather got bad. Enemy armies had attempted to breach the stern slopes of the rockies many centuries ago, but they only ended up meeting an agonizingly slow death by freezing. And they had been lucky.

Mountain lions and snow leopards where abundant in the mountains surrounding the White City, making it their home for millennia before mortals ever stepped onto those ominous lands. Colossal, silver polar bears scouted the snowy inclines, wandering around like silent ghosts on the hunt.

Other, more sinister creatures came out hunting as one reached higher ground. Lethal, white harpy eagles the sizes of two war steeds and wingspans breaching the length of navy military vessels preyed on any unlucky humans that found themselves on the formidable mountain slopes. Duna prayed to the gods that she would never come to face with any of these terrifying creatures. She had enough to worry about as it was.

Cathal hadn't spoken to her at all since greeting the party that morning, acting like Duna was yet another soldier in his ranks, as if his skilled hands hadn't been molding her aching body to his liking just a few hours prior to departing for Morinya.

It was, perhaps, better that way, for she didn't know how she should act around him after their little encounter, even though nothing but some light touches had passed between them. Cathal gave her an easy way out, she supposed, making the decision for her on how to proceed in their non existent relationship henceforth.

She let her mind wander to what could have been last night, to those caresses and sounds that the General's deft hands had elicited from her heated body, to the feelings of wanting to be owned by that man, consequences be damned.

She had to be honest with herself, though, had to realize that even if things had physically proceeded between them, the impressive male would not belong to her. He would still be promised to the princess, and she, Duna, would still be a simple soldier in the General's army, a soldier that had sworn an oath to protect that same woman that now wore the brooding male's ring on her finger.

The one person who the General now desperately chased across the continent to get back by his side.

Disgusted with herself, Duna cursed under her breath, silently reprimanding herself for being so horribly pathetic. Never in her life had she chased another female's man and she would not begin to do so now. She had more pride than that, more self-awareness and self-love. She would not allow herself to stoop so low.

She needed to find a solution to her growing dilemma that had the General's name written all over it, and she needed to do it quickly, before the tiny bud of curiosity grew into a blazing inferno of maddening obsession that she wouldn't be able to quench.

"Be careful that you don't pull a muscle thinking so hard," Petra teased her, riding up beside her chestnut mare. "You're already impossible as it is, imagine if I had to think for you as well, where would the end be."

Duna grinned, thankful for her friend's presence, "I wouldn't mind, you would at least finally use the poor organ for the very purpose that it was designed for."

Looking aghast at the insinuation, Petra demanded, "Are you saying I don't use my brain?"

"When have you ever used your brain?"

"Just last night, while I was contemplating on which part of Rhun's magnificent body I ought to lick first." Her face flushed from her shameful thoughts. "Although, I must say, I wouldn't mind if he licked me first and then I would have to return the favor," she smirked, "It would only be fair, after all."

"You filthy, filthy girl, lusting after the Lieutenant. Whatever shall Moira say?" Laughing out loud at the image of the Captain's scolding face in her head, Duna continued to tease the ginger warrior, "However will our brooding General react if he heard you speaking such blasphemous words about his commanding officer?"

Giggling, they burst into full on boisterous laughs, not being able to hold themselves back even when the others shot them stern, foreboding glances. Kala joined the conversation, adding her two coins to the topic at hand, igniting the hysterics even more.

The women were playing around, enjoying themselves, grinning like three drunken idiots, when Kane decided to make an appearance. "Ladies, you might want to take it down a notch. I'm afraid that if you continue on this way, the General is going to have a fit. He's already on edge as it is."

"Oh, please, there is nothing else for us to do," Petra interjected. "Besides, Morinya is a long way off yet, he surely can't expect us to be silent and well behaved the whole way. We'll die of blandness."

"Don't say I didn't warn you," turning his attention to Duna, Kane winked at her, "So, feeling better, I see. A good night's rest will do that to a body." If he only knew.

Nodding in agreement, Duna turned her face to the front where Prince Edan and Axel were scouting the woods while the rest of the group was wordlessly trotting along on their mounts, looking as glum as ever.

"When do you suppose we'll make camp for the day?" she said. "We've been riding for hours already, we should at least make a short stop so as to at least rest our horses."

"I suppose you're right." Kane rode off to the front, where the General was having a discussion with Rhun, seeming to be in deep conversation. Kane approached the pair, addressing Cathal as he did so. They seemed to have a brief exchange of words before the General turned to an observing Duna, shooting her a look of deep disapproval, before he turned back to the warrior-healer still waiting adamantly at his side for some kind of response.

The General seemed angry about something that Kane was relaying to him, his face set in a deep scowl.

Well, then. Perhaps they weren't going to be stopping for a rest after all.

Kane didn't return to Duna's side as she had hoped he would, instead getting in position beside Bror, while Lir and Kala followed behind them. Duna and Petra were the last in line, riding side by side. The General and Rhun were leading the group, Prince Edan and Axel having gone ahead to scout the area for any potential danger.

It was interesting to Duna how the Prince was willing to risk his life in such a manner, as if he didn't see himself as the second in line to the mighty Tyrossian throne and was therefore – in his eyes at least – disposable. Perhaps that was due to the fact that he was always accompanying the General whenever he went on any missions across the kingdom, finding it his duty to protect the people that his brother, if not him directly, would one day lead.

Sudden shouts rang out, echoing across the path on which the group was travelling.

Petra went down in a flash of black, landing on her back as if struck, breathing but not moving. Duna cursed, lying down low on her horse, steadying the animal by its reins while she searched the area for the attackers.

An arrow shot through the air, hitting Lir in the shoulder, sending him flying off of his mount. Another one followed shortly after, missing its mark.

Madness ensued.

Masked men ran out from the woods to both their sides, blades flashing in the bright daylight. There were eleven of them, some short and stocky, others tall and lanky. They seemed like some type of road bandits, praying on unsuspecting travelers. Little did they know that Duna and her party were no plain commuters.

They dismounted their steeds, engaging their assailants head on with their own swords and blades. Kala and Kane were fighting with their backs to each other, the brother and sister duo slashing at their opponents. Rhun was fiercely trying to protect an injured Lir, who was bleeding profusely from his shoulder where the arrow still protruded, struggling to hold his own ground.

Bror and Axel were fighting by Prince Edan's side, cutting down two of the attackers in the process. Cathal was going at it with three pudgy males with nasty looking weapons, ducking and jabbing and thrusting at the easy targets.

Petra was rolling on the ground, trying to get up after she had been seemingly hit with a stone to back of her head, close to her nape, the slight wound bleeding down to under her collar.

Duna slithered down the side of her chestnut mare, quickly making her way to the wounded female, keeping her head lowered so as to not get shot by some stray arrows. "Petra, can you hear me? We need to move, there's been an ambush. Here, grab onto me." Pulling her arm over the back of her shoulders, Duna helped the woman get behind a thick trunk, making sure that she was still conscious.

Turning around, she examined the scene before her. Lir was leaning against a similar trunk as Petra, Rhun somehow having gotten him out of the way of the fighting. Five of their assailants lay on the ground, some unconscious, some dead. The other half were heavily involved in combat with Duna's formidable comrades.

Rhun had a nasty looking cut on his arm, soaking his leathers through. It didn't look fatal, but infection would most likely be the damning culprit if he didn't get it treated in time.

Seeing her opening, Duna withdrew her throwing knives and threw them at her targets. The blades hit their marks dead on, impaling two of the attackers straight in the forehead, right between their eyes. Not wasting a moment, she found the next attacker.

An ugly, toothless male was baring down on Kala, who was limping along, dragging her wounded leg behind her while blocking blows to her head.

Gripping her throwing knife, she aimed straight for the man's heart. It hit its target with unrelenting speed and precision, throwing the man back with the force of the impact, rendering him dead on the spot. Only three attackers remained.

Duna ran into the heart of the fighting, her double-edged long sword drawn from it's scabbard. Like moths drawn to a flame, the bandits turned their attention to her, smirking, the other warriors – who now stood staring at her, frozen, as if made of stone – forgotten about.

Picking up another sword that lay wasting on the ground, she unleashed her inner monster. "Come get me, boys." She lifted her blades, a wicked grin spread across her stoic features, eyes blazing with bloodlust.

They lunged at her, expecting a weak little damsel who was playing pretend with her toy swords. Little did they know, she was a born killing machine.

She thrust and blocked at the same time while jabbing and kicking, her opponents relentlessly attempting to get near her. She spun her body while simultaneously twirling her swords, lifting them up and slicing, cutting her assailants in the legs and arms, relishing in their shouts and screams. Ducking low and gripping her shorter sword by the hilt, she jabbed upwards, piercing one man through the underside of his mouth, while she plunged her long sword back and into the gut of another male who was running straight at her, impaling himself on the blade.

Blood trickled down her blades, coloring them a deep crimson shade, a tangy copper smell saturating the air around her. She closed her eyes and inhaled. A deep, lungful of air soaked with the smell of blood rushed into her body, igniting her frenzy and need for vengeance.

The last remaining attacker stared at her, eyes wide open with fear, his face a sickly grey color. She smirked at him, a villainous mask playing across her blood soaked face. He pissed himself then, the pungent smell of it mixing with the copper and earthly aromas shrouding them in a thick veil of death. The male threw down his sword, bolting for the tree line. Not giving him the opportunity to get away, Duna threw her weapon at him, skewering him through the back, his body collapsing onto the cold grass.

"Bloody hell. Remind me to never get on your bad side," Kane mumbled, arms by his side, his drenched sword lying casually in his left hand.

"She doesn't have a bad side. This is her only side," Petra chirped in from behind them, holding the back of head where her wound was now blossoming into a beautiful shade of black and blue. "Way to attract the men, don't you think, Kane?" she winked at the warrior-healer, who was leaning on his horse, shaking his head at the woman in question.

"You think she'll take me, Petra?" Kane flashed a smug grin at Duna, rubbing his strong square jaw. "I bet she could teach me a few tricks. Maybe, we'll both teach each other something."

"Enough!" a deep, angry voice barked out, cutting off their banter. "Maelys, Lir and Rhun are badly hurt, go see to them." The General turned to Petra, who was groaning from pain, "You seem to be doing well seeing as your mouth is running so much. Go see Kala, just in case." Petra got up and made her way slowly over to the warrior-healer, rubbing her neck as she went along. "And you," the General finally acknowledged Duna, who now stood alone with the man, "what the fuck is the matter with you? We are not in training camp anymore, this is real life."

The arrogant prick.

When Duna didn't answer him but rather stood stoic and unblinking, Cathal continued, "You are to go back to Scythia along with the wounded. I will not have your life on my conscience."

He started to turn, but Duna cut him off, "The fuck I will. I'm staying right here, General. And there's not a damn thing that you can do about it." She seethed, her temper rising to dangerous levels. Who did he think he was, ordering her around like that.

"What did you just say to me?" Suddenly, he was there, towering over her five foot five frame, his face set in a murderous scowl. "You dare disobey a direct order from your General, soldier?"

She leaned in, her face tilted upwards, her hazel eyes burning crimson into his own glaring ones, "I said, I am not going anywhere. I killed six men today, *six*. That's more than half of the assailants. More than you or any of the other warriors killed, combined. You do not get to send me back to Scythia just because your ego is bruised."

"Do not test me, Duna," he hissed, leaning in close to her face, "I am *this* close–" he gestured with his fingers "–to bending you over my knee and spanking you right here in front of everyone for almost getting yourself killed."

"So spank me, General, what's stopping you?" Duna smirked, crossing her arms in front of her body. "Do you know what I think? I think that you are all talk and no action. A big man with big words, but one that never pulls through." She perused his face, from his lips to his eyes, arching her brow, "Maybe I should ask the Princess. She seems to be the expert on all matters concerning you, no? After all, it's her finger that wears your ring."

"Are you jealous, little monster?" he rumbled, his voice so low it was almost a whisper. "Do you wish to be the one with my ring on your finger?"

She stepped right up to him, arms lowered by her sides, her breasts pressing on his rock solid, upper abdomen. Unaware of what she was doing, she inhaled his leather and whiskey scent, sending her senses raging.

"No," she breathed, before raising her voice, "My finger will never wear your ring. The only man whose ring I'll ever wear will also be the only one who will ever be able to order me around. The only one who I will give my aching heart and slick body to. My very soul. My entire being." She pressed a long finger into his leathers, right over his beating organ, "You are not that man, General Ragnar. And I am not your woman." She backed up, her features a mask of unforgiving exasperation, while her insides cried out in despair, imploring her to return to his body's magnetic orbit.

Fists clenched at his sides, he threatened, "That has yet to be seen."

The two of them faced off each other, their gazes locked in a perpetual battle of will. Neither one of them backed down. They were like two angry bulls fighting in the arena until the last one was left standing, bloody and bruised. Who would relent, it remained to be seen.

"Get on the horse, Duna." When she didn't move he growled, "Now." Shooting him a dirty look, she made her way towards her ride, cursing like a sailor as she went. "Watch your mouth, little girl."

She smirked at him, then taunted, "Make me, big boy."

"Duna!!" he bellowed.

"I'm going!" she yelled back at the dictator. "No need to get your panties into a bunch–" Her restraint was non existent when it came to this devastating, arrogant male, as much as she liked to pretend otherwise.

Of course, she mounted her horse, even if she did so while muttering filthy words under her breath. There was never any doubt in Duna's mind that she would do as he said even before the command was out of his mouth.

Despicable. Absolutely grotesque.

The General watched her until he was entirely certain that she wouldn't get any more ideas before going over to his own steed and getting on the massive animal. Addressing the group, he announced, "Rhun and Lir are badly injured and must return to Scythia. Kala, seeing as you are a healer, you will go with them to tend to their wounds until they get appropriate medical attention at the capitol. Axel will also be accompanying you as your guard, should the need arise. The rest of us will continue on to Morinya, which, if all goes well, we can expect to reach in three days time."

They quickly bid farewell to their four companions, the six of them making their way deeper into the Kingdom of Nissa. Thankfully there were no more surprises for the rest of the cool autumn day. They made a small camp some time during the late hours of the evening, Duna and Petra huddling close to each other for body warmth. The next day passed in the same bland manner, riding, eating, resting. Repeat.

The landscape changed from rich earthly colors to cooler browns and blacks, snow making its first appearance at the end of their second day, when they could just see the vague outlines of the infamous mountains that surrounded the fabled White City. Temperatures dropped to below zero as evening approached, slowing down their horses which were more adapted to the milder winters of Tyros.

Early morning of the third day, a messenger bird arrived, flying straight for Bror. On closer inspection, Duna realized that it was in fact some type of hawk, guessing by the resplendent brown color of it's feathers and typical sharp features which were specific for those majestic birds of prey.

Unrolling the tiny parchment from a miniscule little pouch that was attached to the bird's leg, Bror read its contents and frowned. "This is not good," he turned to the General, brows furrowed together. "The Princess has been seen on route to Navajo. It hasn't been confirmed yet, which means that she could still be in Morinya but that they sent a decoy to throw us off her scent." When no response came, he said, "How do you want us to proceed, General?"

A deeply troubled Cathal took his time answering the bird tamer, strategizing on all the possibilities of the appending issue.

It was Prince Edan that gave them the sought after solution, "Kane and I will go to Navajo. If anything is amiss, we will know. You four continue on to the White City." The giant of a man turned to Bror, "Send word to my younger brother, Valen, he's stationed on the border with the Kingdom of Baqar. Tell him to meet us halfway at the Healing Pool of Niamh, he'll know where that is."

Having decided, the once company of six split up into two lesser groups. Duna, Petra, Bror, and the General continued on to the northern kingdom's capital while the Prince and Kane made their way to Baqar, the smaller of the three kingdoms on this side of the Continent.

Nightfall came and went, the stars shining brightly on the moonless sky. Snow covered the once barren ground, enveloping the valleys and eventually the mountain slopes that surrounded the White City.

As they made their way further into the mountain range, the temperatures got so low that they were forced to make camp and light a fire, much to the General's adamant protestations.

Duna refused to leave this life frozen into an ice cube in the middle of some foreboding rocky slope in the middle of strange territory. She would much rather be eaten alive in her sleep by a mountain lion or snow leopard. So a fire it was then, but not too large for they weren't going to press their luck now that it has been good to them for the past three days since being attacked.

The four of them huddled close around the fire, Duna and Petra plastered against each other under a thick blanket as they sat dangerously close to the flames.

Teeth chattering away, Petra said to her three freezing companions, "What kind of an idiot makes a home in a god damn icicle? It's the stupidest thing that I've ever heard. Sadistic maniacs." She shivered, causing Duna to shudder in response as well. "Let's play a game. Each one of us tells a story that is not known to the others. It can be anything – a memory, a fairy tale, a personal story, a myth. But it must be something that very few people, if any at all, are aware of. I'll go first."

"Does it have to be true or can we make it up?" Bror asked.

"It doesn't matter, as long as the person telling the tale doesn't reveal its authenticity."

Satisfied with her explanation, Bror crunched up into an even tighter ball of clothes and wool, throwing stray glances to the General who seemed to be lost in deep thought, with not so much as a blanket over his sturdy body.

"Once upon a time," Petra began, "in a far away land, lived two brothers. Both were mighty and strong, formidable warriors. One ruled the Lands of the Living and the mortal Forgotten Kingdom, the other the Realm of the Dead and the Underworld. They loved each other dearly, never allowing anything or anyone to come in between them. One day, their father, the King of the Holy Kingdom of the Gods, was murdered by his very own brother, the Lord of the Red Land, the uncle of the two warriors. The Lord of the Red Land cut up the King's body into twenty six tiny pieces and placed them into twenty six miniature wooden crates, which he then plunged to the bottom of the Endless Sea, the underwater currents scattering the parts all over the Known World.

"The two warriors swore to avenge their father's death by hunting down the Lord of the Red Land and every one of his co-conspirators. The eldest warrior, the Lord of the Lands of the Living, cut up his uncle's body into small bits, preserving the heart intact, and threw them all into the pits of the Underworld, where his younger brother ruled. The Lord of the Underworld, the Realm of the Dead, took his uncle's heart and weighed it to see if his soul was worthy to enter the Afterlife. Having been found lacking, the Lord of the Underworld cast his uncle's soul into endless darkness, where the Devourer – a being of infinite shadows – fed on it and will continue to do so for all of eternity.

"Having avenged their father's death, the two warrior brothers had a dilemma. Who was to rule the heavenly Realm of the Gods? The younger brother, the Lord of the Underworld, had no aspirations in becoming a king. He gladly gave up his claim to the throne, swearing fealty to his older brother. Millennia passed where everything was in order. The new King of the Realm of the Gods was pleased with mankind, not once questioning their morals. His younger brother, however, was appalled at how wicked the people had become, their souls reeking with corruption and atrocious acts of violence during their mortal years. He consulted his brother, the King, desperate to see a completion to the never-ending stream of souls that he kept sending into the endless darkness."

Petra paused, searching their faces before continuing, "The King didn't have an obvious solution to his formidable problem. He could see how it would affect his younger brother, for it was not easy for one to damn a soul for all of eternity, and thus, forbidding him entrance into the golden light of the Afterlife. The Lord of the Underworld, the Realm of the Dead, had become so desperate that he was willing to trade his immortality for a mortal life if it gave him reprieve from the gloom that had become his reality.

"His brother, the King, who loved his brother dearly, was not pleased with his suggestion. As Ruler of all gods and the Lands of the Living, he had the power to strip his brother of his immortality, but it would come at a costly price." She stopped, seemingly baffled on how to proceed. "Some legends say that the King granted his brother's wish of a mortal life, rendering him human and him meeting, after many fruitful decades, a mortal's death. Other legends claim that insulted by his brother's refusal at an immortal life, the King cursed him for all of time. The Lord of the Underworld was said to have gone on living as a half deity, living as a mortal but never dying as one, instead being reborn from the ashes, destined to roam this world in a half-limbo for all eternity."

Deep silence followed the completion of her story. Everyone seemed to be in deep thought, even the General who stared at the white hot flames, appearing incredibly still and lifeless.

"How cruel must one be," Duna said, "to damn one's own loyal and faithful brother to an eternal half-life, your soul never resting, only to be reborn and tortured again, until the end of time."

"Sometimes, it is not the knowledge of what awaits but the hope of what could be that damns a person's soul to eternal agony," Cathal rumbled, his gaze somber and filled with hurt.

"Duna, it is your turn to tell a story."

CHAPTER 12

All three sets of eyes focused on her, so she began, "There once was a girl who lived with her grandmother in a small village in a far away land. The women worked the fields, hunted for meat, salvaging whatever coin they could get their hands on. They were close, the grandmother and the child, having no one else but each other in the miserable world that surrounded them. As the girl grew, the elderly woman got more tired, more sick, until she wasn't able to work the fields anymore, settling instead on a small patch of dirt right outside of their humble home. She harvested fruits and vegetables there, making sure that the now young woman always had food in her belly.

"The young woman grew into a formidable hunter, her skill with the bow and arrow unmatched even in comparison to the men in the village, who grew envious of the woman. One day, while she was out hunting, those same men set fire to her home, hoping to frighten her out of their village. Unbeknownst to them, the young woman's sickly grandmother had been asleep in her bed when they lit the fuse. And so, while the fire raged, it consumed not only the humble home but the elderly woman as well.

"When the young woman, who had been out hunting, returned, she was devastated at the sight that greeted her. Her home was in flames, the ground turned black from the scorching fire. Desperation clawing at her heart, she searched the remains for her grandmother, not even suspecting that she had perished in the blazing inferno. At last, she stumbled upon her grandmother's lifeless body, only the silver pendant around her neck left whole.

"The young woman cried her heart out that tragic day, burying her memories and her very soul in the ground where her dear grandmother's lifeless body would lie rotting away, her silver pendant marking the spot for all of eternity." She exhaled a strangled breath, the story of her life finding light for the first time since those dark days some five years ago. She had changed a few facts, not wanting to give her audience a reason to believe it to be a personal tale. Even then, it had been hard for her to speak, to relive those painful days. The day that had changed her life forever.

Bror and Petra whispered amongst each other, appalled at such horrendous acts of human treachery. Duna listened to them, nodding her head in agreement, her mind wondering somewhere else.

She felt eyes on her. Felt her skin tingle with awareness. The tiny hairs on her neck stood at attention. Her olfactory buds blossoming to inhale a whiff of the perpetrator's addictive aroma.

Closing her eyes, she inhaled deeply, the leather and whiskey scent streaming into her nostrils, down her trachea, and into the million little airways and expanding sacks of alveoli. He invaded her, flooding the infinite number of vessels that made up her body, seeping through the pores of her skin where it evaporated into the air, permeating her surroundings only to enter a new cycle of sweet torture.

She opened her eyes then, a pair of glittering aventurine gemstones flashing across the humble fire, a mere few feet away from Duna.

Cathal stared at her, as if seeing her for the first time, an unknown emotion playing across his devastating features. She held his gaze, unable to break its burning hold, not wanting to look away. She could get lost in his eyes forever. She would gladly relinquish what remained of her shattered soul for all eternity to this enigmatic man.

"Get some rest, tomorrow we'll be at the White City," Bror said, already bundled up right by the fire.

Laying down, her body pressed against Petra's, Duna closed her eyes, sleep overtaking her in mere seconds. She slept soundly and peacefully that night, not knowing that a certain dark shadow stood watch over her sleeping form, daring the fates to make an attempt on her mortal life.

To everybody's surprise, they met no wild creatures during their journey through the immense mountains surrounding the capital of the Kingdom of Nissa. Duna was beginning to question the credibility of the tales that had shrouded the fabled White City in a thick veil of mystery and dread. Even their travel through the narrow pass between the icy slopes of said mountains had been, quite frankly, bland and uneventful.

Disappointed at not having met any giant harpy eagles, Duna grumbled along to herself, wishing to have at least some proof of existence of the mythical beasts. The others didn't seem much fazed by the lack of adventure, Petra and Bror going as far as daring to bicker along the tapered path, not bothering to hide the group's presence. The General had quickly shut them up, though, most likely because he too much rather preferred not to be carrion.

They emerged from the darkened mountain pass just before the Sun made it's way to the top of the day sky, the rays blinding them from being in the shadows for so long. When Duna's eyes finally managed to adjust to the light, she gasped at the awe-inspiring sight before her.

A magnificent, mammoth sized palace of breathtaking beauty was perched on top of a massive, boulder-like type of rock formation, the peaks of its nine sparkling white spires breaching the clouds above, as if touching the heavens themselves. Giant, white birds of prey circled the monumental structure where it met the clouds above.

Duna's breath caught, sudden realization hitting her smack in the face. They were the mythical harpy eagles of legends.

A city of crystalline white walls surrounded the palace at the base of the boulder like rock, as if paying homage to the stone god before it. Multiple openings could be seen in the walls of the palace's towers, presumably homes of the numerous predators that flew in formation around the brilliant white columns.

The palace itself seemed to be carved out of a singular piece of stone, a type of clear ivory dolomite with a surface that shimmered and sparkled in the dazzling bright sunlight. Not a single crack could be seen from where they walked toward the grand building itself. It was truly a profound ode to the formidable human mind and ingenious craftsmanship of mortal engineering.

The group of four approached the intricately carved stone gates of the White City, seeking entrance into it's resplendent walls. After stating their business, the guards let them through. They were dressed in heavily decorated white and gold scale mail armor with matching white and gold breastplates, embellished with the ivory harpy eagle insignia of the infamous Royal House of Raidon who had ruled over Morinya and the Kingdom of Nissa from the very beginning of man.

Gauntlets with gloves and ankle length robes in the same colors covered the guards, under which white and gold boots could be seen peeking through. On their heads, they wore a plain, sparkling white helmet that covered the whole face with only two slits for the eyes and a narrow opening above the spot where the nose should be. The face area had an additional layer of armor covering it, shaped into the sharp features of the harpy eagle. At their sides hung narrowly elongated katana swords with embellished golden hilts, the guards hands resting casually on them, observing the group as they made their way to the home of King Lucan.

Duna was enchanted by the sights that surrounded her as they walked through the streets of Morinya. Vendors were selling all sorts of foods imaginable to the human mind. Opulent cakes and pastries adorned the stalls, richly toned breads and buns overflowing from baskets. Specialized cheeses and spices were spread out a little way down the road, while dried meats hung from rafters. Rows upon rows of the most luxurious silks and lush chiffons were suspended from hangers.

It was more than Duna's mind could comprehend, a sight more glorious than any she thought humanly possible. She was in a fairy tale, one which she never wished to leave. If there ever would come a time when she would have the choice of settling down, she imagined that it would be here, in this resplendent, radiant city.

The General introduced their group to the stern guards that were stationed outside the palace gates, adorned in the same striking uniforms as their comrades at the city's walls. After giving their horses over, servants led them to the Throne Room, where – to everyone's surprise – they were greeted not by the King himself, but by the Steward of the White City and the Head Advisor to the King of Nissa, Lord Kaiyo.

"Welcome to Morinya, I hope that you have travelled well," he said. "The King is awaiting for you in the War Room. Please, follow me."

Lord Kaiyo led them through the wide halls of the White Palace, it's name represented in the brilliant white clear dolomite walls that spread out like an elaborate labyrinth through the grand place. Reaching a set of ornate ivory wooden doors, he pushed them open and instructed them to enter.

King Lucan sat directly in their line of sight as they entered the ostentatious room, surrounded by three males and a young woman. All were sitting at an extravagant, light grey round table, its circumference reaching well over ten meters, held up by thick, chunky legs which supported the weight of the heavy wooden structure.

Lord Kaiyo sat down to the left of the King, who was flanked on the right by a burly man in a military uniform – the General, Duna presumed – and a stoic, wrinkled face full of graying black hair. There was an empty seat in between the King and his General, for who, they had yet to discover.

On the other side of Lord Kaiyo sat a stunning woman of delicate features, who if Duna had to guess, was in her early to mid twenties. Long, stick straight raven black hair framed her face, its shine blinding Duna in the sunlight streaming through the many arched windows lining the walls. Creamy skin the color of summer peaches, high defined cheekbones, a straight regal nose. Full, lush, red lips which revealed a set of perfect, iridescent, white teeth. She had eyes the color of blue tourmaline, a rare shade that somehow seemed familiar to Duna but that she couldn't recall from where.

The King of the White City and the Kingdom of Nissa was an elderly version of the young woman, who was, no doubt, the Princess. Instead of raven black hair, the male's head was a mixture of different shades of black, grey, and white, giving away his ripe age. Face wrinkled, he had a matching straight nose and slightly smaller lips, and the same striking eyes. He was well built and slender, an ode to his decade long military lifestyle, proving that he was in fact, a warrior first and foremost before he was a monarch. The level of discipline and meticulous devotion showed clearly on his aging body, appearing more grandeur in stature than some of the much younger men that Duna knew from Captain Moira's legion of warriors.

The remaining two males appeared to be some sort of advisors to the King, having on themselves a similar type of frock as Lord Kaiyo.

"General Ragnar, well met," King Lucan said, a brilliant white smile livening up his stern features. "What brings you to my city?"

"Well met, indeed, Your Majesty," Cathal replied, a matching but slightly smaller smile gracing his beautiful face. "It has been many years since we last stood in this very same room. Do you remember?"

"How could I ever forget, General. You had barged in here that terribly dreadful day, threatening to skin me alive if I didn't do as you say." The King paused, a wicked smirk showing itself, "Needless to say, you survived, as much as it shames me to admit it. To this very day, you are the only mortal who has ever gotten away with such a blatant display of disrespect."

"Desperate times called for desperate measures, Your Majesty."

"How very right you are," the royal paused, a more serious note in his voice, "Let us pray that we never see those sinister days again, General, for I do not know if today's fragile mankind would survive the endless darkness a second time around."

"Let us pray," Cathal said, his face grave, as he held the King's gaze, the males lost in some distant shared memory, as if reliving the past.

Duna stood by Petra and Bror, who seemed equally perplexed by the two males' foreboding conversation. What dark times were they talking about? Duna searched her brain for the history of their continent, trying hard to remember the last time that a large scale war had occurred on these lands.

If she recalled correctly, there was a Battle at Darda that fit the timeline. It had been a small, insubstantial military operation that lasted for merely three days, where the Tyrossian Army had defeated a foreign invading force coming in from the South Sea. It was a battle for telling around fires because it was considered a great military success, having defeated the enemy with barely a dozen fatalities on the Tyrossian side by the end of the campaign. But that couldn't be right, even the location didn't make sense, the Battle having occurred on the most eastern coast of the Kingdom of

Tyros.

She would have to ask Bror about it at a later time.

The doors of the War Room opened then. Three sturdy males and a petite young woman walked in and, having gone around Duna and her company, took their seats at the round table. Two of the men sat at the Princess's side, while the female joined the General of Nissa. The last, remaining male pulled out the empty chair and seated himself directly to the right of King Lucan.

Eyes of the most dazzling indicolite hue crashed into hers, taking her breath away. "Hello, Duna," Madir purred, a deviously satisfied look on his handsome face. "We meet again."

CHAPTER
13

From her early years as a child, Duna had grown to expect the worst from life, to not get her hopes up. To always expect some sinister twist of fate that would have her digging a hole in the cold ground and covering herself up with dirt for once and for all.

There weren't that many things that could surprise her. It came with the territory of being a soldier, one who regularly went on risky missions into both familiar and strange lands. Duna had learned to read people, to recognize subtle signs of the body in order to predict their next strike.

It had saved her life countless times, both while openly sparring with her comrades as well as during real life skirmishes with a wide array of opponents. From lowly thieves playing the big bad wolf with their hunting knives to highly skilled assassins and groups of rioters that were out for bloodlust, Duna had seen it all.

Or so she thought she had.

When the familiar face of Madir stared back at her from across the vast War Room, she thought she was hallucinating. He was even more stunning than she remembered him. His broad shoulders even wider in the granite grey linen overlapping shirt, the warm peach skin of his collarbones and defined pectoral muscles peeking through ever so slightly.

Duna tilted her head, unconscious of what her body was doing as she took in the sights of this powerful man. Her eyes perused him as Madir stood up and sauntered toward her, his loose-fitting, floor length trousers hiding the sturdy, thick thighs that she remembered all too well from that day at the woods.

Stopping a few feet away from her, his hands clasped behind his back, she was struck by how tall the man actually was. He seemed to have grown in size since she last saw him. Standing diagonally from Cathal, they were almost eye to eye, with the General having a few inches on him. Madir's raven black hair was tied in a loose bun at the back of his head, his majestic bluish-green eyes laser focused on her. His strong jaw was now covered with a slight dark stubble, accentuating the chiseled lines of his face. Duna couldn't help but stare at him. He was spectacular.

"I'm pleased that you still like what you see," said Madir.

"I never said I didn't," Duna teased back.

He smirked. "No, that you did not." Then grinned.

"How do you two know each other?" King Lucan interjected from the round table.

"We had a little run in–" said Duna, at the same time that a "She saved my life–" echoed from Madir.

"Like I said," he repeated, still keeping his striking eyes on her, "she saved my life. And so, I owe her mine, father." Of course, he had to be a prince. And the Crown Prince, at that. Why hadn't it ever crossed her mind? One only had to look at the man to know that he was cut from a special sort of genetic make up that only occurred in the royal bloodlines of the northern Kingdom of Nissa. *Stupid, stupid, always so stupid, Duna.*

"Prince Madir," Cathal interrupted, his face grave, "if I may, I was not aware of this. When, exactly, did this happen?"

"Why *should* you be aware of it, General?" the Prince finally acknowledged the grim male, "What business do you have knowing the details of this woman's private life?"

"I make it my business to know, Your Highness," Cathal seethed, then added, "I know everything about the soldiers that serve in my army, especially the ones that stand out from the rest."

"We'll have to agree on that. She is quite something, isn't she, General?" Madir shamelessly scanned Duna's body in front of the whole room. "Quite exquisite, even more so than I remember."

Silence ensued, Duna standing in front of the ravishing heir who was inspecting her for the second time, while the other breathtakingly beautiful male shot daggers at the man as he did so.

If they could hurry this along, Duna would feel much less embarrassed at being so carefully scrutinized by the dark haired prince.

"General Ragnar," Lord Kaiyo broke the tense silence, "we have yet to find out the reason for your visit to the White City. The King is quite pressed for time. He is a busy man, as you know."

Cathal answered, his eyes still on the Prince, "Princess Leila has been taken hostage three weeks ago while on a humanitarian mission to one of our villages. We had received word that she has last been seen entering Morinya, accompanied by a group of five men. One of her ladies in waiting is most likely with them as well."

"And you believe we know where she is?" Madir said.

"No, Your Highness, we simply came to ask for your help in finding the Princess if she is, in fact, here in the White City."

"What kind of help would this entail?" asked the solemn man that Duna had presumed to be the General of the Nissian armies.

"Manpower, searching suspicious places and groups that are known to deal with human trafficking. Any information that you could give us that could ultimately lead to her retrieval."

Madir, who had walked back around and took up his seat by the King's side, cut in, "General, if I may be so blunt," he arched a thick brow as he addressed Cathal, "The Princess, is she also not your betrothed?"

Clenching his fists by his sides, the General answered, "Yes."

"And, yet, you let her get captured." He leaned forward, fingers crossed in front of him on the table. "How very strange."

"There is nothing strange about it. She was taken while I was away on duty. I do not go dragging her along with me whenever I leave for a military campaign, Your Highness. She has no business at such oppressing places. She is the princess, her place is at the palace, dealing with less stressful obligations."

"So you're saying that she is a weak and helpless woman."

"I said no such thing," Cathal seethed, his jaw clenched tight.

"But you implied it." The Prince tilted his head, leaning back. "Interesting." He shot a questioning glance at Duna, who was still standing rooted to the spot. "Tell me, my little warrior," he addressed her, Cathal hissing at her side, "what are your thoughts on this matter?"

"Pardon me, Your Highness, I–" she started.

"Madir."

"Madir," she said, "It is not my place to discuss the Princess. Not only is she from the Royal Family, I do not know her and therefore cannot judge her character. It wouldn't be an accurate assessment."

"Your Highness, I believe–" Madir lifted his hand, silencing Cathal's words.

Still not breaking eye contact, he spoke to Duna, "But you must find it quite strange that General Ragnar did not have his betrothed protected at all times, even more so fiercely while he was away from the capital." When she didn't answer, he continued, "Let us pretend, shall we? Let us pretend that you, Duna, are my betrothed," Duna swallowed while Cathal steamed by her side, "and that I am to be your husband. Do you truly believe that I would leave your side before ensuring your complete and absolute safety?"

"I don't need protection, Your Highness. I can take care of myself," lifting her chin, she stared down the Prince from across the room, not caring about the many eyes that were trained on her."So, as to answer your question, it wouldn't matter if you would leave me unprotected or not. I am not some pathetic, weak little damsel in need of safe keeping. I would never allow anyone, including you, to treat me as such."

"Assuming you were aware of my protection," Madir grinned, clearly pleased with himself, "which, once again, begs me to question the General's allegations that his betrothed has been captured. I find it quite odd that a man of his reputation and meticulous attention to detail failed to ensure the safety of the woman he claims to love." He turned to the King, "Father, may I suggest looking into this supposed kidnapping of a foreign princess before lending our support to the Kingdom of Tyros," then back to Cathal, "One can never be sure of another's motives these days."

Duna glanced at the men and women sitting around the round table, who were clearly sharing the Prince's thoughts. She had never questioned the validity of Cathal's claims. To even think that Princess Leila hadn't been captured or even worse, that she had been taken by the people she trusts as a political move to gain valuable information on the northern kingdom seemed absolutely absurd, even on the verge of insanity.

It was true that entrance into the White City was highly restricted, yet they had entered it without so much as a questioning glance. The General would have had to inform the King of Nissa himself of his motives and proven them sincere and indisputable prior to even being granted consideration for their admittance to Morinya. The King was the only person who could give him permission for such a request; not even the Crown Prince and the Princess of the Kingdom had the authority to do so. She refused to even ponder on the possibility that this was all a very elaborate farce to gain entrance into the White City.

"Father, I will let you work out the details with General Ragnar." Madir rose. " I believe our guests are tired from their long trip, perhaps I ought to show them to their rooms for the duration of their stay."

"Yes, yes, go, leave us." King Lucan replied, visibly agitated at his son's previous insinuation.

Duna, Petra, and Bror followed the Crown Prince of Nissa out of the War Room, accompanied by his three companions, two of which Duna recognized from that day in the woods. Mikella and York appeared healed and wholly returned to their healthy states. The third man was someone she didn't recognize, although by the way the man was staring daggers at Bror, it seemed that the two males were well acquainted with each other.

"Lovas, I was wondering where you had disappeared to," the third man said. "I was beginning to get worried that you had left us without saying goodbye. It would be so very unfortunate if you had."

"Doran Algernon," Bror smirked at the contemptuous man, "always a pleasure talking to you. Tell me, how is your wife doing? Do give her my kind regards. Oh and please–" he stopped walking and turned to the man, "–let her know that I'll be stopping by one of these nights. I am in need of a good adjusting." Bror grinned, clearly enjoying himself. He stalked off completely unfazed by the fact that Doran appeared on the verge of erupting, barely restraining himself from murdering the menacing male.

Petra and Duna exchanged confounded glances, not knowing what to make of the altercation. It appeared that the blue haired warrior was sleeping with Doran's wife.

The group of eight made their way to a secluded part of the palace with Madir in the lead. He showed Petra and Bror to their rooms while a third room he reserved for Cathal. "Mikella, please accompany Petra on a tour of the grounds after she is done making herself comfortable," he turned to his other two companions, "You two deal with Bror and the General. I don't want anyone bothering me for the rest of the day." The Prince turned to Duna, his gaze full of mischief, "I have a little female whose needs have to be taken care of."

Duna blushed at the insinuation.

The man was a shameless flirt. He also had the face and body of a brutal warrior. She was in so much trouble. At least now she didn't need to think about the General anymore. Madir was the perfect solution to her ever-growing problem with the male, the answer that she had been desperately praying for since their encounter at the inn. "Lead the way, Your Highness."

They walked in silence, each to their own thoughts. Looking up around her, Duna realized that they were now in an entirely new wing of the grand building.

Stopping in front of a pair of double white, intricately carved wooden doors, Madir turned to her, only a foot of space between their bodies. "I already told you, it's Madir. No need for formalities between us, Duna. Besides, you should get used to saying my name," he leaned in ever so slowly, whispering, "you will be screaming it soon."

Her mouth gaped open, "Wha–"

"You are a very beautiful woman, Duna," his fingers grazed lightly over her jaw, "I intend to make you mine."

"I...I–"

"I need you to understand," he cut in, his voice a low sensual melody, his long calloused fingers holding her face, "I am not a patient man. I am ruthless," his thumb caressed her chin, right under her bottom lip, "possessive. Demanding. I take what I want without remorse. But for you, my little warrior," he pressed close to her, his hand going around her throat, "I would become whatever you need me to be, until you finally realize that you belong by my side," his thumb pressed lightly against her pulse as he purred, "and in my bed."

Sudden heat flooded Duna's body, pooling in her lower abdomen, igniting her core. She was at a loss for words. Her mouth had gone dry, the air straining against her lungs. She swallowed, then tried again. Madir followed the movement, his hand still gripping her throat.

The bastard knew exactly what his words were doing to her.

Movement came out of the corner of Duna's eye, but Madir didn't seem to notice, or if he did, he didn't appear much worried about it. He stood unmoving, his hand still cuffing her neck, an inch of space separating their wired bodies.

"Your Highness," a voice called out, "The King has summoned you. He is waiting for you in the Throne Room." The servant waited until Madir reluctantly stepped away from Duna and acknowledged that he had, in fact, heard him.

"I will be there shortly."

"I am to escort you there at once, Your Highness."

Madir sighed, placing his hands behind his back. "Fine," he turned to Duna, "We will continue this later. Get some rest." He stalked off, the servant trailing behind him, desperately trying to keep up with the perturbed male.

She entered her temporary living space, not bothering to close the door behind her. It was a lavish space filled with exquisite furniture and soft, pastel colors. A large, four-poster bed stood pushed up against a wall with a mural of a delicate lilac rose painted over the whole of it, reaching the ceiling. Opening her closet, she saw that it was already filled with a wide variety of luscious gowns in soft pastels of luxurious silks and chiffon. Not exactly what Duna would have picked for herself, but splendid nevertheless.

An adjoining bathing chamber was perhaps what caught her eye even more than the opulent suite. It was larger than her whole barracks back at the military training camp. An impressive bath tub lay to one side of the space while a wide, regal glass encased cabin like structure stood in the center of the room. On closer inspection, she noticed something that resembled a silver tray with multiple tiny holes in it hanging from the ceiling in the center of the glass cabin. Duna gasped – it was a shower! She had heard stories of such wondrous inventions. To have one in her own bathroom. It was overwhelming.

Walking out of the space, she was struck by the image of Cathal's imposing presence. His back was turned to her while he surveyed the room around him.

"What are you doing here?" she asked him, not bothering greeting the man. He had an annoying habit of coming in unannounced and uninvited.

He turned to her then, his translucent, green eyes pinning her to the spot. "How do you know Madir?"

"I thought we already went over this back in the War Room."

"I don't give a shit about what that arrogant prick said. I'm asking you. How do you know him, Duna?"

"What does it matter?" she said. "I met him by chance while I was scouting with Petra. Some men were trying to rob him and his two companions, we happened to be close by and heard the commotion. Petra and I fought and killed their assailants, which is why Madir claims I saved his life."

"Why is he acting like he knows you on a personal level?" Cathal said, scrutinizing her.

"Why don't you go and ask him yourself? Besides, I don't see how this is any of your business, General. You are nothing to me but my commanding officer, just as I am nothing to you but another soldier in your army."

Cathal opened his mouth to say something, but then closed it again. Hesitating for the second time, he said, "It's not my intention to tell you what to do, Duna. I just want you to be careful with him. He is a dangerous man, one that I know far too well. He cannot be trusted."

"Much like yourself, wouldn't you agree?"

"I may be a hard man, but I am not a dishonest one. I do not hide my true self from the world; I only show the parts that I wish to be known. I– apologize if I ever made you doubt my sincerity. It was never my intention to make you feel less than you are worth." He came close to Duna, and reaching out a hand, cupped the side of her cheek. "If only you could see yourself through my eyes..."

"What would I see?" she whispered, holding her breath.

His eyes were soft, so very soft as he looked at her, both of his hands holding her face as he searched her eyes. "A brilliant white light in the vast emptiness of forever, shining like a beacon of hope through the ever ending darkness. Salvation. An anchor to sanity," he paused, "The answer to everything."

Duna was mesmerized by his words. His gaze, his touch.

His nearness was enough to make her melt from the heat that his body was emitting. Like a furnace it burned hot, blazing a path around itself. Try as she might to ignore him, she would always be affected by this devastating male. She would gladly give her heart to him, but – it could not be, he was not hers.

"Thank you, for warning me. I promise to be careful around Madir. And, General–" Duna hesitated, "–I, too, apologize for being difficult. I do not ever mean to purposely antagonize you. It's just that I have been... alone for so long, that I don't know how to be nice and gentle and caring."

"You don't have to apologize for being yourself, Duna. You don't ever need to pretend with me." His thumb caressed her cheek while the other hand stroked her hair. "I already told you before, I won't let any harm come to you while you are by my side. I will always keep you safe." Yet he had never told her who would keep her heart safe from him. "Duna, you are so special to me. You must know that."

Silence.

"One day, I will make you see," he said softly.

"There won't be a one day, General. You are to be married to the princess."

"I am," he said, searching her hazel eyes.

"And yet you stand here, claiming that I am special to you."

Lowering his hands from her face, he placed them in his pockets. "Yes." That bastard.

"Am I a joke to you?" Duna said, "Do you enjoy making me feel like a complete idiot?"

"One day, you will understand," he said.

"One day– What does that even mean?!" If she had a knife on her, it would already be impaled in his shoulder. Or one of his kidneys. Or liver. The choices were endless.

"Not yet. You are not ready to hear what I have to say." Turning around, Cathal started to leave. "Now, get some rest. We have a lot of work ahead of us."

"But–"

"Get. Some. Rest. Now, Damaris." Unbelievable. The door shut behind him, leaving an irritated Duna to her own conflicting thoughts.

As the days went by, the group settled into their new temporary home. Duna and Petra had gone into the White City with Mikella and York almost every day since coming to Morinya, and each time Duna was blown away by the sights and sounds that greeted her. But perhaps the most magical experience that left Duna astonished each time as she wove her way through the city streets were the smells. The incredible, rich, mouth watering scents of food and perfumes and numerous vendors selling everything that the mind could conjure up.

She had made it a daily habit of always buying herself a pastry on her way back to the palace. Today, it was a puff pastry with a vanilla cream filling and a topping of caramelized almond flakes. Duna engulfed it before she even reached the palace gates.

As she ascended the multiple shimmering white dolomite steps to the grand entrance, a glimmer of silver through one of the open, lower floor doorways caught her eye. She went to inspect the strange anomaly, only to discover that it was, in fact, a spacious training room. Entering through the premises, she was met with a vast opening filled to the ceiling with an infinite variety of weapons, some of which she had never before seen in her life.

There were blades of every shape and size, of every cut imaginable. She saw steel, and glass, obsidian, silver, and gold, littering the impressive swords and daggers. Throwing knives were hung from scabbards in the walls, spears and maces and javelins right underneath them. Axes and hammers. Crossbows and longbows. Sickles and katar blades. Nunchucks and a wide array of flails. Numerous fearsome weaponized armors with sharp spikes and matching gauntlets furnished mannequins along an entire wall of the room.

She was so overwhelmed that she failed to notice that she was not, in fact, alone.

Doran stood facing her, naked from the waist up, his bronze, sculpted chest on full display. He had a glorious depiction of majestic black wings spanning his entire right arm over his shoulder, and overlapping the top of his right pectoral muscle. He was tall at about six feet, lean but not bulky. His short, wavy dark brown hair was plastered to the sides of his face and neck, wet from the apparently heavy duty training that he had been up to before Duna interrupted him. A pair of elongated swords hung loosely at his sides.

"I'm sorry for barging in like this, I didn't know anyone was in here," she said. "Do you mind if I stay and observe? I promise to not get in your way."

"I have an even better idea, why not join me?" He walked over to the wall of weapons and after briefly inspecting the collection, he picked up a pair of – sticks? They were the length of her entire arm, slightly curved, made from red oak. Throwing them over to Duna, he explained, "These are wooden swords that we use for training." He scrutinized her, then said, "It'll do. Now, let's see what you're made of."

He lunged, she blocked. He thrust, she blocked then with her other arm jabbed the man in the gut. "Good," he said. "Again." They sparred like that for a while, Duna getting the better of the man. She wasn't sure if he was holding back or if he was actually that slow.

"Can you go any faster? I'm getting bored."

He threw back his head, roaring. It was such an unexpectedly deep, thundering laugh that it took Duna a few moments before she realized that it was coming from the male in front of her. It simply did not fit his physiognomy.

"Alright, I guess I can do that. Now, are you sure about this? I don't want to hurt you, little lady," Doran said.

How adorable. "Don't worry, you won't hurt me. Now," she got into position, "let's begin." She flew at him with her two wooden sticks, not giving the man a chance to say anything before he had to block her.

It was a spectacular fight. Duna was in her element now, lost in the movements of her body, her mind sharper than the blade of her formidable opponent. Thrust, block, slice. Feint, jab, block. On and on they went, dancing around each other, never missing a beat. Doran was impressive with the elongated blade, but she found it odd that he would not give her real weapons as well. It would only be fair.

"Why do you get a real sword and I get some wooden sticks?" she said, blocking then thrusting.

"Because, I like all my body parts right where they are."

"So do I, yet you don't hear me complaining about the almost twenty inch long blade that you have flying at my head," she stopped moving as she blocked another one of his jabs. Walking over to the weapons collection, she picked up two double-edged short swords. "Now, where were we?"

They went at it through the rest of the afternoon, only stopping to refresh themselves with some much needed water, not bothering wasting time on food and the likes.

Doran was a worthy opponent, someone that was of almost equal skill as her. She was faster though, more nimble, while he was predictable. She had learned all the ticks and giveaways of his demeanor and body. They were so slight that any other person would have missed them. But Duna was not like everybody else, she played by her own rules and could see right through her opponent's mask.

"Enough," Madir barked through the vast room, "I have been standing here for the past hour, waiting for my turn, and yet you two are still going at it. Algernon, you may leave."

The male bowed to the Crown Prince and then to Duna, "You are a formidable opponent, Lady Damaris." *Wait, what?* " I would be honored to train with you again." Leaving the training facility, he returned his weapon back on the rack in it's rightful place and left her alone with the dark haired prince.

"So, this is where you have been hiding today," Madir said, walking up to stand a few feet away from her. "I have been looking for you everywhere. I was told that you had gone into the city with Petra. Why didn't you come see me once you returned?"

"I wasn't aware that it was required of me to do so, Your Highness," she said, returning her swords to their places. "What did you need from me?"

"I wish to see you whenever you are here, in the palace, Duna. Is that not enough?"

"Don't you have things to do? You know, like be a prince, make important decisions, woo unsuspecting females?"

"The only female that will ever get my attention is already standing right in front of me. Besides, you're not unsuspecting. You are well aware of my intentions with you." Madir stepped up to her then, taking her hand in his.

She blinked. "That you intend to make me yours."

"That you will be mine, Duna." He lifted her hand to his mouth and kissed her knuckles.

"And how will that happen?" she breathed, "I already told you, I don't fall for pretty boys."

He chuckled. "It's a good thing then that I'm not one, for the things that I will do to you no boy will ever even dare to attempt with a woman like you." He lifted her fingers, nibbling the tips of them with his teeth. "Soon, you will be mine. And when you are, your body will belong to me, to do every little dirty and depraved thing that I want with it. I will suck you dry and then fill you up again so thoroughly that every single one of your holes will be leaking with our combined juices."

She choked on air, throat drying up. Her clit was pulsing widely, pressing against the seem of her pants. This man and his filthy mouth.

"Can you just imagine?" spreading each of her digits, he licked and sucked on the skin in between them, "You splayed out wide, your hands and legs tied to my bed, utterly helpless, your slick coating my dick while I pound away into you." She whimpered, her core clenching around nothing. "Yeah, that's it, you'll be screaming my name so loud that there will never be a doubt in anyone's mind about who's fucking you."

Oh, God.

"Now, be a good girl and go to your room." He released her hand, slowly scanning her from head to toe. "Tonight you dine with the King. Be presentable."

CHAPTER
14

"No, absolutely not, I am not wearing this," Duna said, inspecting herself in the mirror.

"Oh, hush," her lady in waiting, Epona, chastised her, "you are exquisite, Lady Duna, the very picture of grace. Now, be still while I finish doing your hair."

"I'm practically naked!" Duna spun around then, examining the back of her dress where the same sheer cream, beaded lace material covered her exposed body. "You can see everything, why bother wearing the gown? I'll just go without it, it would at least be a less of a shock when the King sees me." She was not going like this to dinner with the monarch of Nissa. It was absolutely out of the question.

"Lady Duna, please stop moving around, I will poke you with the pin by accident and then we will have blood all over your gown." Epona twisted her back so that Duna was facing the front again, smoothing out her long chocolate locks which she had styled in soft waves that were cascading down one side of her body, over Duna's covered shoulder.

The gown itself was a true masterpiece. It was a sheer lace material in the softest cream hue. Countless tiny silver beads were woven into the lace, making the dress glitter and sparkle in the light. It had long balloon sleeves that were cut in the middle, revealing Duna's forearms. One of Duna's shoulder and upper arm was bare, the neckline having a lopsided draped cut out that went over one shoulder. The gown itself followed Duna's sensual curves, accentuating her toned, succulent body. It finished in a mermaid style bottom that was slightly longer than her height, giving the effect of cascading waterfalls when she walked.

Duna's issue wasn't with the gown itself, per se, but with the lack of undergarments that she had to abolish in order for the dress to lie on her body the way it was designed to do. The fact that the material was a lace, and that besides a small piece of cloth that was sewn into the area where her private parts were, everything else was on full display. Her nipples, thank the gods, were covered with the overlapping draping of the neckline.

Madir had said to look presentable for the King; surely, he didn't mean this. Maybe it would be best if Duna changed into something less revealing. After all, it was only a dinner.

"Epona, please," she tried again. "I can't go like this. I'm overdressed and exposed and I feel like a complete idiot. I'm not used to wearing clothing like this, I will only make a fool out of myself. Which will also reflect badly on you, seeing as–"

"Lady Duna, did anybody ever tell you that you speak too much?" the elderly woman shot her a stern look. "You *will* wear this dress because Prince Madir had personally picked it out for you. You must always do as he says. Always." Appraising her one last time, she left Duna to herself, apparently satisfied with the job that she had done.

After what seemed like a lifetime, a servant came to escort Duna down to the dining hall. She entered the sumptuous space, examining it. One side of the wall was in fact a row of high, arched windows, adorned with a multitude of sheer curtains and gold drapes. Opposite the windows was a wall filled with paintings depicting people in different stages of cooking and feasting. In the center of the room was a long, elongated oak table with a champagne colored damask table cloth that cascaded down the sides. From the ceiling hung a row of eight massive crystal and gold chandeliers, illuminating the space in soft yellow light.

King Lucan sat at a throne-like chair at the head of the table, sipping on a glass of wine. Duna slightly bowed at the head, not knowing what the appropriate etiquette for greeting the King of Nissa was. He nodded in return, showing her to a place across from an exasperated Madir.

"Your Majesty, thank you for inviting me to dinner, I am honored to be seated at your table." Duna said as she made herself comfortable in the sizeable white chair.

"Lady Damaris, is it?" the King asked, piercing her with his indicolite colored eyes. She nodded while the man continued, "I hear that you have become a regular customer at Rida's Bakery Shop. Tell me, which is your favorite pastry? I, personally prefer her puff vanilla creamed ones."

Duna stared at the King, dumbfounded. "The ones with the caramelized almonds that are sprinkled on top?" She gasped, "Those are my favorites, too! Oh, you must accompany me next time that I go to the White City,

Your Majesty." *Well done, Duna. Maybe you can invite him for tea and a round of gossip after you've finished strolling around with the man. Idiot.*

Much to Duna's surprise, the male laughed at her suggestion, a full on hearty laugh. "My son was correct, you are quite something, Lady Damaris. I don't believe that a woman has ever invited me out for puff pastries before." He sipped his wine. "I'm afraid that I must decline your offer, however tempting that it is. Maybe my daughter," he pointed towards the Princess that was nibbling on her platter of delicacies, "Roesia, can accompany you. You are about the same age, I believe. She can show you around our beautiful city."

They conversed some more, Duna completely blown away by the male. He was so different from what she had pictured a king of a fabled, legendary city to be, so much more relaxed and humbled.

For the first time since sitting down at the dining table, Duna noticed that the King had no crown on his head. Come to think of it, he didn't have one on when he had greeted them in the War Room either. How very strange.

The heavy, wooden doors swung open, cutting of their conversation. Duna knew who it was even before the heady scent of leather and whiskey struck her senses.

Her head snapped around. Her breath caught. Her heart hammered away. All the blood shot to her over sensitized skin, where even the light breeze that was blowing in from the slightly open windows was causing her skin to shiver and quake.

As if her subconscious mind had summoned the very man himself, Cathal walked in, taking all the air with him. Like a vortex, he sucked everything into his field of orbit. He was the Sun and they were the planets revolving around his blazing, bright inferno. Duna would burn with him until her very last breath.

She stared at him, at a loss of words, as he approached her side and pulling out a chair, sat down right next to her. Nodding to the King, he finally looked at her. He was so close, so very close, that she could see the breathtaking color of his eyes. She gasped.

She had never seen his eyes from this close up before; she had never seen eyes the likes of his before. They were a translucent, sparkling sage-green shade speckled with silver. They glistened in the sunlight, making it seem as if a thousand little shimmering silver stars were trapped within them. When he gazed at her like he did at that moment, Duna had the feeling that she was floating through the vast, endless expanse of a glowing green nebula, lost in the never-ending glittering stars.

They stared at each other, completely oblivious to their surroundings, to the fact that the King was addressing them. Duna's mind had not registered that Madir had called her name, that there were conversations going on around them. She could only study the magnificent man beside her, her heart aching as she did so. *He will never be yours.*

She broke their gaze then, getting back to reality. He would never be hers. She would have to remember that, she would have to grip her heart with an iron fist and squeeze all her emotions out of the treacherous organ until it bled him out, until it no longer beat for him. Then she would put herself back together again, to factory settings, to the way she had been prior to laying eyes on him in the General's tent. Before she ever inhaled his addictive scent, which had become engraved into her brain like a brand on her soul.

Duna was doomed from the very start. There was no remedy for this ailment. No reprieve from her ever consuming thoughts about this wonderfully dark, enigmatic man. She could sense him, his soul. It called to her, just like her body called to his.

She ached for him, with every fiber of her being.

But how could she tell him? It was impossible. She was nothing to him. He would only laugh in her face. He was already taken, he belonged to another woman.

And yet, Duna didn't care. Fates damn her, she was a horrible human being for it, but she didn't care. She would let him ruin her for all other men, if only she could be in his arms for a single night. One. Just one. It would be enough to fill her well of yearning, to draw from it to quench her never dying thirst if only for a little while, for the rest of her miserable days in this depressing world.

"General Ragnar, what news do you have about Princess Leila? Has there been any progress?" King Lucan said, bringing Duna back to the present.

"Not yet, Your Majesty," Cathal answered. "Our search of the eastern part of the city has concluded this morning. Unfortunately, we failed to find anything that would even remotely suggest as to where the Princess might have stayed while in the White City. We will resume shortly in a few days, after we re-evaluate our strategy."

They continued discussing the topic at hand, Duna's thought starting to wander again.

How could the gods be so cruel? First, she had lost her parents at an early age, leaving her sickly grandmother to fend for her. Then, that very same wonderful woman was taken away from her in the most horrible of ways; burned, in a fire, a fate so terrible that she would not wish it upon even her worst enemy. And, finally, the man that had imprinted himself on her heart, could never be hers.

Duna's breath hitched. She was being ridiculous. She hardly knew the General, she needed to stop being so overdramatic.

A hand lightly gripped her thigh, calming her raging thoughts. It did no good for her heart though, the organ hammering away like an opiate addict during his high. She dared not turn her head to look at Cathal, lest he see the tempestuous storm in her eyes. She stared ahead at the King, swallowing, her hands gripping the knife and fork like a vise.

The hand moved slightly upwards, then back down again, over and over in the softest caress of the skin. The sheer lace gown did nothing to temper down the violent sensations taking over her.

He increased the pressure in his strokes, gripping her muscles while massaging her thigh. From her knee to her hip he worked her ripe flesh over the nonexistent fabric, taking his time to explore her wired body. It was torture; sweet, magnificent torture.

His firm hold reached the fold of her upper thigh, right where it connected to her lower abdomen and the heated part of her core. He pressed his callused fingers in between her closed thighs, the friction of her lace gown burning away at her skin.

Oh, God.

Releasing the pressure, he placed his whole hand between her thighs and spread his fingers open so that her legs were spread slightly apart, allowing him entrance to do with her as he pleased.

The loose fabric of her gown fell in between her legs where his hand was, the lace covering her soaking wet core and pulsing nub. With the root of his palm, he worked her in circles over her dress, the beads rubbing against her throbbing clit, over and over, relentlessly, all the while he continued to make idle conversations with the King.

Duna sat stoic, liquid heat pouring out of her, drenching her gown and the chair underneath her. She stared at a spot on her plate, her knuckles white from the iron grip that she had on her utensils.

The General increased his tempo, circling and rubbing and pressing as he pleased. The man was the devil himself, pure evil for doing this to her in the middle of the dining hall in front of an unsuspecting audience. She was going to explode in the most violent of orgasms if he kept up his ministrations.

That's it sweetheart, cum for me. Duna's head snapped around at Cathal, dropping her cutlery, the steel making a loud crashing sound as it hit the porcelain plate.

Did she just hear his voice in her head? How was that possible?

He was looking straight ahead, smiling away at something that Princess Roesia had said, appearing completely oblivious to what had just occurred. No, she must have imagined it.

This was not good, she was starting to hallucinate.

"Are you alright, Lady Damaris?" King Lucan asked her, confused about her show of clumsiness.

"I'm fine, my hold slipped," she said, trying desperately to keep her voice steady while Cathal rubbed away at her. He was merciless, utterly despicable with what he was doing to her.

Heat pooled in her lower abdomen, spreading slowly over her entire body. She clenched the table cloth on each side of her plate, gripping it so tightly that her knuckles blanched. A violent wave of numbness suddenly overtook her.

She burst then, a roaring volcano erupting from her core, the magnitude of it sending continuous ripples of ecstasy to the very tips of her fingers and toes. Head lowered down, she closed her eyes, her lips parting in a silent scream, only a low moan escaping from her over stimulated body.

So fucking beautiful. There it was again, his voice. She had not imagined it, Duna was certain without a doubt that Cathal's voice was speaking in her mind.

She could hear his thoughts.

He slowly pulled away his hand, grazing her leg softly to the top of her knee as he did so. Turning around to her, the General chuckled, a satisfied glint in his eyes. "Dinner was very satisfying, Your Majesty. Thank you for inviting me."

Duna flew into her room, crashing the heavy door closed behind her. Bolting the lock, she pressed her back against the sturdy wood and wheezed. She was going to suffocate, she couldn't get enough air into her lungs.

After dinner had finished, the General had left with King Lucan and Madir to the War Room to go over more details about their upcoming search mission for Princess Leila. The remaining royal, Roesia, had invited her along for some late night tea, but Duna had kindly declined. She needed to be alone, to get her bearings together.

She had orgasmed in front of the Royal Family of Nissa in the middle of dinner. To make things even worse, she had a bad feeling that the Crown Prince had caught on that something was happening with her under the table. He kept throwing her questioning glances, irritated that he couldn't catch her eye. She was mortified that he would discover their little indiscretion, not that the man had any claim on her, but nevertheless.

What to make of Duna hearing the General's thoughts in her head? How was it possible? She was human, as plain as they came. As far as she knew, so was Cathal. Apart from his otherworldly presence and breathtaking beauty, he seemed ordinary enough. There had to be a reasonable explanation for this insanity.

A knock came at her door, jolting her to the present. Please, let it not be him. *Please, please, just not him.*

"Duna, are you in there?" Petra's voice came from the other side of the door. Exhaling a sigh of relief, Duna unlatched the door and swung it open. Petra was standing in a light blue, fluffy cashmere robe tied around her waist, her hair down, a pair of matching fluffy, warm slippers on her feet.

"Why do you look like you killed a bunny and wore his fur to bed?" Duna said, inspecting the female. She had never seen her friend in such an absurd ensemble.

"What, as opposed to looking like I just orgasmed under a waterfall?" Petra arched a defined brow, her hand gesturing to Duna's sheer cream lace gown with interwoven silver beads.

Duna grinned. If she only knew. "What do you want, oh Mighty One?"

"The General received news today from Baqar from Kane," Petra entered her room, "The two princes are together at the Grand Palace of King Basel, they have received aid from Navajo in scouring the land for any traces of the Princess."

"Do they have a lead?" It was all very strange to Duna. How could a person as important as the princess of a kingdom as imposing as Tyros just disappear without a trace?

Her appearance alone was unique enough to distinguish her, with her long silver hair and pale alabaster skin. She would stand out in a crowd where ever she went, no cloak or mask could hide her identity. To think that they couldn't get a single, miniscule lead on her was close to impossible. Something else was hiding beneath all of this.

Duna would be damned if she didn't find out.

"Not yet, I just came to let you know. The General made a decision that if we didn't receive any news from Navajo in a months time, the three of us are to join the rest of our company in Baqar." Opening her door, Petra stepped through. "Good night, Duna."

Shutting the door and latching it once again, Duna stared at the tall, arched window at the other side of her room. Walking across the space, she stopped in front of the glass, looking up at the sky. The stars were out tonight, the Moon shining bright in the dark expanse of the never-ending shadows. It was captivating, mesmerizing. Holding Duna prisoner to it's lustrous existence.

"It's stunning, isn't it?" the General's deep, velvety smooth voice reached her from the shadows of her room. "The ancients believed that the Moon goddess Selene, sister of Helios, the Sun god, drives a silver chariot across the heavens each night, pulling the Moon as she flies through the sky, her two snow-white stallions blazing a path through the darkness." He came close to her, his heat radiating behind her back. "You are more beautiful than the Moon," he murmured softly into her ear, leaning down over her bare shoulder. "More exquisite than the star filled sky." Using his firm hand, he gently moved her hair aside, his calloused fingers lightly grazing her shivering skin. "More captivating than the vast, endless universe that surrounds us." He inhaled her then, his nose burning a path from her exposed shoulder, over the curve of her neck, all the way to the back of her ear. "I have been going mad thinking about you, Duna," he whispered, "I have tried to stay away from you, to tell myself that it is wrong. That you do not deserve a man like me."

She swallowed, looking through the window, chest heaving madly. His long fingers trailed a path down the slope of her neck and over her shoulder, gripping her bicep. "I am a selfish man, little one. A bad man. I want what I cannot have." He pressed close to Duna, his tight body pressing against her soft curves, igniting her senses. "But I dare anyone to stand in my way. I will burn the whole fucking world down for you," he gripped her other shoulder as well, pulling her against him, "For just one touch from your exquisite mouth, for just one smoldering embrace in the shadows of the darkest night. For a single gaze from your soul shattering, depthless eyes, I would punish the gods themselves." *You are mine.*

Duna spun around in his arms, gasping. "You did it again," she breathed. She fisted his shirt, staring up at his star-filled gaze, "How did you do that? How can I hear you?"

Cathal seemed confused. His knuckles grazed across her flushed cheek. "I don't understand. What do you mean?"

"Your voice, I can hear your voice in my head," she said. "I can hear your thoughts."

He went utterly still, his hand freezing on her cheek. *Impossible.*

"Yes, well, it should be, but–" she shrugged, answering out loud to his thoughts, "–it would appear that it is not."

Cathal blanched, his hands dropping to his sides. "How is this possible?" *It cannot be you.*

"I can't be who? What are you talking about?" She released her hold on him, spreading her palms over his chiseled chest. "Please, I don't understand what's going on. How can I hear your thoughts, Cathal?"

"I–" he choked, his words lost in his throat. He stepped back then, putting space between their bodies. *I will not sacrifice her, brother.*

"Sacrifice? What–"

He suddenly grabbed her, holding her shoulders tight, eyes pleading with her, "You must *never* tell anyone about this. Not ever, Duna. Do you understand me? I forbid it. I will hunt down any and every damned person that you utter a single word to about this and I will skin them alive right in front of your eyes and make you watch as I shred them to bits, piece by piece. I will become evil incarnate. I will become the Devourer of souls herself if I have to, just to keep you safe." He shook her, "Swear to me, Duna."

Shocked at his confession, she could only nod.

"Use your words, little one. I must hear you say them."

I swear.

He dropped his hold as if burned. Eyes wide open, mouth gaping, he ran his hands through his hair.

"You heard me," Duna said. "You can hear my thoughts, too. Oh, God," she wheezed, hand flying to her thundering heart. "What is happening?" She was not the panicking type, yet she was on the verge of a mental collapse.

"I–I will explain one day, just not yet." He embraced her then, his strong arms going around her shaking body, pressing her against him. "I swear to you that I will keep you safe. I won't let anything happen to you, Duna." *I will live through a thousand more deaths until the end of time if that is the price.*

Duna could only stare at him, dumbfounded and stunned.

He kissed her forehead then, his piercing green eyes imploring her to understand. "Remember, you swore to me." With one last desperate look at her, the General turned around and walked out of her chambers.

CHAPTER 15

"Your Majesty, General Ragnar is here to see you," the servant echoed from across the room while Cathal waited impatiently for the male to leave them to themselves.

King Lucan glanced up from the long parchment that he was reading. Slowly lowering it on the table, he waved the servant off. "General, I cannot imagine what is so urgent for you to come to me at this late of an hour. Surely, even if Princess Leila had been located, you would not dare to interrupt my peace until a more appropriate time."

"I must speak to you," Cathal stepped closer to the man. "It is about Seba."

The King blinked, then stared at him. "You cannot be serious, General," the man rambled on, "That is a myth, a distorted confabulation of a delusional mind. You must not–"

"I was there that day, Lucan, when the bellflower bloomed on those blood drenched fields. You know what I speak of!" Cathal shouted. "It was real, I myself witnessed the future that she revealed to us. She was sane and very much aware of the words that were coming out of her mouth."

"And yet, she condemned us all that day," the King said, his face stern.

"No," Cathal frowned. "She gave me hope that there will come an end to this agony, that my sacrifice was not for nothing. That there is still hope for mankind."

"What is it that you wish from me?" The King stood from his chair, clasping his hands behind his back. "I am getting old, not even the elixir will grant me more time than it already has. Perhaps, if I may pass it on to Madir–"

"No," Cathal interrupted, "You are the Keeper, the one true Guardian. No one else can know. If it dies with you before the next Guardian is selected, then so be it, we will all face the consequences. But Madir cannot be trusted with it, he will doom us all for eternity. He is greedy and ambitious, his soul is tainted. You know this Lucan, do not let your fatherly affections get in the way of your sound judgment."

"Madir could be great, he could do great things for mankind. Do not throw away faith for him just yet, Cathal, he can change," King Lucan pleaded with him, his eyes full of remorse and despair.

"He cannot. He will not. The darkness in his soul grows as the days go by, if he continues this way it will not be salvageable. You know I cannot alter the outcome if it comes to that. Do not ask it of me. I will not do it." Even if he wished it as a final gift to his greatest ally, Cathal would not risk it.

"Yes, it is perhaps better that way..." the elderly man trailed off, his thoughts gloomy. "Why have you come, General?"

"You are the Guardian. I wish to hear the Oracle's prophecy again." He held his breath. The King could, of course, refuse him. It was in his right to do so as the Keeper of Seba. But he would not, for he owed Cathal his life. The man would not be standing here today if it weren't for the General.

The Guardian took off his silver medallion necklace and, placing it in Cathal's open palm, beckoned him to follow. The two males made their way to a small nook in the eastern wall of the bedroom, it's place hidden from view by a familiar plant whose dense vines and colorful flowers seemed to cover the entirety of the secluded space, appearing as if there was nothing behind the greenery but white stone which Cathal realized was actually some type of limestone instead of the dolomite which made up the whole of the White Palace.

Cathal watched in amazement as the vines slithered away as the Guardian softly stroked their leaves, the delicate violet flowers blooming even more under the man's gentle touch. As if bowing to him, they lowered themselves to the ground, revealing an archway large enough for the male to pass through and enter the niche.

On the wall was an intricately carved depiction of a five-pointed line that resembled a starfish, the size of a man's palm. The symbol for Seba, the representation of the constellations, the star-gods.

King Lucan nicked his palm with a pin, a drop of dark red blood appearing on his skin as he did so. Placing his wounded open hand on the symbol, the markings began to react, appearing as if they were shimmering under his skin. Pushing the rock, it heaved inwards under his touch, and then suddenly, it completely disappeared. As if the white limestone had never been there, a substantial black hole now stood in its place, and in it – stars, endless stars, sparkling in the vast darkness that lay beyond.

Realization hit Cathal in the face like a slap of reality. It was a gateway. "You did it." He was stunned. Then a new wave of shock hit him, "This is what you protect in the White City." He had never, in his wildest dreams, imagined that his oldest ally and brother in arms would be the one to finally forge the lost gateway that would take him to the one place that he ached for the most.

His home. He could finally go home.

No, Cathal realized. He could not. His dear brother would take it as a sign of surrender, of his acceptance of the inevitable fate of mortals, of their irreparable souls. He would not doom them so. He would not be that selfish. There was another way, he had to hear the prophecy again. "Take me to her, Lucan. I want to see her."

"I cannot go with you, General. You must go alone. Place the necklace of Seba around your neck and enter through the portal. It will take you to her, but beware, she might appear as one who you might not desire to hear of again. Also, you must not stay long. He will sense you. If you wish to return to this world of mortals, you must never allow that to happen, for he will never let you go again."

Cathal was aware of it; oh, how well he knew his proud brother.

Entering as instructed, he felt a shimmer go over his body, and the niche faded away to nothing. He was standing in an intermingling, luminescent cloud of dust and gas, forming a dazzling two-colored nebula. Constellations surrounded him on all sides, appearing as if he was floating between them.

"Your Highness," a soft female voice spoke to him, "you have returned at last."

"I have not. I have come to ask of the prophecy," he said. "I wish to hear it again from you."

"You are not the Guardian, Your Highness. I cannot repeat the prophecy for you. You know this," the dear voice whispered then, changing to another one that he knew all too well, "my son."

Son.

How long has he not heard that word. How long had he not heard her utter it.

"You will repeat it. I will not ask it of you again." Mother. Dare he say that damned word out loud? Would it mean anything to him after all the millennia that he had been left wandering the cold, barren lands of humans, alone and desperate. Did the word hold the same weight after his own blood had betrayed him in such a cruel way?

"I will grant you your wish, Your Highness, if only to ask of you a small favor in return," his mother said. "Say it, just one more time. I wish to hear the word that my heart has been pleading to hear for almost an eternity. Those two syllables that are meaningless when apart but when spoken together by you, my son, my Lord, they become the very reason of my existence."

Appalled at her words, he seethed, "You betrayed me, along with my duplicitous brother. Do not act like a weeping mother who lost her son by some unfortunate turn of fate. You are nothing to me, not anymore. All the love and affection that I felt as a son for you vanished the same day when you stabbed me in the back." A storm raged in him, his brother would sense him if he didn't control himself. He would need to leave soon. He was running out of time. "Now, the prophecy. Mother." Her form was not visible, but Cathal imagined he saw a glimmer of her ethereal face before him as he pronounced the damned word.

"The prophecy of Isis is one that must never be repeated out loud to anyone outside of the Guardian and yourself. It is explicit that you follow my instructions or it could cause unimaginable ripples in the lives of man. The prophecy is this:

In the midnight hour on the forgotten isle,
the truth will be Shed.
The one who seeks to tame a heart,
so black with gloom and regret.
The mind will know what ears don't hear,
what silver eyes don't Shed but fear.
The end will come when hearts collide,
of Fate he can't escape.
To forge a bond of ever more,
the price that one must pay.
The sands of time will flow once more,
once she has sworn an oath.
Of blood and tears, a soul so pure,
the God may be restored.

"You must go now, hurry!" his mother's voice drifted off as he was pulled back through the portal and into the chambers of King Lucan of Nissa.

Cathal watched, stunned anew, as the gateway disappeared right before his eyes, the vast universe of stars replaced by the white limestone of before.

"It's not possible," he murmured to himself, a new wave of shock taking over his body. Hands running through his hair, he spun on the spot, desperately trying but failing to keep his bearings together. He paced the

King's chambers, thinking over everything in his mind.

But how can that be? It doesn't make any sense. God damn it, he was going in circles. He was not going to accomplish anything in the state that he was in, he had to get some rest.

Bidding the King goodbye, the General went back to his room. Unknown to all but the very man that he had just left, he had relocated his sleeping chambers to one that was right next to Duna's bedroom, their two rooms adjoined by a shared door. He was surprised that she had not discovered it yet; the door nor his new residential quarters.

Cathal did not care for the Prince. He would surely be angry about the move, needing to have Duna all alone and secluded from the rest of her company. He knew what Madir's motives were, could sense them on the male. He was entranced by his little warrior, he wanted to possess her like every other thing that the Prince ever possessed in his life. Except the man did not understand that she was not an item to be purchased and maintained; Duna was a human being, one with such a pure soul that Cathal sometimes found himself in awe of her.

He knew that she had lost her grandmother in a tragic way; the story that she had told by the fire in the mountains had done nothing to hide her grief from him. He had read it in her eyes, in the way they glistened with unshed tears. In the way her chest had heaved and then gone unbelievably still while she had recalled finding the elderly woman's scorched body.

He could still not believe that the village that he had found burned to the ground five years ago while on a scouting mission with his soldiers was her home village, the one that had shattered the General's already frail belief in mankind.

Cathal did not need to be a mind reader to know what went through Duna's thoughts. To feel what her heart ached for with each vicious thump of its muscle. He was so captivated by her that it sometimes appeared to him as if he could observe her for all eternity and still, it would not be enough.

Her beauty enthralled him, called out him. Her body – that succulent, ripe, delicious body of hers – ignited a raging inferno in his groin that he desperately tried to quench by himself, fisting away at his hard cock day in and day out like a hormonal adolescent.

It was not enough, though, his hand did nothing to diminish his ache for her. If anything it made it only worse.

He could already taste the delicious juices that would flow out of her. How he would lick and suck her sweet pussy dry from behind while she squirmed on his face. She would come like that first, at least once, before stuffing her full to the hilt. He would have to make sure she was nice and ready for him before she took his substantial cock.

He imagined her now, bent over; her round, full ass spread out wide while he pounded into her from behind. He would play with her flesh while he fucked her hard, would grip it until his handprints were marking her skin for all to see who she belonged to.

Oh, he would fuck her so gloriously, so ruthlessly. She would be moaning and begging and screaming his name through it all.

But first, Cathal had to end things with Leila. She might be his fated mate, but it was not fair to give her false hope. He was not in love with her anymore. It was a fact which he had long ignored, not wanting to believe that such a thing could exist between mates. It wasn't unheard of, he supposed, but it was a rare occurrence nonetheless.

He could not give himself fully to Duna until he talked to Leila; he owed her that much as a sign of respect for all the decades that they had known each other, for all the years that they had spent as lovers. He would, also, have to break of the engagement; King Fergal would not be pleased with that turn of events, but there was nothing that he could do about it in the end. The King would accept it as he would have no other choice.

Cathal's only worry was for how Leila would take it all. She was fragile, even though she pretended to be strong. He would have to be gentle about it, lest he cause more damage than was necessary.

He went to shower, needing to take down his body's elevated temperature. Leaving his door slightly ajar, he listened to the sounds coming from the little warrior's room. She was obviously sleeping, it was well past midnight.

Getting out from under the cold stream of water, he wrapped himself up in a towel, not bothering with clothes. He might as well get dripping wet into bed, the droplets would steam away from his body at the rate that he was burning up.

Duna, it was all for her. The shower did nothing to ease the throbbing of his cock. It appeared that he would need to take care of himself, yet again.

That was when he heard it. There was a low, whimpering sound coming from behind their joined door. Pressing his ear to the wood, Cathal listened to any signs of distress.

"Oh, God."

He bolted upright, his heart beating furiously. Duna was moaning in that room. Was Madir with her? Were they fucking? He was going to murder someone.

Not caring as to how it would appear and how he would explain himself, he barged into the chambers, not bothering to close the door behind him. The sight that greeted him was one that he had hoped in his wildest dreams to live to see one day.

Duna was alone on her bed, naked, her exquisite body wet and on full display for him as she moaned and moved on her pumping fingers. She had not heard him enter, or if she did, she did not seem fazed by his presence.

Cathal stood frozen by her bed, breathless, his cock at full mast, pressing at the towel that was wrapped loosely around his lower body. He was fucking mesmerized by the sight. He didn't know where to look first.

She was stunning, with curves that went on for days, her thick thighs spread wide, revealing her glistening, completely bare cunt. Her breasts modest in size but so plump with the most mouthwatering pair of perfect, tight nipples that he could just imagine licking and sucking them while he fucked her into oblivion. His throat was so dry that he could not even swallow.

Duna was glorious in her erotic haze. And he wasn't even fucking her yet. He was going to explode just by watching her fingering her tight pussy. He groaned, and that's when she saw him.

She stopped.

His voice a raspy low, he said, "Don't stop, please. Let me watch you."

"Only if I get to watch you, too," she purred, slowly resuming her ministrations. She watched him the whole time while she mercilessly pumped away in herself, her eyes hooded, never leaving his own heated ones.

"I will fuck the mattress if I have to just to see you fuck yourself in that perfect cunt." Cathal took of his towel and threw it over the bed beside her. He took his hard cock in his hand and fisted it tightly. "Spread those pretty thighs wider for me, yeah, just like that. I want to see what that finger is doing."

She did as he told her, following his every instruction to the letter.

"Put another finger inside. Fill yourself up nice and tight for me." She did so. He whipped away on his cock. "That won't do, you can take one more, Duna. Show me," she placed a third finger inside her dripping wet pussy, stretching herself so sublimely. "Now, fuck yourself nice and slow. I want to hear you moan while your slick pours down to your wrist."

She moaned and whined, he pumped and groaned. They worked in tandem with each other, their rhythm matching perfectly. Eyes locked, they increased their speed.

"Play with your clit, don't be shy, that's it. Harder, yeah, just like that." He was ruthlessly fisting his cock, the engorged head a livid, dark color, his veins throbbing at the erotic sight before his eyes.

He was standing right between her legs as he did so, her thighs spread nice and wide right in front of his eyes. He could just picture his massive cock filling her up to the hilt, her juices coating it, overflowing around his hard shaft and onto the mattress below while he pumped her full.

She was moaning so loudly now that he was sure that he would bust just from the sound of it alone. Mumbling incoherently, she moved herself down closer to the edge of the bed where Cathal was standing. "Spread your legs wide, General. I want to hook my knees around you."

Fucking hell.

He did as was told, not hesitating a moment. He spread his legs out wide, still keeping himself steady while he hammered away at his cock.

She moved even lower to the edge of the bed, her legs pushed wide open around his knees, more than he thought humanly possible. Her cunt was on full display for him like this, so close to his cock that he was barely restraining himself from not impaling her on it.

She arched her back then, pushing her hard, erect nipples up in the air. Moaning incessantly, she worked her three fingers inside of herself all the way to her knuckles. Her other hand rubbed away on her pulsing clit. Back and forth, in and out, slow then fast, it went on and on until the sounds that were coming out of her mouth and cunt were so obscene that Cathal wondered if their souls would burn in the endless pit of darkness for all eternity.

"Such a good fucking girl, Duna, look at you. So drenched, your pussy greedily taking three fingers to the full, stretching your glistening cunt wide." She whimpered, her breathing increasing, her hand speeding up as he matched her tempo. "That's right, take it all, take all those glorious inches because once I fuck you, your fingers will never go in that sweet cunt of yours ever again."

She exploded in a serious of loud, erotic moans as soon as the words left his mouth. On and on, her body shaking, the sounds of pure bliss and satisfaction filling the air.

Cathal pumped his cock once, twice, and followed Duna. He detonated all over her stomach, the hot, white cum drenching her hot flesh. It flew out of him in endless streams of white liquid, the intoxicating smell of their body fluids soaking the air around them.

To his amazement, she rubbed his cum all over her skin, spreading it over her breasts, coating herself in his scent. The filthy little vixen was fucking made for him. She sat up then, her legs still locked around his spread out knees. Looking up at his still erect shaft, she licked her lips.

"Not yet, little monster. You will take my cock when the time is right. And you will take all of it, every last inch in that pretty mouth of yours." Lifting her chin up to make her look at him, he said to her, "I will not fuck you until I am free to do so properly, like a woman like you deserves to be wrecked," he caressed her hair, "I will not hide you in some dark corners, you are not going to be my dirty little secret, Duna. Until I can pound ruthlessly away in that tight pussy of yours and make you scream so that everyone knows who you belong to, I will not do so. Do you understand?"

She nodded. "*Yes.*"

He stared at her, both of them naked, vulnerable, yet not hiding from each other. He had heard her thoughts again in his mind. Shaking his head at the impossible reality of his discovery, he answered her back in her mind, *"Give me time to make things right first. I need to do this the correct way. Leila deserves the truth from me before I give myself to you."*

"I know, Cathal. It is the only way," she answered him back, their eyes locked in a war of emotions, neither one of them daring to admit to the other the truth.

She got up then, and placing her hand over his chiseled chest, kissed the skin over his heart. He touched her cheek, his thumb lightly tracing the lines of her face. They parted ways then, each to their own empty room, only a door separating their breaking hearts.

They should have known in that moment that Fate always had a cruel way of interfering with one's plans, with the lives of mere mortals.

Even gods were not immune to her wrath.

CHAPTER 16

The long hours turned into even longer days, the nights seeming to never come as Duna consistently trained and sparred with Doran and even the Prince, himself. Petra and Bror left every day with the General on search missions accompanied by the countless men that King Lucan appointed them for their task. Each time Duna had chosen to stay behind, to be their eyes and ears at the White City should something of importance occur while they were away.

She had not seen Cathal after their heated encounter in her sleeping chambers. She was wondering if perhaps he had regretted it as soon as he had returned to his own rooms, which Duna had finally noticed, was adjoined to her own through a shared wooden door. She knew that a lot of things were spoken between them before they had parted ways, heavy words that could be interpreted in a number of ways, depending on the receiver. Duna wondered if they were honest words, or if Cathal had spoken them in the heat of the moment. She had her suspicions.

She did not have any regrets, she knew what she was doing as soon as he had entered her bedroom. She was not so sure if the same could be said about the General.

Cathal had not come to see her after that night, even though they lived practically in one suite. He had not been at breakfast nor dinner the next day, nor the next. Even after four days of playing cat and mouse with him, he was nowhere to be found. Had something occurred that everyone was keeping from her? She could not see a reason for that if that had been the case.

"Eyes on me!" Doran yelled at her as he managed to, once again, hit her on the shoulder. "You would be butchered into tiny pieces by now if we were on a real battlefield, woman. Get your head out of the clouds." Easy for him to say.

She dropped her sword and sat down on the hard floor. "Where is everybody these days? The palace seems more empty than ever before."

Sitting down next to her, the Master of Arms started, "General Ragnar had received a lead on a possible location for the Princess, they ambushed the said cottage and apprehended a group of men that claim that she has been taken to a secret location outside of Morinya." He inspected her. "The soldiers that were with him said that he went mad with rage when he didn't find his betrothed. They said he thrashed the place, not even the walls were left in one piece after he was done. The men he beat to a pulp, leaving them barely conscious when they left."

Duna blanched, imagining the scope of his destruction. It was not the reflection of a man that had claimed to wish to end things with his betrothed. Not the act of a man that claimed to not have feelings for the Princess any longer.

Stupid, Duna. When will you ever learn? She had been naive, yet again. Chosen to believe what he had told her in thralls of ecstasy instead of looking at his telling actions prior to said encounter. Even the fact that he had not – not once – attempted to seek Duna out should have been a clear sign to her that the General was not sincere in his claim where he wished to leave the Princess.

Not bothering with sparring anymore, she returned to her room. It was a gloomy day, the sky filled with dense, angry looking grey and black clouds.

Duna heard a commotion through the connecting door. It seemed as if Cathal had finally returned. She bolted into his room, wanting to have a word with the missing male. She stopped in her tracks when she saw that it was not, in fact, the man in question making all the fuss, but a maid.

"Where is General Ragnar? I thought he had returned to the Palace," Duna said, irritated.

"You just missed him, Lady Damaris. The General had instructed me to pack at least a week's worth of clothing and rations for his trip. He will not be returning any time soon, my lady." No, it would appear that he would not.

Duna left the woman to her work, closing the connecting door behind her as she went to her high arched window on the other side of her rooms. Gazing out through the glass, she could make out the many brilliantly armed men in white and gold Nissian uniforms riding away through the Palace gates, Cathal leading the line at the front. He was magnificent in the daylight of the dreaded day, armed to the hilt with his own white and gold leathers and armor. He appeared to be going into battle instead of a routine scouting trip across the land to some desolate village.

Duna's soul withered and shriveled up at the sight of the breathtaking, domineering man riding into the darkening day to retrieve the woman of his heart to his side. He had taken an entire platoon of almost fifty formidable warriors just to get her back.

She shook her head, laughing at herself for her own stupidity. She felt pathetic, idiotic. Like a complete half-witted imbecile. It was all her fault though, she had no one else to blame for her mindless behavior. How could she ever believe that a man like that would choose her over the Princess?

It was time for her to take things into her own hands; it was time for her to, once and for all, root out this pestering obsession that she seemed to have developed for the General.

A week passed into two, still Cathal had not returned. King Lucan had received word from his party that a snow storm had raged on for almost five days as soon as they had reached their destination. Only time would tell how long they would be trapped in the remote village somewhere in the land of the snow harpies.

Duna had stayed true to the promise that she had made to herself. She would eradicate the General from her mind and heart. She had been spending a lot of time with Prince Madir since making her decision, growing quite fond of the dark haired male. It helped that he was a very handsome man to look at, not to mention his ever growing fascination with Duna. He showered her with attention daily, bringing her radiant flowers and delicious pastries from her favorite bakery in the White City.

The weather had been kind to them in this part of the Kingdom, barely requiring a light cloak to keep them warm as they had strolled through the many winding streets of the town. Much to Duna's surprise, Madir had a gentle side to him that he rarely showed around other people, as if he was hiding it from the world. He was such a conundrum to her; each day she discovered something new about the intriguing prince.

Today, he was taking Duna to a secluded stream that ran through one of the mountain slopes behind the White Palace. It was forbidden to the public to go near it; only members of the Royal bloodline of the Raidon family had ever set eyes on the ancient creek in all the centuries of its existence.

"I want to tell you a story, Duna, if you're willing to listen," he said.

Duna nodded, curious to hear what he had to say.

"There is an ancient belief that Niamh, the daughter of a sea god, resides in the heart of these mountains," Madir said as they made their way to an iron gate at the back of the palace grounds. "It is said that she rules over the eternal Land of Youth, whose sacred waters flow out from the mountain side, forming a stream of water so green in color that it resembles the precious emerald stones that are fabled to line the entrance to her primordial domain. The legends say that the waters of Niamh are holy, blessed by the gods themselves, and that whoever was to drink from their depths would outlive their mortal lifespan by two fold, at least." He unlocked the heavy gate, showing Duna through.

"When my elders came to this land, they discovered this stream while searching for a place to build their empire. Niamh had, supposedly, granted them permission to make their home so close to her holy spring but only if they swore to her to never drink from the waters themselves. Treacherous and greedy as human nature is, they were tempted to do just that." The pair of them walked toward a stone terrace that seemed to be floating in midair.

"One night, at the stroke of midnight, while a Shadow Moon was showing its face on the star filled sky, my great ancestor broke his oath and drank from the sacred stream. Enraged by his show of deceit, Niamh cursed him and his descendants for all eternity. No two people from his bloodline could consume the waters while the other still lived. The second the other ingested the revered liquid, he would start to age at an accelerated, unnatural rate, withering away into ashes on the wind in a matter of a few nights. Unfortunately, the curse also extended to the people of the land. If anyone else was to drink from the holy waters, they, too, would meet the same fate."

Reaching the balustrade, Duna gasped at the sight that lay before her. The terrace was constructed over a narrow valley between the slopes of two mammoth, snow covered mountains, with steep rocky walls and a stream running through it. The water was a brilliant green shade, shining like the most lustrous emerald gems of royalty.

"So, they closed off the stream of Niamh, building an impenetrable stone wall around its source and enclosing it within the palace grounds. It was the only way to stop the citizens of the newly formed kingdom of not succumbing to the temptation. My ancestor, the instigator of the curse, lived to see two hundred years before he was killed on the battlefield by a spear to the heart." Madir turned to her then, his elbows leaning on the ancient stone. He inspected her face, as if searching for something. "He outlived all of his sons except one, who was as old as him when he, too, died on the battlefield, impaled through the heart by a spear. This seemed to continue for centuries, until finally, my great grandfather, King Alator, noticed a pattern." Madir turned his body all the way around to face Duna, his face grave. "All of his predecessors who had drunk from the stream seemed to have reached the same age of two hundred before they passed on to the heavens. All of them had been struck through the heart by a spear."

Duna held her breath, entranced by his story.

"King Alator searched far and wide for a way to prolong his life, to not meet the same wretched fate," Madir continued. "He met with foreign ambassadors, travelled to distant, long forgotten lands. All in hopes of finding the cure to his ever pressing issue. He was getting old, reaching his two hundred year old mark, and yet, he had no remedy to his ailment. One stormy day, while a battle raged across the Kingdom, he was impaled through the heart by a spear. He was two hundred years old."

Duna stood motionless, her body frozen in place. Had she not heard the story from his lips, she would never have believed it. "What happened after? To your grandfather?"

Madir shrugged, gazing over the vast gorge. "He didn't seem to mind living a life of two hundred, so he didn't waste it away on trivial matters. My uncles died before he did, of course. Only my father remained to succeed him on the throne." He seemed to have drifted off to another place, as if lost in a distant memory. "My father was ambitious, even as a prince. He would go raging into battles, not worrying about his impending death should he get impaled through with a sword. You see, he had not drank the elixir of youth until my grandfather had died. And so, each time he had gone into battle with the risk of dying before he ever got the chance to do so." He stopped, choosing his next words. "He was a true warrior, an honorable man. A magnificent master of weapons. Tales are sung, even today, of his legendary accomplishments on the battlefield. Once my grandfather had finally passed away, my father drank from Niamh's stream, thus commencing the countdown to his two hundred year old mark." Madir walked to a nearby bench and sat on it, patting the seat beside himself, beckoning Duna over.

She did so, taking her seat by the attractive male.

"Darkness spread across the land, swallowing mankind as it went. A great evil from a foreign kingdom from across the sea threatened the very existence of our people. A great war raged on; endless battles of unfathomable losses of human life. It seemed as if all was lost, as if man would not live to see another day. One battle remained. It would be waged on a desolate piece of land that connected our three kingdoms. The Plains of Iphigenia. Where the forces of all Three Kingdoms came together for the first and final time in our mortal history, in a final desperate attempt at relinquishing the evil from our world.

"My father had refused to take part in the final battle, he could not watch his people get butchered any longer. He, himself, had led his armies against the enemy troops countless times. He was sick of the bloodshed. The King, also, had a great dilemma - his two hundred year mark was fast approaching and yet, he was still without an heir. His reluctance to bring a child into that world of doom and despair had seemed to have finally caught up to him.

"One day, a solitary figure came to the White City, cloaked and veiled from the world. He demanded to see the King – my father – threatening to burn down the whole town together with it's inhabitants if the King declined. Needless to say, my father admitted him into his palace, intrigued. Not much is known about what occurred behind closed doors; there are no living witnesses to recall the event; all had died in the War of the Four Kingdoms. It would be the turning point in the history of the war. My father, accompanied by the mysterious visitor, rode into battle with the whole might of our Kingdom's formidable armies, prepared to die for the freedom of mankind.

"If legends are to be trusted, a vast enemy army flooded the Plains of Iphigenia that dreadful, gods forgotten day. As man watched, an endless stream of the most spine-chilling, macabre creatures of the night emerged from the dark. As if crawling straight out of the most horrid of nightmares, they swamped the land, installing fear and despair in the hearts of the human armies. Man had been doomed from the very start, destined to die on those barren fields. Yet, against all odds, the humans prevailed. They fought ferociously, day and night, without ever stopping to take a break. My father arrived to the battle with his fearsome armies, igniting the hearts of the despairing mortal forces. The battle seemed to wage on for weeks, the numbers of human causalities winning over the ones of their enemy's almost a hundred fold. All seemed lost, all except the meek bud of hope that timidly kept blooming in the fragile hearts of man. As the end of the battle drew near, they were ready to relinquish their weapons, to give in to the evil that seemed never-ending. My father's final day of life approached, having reached his two hundred year mark right on that very battlefield."

Duna swallowed, her heart hammering away, her lungs seizing up at the very implication of what the Prince was telling her.

"Through the darkness that encompassed the decimated mortal armies and the vast forces out of hell itself, a solitary warrior appeared, climbing up on a lone boulder in the middle of the plains. The sun emerged at that very moment, parting the black, ebony sky. It shone it's bright light onto the lone man, who lifted his sword to the sky as if cursing the gods themselves for abandoning the humans on those blood drenched plains. All movement ceased, even the dark forces froze as if in a daze. A single, deadly spear blazed through the air over the stoic warriors, headed straight for my father's heart." Madir inhaled, held his breath, then ever so slowly expelled the air from his lungs. "The lone warrior threw his sword at the approaching spear, his weapon flying through the air impossibly fast, hitting its target with immaculate precision. The spear missed its mark, thus failing to lodge itself into my father's still beating heart."

Duna's breath caught in her throat, her gut twisting and turning at the Prince's words.

"The lone warrior had saved my father's life that day, going against Fate itself. Some say that he wasn't a warrior at all but that very same mysterious figure that had come to visit the King of the White City. Others swear that it was a demi-god, or a deity, one of the gods themselves that had been moved by the relentless human heart and infallible courage when placed even in the most dire and impossible of circumstances." The Prince went silent, his eyes roaming over the slowly darkening sky, the Sun making it's long overdue path over the horizon.

"Madir, how is that possible.." Duna trailed off, doing the calculations in her head. "The War of the Four Kingdoms – your father, how old is he?"

He chuckled, amused at her question. "No one really knows for sure," he sighed. "He seems reluctant to give his exact date of birth. I suppose it doesn't really even matter; what are, after all, a few years in the vast expanse of centuries?" He paused, as if doubting himself. "My father is over seven hundred and ninety years old, Duna. Can you just imagine, living that long? To be alive for more than half of a millennium."

She blanched. "What?"

He ignored her, his eyes dazed. "I have tried to make sense of it. To understand how he had done it, how he had outlived all of our ancestors before him. It should not have been possible, yet, here he is, a living proof of the very myth. He has cheated Death himself, has played Fate for an idle fool. I must know how he accomplished it. How he did the unfeasible," he suddenly turned to Duna, "And you are going to help me find the answer."

CHAPTER

17

Almost a week had passed since they had stood over the stream of Niamh, gazing at the sparkling green waters of old. Duna had agreed to help the Prince in the search for the secret to his father's seemingly eternal life. The obvious place to start had been at the Grande Nissian Library, which had been installed in the White Palace since the day that the monumental structure had been built all those millennia ago. Much to Duna's disappointment, however, not much had been discovered in it's ancient tomes. Madir had left Duna to the task of scouring over the many books, him not being much of a history enthusiast himself.

Today had been no different. Duna had found herself, once again, alone in the impressive library while the Prince went off to his royal duties. She had already searched a large portion of the History section of the place, including books about foreign kingdoms, hoping that someone might have overlooked such an obvious source of information.

Aside from learning about the genealogy of the Royal Houses of the Three Kingdoms, it had been a complete waste of time. The only positive thing that had come out of her week long search had been written confirmation of the unnaturally long life of two hundred years that Madir's ancestors had indeed led.

Searching the shelves of the library, Duna found herself wandering off to a secluded section that appeared to not have been used for quite some time. A thick layer of dust coated the vast selection of leather bound volumes. Some of the racks were covered in tangled three-dimensional cobwebs, almost obliterating the valuable ancient tomes. Clearing off some of the spider webs, she carefully read over the many titles adorning the stacks. There seemed to be no specific order to them, as if the books had been randomly placed on the shelf.

Finally deciding on a heavy, intricately decorated volume, she took it off the sill and inspected her selection. The book was embellished by numerous delicate, silver lines and swivels that seemed to form the words of a language that Duna didn't recognize. Cracking it open, she noticed the same cursive writing on the pages lining the inside. As she flipped through the tome, tables with numbers and dates appeared, taking over the text. It seemed as if it was some sort of a reference book for old accounting records.

Placing it back on the shelf, she examined the rest of the selection. A thin, purple, cloth bound novel caught Duna's eye. Taking it down and turning it over, she realized that the book had no title on it. The covering was, indeed, made from some sort of light cloth, however what surprised Duna the most was in how pristine of a condition the book appeared to be in after all this time under the heavy layer of dust and termites. How very strange.

She was even more startled when she opened the small volume and realized that it had been written in the Common Language of the Continent, which meant that she could actually read it.

Excited by her new discovery, Duna snatched up the book and went to a private reading nook by one of the large arched windows. Sitting down on the cushioned bench, she made herself comfortable and began to read.

The text appeared to be some sort of a children's book, the words accompanied by many colorful, life-like illustrations depicting both human-like beasts and mythical beings alike. A half-human half-falcon creature stood beside an equally strange looking mixture of a jackal and a man. On another page, a serpent like demon was shown devouring the Sun while twelve armored warriors impaled the creature with their weapons.

Turning the page she saw an image of an elongated eye as it would appear from a person's profile, with an eyebrow above it and a dark line extending behind the rear corner of the organ. Two additional markings stretched below and toward the back of the eye, one which ended in a spiral like curl.

"The mortal Fourth Kingdom," Duna read out loud, "is believed to reside on the secluded Isle of Ur Chisisi in the most southern part of the North Sea. It is a land inhabited by the descendents of the gods themselves, who had come down from the heavens many eons ago and merged with the humans of the main land. The children which were born from these unions were shunned and exiled from their native homes, showing inhuman capabilities and characteristics that were threatening to the average man.

"Having no other sins but their heavenly origins, the God of the Sky and Ruler of the Realm of the Living gifted them a new land where the blessed children may all live in peace and harmony, away from the avenging and treacherous human beings. The King granted the demi-gods their very own version of his stellar Kingdom of Aharon in the world of man – a mortal extension of his Realm of the Living – providing them sanctuary in exchange for their eternal fealty. Sworn by blood and their sacred vows, they pledged themselves into endless servitude, to answer his heavenly summons whenever called upon." Duna turned the page.

"Many scholars believe that the fabled Forgotten Kingdom is governed from the skies by the God of all gods himself, the mythical King Nkosi. With his brother, the Holy Prince and Lord of the Realm of the Dead and the Underworld, they make up the ruling Supreme Royal family of the heavens. It is highly argued that entry into the earthly Kingdom of Aharon is forbidden to man by punishment of death. No proof for such ostentatious claims has been found. Furthermore, explorations of the North Sea have not provided point of entry into land masses agreeing with the description of the Isle of Ur Chisisi, further questioning the existence of a fourth kingdom."

Duna closed the book, deep in thought. Where had she heard mention of the Forgotten Kingdom before? It was in the back of her mind, nagging at her like a pestilent worm. Then she remembered; Petra had told them a story by the fire when the four of them had been travelling to Morinya all those weeks ago.

If Duna remembered correctly, the legend stated that the Forgotten Kingdom had been ruled by the eldest of the two warrior brothers, the descendents of the former King of the Holy Realm of the Gods that had been ruthlessly assassinated. The older brother had been the Ruler of the Realm of the Living, while the younger brother had ruled over the Realm of the Dead and the Underworld.

It had been the younger of the two brothers who had been responsible for the weighing of the souls of the deceased and their subsequent passage into the Afterlife. Mankind had become so corrupt and tainted over time that the burden of forever forsaking the souls became too much for the younger brother. He had been willing to trade his immortality for a mortal life, just so that he wouldn't have to send the ever-growing sea of worthless souls into the endless darkness where the Devourer would feast on them for all eternity.

The ancient volume that Duna held in her hands had hinted at the identity of the older brother, naming King Nkosi of the Holy Kingdom of Aharon the chief deity in the heavens and the Ruler of the Realm of the Living. That would make his younger brother also a supreme god, and if he ruled the Realm of the Dead and the Underworld, that would make him –

the God of Death.

Gasping at the realization of what she might have discovered, Duna mentally scrambled to put the many pieces of information together. What if this prince, the God of Death, had succeeded in relinquishing his immortality? Would his godly status cease to exist; did that mean that he could roam the earth amongst mere mortals?

Had he wandered their world while King Lucan had been on the throne, giving him the secret to eternal life?

There was, of course, the other version of the myth which stated that King Nkosi had been offended by his brother's proposition, finding it a grave insult to him personally and their supreme heavenly lineage. It could be possible that the King had not stripped away the God of Death's immortality but rather cursed him to a life amongst man, where the Holy Prince could die from mortal wounds but instead of remaining dead, he would be reborn. Each time rising from the dead and resurrecting himself, suffering in agony and pain as he relived each subsequent passing; his soul never resting in peace. Never moving on to the Afterlife.

That would mean that the Prince, even as cursed as he was, would have been alive and walking freely and undetected amongst humans for possibly millennia. King Lucan could have come into contact with him at some point during his two hundred years of life before the War of the Four Kingdoms. The deity could have divulged to him the secret of immortality. He might have even participated in and survived the War itself, not being able to die but being able to succumb to mortal wounds and live through a tremendous amount of pain, over and over again, making him almost indestructible.

Duna felt an immense sense of sadness and injustice for the male. Even as the God of Death, the Prince had felt a great responsibility for the souls of mortals, taking it upon himself as his own personal failure when they didn't make it into the Afterlife. To be punished for having a conscience and by his own blood was unimaginable to her.

She was well acquainted with pain and sorrow. With immense regret for the things that she could have, perhaps, changed had the fates been kind to her. If there was ever an act that she lamented on in her life, besides the obvious tragedy that had befallen first her parents then her grandmother as well, was the fact that Duna had nothing of material value that would remind her of her family. Even the plain, silver pendant necklace that had been her grandmother's she had left behind as a marker for the improvised tomb stone that she was forced to erect to mark the elderly woman's burial place.

There was no point in divulging on events that were in the past, that could not be altered. She prayed with all her broken heart that her lost ones were in a better place now, safe and content.

"That one is a good one," a deep, raspy voice spoke softly behind Duna, startling her out of her somber thoughts. "I personally find it quite relaxing to read the myths of our time. May I suggest this one," King Lucan handed her another pristine cloth bound edition, similar to the one that she was currently holding. "Start with the third chapter then make your way to the end of the book. Only after you have read the last page of the final chapter should you return to read the first two. It will make much more sense that way, believe me."

Taking the impressive volume from the royal, Duna had a sudden idea. "Your Majesty, may I ask you a question?" When he nodded, she continued, "I am very intrigued in the history of your Kingdom. Unfortunately, I haven't had the chance to learn much about the other nations of our vast Continent while I was growing up. My grandmother and I didn't have the means to purchase books, you see, so I'm afraid my knowledge is rather dismal."

"I understand, Lady Damaris," the King said. "How may I remedy that?"

"I was wondering if there was something that is not written in the numerous history books that you have in this resplendent library of yours, Your Majesty. Something that, perhaps, not many people are aware of." She hesitated. "And if such a thing did exist, if you would be so kind as to share it with me. I apologize if I am overstepping–"

"Not at all, my dear," the ancient male said. "You appear to be the romantic type, one who is easily moved by emotions of righteousness and injustice. Perhaps, instead of a history lesson, I will tell you a story. One that a very old and dear friend of mine passed on to me many centuries ago."

Excited, Duna could only follow the monarch as he strolled towards a matching set of burgundy, leather armchairs, his opulent robes trailing behind as he did so. Taking a seat opposite from the man, she placed her two books on her lap, her hands overlapping each other in front of her.

"In a land far away," he began, "even farther than the eye could see, there resides a Kingdom so magnificent that even the brightest stars of our universe are put to shame by it's everlasting, ethereal beauty. It is said to be the home of a group of star-gods, deities that have formed their empire between the very constellations that adorn our endless night sky. They are ruled by a single Supreme God – whose name shall not be revealed – who has the gift of travel between the many realms of the worlds. It is believed that the only way to reach this majestic Kingdom amongst the heavens, is to follow the North Star of our mortal sky. For it is precisely on that very same ever shining jewel that the breathtaking Kingdom of Khalfani lies." King Lucan smiled then, one of the warmest and sincerest smiles that she had ever seen the man display, pausing to let the story sink it.

Duna could only stare back, not daring to move lest she miss a single precious word.

"The Lord of the Kingdom of Khalfani," he continued, "is said to be one of the most powerful gods to have ever been born into existence on the celestial plane. Only one other god has ever been his equal, the Supreme God of the heavenly Kingdom of Aharon, whose considerable, more regal empire occupies the other, larger part of the North Star. Their might comparable in magnitude, the two rulers were faced with a predicament. Who was to rule Polaris, the Realm of the Gods? For there can only be one king.

"Instead of going to war over such an important issue, the Lord of the Kingdom of Khalfani decided that he didn't want the Throne to the heavens. He was satisfied with his own empire, not needing additional lands and titles. His humble domain was sufficient for him and his loyal star-gods, who lived in peace and harmony amongst themselves and the other celestial deities. The Lord of the Kingdom of Khalfani had an additional motive for not fighting over his birth right to the Throne." King Lucan stopped, readjusting himself to a more comfortable seating position in the armchair.

"He did not find himself fitting of such a title, not because he was not honorable or pure. No, it was because he was easily moved by mortal hearts, their souls calling out to him whenever he had to pass judgment on them, pleading with him to take pity on them. He had always been intrigued by humans, by the lives and the choices that they make during their short amount of years in the world. He could not understand how one man could have the purest, most beautiful, radiant soul while another's was so dark that it was dripping with venom, overflowing with malice and greed. The Lord of the Kingdom of Khalfani gladly relinquished his claim to the other contestant, thus making the Ruler of the Kingdom of Aharon also the King of the Realm of the Gods," King Lucan stopped. "Confused yet, Lady Damaris?"

"No, not at all, Your Majesty," Duna said. "It is all very intriguing. But I don't understand, why would the Lord of the Kingdom of Khalfani relinquish his claim? Wouldn't he have been the better choice to rule over all the gods and therefore to be the protector of mortals? His ability to sympathize with man should have given him the necessary advantage to his formidable foe, who doesn't seem to have such cares for human life."

"The gods, my dear, are not like us. They do not waste their time on trivial matters of the heart. They do not sympathize with pain and sorrow, for they no longer have the ability to feel such profound sensations. To them, to show emotion is to show weakness. Could you imagine, being alive since the very beginning of time, and still having the capability to sense despair, hope–" he paused, "love? To relive all those feelings, every day, for all eternity?"

Duna was silent, thinking over his words.

"Would it not drive you mad, knowing that if you were to open your very soul to the world, that it would only ever lead to your suffering again? The most simple solution would be to not feel at all. To grow indifferent." King Lucan leaned in, speaking softly, "That is what the gods have become, Duna. Indifferent to mortal suffering. All except one, one who even after his eons long existence, did not grow dispassionate, who still holds hope in his pure, celestial heart for the souls of mankind."

"You speak as if you are well acquainted with this god, Your Majesty."

The royal smiled again, straightening in his chair. "Only in his mortal form. He has been my greatest ally in the battle against evil in this wretched world that we call our own. He..." the King trailed off, as if lost in some distant memory. "He has sacrificed his very existence for the betterment of mankind, for the salvation of our souls."

Duna was at a loss of words. The King was confessing to her to personally knowing a heavenly being. A deity.

It was astounding. Unfathomable.

"I will tell you a secret, my dear Duna, something that no one, not even my children are privy to. My advisors from the time when I was a young King were the only ones that were ever aware of it," he said, leaning in once again. "It concerns a choice which I had to make in my youth, one that is of no significance to anyone but myself. It does not affect the lives of other people, nor does it alter the fates."

Duna held her breath, entranced, waiting to hear what other profound truth the man would reveal to her.

King Lucan took her callused hands into his own, enclosing them within his weathered palms. Speaking low so that only she could hear, he said, "I have seen the celestial Realm of the Gods. I have walked amongst them, the star-gods; have gazed upon their immortal faces." His blue tourmaline eyes glazed over, overcome with emotion. "Their heavenly Kingdom of Aharon is Polaris itself, the bright star that is ever shining on our night sky. Its splendor and ethereal beauty matches that of a thousand blazing suns, forever shining like a beacon of light in the vast darkness of the beyond. Yet, even in all it's grandeur, the home of the mighty King Nkosi does not even begin to compare to the breathtaking vision that is the glorious Kingdom of Khalfani."

Duna watched, stunned, as a solitary tear finally made it's way down the monarch's pale cheek, followed by an outpour of emotions from the man's soulful eyes. She was helpless to do anything. Awe-struck. Dazed. To see such a powerful ruler be reduced to tears caused her own to form in her already moist eyes.

A new shock struck her then, the implications of what he had just revealed to her reaching her boggled mind. "You have met King Nkosi.

How—" gasping, Duna covered her gaping mouth. "That means – he is real. The myths, they are all real." When the royal sitting across from her didn't respond, she continued, "The Holy Prince, you've seen him, then. That means – the God of Death, he also exists?"

King Lucan didn't respond right away. He searched her almond shaped eyes, appearing to be baffled by her question. "The God of Death exists, yes. He was not, however, in attendance at his celestial home while I was visiting his Kingdom."

"What do you mean? Where was he?" she asked, confused.

Patting her knee, the ancient man stood from his seat. "That, my dear, is not my story to tell." Wrapping himself in his midnight blue robes, he left her to simmer alone in the endless well of possibilities.

CHAPTER 18

The door to her chambers banged open, startling Duna from her deep sleep. Squinting in the moonlit darkness of her room, she tried to make out what was happening, not remembering where she was at that precise moment.

"Duna," Petra's voice whispered close to her ear, "Duna, get up. You have to come with me, now. Quickly!" Yanking her out from under the bed covers, Petra threw her clothes at her.

"Wait–" Duna caught the items before they hit her face. "What is going on?!"

"I can't tell you, you'll just have to trust me," taking her by the elbow, Petra pulled a half-dressed Duna down the unlit hall.

"Where are we going? Where is the General?" struggling to keep up with the half crazed woman, Duna finished getting dressed. "And why are we whispering?"

"There's no time, hurry!" They came to an unexpected stop, halting before a human sized, colorful painting of the stream of Niamh that spanned the length of the great wall.

Glancing quickly at their surroundings, Petra pushed the heavy wooden frame to the side, revealing a narrow tunnel that disappeared into the shadows. Turning her head toward Duna, she said, "Listen to me. We must stay completely silent from this moment on, do you understand? Whatever you see or hear, you must not react in any shape or form."

Duna didn't know what to make of the whole situation. Why were they standing in the middle of a dark hall in the late hours of the night?

When she didn't respond, Petra shook her, "Use your words, woman. Swear to me that whatever happens inside those tunnels, you will remain stoic. You will remain by my side the whole time that we are in there. You will not even breathe until we return to this spot."

Duna nodded then, "I swear." She didn't really have a choice after all. She supposed that she would soon find out what the whole commotion was about, she only hoped that it wasn't something that she would later regret knowing.

Entering the gloom, Petra slid the painting back into place. The two of them didn't move for a few moments, standing still in the vast darkness. As their eyes adjusted to the shadows, Duna could make out the stone blocks lining the tunnel walls.

Yanking her by the arm again, Petra motioned for them to move forward. They walked for what seemed like hours, traipsing through the winding dark passages as if in a maze. A soft voice floated through the air toward them, the melodic tone of it mesmerizing to their hypersensitive ears.

Duna listened, entranced. It appeared to be a female voice, and it sounded as if she was singing in a language that Duna didn't recognize. She didn't need to comprehend the words to understand the deep anguish that the woman imbued in every syllable of her mournful tune. To feel the agony and suffering in her heart. It was as if the earth itself was weeping, the dense air heavy with affliction and misery.

Petra put a hand in front of Duna, halting her in her tracks. They had reached some type of an open archway that appeared to lead to a stern drop to the ground below. Glancing down to inspect it better, Duna realized that it wasn't a drop at all but a series of wide, shallow steps that were forged into the slope of a mountain. The steps descended, converging at the center where a pool of the most captivating, emerald green water could be seen. It reminded Duna of the stream of Niamh, who's dazzling waters had the exact same hue–

She gasped, quickly covering her mouth with both of her hands.

It *was* the stream of Niamh, except that this wasn't a stream at all but a substantial body of water where a stunning woman with hair the color of sunlight sat singing. She was perched on a rock at the very edge of the emerald pool, her face turned up towards the star filled sky. She was completely naked, her long golden tresses flowing over her bare breasts, her long lean legs emerged foot deep in the clear green waters. She was petite, with soft, feminine features; her skin pale, almost translucent in the moonlight.

Duna couldn't take her eyes away from her, captivated by her angelic voice and the ethereal vision before her. Petra seemed to be suffering from the same affliction, her eyes glued to the woman below.

A hooded figure emerged from the darkness, causing Duna and Petra to withdraw further into the shadows of the tunnels. They watched as it approached the golden haired beauty, stopping barely a few feet away from her. She didn't seem to notice the visitor, continuing on with her sorrowful song as if nothing had changed. The figure kneeled then on the grass below, pulling back its hood to reveal the familiar face underneath it.

King Lucan stared at the enchantress, as if hypnotized by her very presence. Opening up his cloak, he withdrew a single violet bellflower in full bloom, its rich color forming such a wondrous contrast to the man's pale skin as he held the plant in his open palm.

Placing it on the ground in front of the female, the King said, "For you, my Niamh, goddess of Beauty and Brightness, daughter of the King of the oceans. I have not forgotten my promise."

"You are an honorable man, Lucan. I have never doubted you, unlike your ancestors who had betrayed me time and time again," the goddess replied, her eyes still fixed at the silver Moon. "Even if you had not been gifted with the Elixir of the Gods, I would have still withdrawn my curse from your blood, my dear friend. I would have allowed you to live for all eternity if you had wished it so, so long as your soul remained pure and genuine as it has been all of these centuries." Niamh finger combed her long golden tresses, gazing at her reflection in the emerald pool. "Have you found her yet?"

King Lucan froze, his eyes suddenly going wide. "Who is it that you speak of, Your Highness?"

Niamh laughed, her brilliant white smile blazing through the night, "You know of whom I speak, Lucan." When the royal didn't respond, she continued, "The one that is prophesized to end the suffering of mortals. The one that the Oracle foretold."

Blanching, the ancient man stuttered. "Im–Impossible. The Oracle does not reveal her secrets to anyone. I do not believe you, Niamh. You know not what you speak of."

"Don't I though?" Strolling over to the monarch, the goddess picked up the violet bellflower and began singing her grief-stricken tune again, except that this time it was in a language that Duna knew all too well.

In the midnight hour on the forgotten isle,
the truth will be Shed.
The one who seeks to tame a heart,
so black with gloom and regret.
The mind will know what ears don't hear,
what silver eyes don't Shed but fear.

The end will come when hearts collide,
of Fate he can't escape.
To forge a bond of ever more,
the price that one must pay.
The sands of time will flow once more,
once she has sworn an oath.
Of blood and tears, a soul so pure,
the God may be restored.

Niamh's fingers closed around the flower, crushing it in her hold of steel. Spreading them open once again, she picked up the ruined petals one by one and began eating them, relishing in their taste.

It appeared as if the King had entirely stopped breathing. "How– It cannot be."

"You seem to forget that I am a goddess, my King. There is not a single thing that I do not know in this mortal world of yours." Engulfing the last of the petals, she licked the plant's juices off of her palm and fingers. "Why has he not come to visit me yet?"

"I do not know, Your Highness," he said. "I don't presume to understand the workings of his mind."

"And yet, you have known him for more than a half of a millennium. Does he not trust you?"

King Lucan laughed suddenly, color returning to his face. "He doesn't need to trust me, Niamh. My loyalty does not depend on that trivial fact. I am honored to be of service to him, in any shape and form, no matter what lies in his shattered heart. I am forever humbled by the fact that the Prince had found my miserable life worthy enough for saving from Fate itself."

It was Duna's turn to be stunned as she watched from the shadows, Petra completely oblivious to the meaning of the conversation that the speakers were having. They had revealed so much in such a short period of time, Duna's mind couldn't even begin to grasp what it was that it was hearing.

"You have still not answered my question," the golden haired beauty said. "Have you found her, the one predestined to break the curse?"

"What makes you think that it is a woman that the Oracle spoke of?" the King replied.

"Oh, please, you cannot be serious, Lucan? Of course it is a woman." Niamh returned to her rock by the pool's edge. "Who else would have the power to tame the blackened heart of our dear Prince? Surely, you of all people, are aware of the power of love."

"Yes, I suppose you are right. But I have interpreted the Oracle's words slightly differently than you, Niamh."

"Of course you did, you are a man. You do not see beyond that which is obvious to your eyes." She started to stroke her sunlit tresses again. "Read between the lines, my King. The truth is always hidden right in front of us."

King Lucan seemed lost in thought, going over the goddess' words. Shaking his head, he said, "The Prince has already given his heart away, the curse should have been broken by now. Surely, it would not take so much time for the prophecy to come to fruition."

"Then perhaps it is not a question of *if* he loves but rather *whom* he loves, Your Majesty." Niamh inclined her head, apparently finished with their conversation. "Farewell, Lucan. Until we meet again." Sliding into the glimmering water, the goddess took one final look at the monarch and vanished under the emerald surface.

Petra and Duna had retreated through the hidden tunnel, emerging into the dark halls of the White Palace from which they had come from. They walked back to Duna's room, remaining silent until the door to her chambers was well shut.

"What the fuck was that?" Petra hissed at her. "Did you understand anything that they were talking about?"

"No," she lied, "but I'm more worried about the fact that you failed to mention to me that there is a hidden passageway leading into the mountains of Nissa. How long have you known, Petra?"

"What does it even matter, it was of no use to me anyway." She sighed. "I found it by accident one day while I was trying to find a way to get out of this damn place and go to a tavern."

"Why not just go out through the front door, like a normal person would do?" Duna said.

"Because, you little shit, I don't want to have to explain to the General that I haven't slept with anyone since we left Captain Moira's barracks and that if I don't have some sex soon I am going to murder someone."

Duna laughed, not believing the words that were coming out of her friend's mouth. "Unbelievable. Just use your hand, what's the big deal? Besides," she winked at Petra, "I thought you had a thing for Lieutenant Rhun."

"Yes, well, he is thousands of miles away, and I like my dick to be available to me whenever the need arises."

"You have such a filthy mouth, Petra."

She snorted. "You're the one to talk."

Duna threw her pillow at her. "Shut up."

"Yeah, that's what I thought," Petra whipped the cushion back at her as she went to the door, opening it. "Sweet dreams, Duna. Speak to no one of what we saw tonight. Remember, you swore to me."

After her sister in arms had left, Duna had thrown herself back into bed, her mind going a thousand miles a minute. She had discovered so much in just that one, singular day. Where to even begin dissecting the multitude of information still flowing around in her addled brain?

Still puzzling over her thoughts, Duna drifted off to sleep.

As she dreamt of the towering, brooding male that had vanished from her life in the same way that he had appeared in it mere months ago, she was unaware of the pair of silver speckled green eyes watching her from the shadows. She didn't see when those same shadows formed into a man of breathtaking features, looming over the edge of her bed, relishing in the peaceful sight of her in deep slumber.

She didn't witness when that very same figure leaned over her and, softly caressing her chocolate locks, inhaled her intoxicating scent; breathing her very essence into his starved lungs. Nor did she notice the little trinket that he silently placed on her bedside table, leaving it for her to find when she woke up.

Duna would remain oblivious to it all, for by the time morning came, he would be long gone from her innocent life.

She woke the next morning just as the sun was making it's way over the horizon, ushering in the start of a new day. Turning her face towards the high arched window, a silver glint caught Duna's eye. Tilting her head to get a better look at the mysterious object, she thought she saw a piece of jewelry curled up on her nightstand. Squinting, then blinking away her haze, Duna realized that she wasn't imagining the item.

Extending her hand, she grasped the object and pulled it into her field of vision. For the millionth fraction of a second, she stared at the necklace in her shaking hand.

Her mind flashed back to that tragic day more than five years ago, to an agonizing moment in time when she had marked her grandmother's grave with a wooden tombstone. One that she had adorned with the very same silver pendant necklace that she was now holding in her hand.

Tears welling up in her eyes, Duna bolted out of bed. She flew through the connecting door to the General's room, her heart beating erratically, sobbing without restraint.

"Cathal!" she shouted from the top of her lungs, desperate to see the man himself, the one that she knew without a doubt in her aching heart, had been the one to leave her this priceless, precious gift. "Cathal!"

Crying profusely, not caring for how she appeared, Duna ran out from his room and into the halls of the palace, her grandmother's necklace gripped tightly in her icy hand.

She ran to the War Room, charging in when she heard voices from behind the heavy, wooden doors. "Where is he?"

King Lucan, accompanied by a group of twelve robed males, stared back at her. "Where is who, Lady Damaris?"

"The General, where is he, Your Majesty?" Duna was growing desperate. "Please, I must find him."

"I don't know, I haven't seen him since early this morning, perhaps—"

She didn't wait to hear the end of his sentence. She bolted before the monarch could finish speaking.

Running like a mad woman, Duna shouted for all to hear, "Cathal!" But no answer came. No dark, imposing male formed from the shadows. No devastating, magnificent warrior came forward to answer her anguished plea. "Cathal!" Walking back to his chambers, she prayed to the gods that he would be in there, waiting for her.

Alas, she was greeted, once again, with an empty suite, no sign of the man anywhere. His bed was in pristine condition, as if no one had slept in it the night before. Duna knew that he had been here, she could feel it in her breaking heart that he had been so close to her last night, yet at the same time, so far away.

She had missed him. Again.

Not holding back anymore, she let the tears flow freely from her eyes.

Duna collapsed by the edge of his bed, her head buried deep in her elbows, resting on the satin covered mattress. She wheezed and cried, all of those emotions that she had buried deep inside of her soul for the past five years pouring out of her to the surface. She had never felt this helpless before, this lost and desperate, as if her very heart would crack in two.

Where was he? Why was he not coming?

Someone touched her then, their gentle hand resting on her heaving shoulders. Spinning around, Duna saw that it was the King of Nissa.

"Why do you cry, my dear? What happened to cause you such sorrow?" he said, his face a mask of deep concern.

"I can't find him," she said, choking on air, "I can't find the General, he's gone. Again."

King Lucan inspected her moist face, the tears freely streaming down her cheeks. "You cry such devastating tears of misery for the General, Duna?"

"Yes, Your Majesty." She couldn't lie to the man. "He–He left me without saying goodbye." A fresh onslaught of tears took over her, causing her to heave and cry out loud. It was becoming an ugly habit of hers to cry over the beautiful male.

"My dear, the General has left for Navajo, the capital of Baqar." The King searched her face, his eyes turning soft. "He had received news during the night from Prince Edan. Princess Leila has been found."

Blanching at his confession, Duna could only stare open mouthed at the dark haired royal. If she thought that she was in agony before, it was nothing compared to the onslaught of destruction that wreaked havoc on her organs at that very moment.

Everything hurt and yet she could not feel anything at all. As if every nerve ending in her over stimulated body had burned out, overcharged by the multitude of sudden shocks that had gone through her system since waking up that dreadful morning. She wanted to cry, but her eyes had dried up, her lacrimal glands not willing to co-operate. She wanted to scream, but no sound would come out of her strained throat, as if her voice was trapped somewhere beneath her trachea.

Maybe if she punched something, it would ease her pain. Yet, when she tried to get up, her legs wouldn't obey, reminding her that she was not in control of her body any longer.

"I will let the General know that you had inquired about him. I am sure that he could relay his orders for you through one of my letters." The King straightened, his hands going behind his back. "Do you wish to send him a message perhaps?"

"No, Your Majesty," Duna said, wiping her eyes, "that won't be necessary. I simply wanted to thank him for finding something that was very dear to me. It is of no consequence, really." She opened her palm then, examining her grandmother's necklace.

King Lucan suddenly snatched up her wrist, lifting her hand close to his face. "Where did you get this?" When she didn't answer, he asked, "May I see it, my dear? I promise to give it back in only a moment."

Reluctantly Duna handed him the silver necklace. Curious as to why a monarch of such a formidable ancestry would bother with a plain piece of jewelry, she watched as the male took off his own royal necklace and examined them side by side. He appeared to be dumbfounded about something, as if the two trinkets were presenting him with a great riddle.

"This is very strange," he said. "Very strange, indeed." Handing them both over to Duna, he continued, "Tell me, what do you see?"

Duna took the two necklaces from the man, inspecting them closely as he had asked her to. They were both made of the same stainless steel material, coated with silver. Both had a coin shaped medallion hanging from the chain, her grandmother's being slightly smaller in size than the one that the King's had. They had an identical star shape engraved in the middle of the pendant, and in it's dead center, a tiny ruby red crystal.

Handing the royal back his necklace, she said, "They are identical, only the size of the medallions varying in size. What does that mean?"

The King didn't answer right away, as if he, too, was puzzling over the very same question. Placing the jewelry back around his neck, he turned and walked to the door of the General's chamber. "What, indeed." He opened the door, leaving Duna alone. Yet again.

CHAPTER
19

Three weeks had passed since Duna had been reunited with her grandmother's silver necklace.

The shiny trinket had adorned her body ever since that very day, not once leaving her neck. Today would mark the two month's time since they had left Tyros and the training camp at the border with the Kingdom of Nissa. Two months since she had first laid eyes on the General.

Duna had struggled to come to terms with the fact that he had simply vanished in the middle of the night, not bothering to even say goodbye. She knew that it would eventually come to this, Duna was not simple minded. Yet, she had hoped that he would have at least had the courtesy to bid her farewell after all the endless hours that they had spent together, after all the heated glances that they had exchanged in the shadows of the night.

It should be expected, Duna had relentlessly argued with herself. He had found his beloved. His Princess. Of course he was not going to wait around a moment longer, wasting his precious time on mundane things. Who was Duna to him, anyways? Nobody. It had been absolutely mind boggling for her to even consider that the General would think about her when the woman that he loved was waiting for him in Navajo.

"Are you ready?" Petra's voice interrupted her train of thoughts. Tonight they were going to a celebration marking the last day of winter, the Spring Festival. The whole city of Morinya had been decorated the night before, the white splendor of the city now covered in red couplets and crimson lanterns that were displayed on the door frames of the many glistening homes.

Inspecting herself one last time in the long, oval mirror, Duna nodded in approval at the image that stared back at her. She was dressed in a floor length, body hugging, mermaid style gown, it's shimmering emerald beads matching to perfection the opulent green shade of the stream of Niamh. A slit went straight up to Duna's hip bone, accentuating her toned, thick thighs whenever she moved. Long, tight sleeves went over her wrists, converging to a single point right beneath her middle finger. Emerald streaks of fabric stretched around her navel and over her modest breasts, avoiding her chest and collar bones as it connected with the sleeves at her shoulders. It gave the impression as if the ocean itself was reaching its fingers over her sun kissed skin, its ripples desperate to cover her lusciously curvy body.

Her silky chocolate strands were loose tonight, her hair parted at the side. Light make up embellished her naturally pretty features, adding a formal feel to her appearance.

Petra was even more stunning, having chosen a simple gold gown that followed her tall, slender frame, shimmered in the moonlight, accentuating her rich, ginger hair and freckled face.

The two women made their way down to the city streets, winding along the many vendors that were selling traditional Nissian foods as well as some more formal dishes that were only ever made on this specific occasion.

Petra grabbed her arm, pulling her along behind her. "They have dumplings! Oh, Duna, let's get some, please!"

"You go ahead, enjoy yourself, I'm going to see what else there is." Duna watched as her friend hurried down the street, almost skipping from excitement, like a child on its way to receive his favorite candy. Strolling down the cobblestone path, Duna was amazed by the many sights before her eyes. Wherever she turned her head, she discovered something new.

Two large, calloused hands wrapped their fingers around her hips, pulling her backwards onto a hard chest. "Find something you like, little warrior?" Madir purred in her ear, tiny goosebumps appearing across her arms. "I know what I want. Question is, will I have it here in front of the whole city or will I eat it in my bed, spread out on my sheets like a creamy delicacy, ready to be licked and tasted until I have had my fill?"

Duna spun around in his arms, liquid heat pooling in her core. The man had one of the dirtiest mouths that she had ever come into contact with. "Madir.." Breathing hard, she could already picture herself on his massive bed, naked, skin glistening, thick thighs spread wide for him while he devoured her from the inside out, over and over again.

He licked his lips, eyes hooded as he gazed at her luscious mouth. "I would start by opening you up like a delicate flower, my fingers playing with your wet folds until so much slick was coating them that I would have no other choice but to clean you up nice and good with my languid tongue." His hold on her hips tightened then, pushing her further onto his front where Duna could feel the hard outline of his bulging cock.

She gasped. He was huge.

Unable to control her raging thoughts, she pictured his impressive member filling her up, her tight little hole wrapping itself around his hard shaft. More wetness gathered at the juncture of her thighs, coating their insides. She fisted his shirt, needing something to hold on to while she imagined him pounding away in her pussy.

"Yeah, you like that, don't you? Of course you do," he chuckled. "Tell me how I should fuck you the first time, Duna. From the back, with your round ass high in the air, while my dick pumps you full? Or you bouncing on my cock, screaming my name while I suck on your little ripe nipples?"

Duna could feel her pussy clenching around nothing, needing something desperately to fill the gaping hole that was growing painfully soaked by the second. She was going to come and the man wasn't even fucking her yet. "I need you to take me somewhere, Madir. Please." Her voice raspy, she was ready to beg on her knees for the male in front of her.

Taking her by the hand, he led her to a secluded alley behind the busy street. He stopped when they reached a covered nook, flaps of red fabric laying over it like openings to a tent. Entering it, Madir pushed her against the wall. "Tell me what you want, Duna. I need to hear you say it."

Chest heaving, her voice low, she said, "I–I want you to taste me."

"Taste what? Say it." He licked her ear, causing her to stutter.

"M–My cunt. I want you to lick me dry until I'm a complete mess."

"You want my tongue in your pussy? Lapping away at your juices?" He sucked on her lobe.

"Yes," she moaned then, not being able to restrain herself any longer.

Not wasting a second, Madir slipped his hand under the slit of her dress, watching as he did so, hissing when he found her naked underneath. "Where are your panties, sweetheart? Did you want me to find you tonight?" He moved his calloused fingers in between her thighs, spreading them nice and wide. Grazing her hairless pussy, he suddenly stopped. His eyes snapped to hers. "You are completely bare." Madir's other hand flew to her neck, cuffing her throat from the front. "Do you know what you've done, woman?" he leaned in, his face an angry scowl. "You have just unleashed a monster, I will fucking kill whoever even dares to look your way." His hand still grasping her throat, he moved his other hand in between her soaked folds, playing with them like he promised he would do.

Duna whimpered, fisting his shirt, pulling him against her heated body.

"Fuck," he hissed again, "you're drenched." His eyes burned through her, holding her captive, watching her face as his fingers crept closer to her pulsing core. "I'm going to wreck you with my fingers tonight, little warrior.

I want you squirming so badly that you're begging for my cock." He plunged his thick finger inside of her wet pussy, slowly pumping it in and out, pulling moans out of her gaping mouth. "But I won't fuck you just yet, no. You'll have to show me how bad you want my cock." He pushed in another thick finger, stretching her tight hole.

Duna threw her head back, moaning incessantly while the Prince increased his speed, pumping away without a care in the world. Mouth wide open, she began to move on his hand.

"That's it, sweetheart, show me how you would milk my cock." She wrapped her leg around him. He plunged a third calloused digit into her dripping cunt, pounding away, knuckle deep inside of her. He was ruthless, pulling sounds out of her that Duna didn't even know she could make. "Louder. Let them hear you getting fingered." He increased his speed even more, obscene slurping sounds filling the air around them.

She fucked herself on his fingers, shamelessly impaling herself over and over again on those glorious, thick digits. She couldn't take it anymore, it was too much. "Madir." she was close, so close.

"Scream for me, Duna."

So she did just that. Body twitching, pussy clenching away, she screamed into the dark night. Madir never ceased his movements, plunging away into her convulsing body as she came down from her high.

"So fucking beautiful," he finally pulled his fingers out of her, licking them bone dry. "Now, to earn my cock, you will have to give me one more."

"Wha–What?"

He knelt down on the hard ground and placing both of her legs over his broad shoulders, he pinned her to the wall. "That was for you, now it's my turn." Not waiting for her response, he gripped her thighs from underneath, right where they met her ass, and spread her legs in front of his face. "Hold on tight. I want what I'm owed." She didn't have time to react, for in the next breath, he was face deep in her pussy. He devoured her, sucking her juices, lapping away inside of her tight hole that was still clenching from her previous orgasm.

Duna gripped his long hair with both hands, yanking at the raven black strands, holding on for dear life as he feasted on her creaming cunt. She moaned, on and on, mumbling incoherently into empty space.

Over to her clit and back down he went, taking his sweet time so as not to miss a single inch of her glistening pink flesh. He fucked her with his tongue, then returned to her pulsing nub, mercilessly flicking away at it. He seemed like a man on a mission, his only aim to turn her into a sticky puddle of cum.

Duna could only take it, her pussy gaping wide open for him, as if preparing itself to be impaled by his impressive cock, clenching at empty air when nothing filled it.

"Such a greedy little cunt, begging to be stuffed full." He chuckled, the vibrations causing waves of heat to spread through her. "Now, earn my cock, Duna. Show me how badly you want it." He pressed down on her clit with his tongue, making full circles around the sensitive nub.

"Oh, fuck." She rode his face, pressing him even deeper into her drenched core. Holding onto his hair, she felt the heat rising up in her, threatening to burst.

He increased his pressure, pinning her wide open to the wall, his massive hands holding her spread out for him. Slurping away, groaning and pumping the air, he destroyed her clit. She exploded over his face, convulsing uncontrollably, screaming her ecstasy for all to hear.

Madir finally released her legs, slowly lowering her weakened body. Licking his lips, he leaned in, his blue tourmaline eyes blazing through the dark. "Be a good girl and hurry along back to the palace, before I fuck you into this wall." He exited their hiding place, disappearing into the night.

Duna could only nod as she watched him leave, her words lost somewhere with the rest of her mind. She was still leaking from her core, her juices streaming down her thighs. Having no other choice, she used the inside of her dress to clean herself up the best that she could. She would have to shower as soon as she returned to her chambers.

Righting herself and making sure that nothing inappropriate was showing, she slowly made her way back to the White Palace.

Her room was dark and desolate when Duna strolled back inside, locking it shut after herself. Leaning back on the heavy wooden door, she inhaled a strained breath.

Why did she feel guilty for doing what she did with Madir? She felt as if she had betrayed the General, even though they were nothing. Non existent. They weren't even acquaintances. More like – two people that had passed through each others' lives, touching it in a brief moment of time.

No, she would not feel bad. She was a free woman. While he – he was betrothed to the Princess. She didn't owe him anything, especially after he had abandoned her in a strange city, far away from her home.

Shaking her head, Duna slowly walked deeper into the gloom of her room. The shadows seemed to be darker than usual, as if all light had been sucked out from the space.

Spinning around in a circle, she watched as the shadows moved, coming closer to her until they were swirling around her entire body, touching her radiant, sun kissed skin. They advanced on her, wrapping her in a cocoon of black tendrils of smoke.

Reaching out, she touched them, her hands intertwining with the translucent strands, like fingers locked together. To her astonishment, they were warm to the touch, as if alive and pulsing with energy.

The shadows seemed to whisper to Duna then; a low, melodic voice emanating from the void, "Do you find him attractive?"

She spun around, searching for the source of that voice. It appeared to be coming from all around her at once, and yet she could almost pinpoint the exact location of it if she only focused.

"Does your heart beat wildly when he is near?" The voice came closer, "Do you stop breathing when he looks at you?" Then suddenly, in her ear, it purred, "Do you get wet thinking about all the ways that he will fuck you?"

"No," she rasped, shame filling her as she thought of Madir.

A low laugh echoed throughout her room, the voice booming, "Of course not. He will never be the one." It whispered, "He will never be me."

Duna's breath caught, her lungs seizing up. She knew that voice. Would recognize it even if she was lost in the deepest pits of purgatory. Her heart hammering away, fists clenching wildly at her sides, she struggled to make her lungs work.

He's here. The thought struck her like a bolt of lightening. As if on reflex, all of her senses went on overdrive, her core heating up to a fiery inferno.

"You see, little monster, you can pretend all you want with me, but your body, it never lies. I can–" the voice inhaled, "smell you when you get aroused. I can almost taste the sweet scent of your dripping cunt on my tongue when I touch you just here." Shadow fingers plucked her bottom lip, pulling at it slightly.

Duna swallowed, her walls instantly drenched through.

Another shadow hand wrapped her in its arms, pulling her close to a hard chest that she couldn't see, only feel against her soft skin. Closing her eyes, she inhaled. Her senses were flooded with leather, and whiskey, and spice. She inhaled again, breathing in the addictive scent of the male that she had dreamt of since the first night that she had laid eyes on him.

She could picture him now, standing in front of her, holding her close to his sturdy body, exploring her mouth with that magnificent tongue of his, then lower, until he finally flipped her on her back and–

"You forget," the voice chuckled, "I can hear your thoughts screaming in my mind when you're imagining me pounding away in your tight hole."

Duna's eyes snapped open, blushing at the revelation of her filthy thoughts.

"No need to feel ashamed. I already told you, you have nothing to hide from me." The shadows came together then, forming a massive, towering figure of the deepest night that loomed over her as it spoke in that smooth, velvety voice that Duna loved so much. "Have you missed me, my sweet

Duna?"

"No," she lied. "I haven't thought about you at all since you left. Besides, what is this? How are you here? I thought you were reunited with the Princess."

"Is that where you would like me to be, in another woman's arms?" When Duna didn't respond, it continued. "Would picturing me in bed with the Princess make you feel less guilty about your shiny, new toy?"

"I don't know what you're talking about," she said. "I don't have a new toy. Not that it's any of your business, by the way."

A low, raspy laugh reached her from deep within the looming shadow of a man. "You know whom I speak of, Duna. There's no need to pretend. I saw you, in the alleyway. With Madir."

"How–" mouth gaping open, Duna struggled to find her words, "How is that possible? You're in Navajo." *And you're talking to a fucking shadow.*

"I see everything, little monster," it taunted, "I *am* everything." A new tendril of ebony black smoke stroked her hair, her chocolate strands responding to it like a moth that is drawn to a flame.

Duna watched as the two intertwined in a thick coil of shadows and silk, her hair floating around her head as if charged.

"Your body calls to me, Duna," the darkness advanced on her, wrapping her up in its strong, muscular arms again. "It always has. I am the only man that will ever be able to satisfy you. The only man that will fuck you like you need to be fucked, long and hard, until your pussy is molded to the shape of my cock." The shadow blew on her neck, right under her earlobe, causing her skin to shiver from the sensation. "Do you want to know what it's like to be fucked by a Prince?"

Her throat dry, Duna could only swallow again.

The shadow chuckled low in her ear, "That can be arranged. But, until you get fucked by a General, you haven't truly been fucked at all. So go, get it out of your system, this little curiosity that you have for the young princeling." Impressive arms went around her waist, their grip threatening, promising deadly retribution to anyone that dared to pull her out of their firm hold. "Know this, though. Once I get you in my bed, you are never leaving it again. I will own you, completely. There won't be an inch of you that I won't lick, suck, or fuck. I will leave my mark on you so that there is never any confusion about who you belong to.

"My cock," it hissed, "will be the only dick that your succulent cunt ever takes, the only one that will ever fill all your holes day and night, until you are a desperate puddle of slick and cum. And then I will do it again, and again, over and over, until you're so completely drenched that you will be slipping and sliding along my pulsing, hard shaft; so that you won't be able to tell the difference between your sweat and your sweet pussy juices.

"And you will love every second of it. Because Duna, once I fuck you, I will ruin you for all eternity. You will be mine, truly and wholly, and I will be yours, until the end of time. I will brand myself on your soul. You will never escape me." Suddenly, the shadow arms released her from their iron firm hold, pulling away from her entirely until they almost blended with the darkness of the night.

"Wait, please!" Duna begged, tears welling up in her eyes, desperation clawing at her heart. She reached out her hand, hopelessly attempting to grab a hold of the shadows. She would do anything, anything at all that the General asked of her, just to be in the his arms again. "Don't go. Don't leave me again, please."

She watched as the shadows dissolved into thin air, as if they were a hallucination of her confused mind. As if they haven't been tenderly caressing her mere moments ago, whispering sweet promises in her ear.

CHAPTER
20

His eyes snapped open, his body returning to a solid form again. It had been some time since he had traveled in the shadows; he had rarely felt the need for it. Until tonight, when Duna's heightened emotions had unsuspectingly sucked him into her own world, like a vortex that swallows everything in its path.

He had materialized in the darkness of that alleyway where Madir had tarnished his little monster. Cathal had watched on from the shadows, barely restraining himself from not shredding the man to tiny, miniscule strips of flesh. He had wanted to murder the male for even breathing the same air as her.

For him to even imagine where the Prince's grimy fingers had been–

Roaring, the General threw a large vase at the wall of his bedroom in Navajo. It shattered into a million little pieces, the water soaking the walls and the floors.

The fucker had just left her there afterwards, not even making sure that she returned safely back to the White Palace. Anyone could have attacked her while she was in such a vulnerable state. Cathal knew that Duna was no weeping damsel, but he was damned if he would allow anything to happen to her. So he had followed her in the shadows as she had made her way back to her rooms, playing her loyal guard dog lest any fool get any stupid ideas.

Cathal still did not understand it. How Duna had managed to pull him into her own energy field, how he had felt her emotions from thousands of miles away.

It should not have been possible. Even his own brother didn't have that capability, and he was the very epitome of a powerful being.

Pacing his room, the General clenched and unclenched his fists. His jaw ticked, irritation and anger showing their ugly faces. It was all his fault, he had left her to Madir's dishonest ministrations. He had allowed Duna to be a pawn in the Prince's thirst for power.

If it hadn't been for Edan's missive, Cathal would have still been in Morinya right now, with Duna by his side.

Princess Leila had not been found, as he had led King Lucan to believe. Cathal had wanted to see Madir's reaction to the news when he divulged the information to his father in the War Room. He had wanted to witness for himself if the young Prince had been involved in her kidnapping.

So he had written to Prince Edan in Navajo, telling him of his plan. Edan was to simulate a false rescue mission where supposedly he would find Princess Leila and bring her to the capital of Baqar. Had Madir been involved in any shape or form, he would have scrambled to send his men to their secret hideout to be sure that she was still his captive.

Unfortunately for Cathal but fortunately for the young heir, no such conspiracy was discovered, raising the question yet again – where was she? She should have been found by now. They had searched every nook and alley, turned up every stick and stone. Each time they had come up empty handed, as if the earth itself had swallowed her up.

Cathal was growing worried as the days passed by.

He had stormed out of the White Palace in Morinya with a platoon of fifty formidable warriors when word had reached him of a possible hiding place for the Princess. He would go to great lengths to secure the royal's safety, not leaving anything to chance. He wouldn't allow even the tiniest risk of something going wrong in their rescue mission.

The General had trashed the home of those imbecile bandits when he didn't find the silver haired princess, had reduced the males to pulp. He wished her safe and sound in her own Kingdom of Tyros, yes. But he had an even bigger, more selfish reason for which he was growing ever more distressed.

Cathal planned to end things with Leila, to finally set both of them free so that he could turn his attention to the little enigma that haunted his thoughts day in and day out, waiting patiently like a silent predator ready to pounce.

The General had been desperate to finally find his fated mate, the woman that he had once loved, to ultimately put an end to this torment. He hadn't even dared to take into consideration the possibility that the Princess might actually be dead.

Cathal stormed into the bathing chamber, ripping his clothes off in the process, not bothering to take off his three chunky rings. Turning on the shower, he immersed himself under the icy cold water. He was burning up, rage and helplessness mixing with utter devastation inside of him like a violent storm, threatening to rip everything in its path to ribbons.

He had no choice but to leave Duna, he had to let her go until he cleared his relations with Leila. Cathal knew that he couldn't expect her to wait for him so he hadn't even bothered asking the little warrior of it.

If he lost her in the process to Madir he would just have to bare it like a grown man and swallow down his pride. It was, after all, Duna's choice in the end. He would honor it, no matter how much it pained him.

The Prince didn't deserve her, however, and not because Cathal was envious of the man, no. He was selfish and self-indulgent; even his actions from tonight had proven so much to Cathal. Once Madir got what he wanted, he disposed of it as if it was meaningless, inconsequential.

Should he ever treat his little monster that way, Cathal would flay him alive until he was begging for him to end his miserable, unworthy life. And he would enjoy torturing the man too, for the General had acquired a great deal of knowledge in the field of physical torment; had experienced it on his own skin during his long, forlorn existence.

Splaying his hands on the glass walls of the shower, Cathal let the cool water wash over his naked body. He was a power house made into flesh, his body the work of art. Every muscle and sinew clearly visible, their outline meticulously defined, perfectly in union as he rubbed away the dread and despairing thoughts from his tightly wound body.

His mind flashed back to earlier that evening, to Duna in that emerald, body hugging dress. He groaned, his cock coming to full attention. She was fucking exquisite, her luscious curves provoking Cathal, pleading with him to rip them out of their confines and wreak havoc on her glorious body.

Then, as if on reflex, he remembered how he had watched Duna mercilessly finger herself, her slick flowing freely down onto the mattress as she had swallowed the sight of him pumping his hard shaft right in front of her spread legs.

Fisting his erect cock, Cathal heard her desperate moans and screams from that night. He imagined them now as he pictured Duna with her ass high up in the air, him spreading those ripe round cheeks of hers nice and wide, drilling into her pulsing cunt. He would pound into her for hours, relishing in the sweet sounds of her moans and screams as he soaked her walls with his cum.

He wouldn't stop there, oh no. He would keep going, fucking her without mercy, on and on, in each and every filthy way possible, until she was a wanton image of erotic destruction.

He picked up his pace as he strangled his cock. His iron grip pumping up and down his hard shaft, as he played out in his mind all the nasty things that he would do to his little monster.

Oh, how he would wreck her body.

Nothing would be left of Duna by the time Cathal was through with her. He would shatter her mind, body, and soul into million microscopic fragments, completely obliterating her previous self from the onslaught of his ministrations.

Duna would belong to him then, completely and wholly. He would piece her back together, imbue her with his very essence, just as she would breathe life into him.

She was his drug, his poison. Cathal would gladly ingest himself with her venom for the rest of his cursed existence if only she would have him.

Groaning, he felt his balls seize up as he imagined Duna's forbidden hole taunting him as he pounded into her drenched pussy from behind. Would she let him fuck her in the ass? Yes, he would make it so good for her. There wouldn't be any hiding from him, he would demand that she give herself up to him without restrictions.

With Cathal, she would never need to feel ashamed of anything.

His mind racing with filthy, depraved thoughts, his hand bruising his granite hard cock, Cathal exploded onto the glass shower wall. Roaring with pleasure, his cum coated the panel, white hot liquid streaming down the sides. *What a waste. This should all be in my little monster, glazing her shimmering, pink walls.*

Soon. He would need to be patient.

Just as he had told Duna, he would let her have her little fun with Madir. Once she's had enough, though, Cathal would be coming for her.

And then – he chuckled to himself – then, there would be no saving her from him.

Making his way down to the training yard, Cathal caught sight of the two brothers sparring. Prince Valen Vilkas was the more roughed up yet at the same time the spitting image of his older brother, Prince Edan. Being the youngest of the three and therefore the last in line for the Throne of Tyros, Valen had a more easy going demeanor. He didn't care much about rules, only the ones that his monarch of a father had incessantly infused in him while Valen had still lived in the Palace in Scythia.

It showed in the intricate artwork that spanned the vast expanse of both of his arms and his impressive upper body and neck, ending only under his chin.

Valen was a large man, tall at about six feet three inches but not bulky like his brother Edan. If one had to compare the three brothers, he would be somewhere in between the massive warrior build of Edan and the more lean, defined shape of the javelin master Cian.

Prince Valen had the same wavy jet black hair, however his was cut close to his head at the sides while the top was much longer, cascading down his neck, stopping at shoulder blade level. He had the same defined facial features and striking grey eyes, ones that seemed to pierce right through to a person's soul.

It was a hot day in the Kingdom of Baqar, its climate more tropical than the one from which Cathal had come from mere three weeks ago. Nissa was known for its snow capped mountains and brutal winter storms, while Baqar was the very opposite.

Thick, heavy jungle foliage covered the entirety of the land, sparse only in places where man had dared to venture to clear out a path for King Basel Achaz's daunting armies. Beasts of old roamed the wilderness of Baqar, feasting on anything that moved, including meek human beings. One didn't leave the safety of the capital of Navajo and its surrounding villages, unless he wanted to be the next meal for the ferocious creatures.

The General stood observing the two royals as they swung their swords at each other, their bodies drenched from sparring in the Sun. Even though it was only late morning in Navajo, that vicious ball of fire was already roasting everything in its path.

"Well, don't you look like shit," Valen said, lowering his sword to his side. "Late night, General?"

"You can say that, yes." Cathal groaned, already knowing where this was going.

"Do I know her?" Valen winked at him, smirking like an idiot.

Fucking hell. "No."

Valen inspected him, his face turning stern. "Are you serious?" When Cathal didn't respond, he turned to his brother, "Is he serious? Wait, what about our sister?" When neither of the males acknowledged him, he shouted, "Will someone fucking answer at least one of my questions?!"

"No," both men sang in unison.

"Any news, Edan?" the General asked the older, more serious prince, who shook his head in a reply. "I'm getting sick of waiting around, doing nothing. We've swept over almost two thirds of the god damn Continent, where the fuck is she?"

Valen shot an apprehensive glance at his brother, then started, clearing his throat, "Don't you find the whole situation highly suspicious?"

"Very. I'm beginning to think that someone is playing with us," said Cathal.

"I was thinking the same thing. Listen, Edan and I have a theory, if you're willing to hear us out."

The General glared at the inked up royal, not even bothering to divulge a conscious reply. He was getting angry just thinking about the possibility that they were being led on a wild goose chase across the entire Three Kingdoms.

Grimacing, Valen finally spoke, "We believe that this is all our sister's doing."

He blinked. "What did you just say?" He must have imagined it, there was no possible way that Cathal had heard the young male correctly. "You think Leila kidnapped herself?" Hissing, he stepped up to Valen, getting into his personal space, "Are you hearing yourself, princeling?"

Valen didn't back up. He stood straight, feet planted firmly on the ground, holding his place against the slightly taller Cathal. "I know my sister better than anyone, General. Even you. I know what she is capable of when she doesn't get the attention that she craves. I still have the burn marks on my skin from one of her childhood temper tantrums, when she decided that if she couldn't go horse back riding with her precious father then neither could I." He hissed back at Cathal, almost nose to nose with the threatening male. "Do you need me to show them to you again, General? Or is my word good enough?"

The two formidable males glared at each other, sparks flying between them as they barely restrained themselves from not strangling one another.

It was Edan that finally broke the tension. "For fuck's sake, enough already. You're acting like two raging adolescents." Stepping in between them, he pushed them away. "Look, Cathal, Valen has a valid point. You've rarely – if ever – witnessed Leila in one of her hysterical outbursts of emotions. Even though you've known her for years–"

"Two decades."

"Fine," Edan sighed, "even though you've known her for two decades, you haven't truly gotten acquainted with her. Besides, it was only five years ago that you moved into the palace and most of that time you've been away with the army."

"Just think about it," Valen interjected, finally cooling off. "No one saw her being taken, and the supposed witnesses that claim otherwise all have conflicting stories. We're getting misleading information from across the whole Continent; one day she's seen in some far away village in Nissa while the next someone's spotted her bathing in one of Navajo's healing pools. It's not humanly possible for her to travel so fast across the kingdoms. Even if one of the hundreds of leads were to be genuine, we would be sure to receive more from approximately the same location over the following days. None of this has happened. We've been running around like headless chickens for the past three months and we've still come up empty handed."

"When was the last time you saw Leila, Cathal? Do you remember what the occasion was?" Edan asked, steering the conversation.

"Of course, it was right after our engagement celebrations."

"What were you doing?" Valen said, crossing his arms.

Cathal glanced between the two princes. "Is this really necessary?"

It was Valen's turn to be irritated, "Just answer the question, what's the big deal?"

"I was fucking her into the mattress, Valen. Is that what you want to hear?" He was getting angry again. This interrogation was getting them nowhere. If anything, it was getting Cathal closer to punching the inked up male in the face.

As if sensing the General's rising indignation, Edan stepped in. "How did you depart?"

"I left in the middle of the night for one of our training camps on the Nissian border."

"You left her in bed, to go visit some soldiers?" Valen scowled his features, his hands running through his hair. "Fucking hell. I knew it."

"This is not good." Edan paced up and down the training yard, his arms crossed in front of his chest.

Cathal watched him as he made his way around the whole area, stopping in front of a massive tree. The Prince shook his head and then, suddenly, punched the thick trunk.

Cathal could have sworn the ground shook under his feet.

Edan strolled back then, completely unfazed, as if his fist hadn't just connected with the bark of an ancient plant. "We need to go back to Scythia. Father will know what to do."

Scrutinizing him, it was Valen's turn to shake his head, "And why would we do that? For all we know, he's part of the grand scheme as well. Our safest bet is to stay right here, until our dear sister finally decides to show up. Knowing her, it shouldn't be too long now. She never was good at being patient."

Unbelievable. "No, Leila would never do something like this," Cathal said, slowly doubting his own words. "She would never stoop so low as to play with people's emotions and in such a cruel manner, too. It would not gain her any favors, especially not with me, if that's what you're implying." He seethed, fury boiling up at the mere thought of such brashness. "I would never forgive her. It would be the ultimate end for us."

"Let us prey then, for her sake, that we are wrong." Valen perused his face, as if searching for proof of such profound claims. "We should send word to Bror in Morinya, find out if he's had any news recently. The more people we keep involved and the wider our net is, the quicker we'll get to the bottom of this and we can finally all go home." He picked up his shirt from a close by bench, pulling it over his head. "Quite frankly, I'm sick of all this drama." The youngest prince left them then, not bothering to wait for a response from the General.

Cathal supposed that he had, truly, had enough of this traipsing around to last him a lifetime. "What if you're wrong?" he asked, turning to the remaining prince.

"And what if we're right? Are you going to truly end your betrothal to my sister?" Edan examined his face, trying to read Cathal's emotions. "My father will not be pleased, you are aware of this, yes?"

"I don't give a fuck about your father's likes and dislikes, Edan. He may be a king, but he's not my King." Turning away, Cathal started to walk back to the Grand Palace. "I answer to no one."

CHAPTER
21

Swinging her weapon, Duna lunged forward. Blocked, then lowered herself to the ground, extending her leg in front of herself and kicking an unsuspecting Doran in the shin. He hissed, quickly recovering himself as he swung his own sword down.

She blocked his hit again, still low on the floor, her other hand keeping her balance as she rested it behind her on the ground below. Extending her other leg this time, she kicked the Master of Arms in the side, the force of the impact moving him slightly away from her, giving Duna the opportunity to get back up on her two feet.

They went on for what seemed like hours, alternating between swords and spears, even the more intense weapons like the war axe and the mace coming into use at one point during their heated session.

"By the gods, you are one hell of a fighter, woman," Doran said, wheezing, his lungs struggling to inhale from exertion. His glistening muscles contracted and released, the tension in his body visible in every movement of the majestic black wings that were inked onto his entire right arm over his shoulder, overlapping the top of his right pectoral muscle. Even the inked on black harpy eagle that lay right under his right ear was contracting over the straining muscles.

"Glad I could be of some use around here. I feel like I'm wasting away in this palace." Placing her weapon back on the wall rack, Duna paced around the training area, her erratic heart rate slowly coming back down to normal. "Which reminds me, have you received any news from Navajo?

How is Princess Leila doing now that she's returned to her beloved?"

Shaking his head, Doran joined her as they made their rounds. "None, it would appear that the General hasn't found the time to send a missive. Must be busy catching up with the Princess," he smirked then, as if Duna would be in on the joke. Which she was, she just didn't appreciate the mental image that she had once his words were out of his yapping mouth.

"Does that mean that the three of us can return to Scythia? I don't see the point of us staying in a foreign kingdom. No offense, Doran."

"None taken, but I do see your point," he said, his dark brown eyes twinkling. "Perhaps King Lucan wishes for you to stay here awhile, I do get the sense that he enjoys your company, Duna. The old man has been sending for you quite frequently."

She supposed he was right; the ancient King had been asking for her to attend his visits to the Grande Nissian Library, which were getting to be a daily habit for the imposing monarch. He never told her the reason for his ever more persistent stops by the place, however Duna got the impression that he was hiding something from her.

The man didn't appear to have a specific task in mind when he went, randomly selecting strange books from the dust covered shelves and stacking them up on a nearby table, only to have Duna read them out loud to him as he perused the rest of the aisle. It was slowly grating on her nerves, this constant repetitive habit of his.

The least the King could do would be to let her know if and what they were searching for.

"I should check in with Bror, he might be able to tell me more about what's expected of us now that the mission is complete." Realizing that she had never actually visited the menacing warrior since they had arrived in Morinya, she asked Doran, "Do you know where I can find him at this time of the day?"

"No," he shot her a daunting glare. "That piece of shit could be lying in a ditch somewhere and I wouldn't care. Wouldn't be the first time anyway." Shaking his head, he turned to leave the training room.

"What do you mean? Does he usually get into brawls or something? Why would he be lying in a ditch, Doran?" Duna said, struggling to catch up to the brooding Master in Arms.

"He has a habit of fucking woman that don't belong to him, Lady Damaris."

"Well, how is that his fault–" she hit a hard wall, only realizing that it wasn't a wall at all but Doran's hard back. "What is with you men and your abnormal, petrified muscles? Do you eat fossilized beings for breakfast, I mean–"

"Stop talking," he said, turning to face her. "It's his fault because he should have the fucking decency of not pursuing women that are taken."

The Master of Arms leaned in, "See, your little friend likes a challenge. He stalks the women incessantly until they are so brain washed that they are led to believe that they can't live without that arrogant bastard. Once he gets what he desires from them, he casts them away like they are trash, leaving them alone to clean up the mess that he, himself, made in the first place."

"I'm sorry, I–"

"Don't." Turning back around, he stalked out of the training space. "He should be back at the palace this evening, General Gavin has called in a meeting at the War Room."

Duna watched as the gloomy male sauntered back into the ancient building, presumably to catch up with Madir, who she hadn't seen since that day in the alleyway. *Thank the gods for that.*

She still didn't know what to make of the steamy encounter that she had with him, and then afterwards with Cathal. Or rather, his shadows.

She still couldn't wrap her boggled mind around it, how Cathal had easily controlled the darkness as if it was some obliging puppet on strings. It shouldn't have been possible; Duna had never, in all of her years, heard of such an ability even existing.

Was it magic? An illusion? Or was it something far more substantial and otherworldly, something that Duna couldn't even dare to consider.

"Lady Damaris," a servant called out to her as she was about to walk into the Palace, "His Majesty wishes to see you."

Looking down at her sweaty clothing, Duna grimaced, "Now? Let me go change at least, I'm filthy from sparring."

"I'm afraid the King was very adamant about you coming to see him at once, my lady. You will just have to bare your grime until His Majesty releases you from his company. Now, follow me, please."

The servant led her to the topmost floor of the White Palace, where a pair of double, ivory, intricately engraved doors could be found, with one side wide open as if waiting for them. Passing through, Duna noticed the white harpy eagle insignia of the infamous Royal House of Raidon on both panels.

King Lucan sat on a luxuriously cushioned bench with an equally opulent backboard, reading a heavy leather bound volume who's title Duna couldn't decipher. Probably another one predating the time of the White Palace itself.

Waiting for the monarch to acknowledge her, Duna took the time to examine her surroundings. The room was long, spanning the length of at least one military naval vessel, if not more. She supposed the whole upper floor of the Palace had been reserved for the King; he was, after all, the most important person in the entire Kingdom, it was only fitting.

Much to Duna's surprise, the whole space was minimally decorated. Apart from the massive four poster bed, the bench on which the King currently sat, and an equally formidable writing desk, no other furniture occupied the considerable suite.

Books of every shape and size lined the entirety of the walls, for as far as the eye could see. A beautiful, lush forest green type of climbing vine with delicate violet bellflowers covered a substantially lesser part of the opposite wall, right behind the opulent bench that the King currently occupied.

Duna couldn't take her eyes off of the exotic flora, as if drawn to it by some unknown force. She had a strange feeling of familiarity with the star-shaped flowers, as if she'd seen them somewhere before.

She inspected the vines, unaware of the fact that her own two feet were moving and taking her toward that very same plant. It wasn't until she was right in front of the violet bellflowers that she realized that King Lucan had been speaking to her.

"Lady Damaris, are you alright?" he said.

Not taking her eyes off of the alluring flowers, she started, "I can't look away from these vines. I don't understand why, it's as if my body recognizes them from somewhere and my brain is struggling to remember from where." Duna swallowed, inhaling the potent scent of wildflowers. Where had she scented that intoxicating aroma before? "I know that's not possible because I have never seen this type of flower before in my entire life, and I was a hunter while growing up; I would have come across a multitude of varying vegetation." She had this horrible feeling, like waking up after being unconscious only to find familiar faces looking back at her while she remained oblivious to their identity.

The King assessed her carefully, coming up beside her where she stood in front of the vines with the star shaped flowers in question. "This is an Iphigenia Bellflower, known only to bloom in one place in our entire Continent, the Plains of Iphigenia. The only problem is, it hasn't done so in almost six hundred years."

"Then how do you have a fully blossoming vine, Your Majesty?" the words flew out of her mouth before Duna could stop herself. *You imbecile, your mouth is always running ahead of you.*

The graying monarch didn't respond right away, as if searching for the right words. "These flowers have been in my family for a very long time, one can say that they are an heirloom of sorts – a very rare and very precious heirloom. They were a priceless gift from the gods themselves for the harrowing sacrifices that my people had to make in the War of the Four Kingdoms."

Silently, Duna rummaged over in her head what the King had just revealed and compared it to the story that Madir had told her while looking over the stream of Niamh.

According to Madir's version, King Lucan himself had led the Nissian armies into battle that day on the Plains of Iphigenia, so it would have been the man himself that the gods had presented to any precious gift, not his ancestors. If Duna actually considered the unfathomable prospect that the gods had even come down from the heavens to visit mankind, then why would they gift the monarch a flower, of all things, that would mark their gratitude to the humans for their sacrifice?

Why not grant the Nissian people formidable weapons or everlasting life or something more substantial–

She gasped, sudden realization hitting her. That's it. The gift of everlasting life. Duna had found the source of King Lucan's seemingly eternal existence.

But how did a rare flower fit into the whole equation? How did it help him live so preternaturally long? And why hadn't the rest of the warriors received the same offering? There had to be more to it.

"I wish to show you something, Duna." The ancient ruler led her to a set of double glass panels. Sliding them open and passing through the doorway, Duna was left speechless.

They had emerged onto a sweeping terrace with white, dolomite stone balustrades. Magnificent lush shrubs with a multitude of exotic flowers and equally regal, towering trees covered the vast open space. A massive, horizontal stone sundial stood in the center of the terrace.

Duna could only stare in awe, her mouth wide open. She had never seen such splendor before. It was as if she was in another world entirely, one that did not belong to the land of mortals.

King Lucan approached a prodigious device standing on three legs, with a black, elongated type of looking glass. Numbers and various symbols surrounded the many dials that could be found around the cylinder of the device.

"This is a telescope, the only one in known existence."

"What does it do, Your Majesty?"

"Take a look for yourself," he said as he motioned for Duna to come closer.

Hesitating, she leaned into the eyepiece. For a split second in time, Duna saw nothing; complete and utter darkness. Then, as the King adjusted a knob on the side of the optical tube, she was struck with an image so divine and breathtaking that she thought that she was looking at the heavens themselves.

Millions upon millions of shimmering iridescent lights were scattered in her field of vision, some so close together they they formed clusters of magnificent, scintillating shapes that seemed to be floating in the most darkest of oblivions.

She tried forming words, to ask this enigmatic man what this masterpiece was, but nothing came out of her mouth. It was as if her mind couldn't formulate the question, as if a conscious answer wasn't needed at all. It called to her soul, pulled her in like a magnet, the force of the impulse to reach out and be one with the heavens so strong that Duna's eyes filled with tears, her heart painfully aching as if its very life was being squeezed out of it.

King Lucan turned the knob once again, changing what lay before Duna's eyes. Gasping, she gripped her tunic with her fists, twisting the fabric to the point of tearing.

Three brilliantly beaming white and yellow stars floated in her field of vision, one substantially bigger than the other two. The largest one was so bright that its dazzling yellow light outshone the dwarf sized one which appeared to be almost glued to it, it was so close. The third star was further off to the left of them, equally luminous but somehow more secluded, as if unwanted in their field of orbit.

"This, my dear Duna, is Polaris, our North Star," he said, his hand still resting on the dial.

"But there are three stars visible, not one. Which one is it then?"

He pointed to the late afternoon sky which was slowly turning to a darker shade as the light of the day began to fade into evening. "When we look at our night sky with the naked eye, only a single sparkling point is visible, which we humans deemed as the North Star. However, the real Polaris is actually a triple star system, as you can clearly see through the telescope." He turned to her, continuing, "The primary yellow supergiant is in orbit with it's smaller counterpart, making them a pair of some sorts. The pair, in turn, is in wider orbit with the third, distant star that you can clearly see standing out at the side of them."

Duna nodded as the royal explained to her the confounding layout of the constellations.

"The North Star is believed to be the brightest star in our night sky. It belongs to the constellation of Ursa Minor, otherwise known as the Little Dipper. It symbolizes guidance, hope, trust and good luck. It always points north, which is why sailors use it when returning home from sea." The King smiled then, as if holding on to a secret that no one else was privy to. "Our ancestors had a different name for Polaris. They named her the Guardian of the Gods, for they believed that the deities themselves reside on the North Star, and that if one was to follow Polaris, she would take them to the Realm of the Gods." He turned the knob again, motioning for Duna to return to her place by the eyepiece.

"This yellow supergiant," he focused the lens as Duna gasped for the hundredth time that evening, "is the heavenly Kingdom of Aharon, the home of King Nkosi, the God of the Sky and Ruler of all gods."

Completely dumbfounded and awestruck, Duna could only stare at the sight before her eyes. A yellow, slightly pulsating luminous star lay shrouded by thick, dark clouds of dust, forming a phenomenal echo of lights in magnificent shades of purples and pinks and blues.

It appeared as if it was embedded in its dusty environment, set against a dark sky filled with innumerable background galaxies.

"Spectacular, isn't it?" the King said, his voice filled with sorrow. "If every man could gaze upon this majestic sight with his naked eye, I believe that humankind would be prone to do more good in this world than evil. That we would strive to be worthy enough as to reach the heights of the heavens themselves, if only to gaze upon them for one single moment in our pitiful lives."

"What is the third, distant star? Why is it so far out from the other two?" Duna asked, trying desperately but failing miserably to wrap her mind around the fact that she was being shown the mythical Realm of the Gods, and by none other than the Ruler of the Kingdom of Nissa.

He, once again, adjusted the dial. "That belongs to the Kingdom of Isfet, where – if sources are to be trusted – the Serpent God, Apophis, is locked away. He is a primordial god; an ancient spirit of evil, darkness, and destruction, believed to be so wicked that even the Devourer of Souls herself spat him out because of his foul soul. Thus, a new realm – the Realm of Chaos and Darkness – was created, where all demon kind resides."

Duna inspected the sky before her through the lens of the telescope. A shining, white, dwarf sized star was masked by a thick blanket of dust, the dense grey and silver screen-like apparition preventing the star from being clearly visible.

"Apophis," the King continued, "is a heinous force of such evil that he cannot be reasoned with. He does not need any nourishment, nor can he ever be destroyed. The Serpent God leads a diabolic army of demons and despicable creatures out of one's worst nightmares, one that feeds on both living and dying mortals alike, not distinguishing between the two."

"Let us pray then that we, humans, never come into contact with him then," she said, shivering from the awful thought alone.

"Oh, but we already had come into contact with him, Lady Damaris."

"What? When?" It was inconceivable. "How am I not aware of this?"

"What do you think the War of the Four Kingdoms was?" The King gauged her face, as if waiting for the puzzle pieces to fall into place in her mind.

She considered what her grandmother had taught her a long time ago, when Duna was barely eight years old. "It was a war that was fought almost six hundred years ago, between the Three Kingdoms of our Continent and a foreign enemy kingdom from across the sea. The assailants sailed to our lands on massive war naval vessels, ambushing the West Coast between the border of Nissa and Tyros."

"Yes, they were led by Apophis, the Serpent God himself," he said.

"What? Why is there no account of this?"

"There is, just in very old texts that are not available to the public."

"How is that possible?" Duna asked, once again, dumbfounded. "How was he defeated then if he can't be killed?"

"He wasn't. He was banished to his Realm of Chaos and Darkness, locked away for all eternity until he is released again." King Lucan turned to the telescope in front of her. "The ruler of the said foreign kingdom had sold his soul to Apophis in exchange for might and weapons of mass destruction, not realizing that in doing so he had doomed himself as well. As soon as Apophis was banished, all of the humans that had pledged their souls to him died, for no mortal can survive in the Kingdom of Isfet. Thus, the War of the Four Kingdoms came to an end."

Try as she might, Duna struggled to comprehend what the ancient male was trying to convey to her. "I still don't understand. You said that he leads an army of demons. How did mankind succeed in casting him out, then, and with what weapons?" She turned to the royal then, "And who was the one that banished him?"

King Lucan was silent, unmoving, as he observed the night sky now overflowing with tiny specks of silver and white.

Duna got the impression that he wasn't going to reply to her ever-growing list of questions, and she wouldn't blame the man; she was inexcusably uneducated – borderline idiotic – in myths and legends of old.

"The answers to those questions are far too complex and harrowing to be divulged in one sitting, so we will leave that for another time, Lady Damaris. I will, however, allow you one piece of enlightenment." He continued to gaze upon the dazzling darkness, contemplating on how to relay his next words. "I was one hundred and ninety nine years old when a man came to visit me one dreadful day," he began, causing Duna to hold her breath in return. "The War of the Four Kingdoms had already been long underway by then. People were dying by the thousands each day, as if being struck down like flies. I, myself, had led our armies into battle for the freedom of our Continent, not caring that I could relinquish my life on those same bloody fields before my time was due.

"You see, my ancestors had a curse placed upon them many millennia ago, one where the goddess Niamh gifted us an unnaturally long life only to die on the day that would mark our two hundredth year of existence." He paused, inhaling a shaking breath. "The man that came to see me that day while I was approaching my deadline was a warrior of old, an ancient being that was sent by the gods themselves to help mankind overcome the darkness that had threatened to overwhelm our world as we knew it. Together, he and I fought side by side, battling relentlessly against the evil that had crawled out of the macabre Realm of Chaos and Darkness.

"On the exact day that I had been destined to die by the goddess

Niamh, my life was saved by that same ancient warrior, the one that had been sent by his kind to drag me into the very pits of damnation on the Plains of Iphigenia." The King turned then to Duna, his gaze filled with deep misery and regret, as if the very memory of that day caused him unfathomable agony. "In turn, as a show of gratitude to the god that had cheated Fate in my name, I sacrificed my blood on those fields of death and despair to be used by him as a talisman that would send the Serpent God back into his celestial cage, to be locked away until the end of time, or until the seal was once again broken."

Mouth gaping open, Duna could only stare at the man in front of her who was the very embodiment of the legendary heroes of old. She couldn't even imagine battling an enemy of such magnitude, facing it head on with such relentless courage and drive.

"It is getting late, Lady Damaris. We shall continue our conversation at another time; we have much yet to discuss," he said, changing the subject altogether.

"Wait, what is that second star, the one hidden from view behind King Nkosi's Kingdom?"

A slow smile spread across the monarch's face, as if he knew some deep secret that only he was privy to. "I believe you can make the necessary deduction yourself, Lady Damaris."

Of course he would believe that, she needed him to tell her directly, though, otherwise her mind would be going mad with the endless possibilities.

The King left her trailing behind as he walked back into his chambers. "In the meantime, I am willing to lend you some volumes from my personal library, so that you may catch up on history. It will make our next meeting much easier for the both of us." He winked at her, hinting at what Duna already knew – she was in dire need of a good education.

Blushing in embarrassment, she followed the man to a high tower of books that were already laid out on his massive table. There were at least a dozen of heavy, leather bound volumes stacked up on each other. Duna prayed to the gods that this wasn't her intended reading material.

"Epona will help you carry them to your chambers," the monarch said as her lady in waiting sauntered into the chamber. "We will meet again in a few days time. Have a pleasant evening, Lady Damaris."

With those final parting words, Duna was escorted out of the royal's living space and into the awaiting real world of the White Palace.

CHAPTER
22

She had flown into her bathing room before the sweat and grime had clogged up her pores. She had been so filthy from her sparring session with Doran that Duna couldn't even imagine what the King had thought of her after having spent half of an entire afternoon together star gazing. It was so embarrassing for her to have been in that state of disarray in front of the monarch, but orders had been clear when the servant had come for her – the King would not be kept waiting.

Duna had remembered that she was to find Bror that evening in the War Room, and just in the nick of time. She had ran up the long flight of stairs to the mentioned place just as the many formidable members of the Royal War Council were making their way out of the grand space. Bror was one of the last ones to exit.

"Duna, what are you doing here?" he said to her as she hurried to walk beside him. "I thought you had left with the General to Navajo."

She snorted. "And why would you think that? I highly doubt that the General would be needing me now that his Princess has been found." *And good riddance to them both.*

"I see," the menacing warrior said, appraising her. "Not sure what that is supposed to mean, but let's just pretend that I actually care.

What can I do for you?"

"You know, I am starting to believe all of the stories that are circulating about you."

"Once again, my care for such trivial things is the same as my love for wasting my time on stupid subjects – nonexistent," he turned away, "Now, if you'll excuse me, I actually have duties to attend to."

"And are you always such a dick?"

"Only when the need arises."

"Alright, if you want to be a pretentious asshole, then two can play that game." Duna stepped right in front of his path of walking, crossing her arms as she did so. "Did the General say how long we had to stay here, in Morinya? Or did he forget that he dragged us to a foreign land in search of his lovely bride and then fucking left us as if we were worthless nobodies once his betrothed had been found?"

"You've got quite a mouth on you, you know," Bror said, rubbing his jaw.

"So I've been told. Answer my question."

"General Ragnar didn't say anything about you and Da'Nyla," he started, "so I'm guessing that it's up to you two ladies to decide where you want to go from here. My duties lie in the White City, so I will not be joining you wherever it is that you plan on travelling, unless the General says otherwise."

"In other words, he doesn't give a shit."

"In other words, no," Bror said as he moved to go around her.

"Fair enough. One more thing, have you seen Madir?"

"Madir?" That got his attention. "Since when are you on first name basis with the Crown Prince of Nissa?"

She chuckled, "Since when are you fucking Doran's wife?"

"Last time I saw him he was in the gardens with Princess Roesia," seething, Bror finally made to escape Duna's attention.

Prideful at her own ingeniousness, she called after him, "See, that wasn't so hard, now was it?"

"Fuck off." His back turned to her, he lifted his middle finger at a grinning Duna, showing just how much he appreciated her little show of wittiness.

Roaring with laughter, Duna shouted to the disappearing man, "Right back at ya'!"

❖

The gardens were located on the far side of the White Palace grounds, extending almost to the mountain slopes that surrounded the city of Morinya. They were a substantial piece of greenery in an otherwise rocky land. Flowers in varying stages of bloom, of all shapes and sizes, not to mention the multitude of bright colors, could be seen growing in neatly organized clusters along the many paths lined with tall, strange looking trees.

Madir was strolling with his sister, Princess Roesia, along one such regal path, with Mikella and York keeping close watch behind them like two loyal guard dogs.

Snorting to herself at the comparison, Duna approached the lot. "Good afternoon, Your Highnesses, I hope that I am not intruding. If I may, I would like to have a word with you."

Madir stared at her as if seeing her for the first time, then glancing between the Princess and York, he said, "Please escort my sister to her chambers. Mikella, you may take your leave for now, but don't go too far. I will call for you when Lady Damaris and I are finished here."

All three did as told, leaving Duna alone with the Prince. "There was no need for that. What I wish to say won't take long anyway."

Madir stood stoic, his face a blank canvas, his hands clasped behind his back. He looked glorious today in a white and gold Royal Nissian uniform, sans the heavy armor and gauntlets. A long, elongated katana-like sword was sheathed at his side, painting the perfect picture of regal poise. His raven hair was tied back with a tie, accentuating the defined lines of his handsome features, while a light stubble covered the bottom half of his masculine face.

"Where have you been, Duna? I have been searching for you the whole day."

"I was with your father, Your Highness. He was giving me a history lesson," she said.

His gaze unwavering, Madir hissed, "Were Doran and Bror also giving you history lessons?"

She was so confused. "Doran was sparring with me, as he does almost every single day. Bror was helping me locate you, actually."

"Next time, let me know where you are. I don't like to be uninformed of your whereabouts." Madir stepped close to her, giving her a once over.

"Not sure I'm understanding, but alright." She straightened, chin high in the air. "I wanted to speak to you about Tyros. I will be leaving for Scythia with Petra in a fortnight's time, if all goes well. I just wanted to thank you for your generosity and your show of affections. I am humbled, Your Highness."

Taking a lock of her chocolate hair, he murmured low, "You know, Duna, I am starting to think that you do this on purpose."

"I don't know what you're talking about."

"No?" He coiled the strand tightly around his index finger, piercing her with his striking blue eyes. "First, you come to me looking like a delectable meal. Then, you give me a taste of the sweetest fucking pussy that I have ever sampled in my entire life." He leaned in. "Do you know what that does to a man, sweetheart? It drives him mad with need. I crave you now like the fish crave water, like the birds crave to fly." He got within an inch of her body, heat radiating off of his hard chest.

Duna's breath caught, trying not to show how much he was affecting her.

Gripping her waist with his substantial hands, Madir pulled her close to his heaving body. "I can't stop imagining you splayed out on my bed with your fucking perfect cunt ripe for the picking. I want to drill a hole in your pussy so bad with my cock that I can't fucking think straight. Do you know what I've been doing ever since I licked you dry in the alleyway? I have been beating my cock day and night, desperately trying to calm this fucking volcano that keeps threatening to explode at the most inappropriate of times." He rested his forehead on hears, closing his eyes as he did so. "I was in the War Room today, where General Gavin was discussing guard duty with my soldiers. I couldn't concentrate on a single word that that wrinkled up man was saying. All I could do was picture you naked, your glistening pink pussy wrapped around my shaft while you impaled yourself on it over and over and *over* again, your tits bouncing up and down in front of my face while I sucked on your tight nipples."

She choked on air then, her nipples turning to hard beads of rock. Her core heated, wetness pooling in between her legs.

"Would you like that, sweetheart?" he purred in her ear, eliciting tiny goosebumps to form on her arms, "To fuck yourself on my big cock? To feel my dick deep in your tight pussy, while you ride me like a race horse?" Licking her earlobe, he then sucked on the skin, nibbling it lightly as he did so.

Moaning, she fisted his shirt, pulling his sturdy body right onto her soft curves.

"I would let you do to me whatever you wanted to, my little warrior. My body is yours to use however you wish. You can sit on my face while I eat you out, make you nice and wet for my cock. Then you can be a good girl and choke on my dick while I feed it to you." He gripped her hips, pressing his massive erection onto her stomach. "I would fuck you for hours in that delicious mouth of yours, your pussy clenching on empty air, until your throat was so sore that you had no choice but to spread your pretty thighs and take my cock in any way I give it to you."

"Fuck, Madir," she rasped, her voice an erotic low.

"Yeah, that's right, I'll fuck you like it's the last thing that I'll ever do in my life. Day and night, without ever stopping, pounding away into your dripping cunt, wrecking every hole of yours with my cock." He grabbed her ass then, lifting her up while she spread her legs around him.

She felt his hard shaft pressing right up to her drenched core, right where she needed him. She moaned as he moved, his rigidness rubbing against her pulsing nub.

Madir walked them to a nearby stone wall that was covered on all sides by a dense foliage of yellow and blue flowers, giving them privacy from prying eyes. He pressed her into the wall, her legs hooked behind him around his back. Still holding her ass while keeping her up against the wall, he started to move against her spread legs.

"Oh, fuck." Duna moaned, the sensation so magnificent.

"We'll get to that, but not here." He rubbed his hard shaft against her aching clit. "I want to hear you beg for my cock before I rip into your tight pussy, Duna. Are you ready to do that?"

She shook her head, not wanting to admit how badly she wanted him to fuck her already.

Chuckling, he increased his pace, moving her up and down his erection by her ass while he pushed his cock into her clenching core from the front. "So stubborn, but I'll fuck that stubbornness out of you. You'll be an obedient little lady by the time that I'm through with you."

She moaned and moaned, her head tilted back against the wall, breathing heavily. He played with her body like it was putty, squeezing her ass with an iron like grip, sweet pain mixing with divine pleasure. Duna grabbed onto his shoulders, holding on for dear life as he ground into her over their clothes, the friction of them making it even more torturous.

"Madir– oh, God."

"Yes, Duna?" he chuckled, the arrogant prick. "Is there something you want to say to me?"

She shook her head again, not giving in. She would not be begging for his cock.

Suddenly, he pressed her against the wall, ceasing all movements. Grabbing her by the hair, he tilted her head to one side, exposing her neck to him. Leaning in, Madir inhaled. "Lavender and almonds, so fucking sweet." He licked a path to her ear, his tongue sweeping and circling every inch of her over stimulated skin.

Her thighs shook, liquid pouring out of her tight hole.

"You like that, little warrior? You like my tongue?" Moving to underneath her chin, he repeated the same on the other side of her neck. She moaned and tightened her hold around his waist, her legs gripping him tightly. "Yeah, you remember what my tongue did to your succulent cunt, don't you? How it cleaned up every last drop of your slick?"

Whimpering and moaning, she started to move on his hard shaft, the seams of his trousers rubbing over her aching clit.

"That's it, feel what you do to me, woman." He pressed his erection into her gaping legs, right over her needy cunt. "Are you ready to beg for my cock?"

"Never," she breathed, her eyes hooded as she continued moving over his huge member.

Chuckling once again, increasing his speed while he lifted her up and down over his front, he purred in her ear, "How's your pussy holding up? Shall I make you scream?"

She nodded while holding on to the Prince, shamelessly moaning like a beast in heat.

"Until you are ready to plead with me to feed you my cock, you can use your fingers to finish up here." He suddenly released her, licking her lips as he did so. "This delicious mouth will be the first thing that I impale, then when you're done gagging around it, I will treat you to a hard fucking." He backed up into the gardens, licking his lips, savoring the taste of her mouth on them. "You're not going anywhere." Smirking, he turned around and without another word strolled away into the White Palace.

Well, I'll be damned.

Duna concluded that she, indeed, was staying right here in the White City. After all, there was no one waiting for her in the Kingdom of Tyros.

Mikella had been standing by the entrance of the gardens when Duna walked back into the foyer. Upon seeing her, the five foot three warrior gave her a once over and grimacing, motioned for her to follow.

"What's with the face?" Duna said, irritated.

"It's not my place to make any comments, Lady Damaris," Mikella said as they made their way to the cumbersome stairs that would lead Duna to her chambers.

"Well, your face seems to be doing enough talking, so just spit it out."

Sighing, the black haired female spun around to face Duna. "His Highness seems quite taken with you. I suggest that you show gratitude for such an honor."

"You mean, you wish to be the one that he's squirming around, and you feel threatened by my presence." She already knowing where the conversation was headed.

"No, Lady Damaris, it is not like that," Mikella admitted, her face a solemn canvas of features. "The two of us, together with York, went through military training together. The Prince is like a brother to me, and that is all that he will ever remain."

Well, now Duna just felt plain stupid. "I apologize for my snide remark, then. I'm not really used to talking to people, to women especially."

"I understand," Mikella said as her hand rested on the hilt of her katana sword.

"No, please, let me explain." Hesitating, Duna started, "I have been surrounded by constantly aroused males for the past five years of my life, the only females that I ever came into contact with were usually rude and obnoxious towards me for no apparent reason other than that they felt intimidated by my very existence. Other times they were trying to take their frustrations out while sparring with me in the fighting pit of our barracks. So, once again, we were always in some sort of competition." She sighed, feeling embarrassed at how she had spoken to the sincere woman. "I find it highly unusual when a female wishes to have an honest, open conversation with me, without the tedious bickering and attempts at backstabbing."

Mikella smiled then, her face lighting up from the mere appearance of such a heart warming grin. "Perhaps we can be friends, Lady Damaris. I, too, am in much need of female company."

"I'd like that, Mikella. And please, call me Duna. I'm a warrior, just like you."

"Very well, Duna. Let's get you back to your rooms. We don't want the Prince getting his panties into a bunch." The grey eyed beauty winked at her, leading her up the flight of stairs.

"Oh, I like you." Excited at finally having someone other than Petra to talk to, Duna asked, "How well do you know Madir? Is he always so serious?"

Mikella glanced at her, an unreadable emotion playing across her features. "As I already mentioned before, he is like a brother to me. He's serious about the things that matter to him, you being one of those things."

"He hardly knows me, though."

"Don't let his outward appearance fool you," the female said. "Madir knows everything that there is to know about you; from what you eat, to who you surround yourself with, to where you spend every waking minute of your day." She stopped in front of Duna's chambers, her face stern. "He is very dedicated to the safety of the people that he cares for. You're one of those people now, Duna."

"I'm not sure how I feel about that, to be honest. I don't appreciate being followed around, I'm not his possession." What was going on? Other than the intense physical encounters that they've shared, Duna hadn't gotten the impression that Madir had become so invested in her.

"It's not your decision to make." Opening the door for her, Mikella added, her voice a low rumble, "You should get used to it if you plan on staying here in Morinya." Bidding Duna goodbye, she left her to her own worrisome thoughts.

What had she gotten herself into this time?

CHAPTER 23

Duna had been catching up on the literature that the King of Nissa had bestowed upon her, painstakingly divulging the never-ending information that seemed so foreign to her that she sometimes had the feeling that she was reading in another language.

Stars and constellations, planets and orbits, it was all so new to her. Nebulas, galaxies, supernovas, all terms which she had never in her life of twenty eight years ever come across. What was the point of knowing about these phenomena when she would never actually witness them with her own two eyes?

Chastising herself for willing to be so despicably ignorant, she opened up the heavy volume that she had been roaming over for the past two days, desperately trying to understand what on earth she was reading. It was a book about gateways and portals into other parallel realms that surrounded the unsuspecting mortals of the world.

Taking up a seat by the high arched window, Duna began to read out loud. "Gateways are formed when two or more parallel worlds align in time and space at the exact same point of rotation of their axes, where all four vectors must coincide with one another, thus creating a four dimensional overlapping space void of all matter in the participating realms where one can enter and leave without consequences to the person's system."

She shut the large volume, anxiety wreaking havoc on her organs. What the hell did she just read? Perhaps it will get more comprehendible going forward.

"There are two types of gateways in the known universe," the text stated. "A naturally formed one, which can be found in places with a high energy field such as bodies of water containing limestone, volcanoes, or at the intersections of ley lines. The other type of portals are artificial ones. They are made using objects of specific electromagnetic properties whose natural radiation resonates with that of the parallel world which one wishes to enter. They can be forged using any number of materials, the most effective being those of iron, cobalt, and steel." Unconsciously, Duna clutched her grandmother's necklace and started playing with it.

"Once a portal is forged," she read on, "it will remain open for all eternity. Natural gateways act differently to artificial ones, not needing the object with which they were made with to act as a conductor to its wielder, meaning that it is enough for a person to have on his body any item of great electromagnetic properties in order for him to pass through the portal. On the other hand, an artificial portal can only be opened and closed if the wielder has the precise object with which it was forged with on him at the time of desired entrance.

"Many gateways have been discovered in our universe, however evidence of their actuality including their precise locations have been long lost to mankind as a result of the numerous natural disasters that had swept over our Continent throughout our long history, erasing all knowledge about them from existence." Sighing, she closed the leather bound book. It was all of the educating that Duna's simpleminded brain could take for one day.

A knock came at her door then, giving her an additional excuse to relinquish the circumstantial piece of literature. Opening the carved wooden panel, she found the Crown Prince leaning on its frame.

"Hello, beautiful. Miss me?" he smirked, strolling into her chambers.

Closing the door behind her, Duna approached the high arched window where the man now stood inspecting her reading material. Today he was in a matching stone gray ensemble, with a button up shirt whose sleeves were rolled up to the elbows and loose linen trousers. His hair was let loose, his straight raven strands reaching almost to his sturdy shoulders.

Duna perused the powerful male, once again taken aback by how ruggedly handsome he was. Not seeing Cathal every day made it much easier to put Madir into better perspective, she concluded.

"Have you been catching up on some light reading?" he said as he flipped through some texts.

She nodded. "I haven't discovered much about that issue concerning your father, however. I'm sorry."

He waved a dismissive hand in the air. "Perhaps I can help you get your mind off of such boresome matters." Extending a hand, he reached out and wrapped his fingers around her own, pulling her against his hard body.

"Come dancing with me," he purred.

"Your Highness, I–"

"I won't take no for an answer, Duna." He stroked her chocolate hair, winding a strand around his callused digit. "I promise to have you back at a decent hour."

Grinning, she nodded. "Alright, let me get changed first." Walking over to her closet, she rummaged through the opulent gowns, finally selecting a champagne colored one with tiny star shaped beads intricately woven into the fabric. It was one of the prettiest ones that Madir had sent to her via Epona merely a week ago, before their steamy encounter in the gardens.

"No, that won't do. Here, this one." He brought forward a canary colored halter style sleeveless gown. It was so extravagant that Duna worried the dress would be too excessive for her simple tastes.

"It's a bit too much, don't you think? I wouldn't be comfortable wearing it," she said, frowning at the luxurious gown.

"Wear it for me, then. I had it made especially for you." Madir extended the gown towards her, forcing it into her relenting arms.

She took the gown from him and went to change into her bathing room. Emerging back to where the Prince stood waiting, she glanced at herself in the intricate oval mirror and gasped at the sight of herself.

Floor length chiffon the color of the ripest lemons hugged her body, her arms bare as the material tied around her neck, leaving an ample cleavage to the curious eye. Hundreds upon thousands of miniscule golden beads embellished the already glowing gown, making it seem as if Duna was covered in the purest shimmering form of the priceless metal.

"Absolutely stunning," Madir pressed his front to her back, staring at Duna's form in the mirror in front of them. His arms went around her waist, pulling her onto his chest. Leaning in to rest his head on her shoulders, he purred, "It will look even better once it's lying on the floor." He licked her earlobe, sucking in the delicate skin, lightly nibbling on it.

Squirming in his arms, Duna tried to cool down her body's rising temperature. What was it with this man and her betraying body? She needed to remember the promise to herself; she was not – under any circumstances – going to beg him for anything.

As if sensing her train of thoughts, the devastating man chuckled, his hold on her increasing. His voice an erotic low, he rasped, "The night's still young, sweetheart. Never say never."

The two of them left the White Palace hand in hand, Madir gripping her fingers with an iron hold, not letting her get a single step ahead of him. Guards observed them as they made their way through the front gates, not one daring to stop them as they headed toward the bustling city of Morinya.

It was a pleasant night, the warmth of the spring season slowly infusing itself into the late evening hours. Duna hadn't bothered to bring a shawl with her to cover her bare shoulders, her excitement about the upcoming soirée overriding all sense of self-preservation.

Strolling through the crowded city with Madir's fingers intertwined with hers, Duna felt a strange sense of peace. As if finally, she could breathe. Shamefully, she realized that there hadn't been any drama ever since the General had left for Navajo. Was he the ultimate cause of her unstable moods? Or was Duna, herself, the one to blame for her ridiculously overwhelming reactions to the man?

It didn't really even matter anymore, he was gone, he had left her to be with the woman that he loved, and no vows or promises that he had spoken to her in the dead of night could convince her otherwise.

She had cried her eyes out for that enigmatic man, had departed with a piece of her soul as he had abandoned her for the second time that night all those weeks ago; even though he had been covered in shadows, Duna knew without a doubt in her heart that it had been Cathal. It had been quite a revelation to her, actually, to come to terms with the fact that she was so easily disposable.

Once again, she had been naive when it came to the General; he had reunited her with her grandmother's necklace, as a show of humanity and generosity. Had gifted her a part of her lost childhood back in that one simple act of kindness.

Duna had, as usual, read into it too much, made it out to be something far more substantial than it actually was. Like a stupid girl she had thought that it signified a special bond between Cathal and herself, that the numerous heated glances and fervid interactions held a special meaning to him as it did for her.

She had had enough of her own sulking after the brooding male. It was time that she got on with her life, even though there had never been anything to move on from.

"What are you thinking about so hard, little warrior?" Madir taunted, his voice a deep low. He guided them toward an arched bridge made of pure white dolomite stones with matching parapets decorated with waist-high balustrades.

"I was just wondering where you're taking us, Your Highness," she said, examining the structure that seemed to shimmer under the moonlight as they got closer to it.

"When are you going to stop addressing me in such a formal way?"

"When you stop being a prince," she teased back as they came to a stop on the highest point of the arch. Peering over the parapets, Duna glimpsed a narrow river of crystal clear blue waters flowing underneath the stone architecture.

Madir leaned on the balustrades with his back and elbows resting on the stone, his neon-like blue eyes luminous in the dark as he pierced her from a mere feet away. "I've had my fingers and my tongue in your pussy, I think we're way past formalities."

Grinning like an idiot, Duna dared to play the game. "Then perhaps once I've taken your cock I'll stop."

"Yes, perhaps." Grabbing her by the elbow, he pulled her onto his rock hard body, every dip and edge of his muscles coming to Duna's full attention. "I knew you were made for me the moment I saw you playing with that imbecile in the woods. No other woman has captivated me to such an extent that I can't function properly without knowing everything that you're doing at every waking hour of the day."

"You hardly know me—"

"I want to be good for you," Madir interrupted, placing both of his impressive hands on the small of her back, slowly caressing the curve of her spine. "I want to be patient and understanding, to be the only man that you will turn to when you are in need of a companion. I need to be your rock and your shield from this dreadful world." His fingers traced the outline of her spine from her lower back to her nape and back down again, over and over while he spoke. "You are the only person that has ever succeeded in achieving the impossible, in turning me into a complete love struck idiot. I feel like an adolescent again, one that is experiencing his first ever real infatuation."

She was at a loss of words. "Perhaps you are mixing your feelings of gratitude towards me for saving your life with those of actual affection. It wouldn't be the first case of the sorts in history, it's a known syndrome among soldiers and warriors. I recall Lieutenant Fendergar—"

Madir was on her in the next second, grabbing her by the throat, cuffing her neck lightly as he hissed into her face. "Do *not* speak about other men in my presence, Duna. I am willing to be a tolerant man for your sake, but even I have my limits."

Fuming, she said, "That is absolutely ridiculous. I will speak about whoever I want, you can't tell—"

His mouth crashed onto hers, cutting of her words. Their lips melted together, his tongue seeking entrance as he swiped it over her swollen pink flesh.

She whimpered, opening wide to allow him access, his skillful tongue pridefully sweeping in to play with her own wanton one. She met him stroke by stroke, lick by lick, fisting his shirt as his grip on her neck tightened.

He groaned, sucking in her bottom lip, pressing his giant shaft against her stomach. She moaned shamelessly when she felt how hard he was, biting him lightly in return when he released her flesh. Their tongues met again, a perpetual dance of need and desperation playing in the miniscule space between their heated bodies.

"Fuck," the Prince breathed, "that mouth of yours. I am going to rail you right here on this bridge if you keep kissing me like that." He pushed his erection into her again, grabbing her ass as he did so, holding her steady with his substantial hands.

"Not until I beg, remember?" she grinned, enjoying the effect that she was having on the robust male.

"By the time this night is through, you'll be on your knees, pleading for mercy," licking her lips one more time, he massaged her round ass over her dress.

"Is that a challenge?"

Chuckling sweetly, his voice an erotic low, he said, "You want to play, sweetheart?" He rubbed her front over his hard shaft as his grip tightened. "Let's play."

Taking her by the hand, he led them back the way they had come, but instead of returning to the palace, they made a sharp turn into a secluded street and headed straight towards a tavern overflowing with patrons.

Loud, boisterous music emanated from the inside of the complex, spreading through the air like wildfire. High-spirited singing competed with waves of cheers and roaring laughter, the noise becoming so lively that Duna had a hard time hearing her own thoughts.

Madir held tightly onto her hand as they wound their way between the gyrating bodies of the vivacious crowd. Scantly dressed women sat in the laps of half drunken men, their fingers running freely through the males' hair while other couples were downright in the middle of some heavy action.

Duna's mouth gaped open, entranced by the scenery playing before her very eyes. She watched, transfixed, as one of the men unlaced the bodice of a woman that was straddling him and taking out one of her breasts, started to lick and suck on her nipple. He released the other one as well then, giving it the same amount of attention before she started moving on him.

"Are you enjoying the show, pretty lady?" a man murmured in her ear as he grabbed her by her elbow, attempting to pull her away from the prince. "I can make it so good for you." He leered at her, licking his lips as his eyes roamed over her body.

In an instant, Madir was on him.

"Do you want to be three feet under ground?" he hissed in the lecherous male's face, grabbing him tightly by the throat. "What ever gave you the idea that you could fucking touch her?"

The imbecile was still holding on to Duna's elbow, obviously not aware of the impending danger to his very existence. "Easy man, we can share, no need to get so worked up." Patting the Prince on his shoulder, he grinned a half-toothless smile, satisfied with himself for being so generous.

"You are still touching her," the Prince increased the pressure on the man's neck, his veins straining against the force. "I don't like repeating myself, so I'll say this only once. You have one fucking second to take your dirty hands off of her or I will beat you to a bloody pulp." Cocking his head to the side, his hold on the man's throat iron strong, he rumbled, "One."

Without warning, Madir pounced, his fist connecting with the male's nose. His hold on Duna instantly gone, the man miserably tried defending himself, but it was no use. The Prince was like a raging bull, destroying everything in his unfortunate path. He punched the male again, and again, hitting him in the face and head until blood flowed from every one of his cavities. The male went down on the ground, helpless against Madir's unforgiving fists.

Duna blanched, not being a stranger to blood or violence, but to the sight of the poor drunken idiot who had been at the wrong place at the wrong time.

"Stop!" she yelled at Madir, trying to grab a hold of his arm as he swung it down again at the still male. "Enough already! Madir!" Struggling in her useless dress, she cursed the ignorant fool lying on the blood drenched ground. Pulling on the Prince's arm again, she finally managed to separate him from the beaten body sprawled out over the floor.

Spinning on the spot and grabbing her by the shoulders, Madir leaned in, seething in Duna's ear, "No one can touch you, do you understand? No one. I will kill every fucker who so much as tries to go near you."

"I don't need you to be my protector, Madir, I can take care of myself." She tried to soothe the volcano that was threatening to erupt inside of her, the very idea of someone treating her like a helpless little lamb igniting a new kind of flame within her.

"You don't seem to understand, Duna," he said, his tourmaline eyes burning a hole in her. "I am not asking you for permission. You are mine and mine alone. I don't take kindly to my things being meddled with. The sooner that everyone learns that, the better for them."

"I am not your possession," her anger rising to the surface, Duna clenched her fists, trying not to strangle the maddening male in front of her. "I will not be treated as one."

"Get it through your thick head once and for all, little warrior. You belong to me. You did so from the moment you stepped foot into my Kingdom." Grabbing her by the hand, he dragged her out of the tavern and onto the bustling street where another brawl was well under way.

They made their way back to the White Palace, his hold of steel unrelenting as Duna struggled to keep up with him in her ridiculous dress. Not a single word was spoken between them as the Prince led her through the palace gates and up the stairs leading to her chambers. Swinging open her door with his free hand, he barged right in, releasing her only when they were well inside the space.

"You are to stay in these rooms until I tell you otherwise. No one is to visit you without my consent," Madir said, his powerful body radiating from tension, his face a deep scowl.

What in the ever-loving fuck. "You can't keep me in here, I won't allow it," she said, crossing her arms across her chest.

"Do not test me, Duna. You do not know the lengths that I am willing to go to in order to protect what is mine." With those final words he left, banging closed the door behind him.

Just as she was about to go after him, she heard the sound that would stop her dead in her tracks, her blood freezing over.

The lock turned, caging Duna inside her opulent chambers.

CHAPTER
24

The next day, Epona had brought Duna her meals to her room, bolting shut the door behind her as she went back to her duties in the White Palace. The elderly woman had not had said a single word to her as she had hastily carried the full trays of delicious foods back to the kitchens, nor had she commented on the fact that Duna appeared to be calmer than usual.

Little did the woman know that Duna was not the hysterical type, she did not succumb to outbursts of violence and rage when faced with injustice. No, she was the silent type, the deadly predator that stalked from the shadows, waiting and biding her time for the opportune moment to strike.

Duna would have her chance, and when she did, she would seize it by its throat.

She hadn't bothered eating the food nor drinking the water, either. It was embarrassing for her to be treated with such blatant displays of disregard to her person and integrity. No one had ever treated Duna this way, as a petulant, disobedient child, who was to do as was told by her orderly or deal with the consequences.

So she had not bothered dressing, spending the entirety of the day in her lavender satin slip of a nightgown, her hair cascading down to the middle of her back. She sat on her armchair, feet up on the seat, curled up under a light blanket, glancing out at the evening sky.

The stars would be out soon. She could already imagine Polaris as it had appeared under the telescope, its three stars resplendent against the darkness beyond. Having had the whole day free to ponder on such matters, Duna had finally concluded that the smaller star that had been hiding behind the yellow supergiant had to be none other than the home of King Nkosi's brother and the Ruler of the Kingdom of Khalfani.

She would have to ask King Lucan about it for confirmation; that was, as soon as she was allowed respite from her confinement. Would the monarch scold his son for such despicable behavior? Was he even aware of what his heir did in his free time, how he treated their guests?

A knock came at her door, bringing Duna back to the present.

She didn't bother getting up, laughing low under her breath from the irony of the situation. She remembered her time back in Captain Moira's barracks. How long ago it seemed to be now, as if an eternity had passed since she had desperately strived to have people asking for permission prior to entering her private abode.

Now, when her wish had finally come to fruition, she was locked in, like a bird in a cage, unable to decide for herself if she would allow her visitor free entrance into her chambers or not.

The knock came again, more urgent this time. Groaning under her breath, Duna adjusted her position in the bulky furniture, waiting patiently for the interloper to cease his annoying habit. After a brief moment of silence, she had concluded that he had in fact surrendered, when the lock turned and her intruder barged in.

"Did you not hear me knock?" The Prince rumbled behind Duna as she sat staring at the Moon.

Not bothering to turn around, she mockingly replied, "Was I supposed to get up and open the door for you, Your Highness?" When he didn't reply, she added, "I'm busy, so if you can go back to wherever it is that you came from, it would be greatly appreciated."

He barged right up to her, leaning over the backrest of the armchair in which she was comfortably seated, "I am not leaving until I have a talk with you." When she didn't bother turning around, he crouched down beside her. "Please, Duna."

Contemplating the Moon, she remembered a similar time when she had been observing the luminous planet, when Cathal had snuck up behind her, whispering sweet words in her ear. The time when she had discovered her ability to hear his deepest thoughts. She had thought that she would burst from joy then, from having him merely in her vicinity.

How foolish she had been then, just as she had been with Madir.

"Look at me, damn it." Grabbing onto the legs of the armchair, he spun it around, forcing her indifferent gaze to finally meet his despairing one.

Staggering at the sight of deep sorrow and regret in the Prince's striking blue tourmaline eyes, Duna felt her heart ache. Perhaps she had overreacted to the whole situation. After all, no physical harm had come to her. She had been given food and drink, and she had a roof over her head, so it wasn't as if she had been abandoned somewhere on the side of the road.

"I'm sorry, Duna," Madir's voice broke, his eyes turning downwards as he searched the ground beneath her feet. "I should not have kept you in your room. It was wrong of me to do."

"Then why did you?" she seethed, her emotions ambivalent as she observed the despairing male kneeling at her feet. "No one forced you to lock me up like a prisoner. I haven't even done anything to warrant such disgusting behavior."

"You're right. There is no excuse." Taking her hands, the Prince kissed her palms with his velvety smooth lips, murmuring softly to Duna, "I am ashamed of how I have conducted myself. Forgive me, little warrior. It will never happen again."

Duna examined him and his disheveled appearance. He was still in the grey ensemble from the night before, his shirt half buttoned up, wrinkled at the collar, as if he had been constantly pulling on the material. His hair was tousled, the light stubble on his face more coarse than before. He appeared as if he hadn't slept since the night before, the slight bags under his eyes a silent ode to the fact.

The Prince stroked her hand with his thumb, his indicolite eyes burning as he looked up at her in her satin nightgown, her bare legs glistening right in front of his handsome face.

"I was nine when my mother was assassinated," Madir said suddenly, shocking Duna with his confession. "We were returning from a nearby village that had been that year's host of the Summer Festival. The celebrations had been a success, the people had received a great sum of funds from our Royal Coffers for organizing the whole event and as an incentive for the upcoming year." Dropping her hands back into her lap, he caressed her feet.

"What happened?" she said, stunned from what he was revealing to her.

His sizeable hands swept upwards to her knees, stroking her calves in smooth motions and then back down to her ankles, repeating the process as he spoke softly, "My mother was a kind person, a gentle soul. She was always putting others first, even at her own expense. My father had been so in love with her that they had rarely separated from each other, even when going on different missions across our kingdom." He resumed his clever ministrations, softly rubbing Duna's sensitive skin. "He could not accompany us that day to the Summer Festival. A foreign ambassador was to visit, and so he had sent me to watch over my mother in his stead."

"You were so young, though," Duna said, astounded at the amount of responsibility that had been put on a nine year old boy.

A slow, grieving smile spread across the Prince's solemn features, coating his face in melancholy. "Yes, I was. But I believed myself to be indestructible. I had begged my father to let me go with my mother, to be the one guarding her in the carriage instead of General Gavin."

Leaning in, he softly kissed Duna's right knee, then her left one, his hands continuing their thorough perusing of her calves. "My father was pushing for reform, much to the grievances of our Minister of Coin at the time. You can imagine, what power thirsty men are capable of doing just to reach their ultimate goal."

Duna's breath hitched, from what the Prince was implying and from what his mouth was doing.

His deft hands grabbed her by the knees then, spreading her legs in front of his face. His eyes darkened as her nightgown hitched up to around her hips, revealing her thick thighs and lilac colored lace panties.

She inhaled, the air straining against her heaving lungs, as he leaned in, his lush lips moving to the inside of her right thigh, right over her knee. "My mother died in my arms in that carriage, bled to death as I miserably tried to stop the flow of blood. I was helpless to do anything but stare on as her life left her weakening body."

"Madir–"

"My father refused to wear the Crown ever again, blaming himself for my mother's death," he said, interrupting her words of condolences. "I swore to myself that day that I will never again let another person that I care about be hurt. That I would do everything in my power to protect the people that I love from this merciless, cruel world."

Duna's lips trembled, suddenly remembering her own oath to the heavens as she had buried her grandmother's scorched body in the cold ground all those years ago. Those were the exact same words that she had spoken out loud, the ones that had sent her running to the nearest military training camp of the Tyrossian Royal armies, committing herself to a life as a warrior.

"I need to know that you are well," the Prince said as he licked a trail up Duna's inner thigh. "That you are safe. I won't let anyone get near you, I swear to you." He spread her legs even more then, his tongue stroking her heated skin, getting dangerously close to her pulsing core.

Chest heaving, heart racing, Duna gripped the armrests of her chair as she observed the vigorous male in his lusty ministrations.

His punishing hold on her thick thighs increased, pinning her down as his head of raven hair went between her spread legs. Hooking a callused finger in her panties, he purred, "Lift yourself up, sweetheart. I want nothing blocking my way."

She did as told, lifting her ass as he slipped the nonexistent fabric over her hips and down over her ankles, throwing it aside once he had it free of her body.

Air caressed her bare skin, her slick running freely down onto the cushion of the armchair on which she was sitting on.

"You're so wet, little warrior," he breathed as he gripped her under her knees and pulled her closer to him so that her wide hips were hanging down over the edge of the seat, her glistening cunt right in his face. "Do you forgive me, Duna?"

She didn't get a chance to reply, his mouth was on her in the next instant.

Hooking his strong hands under her knees, he lifted her legs until they were all the way back at her sides, folding her in half, opening her up impossibly wide.

His tongue licked a trail up from her cunt to her throbbing clit, circling the pulsing nub with confident strokes. She moaned as he did it again, spreading her own pussy juices over her mound, the feeling so incredible that she creamed as he increased his pressure.

"Oh, fuck, Madir," she whimpered, her head falling back against the backrest of the chair.

"Say you forgive me, Duna."

He ate her cunt out like there was no tomorrow, lapping away at the slick coating her ripe, pink insides. Returning his attention back to her throbbing clit, he spread his tongue and picked up his speed.

"Oh, God." She was going to explode and he had barely even began licking her. Her hands flew to his raven strands, pulling at them as his face disappeared into her center.

Like a man starved, he devoured every last inch of her succulent pussy, attacking it with his experienced tongue, sucking and licking, nibbling and licking again as he cleaned up every last bit of her sweet juices.

"You're not going to come until you say you've forgiven me," Madir said, pulling away from her drenched core.

Lifting her up in his arms, he carried her to her opulent bed, gently placing her down on the satin covers. He unbuttoned his shirt, revealing a chiseled chest and impeccably defined abdominals.

She salivated at the sight of him. He was magnificent.

Unbuckling his belt, he slowly unzipped his pants, his erection springing free from its confinement. Duna's throat dried up. He was huge.

Licking her lips, she swallowed, shamelessly inspecting his sturdy cock. Unconsciously, she spread her legs nice and wide right in front of him, inviting him to impale her with his impressive member.

"Sweetheart, you better close those pretty thighs before I fuck you right through the sheets," the Prince said, his voice raspy with lust, as he fisted away on his cock. Precum leaked from the tip, glistening in the moonlight.

"I want you to fuck me, Madir," she purred, slipping out of her nightgown, barring herself completely to the virile male strangling his erect shaft. She massaged her breasts, pinching her tight nipples as she did so, her eyes locked on his heated ones.

Stepping out of his pants, he approached her then, his fingers wrapped around his dick as he pumped up and down, once, twice. Releasing himself, he got on the bed in between Duna's wide spread legs, staring down at her face.

"Last chance to change your mind, sweetheart. Once I fuck you, there's no going back. You'll belong to me and only me."

Shaking her head, Duna breathed, "I'm sure, I want this. I want you, Madir."

Aligning himself up with her drenched opening, his eyes focused on her face, he pushed his cock all the way in to the hilt. She gasped when she felt her pussy clenching around his hard shaft, straining to accommodate his impressive size.

"Yeah, that's it, take me like a good girl. Wrap your pussy around my dick, little warrior." Placing his hands on either side of her head, his muscular body looming over her, he began to move.

Pushing all the way in until her pussy swallowed his whole shaft, then pulling all the way out, only his tip remaining in her tight hole. He plunged back in, then out again, over and over, mercilessly pumping her full to the hilt every time, making her gasp and moan as he plundered her soaking wet cunt.

He increased his speed then, never breaking his piercing gaze from her hooded eyes, soaking in the sights of her face and the sounds of her incessant moans. His muscles bulging from the force of his thrusts, he pounded into her without remorse.

"Oh, yes, it's so good," Duna moaned and moaned, slipping her arms around his back, grabbing onto his defined ass with her hands, sinking her fingers into the flesh as he fucked her into oblivion.

"Do you forgive me, Duna?" Slipping a hand around to her front, he wrapped his long fingers around her throat. "Say it, or I won't let you come." His hold on her neck increased, slightly cutting off her air supply.

"Oh, God," she moaned again, not caring for the obscene noises that were coming out of her soaked pussy, her juices dripping out and around Madir's thick shaft, wetting the duvet underneath her.

"Say it, little warrior," he hissed, his face an angry scowl. "I–" thrust "forgive–" thrust "you," thrust, thrust, thrust. Obliterating her pussy, making her grab onto his ass for dear life as he destroyed her.

She couldn't take it anymore, it was too much. "I forgive you," she blurted out, as she felt heat rising up in her lower abdomen.

Pounding away into her, his fingers cuffing her throat, he demanded, "Now, scream for me."

She exploded in a violent orgasm, her walls clenching and unclenching around his stone hard shaft, milking his cock as she screamed her ecstasy for all to hear.

He kept thrusting through it, never letting up, until finally, he groaned and erupted inside of her, coating her walls with his seed.

Pulling himself free of her tight canal, he leaned in close to her ear, his voice low and menacing, "You belong to me now."

The Prince stood up then and picking up his clothes from the floor, walked out of her chambers completely naked, not sparing Duna a second glance as she lay spread out on her bed, her body spent from their throws of passion.

CHAPTER
25

The following seven days had gone by in a blur. It had been the same repetitive routine day in and day out. Each morning she would train with Doran before breakfast, after which she would visit King Lucan on his terrace where they would discuss the many books that she had finally almost completed reading.

She would then go wandering with Petra through the White City only to return in the evening at which point Madir would come to her rooms and fuck her until they were both sated.

He would leave right after, as usual, not bothering with dressing as he strolled out of her chambers and back to wherever it was that he went when he left Duna lying completely naked on her bed.

The man had a healthy appetite if ever there was one, and was not at all shy about all the filthy things that he promised to do to her while he pounded away into her body.

On the eight day of the same tiring regime, Duna decided to change something.

So, when she woke up, she didn't go down to the training room to spar with Doran. Nor did she visit King Lucan after breakfast. She also ignored Petra's invitation after lunch to go to strolling through Morinya.

Instead, Duna got dressed in a simple cream linen blouse and a pair of earth colored leggings, buckling up her thigh garter belt with her sheathed seven inch blade sticking out at the side of her leg as she walked. It had been weeks since had worn her dagger, not realizing until that very moment how bare she had felt without it on her body.

Her hair had grown substantially in the months since coming to the White City, but she had not wanted to cut it for Duna felt as if the water that flowed from her shower head had a healing effect on her scalp and was thus causing her chocolate locks to grow faster and healthier than was usual.

Tying her long hair up in a high ponytail and braiding it down to the small of her back, she made her way to her door where a pair of brown flats awaited her. Slipping them on, she materialized from her chambers.

She weaved her way through the many labyrinthine halls of the palace, finally emerging into the brilliant white light of the late afternoon. No one stopped her as she strolled through the gates, nor when she turned sharply toward a more secluded part of the city.

Morinya was truly, in all sense of the word, spectacular. Not one piece of trash could be seen littering the ground, not one stray leaf could be seen blowing away on the lush, green grass. It was as if nature cleansed itself here in this marvelous land of the legendary harpy eagles and dazzling white dolomite stone structures.

Duna wandered down the cobblestone path, letting her feet carry her on their own accord. She didn't realize when the path stopped abruptly and turned into – a rainforest? *What in the world?*

What was a rainforest doing in the middle of the capital city of Nissa, which was in turn known for its naturally chilly climate and raging snow storms that covered almost two thirds of the Kingdom's seasons year round?

Immersing herself in the dense foliage, she led herself through the many intervening trees and branches, not daring to look away from the path lest she get lost in the forest.

Chi-chi-chi.. chi-chi-chi. Duna spun around on the spot, searching for the source of the sound. The chirps seemed to be coming from somewhere to her left. *Chi-chi-chi. Chi-chi-chi.* There. She could have sworn–

A massive, almost entirely white raptor swooped down from the thick canopy that covered the clear blue sky, lowering himself right in front of her. Broad wings spread out from its sides as it flapped them up and down while standing on its two legs, its corresponding four blade-like, yellow talons digging into the ground.

It's head a pale grey, it was adorned with a double crest, as if a crown of feathers perched on top of it. The upper side of the bird was covered in silver-grey plumage while the underside was mostly white, except for the feathered tarsi, which were a mixture of grey and black. A broad silver band went across the upper breasts, separating the grey head from the white belly. The tail was dark grey, with three white bands spanning across it.

Duna's breath caught as realization hit her. *It's a harpy eagle.* Blood red irises stared down at her over a slate-black downward curved beak, piercing her with their predatory glare.

She froze, not daring to move as the three meter tall bird inspected her from across the forest floor. Tilting its neck, it opened its bill and let out a goose-like call, flapping its wings as it stalked close to her, repeating the rapid chirps, as if trying to convey something to her.

"I–I don't understand," she stuttered, adrenaline pumping through her veins as she stared at the mythical harpy eagle of legends, not believing her own eyes.

The raptor flapped its wings again, coming even more closer to her, letting out a procession of rapid chirps and occasional sharp screams. She didn't get the feeling that it was being hostile towards her, but then again, she wouldn't know, having no experience with such creatures.

Duna held her breath as it stopped a mere arms length in front of her. She had to take a step back as she craned her neck just to be able to look at it, the beast was so enormous.

Please don't eat me. She prayed to the gods. *I will be your faithful servant, just please let me live to see another day.*

As if hearing her thoughts, the impressive bird tilted its head and let out a low cackling noise. It sounded like – it was laughing at her.

Stunned at such a possibility, Duna placed her hands on her hips, irritation rising in her. "You think that's funny? Well, at least I don't look like a giant chicken." She lifted her chin up, staring down the formidable predator.

A series of shrill screams and rapid cackling sounds erupted from the creature, its wings beating rapidly at its sides, his head thrown back, eyes closed shut. It *was* laughing at her.

"Well, that's just great. A mythical bird finds me entertaining." Spreading her arms out at her sides, she spoke to it, "I'm glad that I'm so amusing to you. Now, can you move? You're in my way." Attempting to step around the harpy, Duna stopped dead in her tracks when the eagle didn't budge.

Instead, it lowered its head towards her, its sharp black beak barely an inch from Duna's face. Its striking red eyes dead set on her, it let out a series of chirping sounds.

Not knowing what to do, Duna had no choice but to stand there, frozen in place, running through all of the available options in her head.

Suddenly, the huge bird spread his wing out right in front of her, lowering it to the ground so that it was level with her feet. With it's beak it nudged her in the side toward his feathered limb, as if inviting her to – climb on?

"Oh, hell no," Duna breathed, sweat trickling down her spine, "you're not serious, are you? I can't get on that, I–I–" Swallowing a dry lump down, the bird nudged her again towards its lowered wing, this time more forcibly as if losing his patience with the cowardly human.

Finally mustering the courage, Duna stepped up to the broad limb, crouching down low as she climbed onto the thick plumage and gripped the soft feathers for some purchase. The creature lifted its wing then, forcing her head first onto its silver back. She grabbed the feathers with both of her hands, clenching them tightly as she adjusted herself on the bird's back, spreading her legs over its sides as she straddled it.

"You better not drop me, or I swear to God–" The harpy eagle spread its formidable wings as it ran forward, flapping away and soaring through the thick canopy of the rainforest.

Duna gripped the feathers around the mighty beast's neck, holding on for dear life as it beat its wings, rising higher and higher over the rainforest below. Looking down, her stomach plummeted.

The White City lay below her, its winding streets spreading out like narrow threads of silk, the homes and its inhabitants getting smaller by the seconds as she was lifted to the skies above.

The pair of them soared through the clouds, the wind blowing in Duna's face, whipping her hair out of her braid, the long chocolate strands dancing on the waves behind her.

It was such a spectacular sensation, to be so high above, looking down at the land, breathing in lungfuls of fresh, mountain crisp air.

She felt so liberated. Her troubles laughable when compared to the grand scheme of life.

The harpy swirled right then, its impressive wings stretched out, giving Duna the impression that the whole of the world could fit under its colossal wingspan. A winding emerald green serpent caught her eye on the ground below, it's sparkling crystal waters reflecting the Sun's brilliant rays.

A shrill scream echoed through the air, piercing Duna's ears as she was carried on the raptor's back. Another one answered back, then a third high pitched screech followed. Snapping her head around, she was shocked by the sight at their backs.

Three giant, equally glorious harpy eagles trailed behind them, their wings flapping on the wind as they soared through the air. A procession of screams and shrieks began as an endless array of the mammoth birds joined their flight through the Nissian sky.

Duna choked on air, tears of awe flowing freely down her cheeks, soaking her face. She never knew such joy, her heart expanding in her chest cavity, threatening to explode from the shear bliss.

She felt such immense honor for being allowed to be a part of something so precious, for being chosen by these mighty birds of legends to be carried on their powerful backs.

Leaning in, she rested her head on the soft white plumage, her arms going around the harpy's thick neck, intertwining her fingers under its sharp beak. She closed her eyes, relishing in the melodic song of the mythical beings, her heart hammering away as the cool air caressed her skin.

The world faded away, only her harpies and the wind remained.

"Lady Damaris," a man's soft voice murmured in her ear, "wake up." Slowly opening her eyes, Duna saw the King of Nissa leaning over her, his face radiating from pride and admiration.

"What happened? Where am I?" Sitting up to a half-position, she carefully searched her surroundings.

"You're in my chambers, my dear," he said as he brought a chair to the side of the bed. "The harpies brought you to me when you fell asleep on Shah's back."

"Shah? Who's that?" Blinking away, she tried clearing away the haze from her sleepy eyes. She couldn't remember anything other than soaring through the sky on a pair of magnificent white wings.

"Shah is the King of the Snow Harpies, Lady Damaris. The giant raptor on which you rode over the entirety of my kingdom on." He sat down then, his fingers crossed in his lap as he examined her. "He is an old acquaintance of mine, if you will. I have known him for – well, for a long time. I have never known him to carry a person on his back before. It would appear that he is quite fond of you."

She snorted. "I hardly doubt that, Your Majesty."

"Oh?" the graying monarch lifted a thick brow, "Is that why he is perched on my terrace, waiting on you?"

She blanched. "Wha–what?" Her gaze flew to the high arched windows overlooking the snow capped mountains of Nissa, as if expecting a giant bird to sweep by the glass panel. "Why would he be waiting for me?"

"I have no idea, my dear Duna. Like I said, this has never happened before."

"I don't understand. What should I do?" Panic seized her chest as she contemplated on her next move. "When will he leave?"

"Perhaps you should go and ask him."

Laughing at the preposterous idea, she said, "You can't be serious." When the man didn't join in her amusement, Duna's face fell. "You're serious."

King Lucan stood from his seat, his hands clasped behind his back as he sauntered over to the double glass panels leading to his terrace. Opening them, he disappeared from her view. A shrill scream erupted from the outside, jolting Duna from her stupor.

Not wasting a moment, she flew through the open doorway, afraid she'll find the King's decimated limbs thrown across the sweeping dolomite expanse. Breathing a sigh of relief when she found the man intact, she inspected the scene before her.

King Lucan stood facing the substantial bird, his arms crossed in front of his chest as he stared at the animal. Shah glared right back at the man, his distinctive blood red irises laser focused on him, his eyes unblinking as if in a trance. Neither seemed to move, as if sizing each other up.

Duna slowly made her way towards the monarch, being careful so as not to make a noise as she crept close. As soon as she entered the raptor's field of vision, his head snapped to her, his eyes trailing her every step as she carried herself closer to the human.

Emitting a rapid procession of high pitched shrieks, he flapped his wings frantically at the King, as if preparing to launch himself at the male.

Afraid for the ancient's life, she jumped in between them, her arms raised up as she faced Shah, shouting at him, "Stop!" When he didn't relent, she added, "He's not going to hurt me!" The mighty bird ceased all movement, his sharp gaze penetrating Duna as she slowly lowered her arms and strode toward him.

"It's alright, Shah. I'm alright." The bird cooed then, a low sweet sound rumbling from his chest as she grazed the plumage covering his neck, caressing the soft feathers with her fingers. "You like that?" Laughing at the impossibility of the situation in which she found herself in, yet again, Duna splayed her fingers over Shah's velvety smooth neck, sinking them in as she stroked the fabled raptor of legends.

"As I said, he seems to be quite taken with you, Lady Damaris," King Lucan said from behind her, his voice filled with determination.

"It would appear so, yes. He's not the first wild beast to be so, though," she said, her mind wandering off to that dire wolf that had purred when she had petted him. "I've never even heard of such instances where feral creatures react in such a manner towards humans. I wonder if it means anything."

King Lucan contemplated silently on her admission. "There is one legend that I remember reading when I was a young boy. Now, mind you, that was many centuries ago so my memories might not be completely accurate."

She shrugged. "I'd like to hear it, Your Majesty."

"Well," he started, "the tales say that there once was a protective god known as the One Who Rescues, or The Enchanter, who was believed to be a master of wild beasts and weapons of war. It claimed that he was particularly accomplished with the bow and arrow, pursuing and killing dangerous animals that threatened man, especially children."

"What happened to him? I thought gods were immortal, and hence couldn't ever die," she said, still caressing the bird of prey in front of her.

"If I recall correctly," the monarch said, "it was written that King Nkosi proclaimed him a general god of protection against all illness and harmful magic, birthing him another name in the process, thus leaving his previous role vacant until a new god was appointed the title," he trailed off, trying to force his memories.

Duna pondered on the King's words, rolling them over in her head. "Are you suggesting I apply for the role?" Chuckling to herself at the absurdly sarcastic remark that she made, she added, "Joking aside, I highly doubt that I have such an enchanting effect on wild animals, Your Majesty. Two such instances don't make it a general rule."

When the man didn't answer, she turned her head to ask what was going on, but the King wasn't there. *Where did he go?*

Going around the massive, horizontal stone sundial that stood in the center of the terrace, Duna strolled back into the royal's chambers, leaving Shah perched outside.

Examining the expansive space, she found the King seated on a cushioned bench, bent over a heavy, leather bound volume. He was reading something, his eyes rolling over the ancient text.

His head snapped up, his indicolite eyes locked on Duna.

"What is it?" she said. "What did you find?"

King Lucan sat utterly still, his chest barely moving as he inhaled strained breaths. His hands were shaking, desperately trying to hold on to the substantial book in his lap. "I–I found his name," he stuttered, attempting to regain some composure, his eyes inspecting the words once again as he muttered under his breath, "I don't believe it. She was right."

Duna stood waiting, pretending not to hear that last part. *Patience be damned.* "Well, what is it? His name?"

The King blanched, his knuckles joining in the change of color as he opened his mouth and murmured low so that only Duna could hear, "His name was Shed." His gaze pierced her. "The Savior."

Duna had been ushered out of the royal's chambers as soon as she had convinced Shah to return to his nest. The mighty bird had been reluctant to leave her side, as if danger was lurking just around the corner, waiting for her to be alone before it pounced.

She didn't understand it, this strange connection that she had with the raptor. Had it been mere coincidence that Duna had stumbled upon the harpy eagle's nest in the rainforest? Or had Shah sensed her and thereafter sought her out?

It was such a wild idea that Duna laughed out loud as she made her way to the training space in the White Palace.

Petra and Mikella were going at it like two wildcats, ready to lash each other's throats out at a moment's notice. Both women were formidable opponents, relentless and unforgiving in their onslaughts.

"How was your stroll through the rainforest, Duna?" Mikella chirped as Duna approached the pair. "I heard you met our Bird King."

"Who told you that?"

The female warrior smirked, appraising her from behind her sword. "Everyone in the whole city knows. You were seen riding on Shah's back through the Nissian sky. You've actually become quite a legend." Sheathing her sword, she added, "His Highness isn't very pleased about the whole thing."

"That's ridiculous, he has nothing to be angry about," Duna said, her hands on her hips, "Besides, it's not like I had a choice. The beast practically pushed me onto his back. It was either that or be eaten." She turned to Petra, clearing her throat. "There was something that I wanted to talk to you about."

"Just giving you a friendly warning," Mikella interjected. "I'll let you two ladies speak in private." Bowing slightly at the neck, she returned her weapon to the wall and strolled out of the training room.

"That one is trouble, I'll tell you right now." Petra pointed the end of her sword in the direction in which the dark haired woman had just left. "She's hiding something. And I'm willing to bet on it that it has something to do with that Prince of yours."

Duna lifted an arched brow, scrunching her features in confusion. "Madir? They're like siblings, it's fine."

"Then why are they always speaking in hushed tones whenever I see them, only to quickly end all conversation and have Mikella leave his side? And for fuck's sake, what's he got to be so mad about?" She shook her head. "Something isn't right. I can just feel it in my bones."

"Yes, well, I'll let you figure that out on your own. I wanted to speak to you about our trip to Scythia." Duna paused, taking a deep breath. "I–"

"There's been a change of plans, actually. We won't be going to Scythia after all." Placing her sword back on it's rack, Petra turned back to her. "Bror received a missive this morning. The General has summoned us to Navajo. We leave in the morning."

Staring at the woman, Duna had a hard time coming to terms with what had just come out of her friend's mouth. "I won't be going with you," she said, lifting her chin up. "I've decided to stay here, in Morinya."

"What? Why?" The ginger warrior scrutinized her, her eyes filled with confusion. "Does it have anything to do with that princeling?" When no reply came, she continued, concern coloring her features. "Look, it's your life and you can do whatever you want, but something is off with that man. I don't trust him. You need to be careful with him."

"You're overreacting, Petra. He's just different than what you're used to."

Her friend shook her head. "No, he's too quiet, I don't like it. And if you're staying just because you're avoiding the General, then you need to grow some balls and face him."

Huffing, Duna pretended she didn't understand. "What are you talking about? Why would I be afraid of seeing the General?"

Petra came close to her then, leaning in as she focused her bright green eyes on her. "You forget, I have known you from the very first day since you arrived at the barracks. I know how you breathe, woman. Don't think I don't know what you hide in here." She pressed her finger into Duna's chest, right above her beating organ. "You have nothing to be ashamed of. You can't dictate who you give your heart to."

"You're wrong," she said, trying to temper down her emotions as she thought of Cathal. "My heart belongs to Madir. He is the only one that I have ever been interested in since that day in the woods." She inhaled a calming breath. "I wish you a safe journey to Navajo. My decision is final."

Nodding her head, Petra turned to leave. "As long as you know what you're getting yourself into." She stopped at the open doorway of the training facility, her back to Duna. "Don't ever change yourself for a man. If he truly cares for you, he'll accept you for the way that you are. Not for what he wishes you to be."

With those final words, her friend and sister in arms left her to her own miserable thoughts, not knowing when and if Duna would ever seen her again.

CHAPTER 26

He paced up and down the long, open corridor leading to the Reception Room at Dasan Hall of the Grand Palace at Navajo.

Almost two weeks had passed since Cathal had received confirmation from Bror that they would be joining him at the private residence of the Royal Achaz dynasty.

Two agonizingly long weeks, where he had thought that he would eat himself alive from worry and agitation. He could not rest until his little monster was safely beside him, even if he had to pretend to not care about her, while she imagined the worst of him.

Cathal would be fine if she hated him for the rest of her life for leaving her in Morinya, as long as she was out of harm's way. That was all that mattered to him.

"What's taking them so long? Where the fuck are they?" Mumbling under his breath, he failed to notice that Valen was observing his anxious behavior, and by the look on the young prince's face, it would seem that he was confused about Cathal's state of restlessness.

Ignoring the youngest son of King Fergal, Cathal stopped his pacing and searched the horizon through the open pillared hall of stone for any signs of the three warriors whose arrival was already long overdue.

Why aren't they here yet? Bror would have sent a bird if a delay had occurred, and yet there had been none for the past day since receiving word that the trio was entering royal grounds.

Cathal had regretted abandoning Duna at the White Palace. He had been wringing his hair day in and day out for being so foolish, for believing that time and distance would push her out of his mind and heart. That he would be able to go on living the life that he had led prior to meeting the little monster.

How incredibly stupid and inconceivably naive to think that he would be able to squeeze her out of his wretched system.

Shaking his head, Cathal leaned on the balustrade, his fingers gripping the white stone. "Something is wrong. They should have already arrived by now." He needed to get his horse. Rais would take him to her; he would find Duna even if she was hiding in the most desolate place on earth.

"What's the rush, General? They'll be here, just relax." Valen came up behind him, clasping him on the shoulder. "Prince Kalad had received news this morning. You're not going to like it, though." Scratching at the back of his neck, the heavily inked up male hesitated, his face a deep frown. "His captain has found a lead on a possible location where my sister could be in hiding. They're investigating it as we speak, which means that if all goes in our favor, we could have her here at the palace in a week's time. And you could finally get to the bottom of this whole charade."

"She's not holding herself captive, Valen. I refuse to believe her capable of such despicable scheming." His knuckles turned pale as he gripped the stone almost to a breaking point. "I refuse to believe that I have been so thoroughly deceived all these years as to wrongly consider your sister to be an honest and righteous person."

The very thought sent Cathal's insides boiling.

You're wrong, brother. My sacrifice was not in vain. Mankind was redeemable. It had the potential to be great again, to be just and fair and honorable, as it once was, all those millennia ago.

"Like I said, I hope–" The Prince's words were cut off as a stream of riders appeared over the horizon. Flying down the dozen steps that led to the courtyard, he didn't wait to see if the General was following along.

Cathal stood by the intricately carved stone pillar of the open hall, examining the many faces that had just arrived.

Bror ran up to him then, obscuring his view of the crowd. "General," he inclined his head in greeting, a broad smile spreading over his face. "Now there's a face that I've longed to see." He punched him playfully in the shoulder. "Where are the others?"

"Edan and Kane are out with the two princes on assignment. They'll be back shortly." Searching the group that had just arrived, Cathal's pulse raced. *Where is she?* "Did you have any troubles on the road?" Perhaps they had separated and were coming in via two smaller groups. "I don't see all of our people here."

She better fucking be here or he was going to murder someone.

"No, we're all here." Bror clasped him on the shoulder, his almost black eyes appearing to bore into his soul. "How's your beloved? Have you caught up on lost times?" He winked at Cathal, a mischievous little grin playing on his face.

"Stop talking," Cathal hissed, his temper rising to dangerous levels. "I thought I was explicit in my order that all were to come to Navajo, no exceptions."

"Like I said, we're all accounted for. There was no trouble on the road, we had good weather and made–"

Fisting his shirt and lifting him off the ground, Cathal raised the assassin until he was eye level with him. "Do you take me for a complete imbecile? Where are the women?"

"General Ragnar," Petra's voice called out from the crowd behind Bror, cutting through his maddening thoughts. He reluctantly released the spy master, turning his attention to the slender woman that was standing at the bottom of the steps. "Asking permission to withdraw to my sleeping quarters. The road was long and tiring, I could use some rest." She stared him down, not once blinking as he appraised her.

Cathal glanced around the awaiting female warrior, expecting to see another one sauntering by, the one for whom his heart beat frantically at the mere mention of her name.

His little monster was nowhere in sight.

"Where is she, Da'Nyla?" Clasping his hands behind his back, his fingers digging into the flesh, he desperately tried to calm the darkness that was slowly taking over him. *This is not the time, damn it.* He could not turn into shadows now, in front of all of these people. He had to control his emotions, before all hell broke loose.

"Who are you talking about, General?" Petra flashed him a devious smirk.

Yeah, you know who I'm talking about. Smirking back, he descended the stairs, stepping up to the ginger female. "Perhaps a slight incentive will refreshen your memory. How does kitchen duty sound during your entire stay here at the Grand Palace?"

Blanching, Petra mumbled incoherently, "That won't be necessary, I seem to have remembered – besides, I can't exactly know which 'she' you're referring to – and where is Princess Leila, anyway? I swear, that woman is like a ghost, one minute she's here, the next gone – poof!"

Chuckling at her own idiotic ranting, wringing her hands in anxiety, she looked like a rambunctious child that was desperately trying to get out of punishment for doing something that it was explicitly told not to do.

Raising his hand, Cathal silenced the woman's annoying banter. He glanced between her and his spy master, trying to work out what they were hiding from him.

"Where. Is. She?" He cracked his neck, the storm threatening to take over. In another time, it would take only one wrong word, and he would turn the whole world black.

As if sensing the danger, neither warrior dared to speak. They shot warning glances at each other, wordlessly communicating, begging the other to keep their mouth shut. Their faces pale, they stood stone still before the General.

His patience worn thin, Cathal closed his eyes, inhaling mouthfuls of humid air. He imagined his little monster, that beautiful face of hers, with those soulful hazel eyes. Those delicious pink lips that he never had the chance of tasting. Her lavender and almond scent faint yet ever-present, embedded eternally in his brain's cortex, overflowed his lungs as air entered his airways.

He opened his eyes slowly then, focusing on the female in front of him, attempting to keep his cool.

"General," Petra said, hesitating, as her voice shook, "Duna is not with us. She stayed behind in Morinya." She winced, as if the very word caused her agony.

His voice a deadly low, Cathal simmered, "Do you mean to tell me that you disobeyed my direct order?" His blood boiled once again. His heart hammered away. "I explicitly stated that all *three* of you were to come at once to Navajo."

"She refused to leave Prince Madir," Petra blurted out, taking a step back when she saw the murderous look on the General's face. "She would have stayed in the White City for him even if you hadn't summoned us."

I am going to kill that little cockroach. "Leave." The hold on his rage slipped. "Now." The words were barely out of Cathal's mouth before the two warriors bolted away to safety, leaving him alone in the desolate courtyard. And not a moment too soon, for in the next second he slipped into darkness, his body turning to black swirls of shadows.

It was time that he went hunting.

The murky tendons of night stretched over the land, engulfing everything in their path. They flew at the speed of light past unsuspecting humans as they went about their evening, not noticing the snake like ligaments of gloom.

In a mere instant of mortal time, the shadows reached the gates of the White Palace, slithering between the iron bars, encroaching through the miniscule cracks in the dolomite walls of the ancient building.

They crept up the numerous steps, not once breaking form until they finally reached a pair of double doors. Sliding beneath the heavy wood, they came together, creating the imposing shape of their Master, the Lord.

Opening his shadow eyes, he examined the space.

The room was wrapped in darkness, no light coming in through the high arched windows. The bed stood undisturbed, where not even a wrinkle could be seen in the satin sheets. There were no personal items laying round, no singular object that would give away the owner of the suite.

The closet doors stood wide open, as if left to vent out the dust and stuffy air from inside. Not a sole piece of clothing could be found anywhere on the premises.

Moving on to the bathing chamber, he noticed that it, too, stood empty. No shampoos, no bath oils, not even a towel garnished the place. It was as if the owner had been swallowed by the ground itself, as if he had never even lived in the space.

The Master of Shadows dispersed back into smoke, the appendages extending far and wide through the tiny holes and crevices, covering the ground in a thick fog as they moved from chamber to chamber, searching for the missing tenant. Not a stone was left unturned, not a pebble left unmoved.

They reached their final destination, the one which he dreaded to explore. The results of his search would determine the future, and how he would proceed henceforth.

The royal insignia of House Raidon stared back at the mist, daring the droplets of night to enter the suite. Creeping under the door panel, they emerged on the other side, materializing, once again, into the terrifying figure of the Lord.

He stared at the two humans that lay sleeping in bed, their bodies intermingled, the silky sheets haphazardly thrown over their naked bodies.

Stepping up to the expansive bed, he saw that the female was turned away from the male, whose arms were wrapped around her waist in a deadlock, her body pulled back against him.

Possessiveness shot through him suddenly, showing its ugly teeth, snarling like a vicious animal in his veins.

Crouching down low so as to be level with the woman's closed eyelids, he inspected her face. Large eyes with long, dark lashes grazed her sun kissed cheeks, her plump pink mouth parted ever so slightly as she breathed in air. Her long chocolate locks were spread over her bare shoulder and down the length of her back, cascading in rivers of shimmering silk over her smooth skin.

Leaning in, he closed his eyes as he inhaled her addictive scent.

The lavender and almond fragrance awakened his soporous senses, igniting the many neurons in his brain, forging new synapses in his body's composition. It was an aroma which would forever be embedded in the make up of his genetic sequence, one which could never be erased from his celestial being. She had become a part of him, had unknowingly infused herself into his very spirit.

"Cathal.." her soft, feminine voice whispered, her eyes shut, like a silent prayer in the night. He froze. Searching her face, he realized that she was still asleep, dreaming.

"Until my very last breath, I will wait for you, my little monster," he vowed out loud, murmuring softly in her ear. "If not in this lifetime, then in the next, I swear to you, we will be together." Brushing her cheek with fingers of gloom, the Master of Shadows memorized her peaceful state of rest, where not even he could enter her blissful dreams.

He would gladly give himself over to the Devourer herself if it meant that this pure creature that slept soundly on a bed of clouds would be safe and taken care of until the end of time.

He would burn in eternal damnation for her salvation.

"I will gladly die a thousand more excruciating deaths if that is the price that I must pay so that I may finally, one day, hold you in my arms. There is nothing that I wouldn't surrender for you, nothing that I wouldn't endure just to have you gaze upon me with love in your eyes." Lips of smoke caressed her soft skin, leaving a trail of shadows behind. "I will fight Fate itself, for you are mine, and I am yours. Not even the gods themselves can keep us apart." *I will wipe the Realms from existence if any dare stand in our way.*

Retreating into the dark corner of the chamber, the menacing form observed his little human for a while longer before dissolving back into tiny droplets of black mist, flying back to his place of residence, the wind carrying him away from the one who had captured his tortured soul.

He didn't see the brilliant beams of silver that shone through the glass panes, merging into an ethereal shape that descended onto the sleeping male's body.

Stepping out from under the moonlight, he ascended the many stone steps that led to his living unit, the one which was located in the East Wing of the royal residence, secluded from prying eyes.

The shadows seemed to follow him as he walked through the unlit corridor, bending and swirling around his towering shape. He entered the desolate chambers, not bothering to ignite a light. He didn't need one to see in the dark; his eyes of the purest green aventurine shone like a beacon in the forbidding blackness.

Casting his clothes aside, he changed into a pair of light garments, ones which would allow his skin to breath in the humid Navajo climate.

He would have to be quick if he wanted to speak to the heir of the Kingdom, for it would be midnight soon and Prince Faiz Achaz would be leaving for his seasonal tour of the many healing pools of Baqar.

Cathal flew up the stairs to the third story where the royal's private suite was located, stopping only to announce himself to the many guards that were situated on the wide floor landing directly in front of his chambers.

The four men assessed him from head to toe, each one of them taking their time in evaluating the level of danger that he would present to the Crown Prince. The General, too, took the opportunity to inspect them from where he was standing, awaiting admittance.

The males were dressed in the official Baqarian uniform with opulent ruby red, long sleeved tunics that went down to their knees, white cotton trousers that swept down to their ankles, and a pair of plain black slippers. A band of gold cloth was wrapped around their waist and knotted at the back. Matching gold turbans were worn on their heads with their dark hair tied in a low bun at the nape. Each held a six foot long spear in one hand, with a large, heavily curved dagger at waist level on the right thigh.

After a few moments, the solid silver doors opened, permitting him entrance.

Cathal strode into the splendid peacock-themed space, with numerous beautiful pieces of art decorating the many walls and a stunning floral mandala in brilliant shades of blues, purples, and browns painted onto the marble floor. Stained glass windows lined the walls opposite from the works of art.

"General Ragnar," a deep, raspy voice echoed from behind the wooden table that was located to the left of where Cathal stood. "To what do I owe this pleasure?"

Turning to the sound of the voice, Cathal mentally prepared himself. "Your Highness, I wish to speak to you about Princess Leila."

"Ah, yes, but of course. What is it that interests you?"

He hesitated. "Prince Valen has informed me recently that your brother may have a lead on a possible location for her. Has a search party gone out yet?"

Resting his left arm on the table, the Crown Prince drummed his fingers as he appraised Cathal. "Yes. And they have already returned." He tilted his head then, taking in the General's calm demeanor. "You are not alarmed by these news."

I'm sick of it, that's what I am. "What have they found?" He placed his hands behind his back, clasping them so as to block the urge to clench them from agitation. *When will this madness end?*

Standing up from behind his desk, the male sauntered over to where the General was standing. At six feet high, the male was substantially shorter than Cathal's towering height. With a head full of brown black curls that ended just under his ears and a neatly trimmed beard and mustache, he was the very picture of the infamous royal bloodline of the ancient Achaz dynasty. Straight wide nose with a single gold hoop decorating it, eyes the color of burning copper and a square jaw with a slight indentation in its middle embellished his defined facial structure. His skin the color of rich almonds glowed in the light of the many chandeliers hanging from the ornately carved ceiling.

He was a substantial male, with an elegant yet impressive stature, an ode to his ancestors' warrior heritage.

"It would appear that the Princess had, indeed, been occupying the small hut as of recently." His eyes pierced Cathal's, his stare laser focused on him. The gaze of a hawk that's spotted its prey. "Do you want to know what I think, General?" Cathal nodded. "I believe that your beloved is very close to the Palace. In fact, I will be so bold as to assert that we will be seeing her very soon." He lifted a thick eyebrow. "In a matter of days, in fact."

"How can you be so sure?"

He chuckled. "I have a gift, if you will, for such things. I can – foresee what the future holds." Tucking his hands into his purple and gold tunic, the heir sauntered back to his desk. Opening up a drawer, he pulled out a rectangular shaped parchment and walking back to Cathal, handed the mysterious piece of paper to him. "This was found inside the shed, it was addressed for you."

Unrolling the sparse bit of fabric, the General read the few lines of words that were written on it. *"At the strike of twelve we will meet again."* His fingers tightened around the parchment, crumpling it in his fist as anger boiled in his blood.

Someone was playing a very dangerous game with him.

"As I said, I am excellent at foretelling the future." Prince Faiz stepped up to the General, having no problem with the height difference as he stared him down. "We have a saying here in Baqar. The saddest thing about betrayal is that it never comes from your enemies–"

"–but from those who you trust the most," he finished the male's words.

"Indeed," the Prince smiled, a feral expression on his face, "and we deal with traitors accordingly."

"That won't be necessary."

"In due time, General," walking away, Faiz stopped only once he was standing in front of a three by two meter ominous painting showcasing the beheading of a foreign queen. "In due time."

Coming up beside him, Cathal inspected the disturbing piece of art. "This is a very interesting choice of decor to have in your personal chambers. Do you not have nightmares when gazing upon it before closing your eyes?"

"Not at all. If anything, it gives me a clear perspective of the world which I want to build once I am King." A serious look passed his face. "It is an homage to our ancient dynasty. My family is forever indebted to those who have stood by us throughout the kingdom's long and bloody history."

Both males' eyes lingered on the far left corner of the artwork, where a menacing figure cloaked in black was depicted standing behind the crowd, overlooking the beheading of the said queen, a pair of scales in his right hand and shadows of gloom swirling around him.

"Achaz will never forget the sacrifices that were made for our people." Faiz turned towards Cathal, amber eyes boring into him. He kneeled then, his body bowing down low until his forehead touched the ground, his hands splayed flat at the sides of his head.

"Until my very spirit leaves this land of the living and enters the endless void that is death, I eternally pledge myself to you. May you judge my heart worthy."

Cathal observed the future ruler on his knees in front of him. "Do not waste your breath, princeling. You are swearing yourself to the wrong man." He turned then, his long strides taking him out of the royal's chambers, tendons of black mist following in his wake. "Safe travels, Your Highness. We shall meet upon your return."

CHAPTER 27

The ancients believed that Navajo was once inhabited by one of the Supreme Gods himself. That it was a holy place where, once long ago, evil was destroyed and thus humanity was set free from its chains.

As a show of gratitude for their breaking from said evil, the rulers of the olden days had constructed over twenty thousand temples across the now bustling cosmopolitan, breathing life and hope into the once desolate land.

Its legendary name, Varanasi, was derived from the two rivers that flowed at its two borders – the Varuna river in the north, and the Assi stream in the south. Religious ceremonies and varying rituals were performed on the banks of the Varuna, where embankments made in steps of stone slabs along the river bank were carved for pilgrims to perform their ritual ablutions.

Apart from it being a center of worship in the ancient world, Navajo had always been an important site for cultural, musical, and educational enrichment. From silk weaving and carpet crafting to mysticism and poetry reading, it was all contained in the marvels of Varanasi.

It was truly a city that never slept, with its luminous lights blazing without a pause, holding proudly onto its title as an eminent seat of learning and religious devotion.

Kane was taking Cathal on a tour of the ancient City of Lights, having visited it many times during his stay in the capital of Baqar on countless occasions before. The General didn't have the heart to tell him that he had seen it all and then some – the healer-warrior seemed excited at finally having the General at his full disposal. Little did he know that it was, in fact, Cathal who was taking him along as he searched for a certain shrine.

"This is the Temple of Durga, the warrior goddess of strength, protection, and destruction," Kane began as they reached their next place of interest. "She is seen as a motherly figure and is often depicted with numerous arms carrying a weapon with which she defeats demons. She is always portrayed as a beautiful woman riding a lion or a tiger, and is believed to be invincible."

They stopped in front of the place of worship, its multi-tiered spires and ochre red walls standing out against a clear blue sky. To the right of the temple stood a rectangular body of moss green water, a pool of some sorts, with stone stairs on all sides and watch pillars at each corner of the pond. A vast amount of monkeys could be seen loitering the shrine, completely unfazed by the presence of humans.

"Well, at least now I know why then call it the Monkey Temple," Kane muttered, strolling into the building, not bothering to wait for Cathal.

Upon entering the place, they noticed many elaborately carved and engraved stones surrounding a central icon of the goddess with eight arms holding various weapons.

"Can you imagine having so many arms? The things that you could do with those hands–"

Cathal grabbed him by the shoulder, squeezing his flesh. "Get out."

"Apologies, General. I was out of line, it won't happen again."

Releasing him once more, he strode onwards deeper into the shrine, breathing in all the sights that lay before him. A sheepish Kane stayed behind, apparently having decided that it would be for his own benefit to keep his distance lest he get any more inappropriate inspiration from the artwork.

Cathal walked on, pausing at a depiction of the goddess on a lion with nine planets circling around them. *Interesting.* He had never noticed that before during his prior visits to the shrine.

An elderly monk dressed in orange robes came up beside him as he appraised the sculpture. "The Navagraha are nine heavenly bodies and deities that influence mankind. They are the Sun, the Moon with its two nodes, Mercury, Venus, Mars, Jupiter, and Saturn. In fact, the seven days of the week correspond with the seven classical planets." He turned to the General, his breath catching. "But you already knew that, didn't you?"

Cathal stood silent.

"Tell me, have you found what you've been searching for?" The white haired man waited patiently beside him, his hands clasped together as they rested on his stomach.

After a few moments, Cathal finally answered, "No, not yet." If Prince Faiz was right, he would soon be reunited with Leila, and then he would finally get the answers to the endless questions that haunted him.

"The truth is always right in front of our eyes, one only has to open them and it shall be revealed."

"It is not always so simple."

The old monk smiled. "Life is *always* simple. It is man who complicates it needlessly. Even in everyday decisions, we always ponder if maybe we are making a mistake when choosing one of the many choices that are offered to us. Why waste time and energy on worrying about something that we've already decided, something that's already done and cannot therefore be erased? Why not use that same energy to make the most of the choice that we made?"

"Sometimes it is not our own decisions that bring us hurt and regret but that of another's."

Hazel eyes seared through Cathal's. "If you could alter Fate, would you do it? Would you be willing to go back in time, all the way to the beginning, and change the entire course of your existence just for a chance at a different destiny?"

"Fate is a fickle thing, monk. It does not like to be tampered with." Even the gods seldom dared challenging it.

"And yet, you had accomplished that which no one else had ever succeeded in before." The tiny old man stepped closer to him, his shoulders barely reaching Cathal's upper abdomen. He was like a child compared to his towering figure of almost seven feet. "What was her price?" he murmured low, "What did she ask in return?"

"You have inhaled too much incense, old man." The General turned around, walking back the way from which he had entered the shrine.

Running after him, the orange clad cenobite shouted, his raspy voice breaking. "Please, holy one, my brothers and I have devoted our whole lives to the worship of those who had relinquished mankind from great evil. We are forever indebted to you, my Lo–"

"You do not know what you speak of, monk." He hissed, his back still turned to the man as he desperately tried to keep up with him. "Go back to your temple of worship."

"My Lo–" the elderly male finally caught up with him, how he managed it Cathal didn't understand. The man was most likely almost ninety years old and barely walking.

He threw himself on the ground at Cathal's feet, his forehead touching the cold marble floor, hands splayed wide at the sides of his head. *For fuck's sake, not this again.* "Please, forgive me if I have insulted you, holy one. Who am I to pass judgment on you? I am but a humble servant of yours. If anything, I understand why you hide yourself from the world," his voice shook, "I simply meant to aid you in your ailment, for I sense that a great worry is etched into your spirit."

Cathal's face was a mask of indifference. "As I said, you are mistaken. I am not whom you believe me to be."

The old monk's head snapped up then, disbelief and awe mixed up in his features. "I observed you from afar, watched as you moved between the icons and sculptures of Durga. I admit, I wasn't quite certain that it was you at first, but now there is not a gram of doubt in my aging mind. I would recognize you anywhere, holy one, in any shape and form, for your divinity, it cannot be hidden by any simple body of the flesh."

Cathal crouched down in front of the raving elder, gripping him by the back of his neck. "Listen to me, and listen well. I am not this holy being that you keep mentioning. I am a ruthless and merciless killer. My very purpose is to serve out punishment. Do not taint your pure soul by interacting with one whose is as wretched as mine. Your gods would not approve." He stood up.

The monk struggled as he straightened to his full height. "Holy one, please, you must listen to me. You must go to the Temple of Kashi. You will find all of your answers there. Look to the sky when the next Shadow Moon appears—"

Cathal didn't wait to hear the rest of the man's sentence. It was grating on his nerves, this constant need for people to bow to him as if he was some type of noble king or mighty emperor. He had barely managed to convince Faiz that he was not the savior of his people as he had previously led himself to believe. Now this monk, a complete stranger whom he had never seen before, had done the same.

If another human was to kneel at his feet, he was going to hurl someone into the Varuna river.

"General—"

"What?" he snapped at Kane, who had appeared behind him as he had exited the shrine.

"Bror sent word. You are expected at the Marble Pavilion."

"Fine, let's get a move on."

They returned to the royal grounds. It never ceased to amaze Cathal how magnificent the Grand Palace actually was. The three-story stone structure had multiple dark pink domes, turrets, expansive arches and colonnades, all blended together to form a splendor of unimaginable proportions. In the center of the palace was a five story tower with a gold-plated dome, and around the monumental building an expansive geometrically laid out garden.

A group of Baqarian guards escorted them through the East Gate which was reserved only for dignitaries and foreign ambassadors. They reached a set of solid silver doors.

"You are to leave all weapons here. No arsenal is permitted inside the Marble Pavilion," one of the guards informed them, holding out his arms, waiting for them to surrender their belongings.

Once that was through, the General and his companion were permitted entrance. The doors opened, and immediately they were hit by a brilliant silver light that reflected off of the immaculately polished white and grey stone floors.

The Marble Pavilion was indeed exactly as the name depicted; all made of marble. From the floors to the walls to the countless pillars that seemed never-ending in rows upon rows over the vast open space. Only the places occupied by windows and doors leading into adjoining rooms were spared.

Several paintings of former rulers could be seen hanging from the white marble walls. A cannon and a gigantic sword were placed on a type of podium beside one such piece of art. A medium height figure stood examining the intimidating weapon, its back turned to them.

"I was told that you had visited the Temple of Durga," a melodic voice echoed from the person. "Do you always leave a man of worship in the throws of despair, General Ragnar?"

"With all due respect, that old man has lost his touch with reality. I did nothing except point out the obvious to him."

The figure turned. Eyes of blazing amber burrowed into him. "Do you mean to tell me that your act of disrespect of a holy man was warranted? That you could not find it in yourself to be civil with him at the very least? Must you always be so cold and distant?"

"Maelys, leave us." When Kane left, Cathal turned to the person steaming from anger. "Princess Arela, I have no intention of repeating myself, not even to you. You summoned me, therefore I came. What is it that you wish of me?"

The youngest child and only daughter of King Basel Achaz cut an imposing figure even at a much shorter height than him. At five foot six and sultry curves that would leave any woman jealous, she was a stunning creature of the opposite sex.

Straight hair the color of dark truffles reached down to her hips, her rich almond skin in perfect contrast to their pale marble surroundings. High cheekbones and a narrow nose stood over voluminous brown lips. But it was her gaze that spoke to any man or woman who dared to question her authority.

Her eyes were the exact same shade as those of her two older brothers and the entire Achaz bloodline. A molten copper color that appeared to be alive when one stared longer into them. To any lesser man the intensity of having such eyes focused on them would be extremely unnerving. But Cathal was no ordinary man. He would not be intimidated by anyone.

"Why have you not come to see me, Cathal?"

He sighed. "Arela, I don't have time for this."

"It's a simple question. I require a simple answer."

"There is nothing to say, Arela. You know that we cannot be together. I had made that perfectly clear from the very first day." He took a step closer to the Princess. "You are an exquisite work of art, you do not need a man like me."

"I will decide what I do or do not need, General." She closed the distance between them, her turquoise robes billowing around her. "There was a time when you worshiped the ground that I walked on."

"I have always respected you, as it should be. You are a formidable ally. A worthy diplomat. I would be a fool to not acknowledge such a brilliant personage."

Her molten eyes perused him from head to toe and back up, shimmering with delight as they returned to his face. "I always wondered, if Leila had not come in between us, would we have worked out?"

"Arela–" She silenced him with a finger to his lips.

"Shh. It's alright. I already know the answer." She lifted up on her toes, her hand going around Cathal's neck, pulling him down towards her. Leaning in, she murmured softly in his ear, "I have a little gift for you, General." The doors flew open. "An early wedding present, if you will."

Six guards marched into the Marble Pavilion, armed to the teeth. Lining up in a single row in front of the two of them, they formed an impenetrable wall to the other side entrance of the place. Those doors, too, swung open, revealing a very familiar silhouette.

"Now, say thank you like a good little boy," Arela purred, pulling his face down towards her, her lips grazing his mouth.

"What the fuck is this?" he hissed, a violent volcano threatening to erupt. Grabbing her by the shoulders, he shook her. "What did you do?"

"She helped me." Cathal's head snapped up at the voice. "After all, what are old friends for?" The figure stepped into the room.

Cathal's hands dropped from Arela's shoulders as the woman that he has been searching for for the past four months walked right up to him, grey eyes glued to his face.

"Hello, my love. Have you missed me?"

CHAPTER 28

"Oh, that's so pretty!" Princess Roesia exclaimed as she leaned over Duna's shoulder. "You're doing so well. My brother is going to be so proud of you."

Placing down her needle, Duna inspected her handiwork. She had decorated a square piece of ivory linen with gold and black thread that weaved through the light fabric, forming the intricate shapes of wildflowers and randomly shaped leaves. It was a piece which she had meticulously worked on for the past five days, determined to prove to herself that she was capable of mastering the art of embroidery.

"Shall we go for a walk? I hear the nightingales sing most beautifully at this time of the day."

"Yes, let's." Taking the Princess by the hand, the two women made their way down from the craft room to the royal gardens.

It had been an exceptionally warm day in the White City, summer still a month's time away. Epona had dressed Duna in a splendid moss colored dress that flowed around her as she moved, in complete contrast to the body hugging bodice and sleeves that seemed as if plastered onto her. Yellow dandelions were woven into her hair in an intricate braid that went like a crown around her head.

Roesia was dressed in an equally delightful pale pink chiffon gown that went down to her ankles, her hair let down to flow freely behind her. A delicate silver crown with matching gemstones was perched on top of her head of raven black tresses.

"Did you know that it is in fact the males that sing and not the females as people usually assume?" Duna shook her head. "Oh, yes. And only the unpaired males do so and *only* at night when few other birds are singing and therefore their song will be heard far and wide by any potential partners."

A loud whistling crescendo descended over the gardens, followed by a sweet symphony of trills and gurgles. Duna closed her eyes, soaking in the soulful melody.

"Isn't it marvelous?" Roesia beamed, those brilliant blue globes of hers lighting up as she listened to the brown bird's song. "It is said that the rose is it's fated mate and that the nightingale sings its sweet tune to woo the flower in hopes of winning it's affections."

Duna snorted. "Then perhaps someone should tell it that there is no such thing as fated mates. The bird is wasting it's time."

The Princess gasped, her hand flying to her chest. "Do not say such terrible things! They are extremely rare, yes, but that doesn't mean that they don't exist." She took Duna's hand in her own, enclosing it with her delicate fingers. "My parents were fated mates. There are songs written about their love." Her voice shook, murmuring softly, "My father, he was devastated when my mother died. I was only four at the time, but I will never forget the gloom that was etched into his very being. He was like a walking wraith. To this day, he has still not recovered from that tragedy."

"I am sorry for your loss. I realize that it has been decades, but I know that the pain never really leaves a person." Oh, how well she knew the living despair that still lingered in her broken heart.

Roesia nodded, her eyes downcast. "Madir had it worse. He was with her when she was killed. I think it traumatized him for life."

The two females made their way around the gardens, the nightingale's melody following them. The Sun had gone down over the horizon, leaving them in half shadows. After a while, the Princess turned to face her.

"There are many things that he hides, Duna. I don't believe it to be intentional. He has had a hard life, even as a prince. Much was expected of him and is still to this day. He is the only heir to our throne, the pressure to follow in our father's footsteps is immense."

"I can only imagine, those are some mighty big shoes to fill."

Roesia cocked her head as she took in Duna's worried look. "You know about my father." A slight smile bloomed on her radiant face. "I underestimated my brother. Good for him." She glanced up at the sky. "I suppose we'll be hearing wedding bells soon enough."

Duna choked on her own saliva. "Wedding bells? What are you talking about?"

"Oh, come now, you are practically living together, Duna. It is only the next natural step for a couple."

Laughing out loud, she tried to calm her racing heart. "You're getting ahead of yourself, Roesia. We've known each other a little over a month now, and we're not living together. I just happen to be in his room often, it's simpler that way."

"Like I said, you live with him."

"No, I just told you, I am there every night–"

"As you are there every morning and every afternoon when I come to visit." Roesia stopped her stroll, an amused look on her face. "And it is Madir's rooms where you will be returning to after we leave these gardens, is it not?"

"Well, yes, but–"

"There is no shame in admitting the obvious, Duna. I don't understand why you are so opposed to others being aware of your relationship. Everyone in the whole city already knows that you two are together. I don't see what the big deal is if you acknowledge the fact that you are no longer a free woman. There is no shame in being dependant on a man."

Placing her hands on her hips, Duna's blood simmered from irritation. "I will do no such thing, for it is not true. Nor am I ashamed of anything, I have done nothing wrong. However, I refuse to admit to something so ridiculous as to being reliant on your brother. I am my own person, not some mindless puppet that does as she's told."

"Is that why you wore that dress that you have on? Because you picked it out yourself?"

"What?" Duna glanced down at her soft green attire, then touching her hair realized that she had dandelions in it. "Epona kindly suggested it, I see no problem with humoring the old woman."

"Of course, which is why you also took up embroidery."

"You told me that it would please Madir to see me out of the training room for a change!"

"How very thoughtful of you," her voice dripping with sarcasm, Roesia stepped close to her. "Because you have always cared for my brother's wishes. And Epona's, and mine. Let's not forget that you haven't picked up a sword in the last three weeks either. How very kind of you to think of how it would appear to the general public if the Crown Prince's beloved was seen gallivanting around the kingdom in trousers with blades strapped to her side." She spoke lowly, eyes piercing Duna's. "It is most fortunate that my dear brother has found someone that is so easily malleable. Someone that will obey him without question. Tell me," she leaned in, whispering in her ear, "how does it feel to lose yourself? To know that every choice that you ever made was not, in fact, your own, but the result of another's masterful manipulation of your emotions?"

Duna blanched, her mind racing at the insinuations that were being thrown at her. She stepped back. "I refuse to carry on this conversation with you. I wish to return to my rooms."

"You mean, my brother's."

"No, I mean my own."

"You no longer have them, Duna. Or were you not aware that Madir had your things cleared out from there almost two weeks ago?"

She frantically tried to remember when the last time was that she had actually spent some time in her old chambers. "You're lying."

Roesia laughed, a loud boisterous sound coming out from her petite frame. "I would never dare make such a despicable remark were it not true."

Duna refused to believe it. She had to see for herself. "Prove it. Take me to my rooms."

"No."

"Then I demand permission to leave the gardens and go by myself."

"Are you hearing yourself, woman?" Roesia grabbed her by the shoulders, hissing in her face. "When have you ever asked for permission before? For anything, especially for leaving a situation that is making you uncomfortable?" She shook her. "Has my brother brainwashed you so thoroughly that you are willing to put yourself in harm's way just to please him?"

Shock washed over Duna as she stared at the Princess holding her hostage. She had never seen this side of the woman before, it was like she was a completely different person.

"Wake up already, before life does it for you!" Roesia shouted at her.

Duna pushed the Princess off of her, panic seizing her mind. She had to get out of there. Turning to the gardens' entrance, she bolted for her old rooms.

Running as fast as her legs would take her, she flew up the many steps that led to her suite. The halls were dark except for the occasional lantern that the servants had left burning during the night. Not having a clear view in the shadows, she didn't see her long gown as it slid under her slipper while she rushed to reach her doors.

Her sole caught on it, tearing the light green fabric down the side all the way to the middle of her thigh. In a matter of seconds, she face planted on the hard marble floors, her forehead connecting with the stone.

Pain lashed through her head, the sensation so great that she could only remain lying on the cold ground. *Get up, damn it. You are an embarrassment to yourself.*

She finally did so, not caring for the ugly bruise now blossoming in the middle of her forehead. Glancing down, she saw the floor littered with yellow dandelions. Her hair had fallen out from its braid, adding to her disheveled look.

Reaching her door finally, she pushed through, stopping dead in her tracks at the sight that stood before her.

Her room – or what was left of it – was completely void of any of her belongings. The closet lay wide open, not a single piece of clothing hanging in it. Her bed was stripped of all covers, not even a pillow decorating it once opulent bedding.

She flew into the bathroom then, expecting to find at least some of her old shampoos and hair oils that she had carefully carried with her all the way from Scythia all those months ago.

The cupboards and shelves stood empty. Not even her comb remained.

Devastated, she dropped down to the floor, tears welling up in her eyes. It was gone, all of her personal items – missing, as if her very presence had been erased from these very chambers. Her lavender and almond scented soaps, the ones which she had painstakingly saved up for over the span of an entire year – vanished.

Her heart ached, fingers of despair clenching around the bloody organ.

"Why are you on the ground, Duna? Get up," Madir's voice boomed from behind her. When she made no attempt at doing as told, he grabbed her by the arm, pulling her into a standing position.

"Don't touch me," fuming, she whipped her arm from his firm hold. "What have you done with my things?"

"I gave them away."

Rage consumed her, overriding her feelings of anguish. "You did what?"

"You have no need for them, I will give you whatever it is that you require."

A sudden urge to hit something shot through her. "You had no right to touch my things, let alone give them away without my permission."

He laughed. The arrogant prick actually laughed at her. "You seem to forget that I am the Crown Prince and heir to this kingdom. I do not need anyone's permission for anything, especially not yours."

"What the fuck is that supposed to mean?"

He pointed a callused finger at her. "Watch your mouth. That is not the way a lady speaks."

"Good thing then that I am not a lady."

Pinching the bridge of his nose, he inhaled then exhaled through his mouth, as if trying to calm himself. "Stop acting like a spoiled child and come to bed." Grabbing her arm again, he pulled her out of the bathing chamber.

She struggled against his iron grip, her feet not listening to her mind's command to cease all movement as she was dragged to her front door. His hold on her increased, pain lacing through her flesh. "You're hurting me."

Ignoring her, he continued to pull her along after himself, not once turning around to witness the state of agony that was clearly etched onto her face. She tried yanking her arm out of his clutches, but everything that she did was in vain.

"I'm not going with you," she said, putting all of her weight into her lower body, attempting to lower herself to the floor. "I will be sleeping in my old rooms from now on. Please inform the servants to bring up some bedding and a change of clothes."

He stepped up to her then, a deep scowl on his handsome face, as he took hold of her other arm as well. "Do you hear yourself?" he hissed. "The only bed that you will be sleeping in is mine."

"No."

His head came down then, his face barely an inch from her own. Growling, he snatched her up, "What did you just say to me?" Hatred simmered in his blue eyes, as if all sense of restraint had left him. "You dare disobey me?"

There had never been a moment in Duna's life when she had been truly afraid. Even when facing deadly mercenaries with blades that could cut her in two, she had not known true fear. Until that very moment, when she saw the pure rage that was reflected in the Prince's eyes. He appeared on the brink of a violent breakdown.

As if a single wrong word would send him over the edge.

"You cannot order me around. I am not your slave." She whimpered as his fingers dug into her flesh. "You're not yourself, Madir. Please, let me go. You're hurting me."

Without another word, he dragged her out of her old rooms and through the entire palace where only the guards seemed to be awake, not bothering to ease up on his severe grasp of her arm. She could feel his fingernails digging into her skin, breaking the surface as they prodded into her flesh.

They finally reached his private abode, the place where barely hours ago, Duna had found peace and joy. Now, as she was shoved into the room, she had the feeling of being in a cage, one where she was sure to wither in and die.

Releasing his firm grip on her, he locked the heavy wooden door behind him. She glanced down to the place where his fingers had been, gasping when she saw the bloody crescents embedded into her heavily bruising arm.

Her mouth hanging open from the devastating sight, she lightly touched the outlines of where his nails had left their mark. Tears of shock and anger formed in her glistening eyes as she caressed her agonizing flesh.

"What have you done?" she muttered low, her voice betraying her.

"You made me do this, Duna. If you had only listened to me, this never would have happened."

Her breath caught as she slowly willed her gaze to meet his. He stood towering over her, his massive build appearing to have grown in size over the course of their altercation. "You cannot truly believe that." When no answer came, she shouted at him, lifting her arm up to his face, "Look at what you did to me!"

"It will heal, it is only a scratch." He moved around her, taking his clothes off and throwing them onto a nearby armchair. "Get in bed, Duna."

The man was utterly insane. There was no other explanation for it. "You can't be serious." He continued with undressing, not bothering with what she was saying. "This was a mistake." Turning, she bolted for the front door.

In a matter of seconds, he was on top of her. Hooking his arms around her middle, he lifted her up. "Where do you think you're going, hmm?" he rumbled in her ear, his voice dripping with disdain, "Do you want me to murder someone as punishment for your little show of disobedience tonight?"

The space around them blackened, as if a shadow was passing over the brightly lit Moon. Thrashing in his arms, Duna tried with all her might to get out of his punishing hold. He threw her on the bed, looming over her as he started to undress her.

"What are you doing?" she demanded, panic setting in as he began to lower her bodice over her upper body. She slapped his hands then, scrambling up the bed until she reached the headboard. He grabbed her calf and yanked her back down to where he was kneeling on the bed.

"I asked you nicely. Since you didn't listen, then we're going to do it my way." Hooking his fingers in her neckline, he ripped the light fabric off of her body, exposing her undergarments beneath. "Shall I do the same with these, or are you going to be a good girl and take them off yourself?"

Her throat dried up. This could not be happening. This had to be a nightmare. Her body shaking, she pleaded with the man that she had once believed to be misunderstood and hurting from the childhood loss of his mother. "You wouldn't, I know you're not capable of such an atrocity, Madir. Please, let me go back to my rooms, we can talk calmly about everything tomorrow."

His indicolite eyes pierced her as he silently thought over her offer. Hope bloomed in Duna's chest, the delicate bud beginning to take root in her breaking heart.

"No."

All shattered in her as that two letter word left his beguiling lips. It crushed all feelings of good in her, all the care and devotion that she had began to develop for the heir of Morinya going up in smoke.

A violent storm erupted outside, the wind blowing leaves and debris onto the glass panels of the high arched windows. All light vanished, as if the very Moon and all the brightly shining stars had been sucked out of the night sky.

Feelings of repulsion consumed her as she gazed up at the face which she once deemed so devastatingly stunning. "Get off of me." The man didn't budge. "I said, move!" She pounded onto his chest, giving it her all as his substantial body crushed her beneath him.

He tried grabbing her wrists, but to no avail. She was simply too fast for him. Her training kicked in, all those long hours that she had spent for the past five years drilling herself to near death finally showing its face.

Locking her legs around his waist, she head butted him in the nose, blood flying out from his nostrils and onto her naked skin.

"Fucking hell," he cursed as he lifted himself off of her just enough to give Duna enough space to slide out from underneath him. Taking her chance, she grabbed his shirt, pulling it on as she raced for the door.

Turning the knob, she was hit with a fresh wave of panic when the wood didn't budge. It was locked. *Where the fuck is the key?* Shaking the handle again, she realized that she was caged in. There was no getting out of there.

"Looking for this?" Madir's deep voice taunted in her ear as a gold key appeared in her peripheral vision.

She spun around with the intention of negotiating with the male for it, when his fingers locked around her throat, squeezing it like a vice. Her vision blurred as she pounded on his hand, the images in front of her going hazy.

"Time to go to sleep, little warrior," Madir purred as her eyelids slid closed and her entire world descended into darkness.

CHAPTER
29

The sweetest melody swept through her mind, enveloping her in feelings of warmth and pure bliss. It filled her with a sense of peace, as if that simple whistling crescendo had the healing powers of the gods themselves.

A tear slid down Duna's cheeks as she listened to the nightingale sing his heart out to the shining Moon. How oblivious he was to her state of despair, to her spirit that was slowly shriveling away.

As she lay in the dark, her eyelids pressed tightly together, she failed to witness the disheveled state of the once beautiful man that was sitting in the armchair by her side, observing her in bed.

She didn't see the dark circles under his eyes, the black beard that had grown out from his previous light stubble. Nor did she notice his bloodshot gaze, the once brilliant tourmaline color faded to a dull hue, as if void of all life and joy.

No, Duna would remain oblivious to it all, for the soulful symphony that swept across the vast royal chambers invaded her senses, holding her captive to its world shattering tune.

"Madir," a female's voice cut through the haze, "we must get going. It has been days, the soldiers are getting restless."

Silence, and then, "I can't leave her like this."

"There is nothing that you can do, she'll wake up once her mind has healed."

"I need to speak to her, I have to make her understand."

The woman sighed. "You have to bear the consequences of your actions, brother. It is too late to feel remorse now."

"I swear to you, I wasn't myself. I would never have hurt her, Roesia," the Prince's voice broke as he spoke into the night. "When she refused to come with me, I panicked. I didn't know what to do, how to make her see sense."

"Be a man and own up to your actions." A slight note of – irritation? – entered the Princess' otherwise calm tone as she reprimanded the heir. "Time will tell what the outcome of your recklessness shall be, but now you must do your duty to our kingdom."

He lowered his head between his legs, pulling at the strands of his long raven locks. Shooting up from the seat, he came to kneel at Duna's side by the bed. "Please, forgive me, little warrior." He took her hand in his own, beseeching her, "I will do anything that you ask of me, *anything*, just please, come back to me." He kissed her hand, inhaling her scent. "Wake up, my love, let me see your beautiful eyes."

The nightingale's song swept over her, blurring out the Prince's words of sorrow. *What a lovely melody.* She imagined herself soaring on a pair of magnificent white wings through the vast blue sky, reaching the heavens on Shah's powerful back.

Where was the king of the harpies now? Was he roaming free, blazing towards the Moon with his fellow raptors?

How Duna wished to fly with him. If she could ask for anything from the gods, it would be that. To see that mighty bird of prey one last time before she departed from this dismal world.

"Madir," Roesia came up behind him, placing her hand on his shoulder, "we must go. Now."

The Prince kissed her hand one last time before finally standing up and releasing it. Gazing down at Duna, he pledged to the void, "I will make things right."

The doors shut behind the two royals, leaving Duna alone in the gloom filled chambers. Only the sound of the nightingale filling the air around her.

A beam of silver radiated onto her closed eyelids, stirring her awake from her deep slumber. It engulfed her, spreading over her entire being until she finally willed herself to open her eyes.

The shape of the Full Moon greeted her through the glass of the high arched window that was situated right in front of the substantial bed in which she lay unmoving. The massive luminous globe shone down on her, luring her in with its white glow. It called to her as she focused her eyes on the captivating planet before her.

Her thoughts wondered to that terrible night, when she had seen Madir's dark side. The one that she had believed to be nonexistent.

She sobbed, the tears coming in rivers as she remembered the panic and absolute fear that had washed over her as he had torn her clothes off from her body. Would he have violated her, had she not managed to get away? She couldn't bring herself to believe it.

Glancing down at her arm, she realized that the crescent shaped marks were barely visible, reduced to pink scars. How much time had she spent asleep? It must have been at least ten days for her skin to show so little of the previous bruises and scabs that had decorated her flesh from that night.

A new wave of anxiety took a hold of her body as sudden realization hit Duna – she was completely alone. Wheezing from horror, her body shaking from the hysteria that was threatening to consume her, she bolted from the bed.

Her legs gave out underneath her from having been in a horizontal position for almost two weeks with barely any food going into her atrophying muscles. She lay on the cold ground, her silk robes spread out around her as she struggled to stand. *Get up, damn it.*

She crawled to the terrace doorway then, alarm causing her mind to race as she had a new thought – who was to get her out of this hopeless predicament in which she currently found herself in?

You don't need anybody, Duna. You have always been enough. And she had. She would be so now, too.

Arriving at the closed glass doors, she reached her hand up, her fingers latching onto the intricately carved knob to pull herself up. Using the last atom of strength she turned it, the door swinging open violently as she rested her upper body on it's panel. By some miracle she remained standing, barely holding on as a light breeze swept over her, awakening her drowsy senses.

Cursing out loud, she began to walk. Step by step, she gradually made it out onto the wide terrace, the Moon shining down on her, as if encouraging her to keep moving.

Suddenly, the wind picked up, a wild torrent of air attacking her from all sides. Her hair was whipped up, the long chocolate strands dancing around her like brown snakes. Goosebumps covered her bare skin as her nightgown became plastered to her frail body, chills spreading over her as icy cold air charged through the night.

She was thrown about like a leaf, her human flesh nothing compared to the raw power of nature. Darkness descended around her, as if the Moon itself with all the accompanying stars had been sucked into a black hole, no light remaining in the sky.

Closing her eyes, she surrendered to the fervent emotions flowing through her. Fear and helplessness turned to sorrow and despair, leaving her body in streams of moisture, cleansing her insides like holy water.

The agony which she had felt when first her parents had died and then her grandmother returned, reminding her that she would always be at the mercy of those painful memories. Like a vicious concoction they meshed together with the fresh dread that swept over her entire system whenever she thought of Madir.

As if in mocking, the storm raged on, proving to her just how feeble and inconsequential her very presence was. It was humbling to be placed into perspective, to become aware that no weapons of man, no level of skill or brilliant mind could outmatch the ruthlessness of nature itself.

A shrill scream cut through the night.

Her eyes snapped open. She knew that sound.

Glorious white wings appeared over the horizon, illuminating the dark sky. They flapped wildly as the mighty bird caught sight of her, the sheer power of its movements sending it blazing at the speed of light towards an awaiting Duna.

In a matter of seconds, the King of the Snow Harpies was in front of her, his majestic wings spread out as if protecting her. He let out another short shriek as she made her way towards him.

"Shah," she cried, her legs shaking from exertion, "Oh, Shah!" Throwing herself at him, she disappeared into his thick plumage, burying her face in the soft down. "I've missed you, my friend."

The massive raptor enveloped her in his wings, cocooning her in under his sharp beak. Another scream echoed from above them, joined by a chorus of equally lethal sounds.

Shah nudged her with his wing, pulling Duna out of her trance. Lowering it to the ground, his blood red eyes piercing her through, he demanded she climb on his back.

Without a word she obliged, already in tune with the menacing bird of prey from the many secret adventures that they had during her short stay at Morinya. She had never indulged anyone about her private meetings with him, had covertly kept them to herself.

Not wasting a moment, Shah spread his wings wide and together, they soared into the sky, leaving the White Palace and it's unsuspecting inhabitants behind.

She awoke to the sound of rushing water. Opening her eyes, she was struck by the fact that she was no longer surrounded by snow capped mountains. Gone were the white city walls and splendid spires of the White Palace.

Glancing down she realized that she was still perched on top of Shah. She must have fallen asleep while they were airborne. "You silly bird, why didn't you wake me?" A chirrup of noises came in response as she slid down from his back. "And how am I to get back to Morinya now?"

She gasped when the thought hit her. She had made it out of the White City. *I'm free.* Her heart raced as a wave of relief washed over her. She wouldn't have to face Madir now, wouldn't have to relive that terrifying night again.

Tears welled up in her eyes for the hundredth time since waking up in those dreadful chambers. *For fuck's sake, stop crying.* Wiping the moisture from her face, she took a deep breath. There was no point in pondering on the past; she had to look forward from now on, had to figure out what she was going to do, how she was going to find some form of human civilization.

Glimpsing around, Duna saw a thick wall of lush vegetation blocking her way forward. The contrast was so stark, as if an invisible barrier had been placed on the border between two very different climates. Behind her were the grassy fields and high rising mountain peaks of Nissa, while in front – *the wild jungles of Baqar.*

"What did you do?" she murmured to the King of the Snow Harpies, who was observing her as she perused her surroundings. "You want me to go to Navajo?" He shrieked. "What's in Navajo, Shah?"

No reply came. His crimson gaze was laser focused on her, silently communicating his intention for her to go into those intimidating trees. The mighty bird took a step towards her, nudging her from behind with his sharp beak. When she made no attempt at moving forward he did it again.

"Alright, I get it, stop pushing me." She closed her eyes, inhaling a lungful of crisp morning air. This was it. Her chance at a new life.

Soft feathers brushed her cheek. She pressed herself into them, the addictive scent of the raptor that had possibly saved her very life invading her senses. "Thank you, my dear friend," her voice broke, "I will never forget you." Tearing herself from his grasp, she ran for the thick jungle foliage.

Her heart shattered into million little fragments the further she descended into the vegetation and away from her loyal companion. She dared not turn around lest she change her mind at the sight of the awaiting harpy.

Ear-splitting screams cut through the air, followed by a symphony of blood chilling screeches. Her head snapped up to a patch of blue sky peeking through the dense canopy. Magnificent white shapes soared over her, like brilliant pale ghosts haunting the lands from above.

We will meet again. She promised to herself. *Whatever it takes.*

Twilight descended upon her as she slowly wound her way through the jungles of Baqar. It had been days since she had departed Nissa. Not having any supplies on her, she had managed with wild fruit and the occasional stream that she happened to stumble upon.

She was lucky, she supposed, to be lost in a kingdom where food and water was abundant. Where the climate was humid and hot, making her runaway choice of clothing ideal. *Petra would be so proud if she could see me now.* She snorted. Then stopped dead in her tracks, her hands flying to her head.

Petra. She was in Navajo.

Duna had been so consumed with Madir and their altercation that she had completely forgotten about her sister in arms. Her mind had falsely placed her back in Scythia with Captain Moira and the rest of her legion.

Then another realization hit her. Cathal was also there. With his Princess. *Fucking perfect.* Just what she needed – more drama.

Sighing heavily, she continued with her journey. Maybe the General had returned to Scythia once he had been reunited with his beloved, it wasn't so far fetched. After all, what business did he have in the capital of another kingdom when the sole purpose for him visiting it in the first place had been to find his betrothed?

It doesn't matter. You're going to stay away from him either way. She was over men. Especially devastatingly breathtaking ones, ones that would only leave her in shambles, her soul shattered and broken. Cathal was the very epitome of that type of man. Madir didn't even graze the tip of the iceberg when it came to the power that the General had over her.

Her heart raced as an image of him looming over her cloaked in shadows blazed through her mind. She had been having that same eerie dream for the past four weeks, one that felt so real, as if it wasn't a figment of her imagination but a very real memory looming in the back of her subconsciousness.

She could swear on her life that she still felt the soft caresses of his black tendons on her supple skin, could hear his velvety smooth voice in her mind as he murmured sweet promises into her ear.

That vision had haunted her relentlessly. It was like a fifth limb, draining the blood from her organs but completely useless in the grand scheme of things.

Like poison Cathal's essence slowly spread through Duna, affecting her entire being. Her feet planted firmly on the lush Baqarian earth, her body refused to move forward. Her lungs began to hyperventilate, sweat breaking over her already moist skin. *What is happening to me?* The beating organ in her chest cavity increased it's pace, beating frantically to the point where she thought it would explode.

She needed to get help. How far was she from Navajo?

Duna didn't even know if she was heading in the right direction. For all she knew she could be walking in circles, doomed to roam the wild jungles until the end of her days.

A shock of black flew past the line of trees to her left. Her head snapped around, her brain zeroing in on the potential danger as her eyes focused on the looming shapes in the thick vegetation. A rustling came behind her then, igniting her flight or fight reaction.

She bolted, her long chocolate strands trailing behind her. Her bare feet scraping against the jungle ground, cutting her feet as she flew from her invisible assailant deeper into the unknown.

After what appeared hours to Duna, she finally slowed, all signs of the threat seemingly gone. Breathing heavily, she came to a stop, her chest heaving as she rested her hands on her narrow waist.

A shape emerged then from behind the tree line in front of her, causing her breath to catch as she caught sight of the familiar silhouette.

"Hello, Duna," the voice taunted, "You didn't really think that you could actually get away from me, now did you?"

All blood drained from her face as she backed up. "No." It wasn't possible. "How are you here?"

The figure chuckled, chills shooting down Duna's spine. "Hasn't anyone ever told you? I always catch my prey, darling."

CHAPTER
30

He sat at the extensive wooden table filled to the brink with opulent foods of every texture and flavor imaginable to the human mind. He had lost his appetite long before Leila and him had been led to the vast dining hall where they had been ushered to sit side by side as guests of honor close to the royal Achaz family.

Cathal had refused to share a room with the Princess upon her return. He had his suspicions about her mysterious disappearance all those months ago, and until he had the whole situation cleared up he was reluctant to go anywhere near her. Even the current seating arrangements left a sour taste in his mouth.

Something was terribly off.

He could feel it in his bones, this constant nagging sensation that wouldn't ease up. It kept tugging at his insides, twisting his guts to the point where he thought he would take a knife and stab himself just to relieve the constantly building pressure.

It had started a few nights upon Leila's return. Out of the blue, a sharp pain had first zipped through his mind, causing him to drop the spear which he had been using to train in the yard. Just as quickly it had disappeared, leaving a somewhat dumbstruck Cathal to halfheartedly finish up his sparring session.

The sharp pain had later grown into an oppressing headache which he felt even now as he sat staring at his empty plate. His whole forehead felt like it was on fire, as if his brain was boiling to mush inside his skull.

A hand grazed his thigh. Picking it up with his own, he wordlessly moved it back to it's owners side.

"Cathal, please, you have been avoiding me since my return," Leila's soft voice spoke in his ear as she returned her delicate hand to rest on his leg. "I've missed you."

He said nothing as he stared ahead, his gaze landing on the almost full Moon shining brilliantly through the open pillared terrace of the vast dining hall. It captivated him, this brightly lit globe in the sky. Held him prisoner to its ethereal presence.

Leila's hand moved up his strong thigh, her long fingers grazing the outline of his muscles over his pants. He grabbed her hand before it could reach his groin, pressing it firmly. "This is not the time nor the place."

"It never stopped you before, my love," she murmured as she leaned over to his side, resting her chin on his broad shoulder as her grey eyes pierced him. "Why haven't you come to me, Cathal? I have waited patiently for you for the past three nights." She slipped herself out from his firm hold. "Three agonizingly long nights, where I had to use my fingers to bring myself pleasure." Her hand cupped his bulge, massaging it lightly. "I haven't felt you inside of me for so long."

His unyielding grip flew to her lithe wrist, tightening around it like a lethal vice, stopping her persistent ministrations. "Do not–" he threw her hand back onto her lap, "–touch me." Turning towards her, he smoldered, "You have yet to explain to me where you have been for the past four months."

A flash of hurt passed over her graceful features. "I don't know what you mean. I'd been kidnapped, held hostage in random places across the Continent." She turned her face forward, her eyes not meeting his questioning gaze, her chest heaving.

"So you say," he hissed, "yet I find it hard to believe. I have searched everywhere for you, Leila. *Everywhere*. Even places where it wouldn't be humanly possible to reside, and yet, my men and I managed to scour them."

The Princess took a sip of wine, her voice turning to ice, "We shall continue this conversation later on General, when there aren't so many ears listening in."

"I don't give a shit who's listen–" Sharp pain laced his arm, cutting off his words. He forced his eyes shut, clenching his teeth in agony. It was like five serrated knives were being pushed into his skin simultaneously, mercilessly impaling themselves in the flesh.

All of a sudden, the sensation disappeared. *Bloody hell.*

Sweat broke along his spine, his heart beating frantically. He shot from his seat, not caring for the strange looks that he was getting from the many guests in attendance.

"Where are you going?" Leila demanded, glancing at the staring courtiers. "The feast is in our honor. As your fated mate, I forbid you from leaving me here alone."

"No, it's in *your* honor. I'm not the one who's returned from the dead." Not waiting for a reply, Cathal's wide strides took him out of the dining hall and directly to one of the more secluded luxurious gardens at the side of the palace. Unbuttoning his shirt collar, he breathed a sigh of relief as fresh air entered his straining lungs.

He cracked his thick neck then as his muscles began to go into lockdown from the sudden onslaught of tension. His powerful body pulsed as an intense need to defend himself overtook him.

Trepidation washed over him, his mind going into a frenzy as he fought an internal battle with his conscience. *What the fuck is happening to me?*

Dense shadows erupted from his over strung body, engulfing him and the lush gardens in an unyielding membrane of black tendrils.

Collapsing onto his knees, he roared, his hands gripping his throbbing head. He clenched his teeth as tens upon hundreds of thousands of sharp needles stabbed his inflamed skin, his bones stretching to the point where he thought his skull would explode.

A thick veil of gloom descended upon him. His pupils dilated, bleeding over onto his irises, turning the entire organ the color of the darkest night. His vision blurred, then turned laser focused as his eyes adjusted to his pitch black surroundings.

Throbbing ebony flames radiated from him as he straightened to his full intimidating height. His fingers elongated, becoming razor sharp claws. His clothing was shred to strips as his muscles inflated, his impressive body growing even more menacing in stature.

Stretching his limbs, he smirked, satisfaction filling his system. *It seems you've grown sloppy, brother.*

Grinning widely, he spread his arms out. Murky tendons lashed out towards the luminous Moon, stretching over it across the night sky like a dense mesh of interlacing latticework, blocking out it's heavenly glow. In a matter of seconds, it was completely obliterated from view, as if the very planet itself had been wiped out from existence.

Cathal stood admiring his handiwork. He felt as if something was still missing. Then he remembered. *Polaris.* His gaze slid to that ever shining point in the sky. *Let's see just how badly you've slipped up.*

Chuckling to himself, he closed his eyes. Inhaling a deep breath, he lifted his strong hands to the heavens. A surge of wind burst from his vibrating body as he stirred the currents of energy with his mind. It picked up, turning into a violent concoction of dread and gloom.

Raw fury simmered in his blood, taking over his senses. A need for vengeance filled his blackening heart.

His eyes snapped open.

Honing in on the North Star, he channeled his rage toward that one being who's betrayal had devastated him the most. His gaze unwavering, his power radiating from him, Cathal watched as the star's brilliant white light dimmed in the sky, then was completely extinguished.

As if sent into his mind by the gods themselves, Duna's stunning face flashed before his pitch black eyes, cutting through his unforgiving wrath. Except her lovely image was no longer filled with joy and peace, but alarm and terror.

Panic seized his pounding chest as he witnessed a mask of horror slide over her agony stricken features. His hold on Polaris slipped as his power began to fade.

Something was wrong, his little monster was in danger.

Her frightened face disappeared just as quickly as it had shown itself to him, leaving him stunned and desperate for more.

His body soared into overdrive. He bellowed as a blazing inferno erupted inside of him, threatening to burn everything in its path. Cathal knew without a doubt who had sent him a vision of Duna. There was only one being in existence who had the power needed to break through his mental shields.

Releasing his grip completely from the heavens, he withdrew the enveloping shadows from Polaris. *Let this be a warning to you, brother. If you so much as look her way, I will obliterate your precious kingdom.* No one would be safe from him then. He would turn the entire universe to ashes for her.

His abilities spent, he returned to his mortal form. It would be time before they recharged again, but he would be patient. Something had caused a surge in energy in the magnetic fields surrounding the planets, affecting his brother's hold on his powers. Which meant that it wasn't infallible.

Cathal would figure it all out eventually, like he always did. After all, he had a surplus amount of time at his disposal. His only issue now was getting to his little monster and helping her.

Turning around, he charged back into the dining hall of the Grand Palace. Taking a guard's robes from him and after inspecting the many seated guests, his eyes finally landed on the one who's skill of acquiring delicate information he currently needed the most.

He marched right up to the spy master. "Lovas." The menacing man turned to him. "Come with me. Now." Following Cathal out of the opulent space, they came to a spot in a secluded part of the open pillared terrace. "I need you to send a bird to Morinya."

"Has something happened?" The man looked him over in his strange attire.

"You're going to tell me. How fast can you get me the details?"

Bror contemplated on the question. "I can get a hawk airborne as soon as I write up the missive, an hour perhaps."

"You've got half of that." He stepped up to the male, his eyes of green aventurine boring into him. "No one is to know about this, do you understand?"

"Of course, General." Bror flew down the many steps leading to one of the many royal aviaries, not wasting a single precious moment. After a while, Cathal watched as a formidable bird of prey soared from the roof top towards Nissa.

Clenching his fists at his sides, he let out a strained breath. Now all he had to do was wait.

Hours passed before Cathal finally received some news from Morinya. His long time companion rushed into his chambers, not bothering with knocking, a parchment clenched tightly in his hand. He was pale as a ghost, breathing heavily as he appraised the General on his covered balcony.

Cathal ground his teeth in annoyance. "Are you going to stand there and stare at me or are you going to tell me what you found out?"

"I–I don't know how to say this." The otherwise menacing male appeared like a scared child, as if he was dreading the next words that would have to come out of his mouth.

Cold washed over Cathal. "What is it?"

"It's, uh–" Bror cleared his throat, not meeting his eyes. "It's Duna. She's, uh, she's–"

"For fuck's sake! Spit it out already!"

"She appears to be in some sort of a state of vegetation, General." He winced when he saw the murderous look on Cathal's face. His voice shook from anxiety, "They don't know what's wrong with her. One minute she was fine, the next she fell unconscious and refused to wake up."

"Are you hearing yourself? A person doesn't simply just fall into a coma." Anger shot through him as he imagined his little monster lying in some strange bed, alone, unprotected. "What aren't you telling me, Bror?"

The man swallowed. "No–Nothing. I've told you everything." He held out the parchment. "Here, have a look for yourself."

Snatching the paper from his feeble grip, Cathal read over the few lines of words that were inked onto it. "This is all that you've discovered? No cause for her ailment, no details about her whereabouts prior to blacking out, no mention of names as to who was with her at the time?" He threw the small piece of fabric at Bror's face. "You're hiding something from me."

The heavily pierced male shook his head, backing up as Cathal sauntered toward him. His eyes burrowed into Bror, like a predator locking in it's prey.

"Please, General, I don't know anything, I swear–"

"Do you know what they do to traitors here in the City of Lights?" His voice dropped low, dripping with disdain. "They string them up by their ankles and leave them hanging from wooden beams in the middle of the jungle."

Bror whimpered, Cathal's foreboding presence towering over him.

"Have you ever seen a vulture eat an animal's carcass? No? He picks off every miniscule piece of flesh until there is nothing but the skeleton remaining of the dead animal." He leaned down, tilting his head as he inspected the assassin. "Do you know how traitors get eaten? Their blood is first sucked dry from their cavities, and then, when there is no juices left in their system, the creatures take their sharp claws–" he scraped his nails on the side of Bror's face, directly under his right eye where his scar lay, "–and flay the skin from the person's still breathing body, until only the meat remains. The beasts then take their turn tearing the limbs apart until only the feet remain, dangling from the ropes with which they were tied with. Those they leave for last, roasting in the oppressing sun, where larva and all kinds of insects make their home in the flesh until they, too, are ready to be devoured. Not even a single shard of bone is left behind by the time the jungle critters are through."

He circled around the shaking male. "Are you lying to me?"

"No, never. General, please, I swear to all the gods that I have told you everything that I know."

He contemplated on the man's words. "See, I still don't believe you."

Bror swallowed hard, his Adam's apple moving up and down in succession. "Please–"

"He speaks the truth." Both males' heads whipped around at the voice. "Leave us."

Cathal waited until the spy master closed the door behind him. "What is the meaning of this?" How dare she interfere with his orders.

"I forbade him from disclosing anything else other than what he already told you." Leila's long silver locks cascaded down her back as she strolled towards him, putting more sway into her hips than was normal. "You have no business inquiring about some soldier that has chosen to remain in the White City. Especially, since you and I are betrothed. It does not look good in front of the people, Cathal." Reaching him, she placed her arms around his neck, locking her fingers behind his head. "I finally have you all to myself, my love."

"Leila, we need to talk." He gripped her arms gently, attempting to lower them from his body, but she wouldn't budge.

"No, we need to fuck," she pulled his face down towards her, gazing erotically into his stunning eyes, "I want you to rip into me like a wild animal. Make me beg for mercy." She kissed him, her lips melding against his own unresponsive ones.

"Stop–" he straightened up, pushing her away. "I can't do this."

"Of course you can. I'm to be your wife soon." She hooked her arms around his neck once more, preparing to launch herself at him all over again.

"No, that's not–" She licked his lips. He snapped, grabbing her by the shoulders, "Just listen to me, god damn it!"

"What is the matter with you?"

"This was long overdue–" He fervently rubbed his face with his palms, apprehension and guilt blooming in his chest.

"What are you talking about?" Her eyes went wide. "Cathal?"

"Leila.." Trailing off, he sighed. "Come here." Leading her by the hand, they sat down in the two armchairs by the open doors of the balcony. "We have known each other for more than twenty years. I will always be grateful for you, for the love that you've shown me. For everything that we've been through together. You have been a true friend to me, and that will never change. Whatever happens between us from now on, I will always keep you safe."

"I don't understand. What are you saying? Do you not want me anymore?" Leila's eyes glazed over, her voice barely audible, "But, we're fated mates. We belong together."

"Princess," he softly caressed her hand, doing his best to not upset her even further, "sometimes even Fate gets things wrong."

"But – how is this possible? Mates can't turn their backs on each other. Their souls are bound together for all eternity."

"I don't think that that's how it works, Leila." He gently tucked a stray piece of silver hair behind her ear. "A mate can be rejected, it's not that unheard off. It would only lead to the bond eventually dying out, maybe only a trace of it remaining in the subconsciousness of the two people involved."

"I don't want us to be a distant memory in my mind. My heart wouldn't be able to bare it."

"Princess.." he kneeled in front of her, gazing up into her moist eyes, "I know that this is hard for you. It hasn't been easy for me, either. I have tried to dismiss this foreboding feeling that I kept having in my gut ever since we became betrothed. It became unbearable at one point, so much so that I had to leave you to clear my head. Then when I thought that I would finally get some answers, you vanished without a trace."

"I was taken hostage, Cathal."

"And I will find your assailants, if that is the case." He shook his head. "It doesn't really even matter at this point anymore. Your absence made me realize that we're two very different people, Leila. We've grown apart. It wouldn't be fair for me to keep dragging you down with me, you deserve better. A man that will cherish you and be grateful for everything that you are. One that will value everything that you give him."

"I don't want a better man. I want you, Cathal. You're good enough for me." She slid down the chair onto the floor beside him, her pale blue gown spreading out around her like waves.

"You shouldn't have to settle, Princess." His eyes softened, admiring the being that he thought he had loved with all of his heart. "You are a stunning woman, any man would be lucky to have you. I am not that man."

Tears formed in her large eyes, threatening to overflow as she stared at him. "Is there someone else?" A deep frown formed between her eyebrows. "Have you found another woman? Is that it?"

"This has nothing to do with anyone else except me. My feelings have changed."

"You're lying. I could always tell when you were lying to me."

"I don't want to be cruel towards you. Please don't do this."

"Just tell me the fucking truth then!" She shouted at him, bolting upright. Grabbing a vase she threw it at the wall. "Is there someone else? Is that why you're breaking off our engagement and leaving me out in the cold?"

He stood up, anger simmering in his veins. "Do not test me, Princess. I have tried to be honest with you, to let you down gently, to not drag you along like most bastards would do just because you're royalty and because of the free pussy that they would get from you. Do not make me regret telling you."

She screamed at him, her face a deep scowl, "Damn you! I have done everything for you! I changed myself, just so that you would accept me, just so that you would love me like I've always loved you. From the very first day, I have only ever done what you demanded of me."

"What the fuck does that mean?" His voice dropped as he froze, observing her as she ranted on.

"It means that I've suppressed myself, my needs and wants, *everything*, just so that you wouldn't be displeased with me!"

"I never asked that from you."

She laughed then, an ironic sound coming out of her down turned lips. "I did it because I wished it so. I didn't want my mate to be disappointed in the woman that Fate chose for him."

He had a sudden urge to strangle the woman. Humans and their idiotic need to live up to their ridiculous concept of destiny. He tried taming down his anger. "You should never have to change who you are for anyone, Leila, especially not me. I would have accepted you the way you are."

"Yes, well, I guess we'll never know now, will we?" Inhaling a strangled breath, she wiped the moisture from her eyes. "Is it Arela? Are you replacing me with her?"

Unbelievable. "I know that it will take some time getting used to our new circumstances. I shall accompany you back to Scythia, should you require it, to break the news to your father."

"What news?"

Pinching the bridge of his nose, he answered through pressed teeth, "Leila, do not pretend to not understand what I'm talking about. It is beneath you to play these games."

"I have not agreed to terminate our betrothal, General."

"I am not asking for your agreement. I am letting you know that we will not be getting married, Leila. It is not negotiable."

"No." Stepping up to him, she began to smooth out the nonexistent wrinkles from his shoulders. "You will remain my lover and my future husband, and we *will* be getting married. You are clearly not in you right mind. The four months that we have spent apart has left you confused. I will give you the time that you need to rectify that."

Grabbing her wrists, he leaned down until their faces were an inch apart. "You can give me a fucking eternity, I would still feel this way. Do not make me say things that I will later regret. Walk away with your dignity intact."

"I am a princess," she seethed, pulling her hands out of his tight hold, "You do not get to walk away from me like I'm some lowly commoner." Not waiting for a reply, she stormed out of his chambers, leaving a frustrated Cathal alone with a new unsolvable dilemma on his hands.

He stood in the middle of his opulent suite, his hands resting on his hips, his head bowed down as he contemplated on his next move. *Bror.* He had completely forgotten about the male.

Bolting through his front doors, he searched for the spy master. *Come on, where are you?* A shock of silver caught his eye as he flew through the substantial royal grounds. There, just behind one of the palm trees, he caught sight of him. He was talking to someone in the dark.

Cathal slowly crept up to the pair, keeping to the shadows as he did so.

"You have to tell him. If he finds out you're hiding something, he's going to flay you alive." A female spoke, keeping her voice low. "Why didn't you just give him the rest of it?"

"I would have had the Princess not caught me. She took the other part of the parchment with her." The man sighed, obviously distraught. "What the fuck do I do now, Petra?"

Da'Nyla. Of course. Shaking his head, Cathal stepped out into the light. "You're going to tell me everything, and you're going to do it right now." His eyes blazed with fury as he inspected the two scheming individuals.

"General," Petra gasped, all color draining from her face.

He raised a callused finger, "Do not speak until I've given you permission. And you," he turned to the spy master, "you have three seconds to tell me what it is that you're keeping from me before I feed you to the beasts. One."

"I can't–" He glanced at Petra, pleading with her to help him out.

"Two."

Blanching, Bror stuttered, "I– I had no choice, she made me keep my mouth shut. I swear–"

"Three."

"Wait! Fine, I'll tell you everything!" Cathal lifted a thick eyebrow, waiting for him to continue. "Duna was with Prince Madir when she lost consciousness." Breathing heavily, he bent at the waist, his arms resting on his knees. "Oh, gods, I'm going to be sick."

"And?"

"And he was seen dragging her through the palace before that."

I am going to murder that little fucker. "Did he hurt her?" he demanded, his face a deep scowl, barely keeping his rage from boiling over.

"I don't have that information. Everyone is keeping their lips shut, no one knows what really happened." Turning a sickly shade of grey, the spy master hurled his dinner onto the grass.

"Take him to a healer, Da'Nyla."

Cathal watched, unfazed, as the pair limped to the closest gate. He had expended his abilities tonight. It would be days before he could turn to shadows again. But he would be patient, he would wait until the time was right.

Closing his eyes, he inhaled the humid Baqarian air, his lungs expanding from anticipation. Grinning, he walked back to his private suite.

He had a princeling to catch.

CHAPTER 31

The Full Moon hung low in the brightly lit Baqarian sky. Millions of countless stars speckled the night, shining down on the expansive jungles of the eastern kingdom.

More than a week had passed since the General had attempted to break off his engagement to the Princess of Tyros, but to no avail. She still behaved as if they were betrothed, not bothering with knocking whenever he was in his chambers, or even worse, joining him in the water when he was bathing.

It was grating on Cathal's nerves.

He refused to have any sexual relations with Leila. It felt like it would be a tragic betrayal not only to himself, but to his ever-growing feelings for Duna.

He couldn't get her beautiful face out of his mind. Her addictive scent was impressed into his brain. He craved to touch her, to stroke those maddening curves and hollows that were made for his abled hands. To taste, at last, those delicious lips of hers. To hear her scream his name out loud for the whole world to finally know, once and for all, who she belonged to.

She was his, even now, while she wasted her precious time with that arrogant prick of a male. Cathal would wait for his little monster for as long as it took her to realize that her place was by his side. And once she surrendered herself to him wholly, he would never let her go again.

She would never be free of him, for all eternity.

He had tried to be understanding of Leila's feelings, to give her the necessary time to adjust to their new situation. But he'd had enough. It was long overdue that the princess, finally, once and for all, understood that she was no longer the woman of his heart.

He hadn't received any more news about Duna. It was as if everything was being kept under a big veil of secrecy. A heavy feeling of dread had followed him along since discovering about her ill state. It was as if he had a sack of rocks in his gut, weighing him down constantly.

He kept having the same nightmare over and over again, each night, haunting him even in his waking state. Visions of his little monster screaming as she fought an invisible assailant in the dark tormented him to the point where he could no longer take it.

Tonight, he would finally discover the truth of the matter.

Tonight, he would pay a certain dark haired male a little visit.

Stretching his limbs, he let the darkness wash over him. He became one with the shadows, dissolving into the night as tendrils of gloom enveloped entire kingdoms, covering the Moon in an almost ebony membrane.

In a mere flash in the sands of time, he materialized on the vast dolomite terrace belonging to the heir of Nissa. It was in these exact chambers where he had last seen his precious warrior, in the arms of that undeserving man.

Clenching his jaw tightly at the bitter memory, he ground his teeth as pure possessiveness encroached his volatile system.

He was an idiot for abandoning her here, in the clutches of these unpredictable and treacherous royals. Only the King of Nissa was a worthy male, an honorable warrior and trustworthy ally.

Stepping through the open terrace doorway, he entered the darkened chamber. It was empty. Not a single trace of his sweet Duna. He searched the adjoining rooms. *Where is she?*

Not bothering with returning to his shadow form, he burst through the front doors and went straight to King Lucan's private residence. No guards stopped him on the way nor when he stormed into the monarch's chambers. *That's not right.*

The General found the ancient male sitting in his usual spot on a bench, piles of books stacked high on a table nearby. His head was buried deep in some old volume, completely unaware of the company that he had.

"That seems highly stimulating, to be reading it at this late hour." Strolling over to to the monarch, his hands in his pockets, he picked up a random book from the stack, inspecting its contents.

The King's eyes never left the words on the page as he spoke, his voice filled with irritation, "Do you mean to tell me that I'm too old to realize that I'm no longer alone?"

Cathal chuckled. The man still had his wits about him. "I would never dare insult you so, Lucan."

"But you would barge in here, uninvited."

"Why aren't there guards in front of your chambers?"

Finally placing down the text, the King sighed. "My son has gone on a mad rampage across the kingdom, taking every available soldier with him. It would seem that he lost something very dear to him."

"He shouldn't have left you unprotected."

"I'll be fine. I'm no use to anyone at my age." A sly smile bloomed on his wrinkled face. "Besides, I have you to keep me safe. Who would dare attempt anything when the mighty General of the Tyrossian armies is by my side?"

Cathal appraised him from the corner of his eye. "What did he lose?"

A moment passed, then two. The King stood up, coming up to stand in front of him. "A woman. A very *special* woman."

"What the hell is that supposed to mean?"

"It means, General, that your little companion has disappeared in the middle of the night. Not merely hours ago." The King walked over to his violet bellflowers, stroking their soft petals. Cathal's stomach dropped as awareness hit him. He was too late, he had missed her. "Where did you find the necklace that you gifted her?"

Confused about the sudden change of topic, it took Cathal a few moments before he finally realized what the old man was talking about. "It was her grandmother's. Duna had left it as a tombstone marker when she buried the woman."

"Yes, but – why did *you* have it?" He plucked a single flower from the vines. "It seems an awfully interesting happenstance, wouldn't you agree?"

"I don't believe in coincidences nor do I believe in fate, so whatever it is that you're implying, just spit it out already."

"Have you inspected the necklace before you gave it over to Lady Damaris?"

"Only briefly. It's a plain silver pendant trinket with a red gemstone in the center. Nothing special about it. Why?"

"For one who is known for his meticulous attention to detail, you surprise me, General. Has time finally taken a toll on you?"

This was getting them nowhere. "Are you going to just tell me whatever it is that you find so amusing so that we can get on with more important matters? Like why Duna would leave the palace? What did your son do to her?"

"You'll have to ask him that yourself – that is, if and when he returns. I don't believe we'll be seeing him anytime soon. He's developed quite the obsession with that woman." Turning back to Cathal, the King focused his ancient stare on the imposing male. "The more pressing issue is the fact that the necklace that you gifted Duna, the one that you say belonged to her grandmother–" he withdrew his own shining silver pendant from beneath his robes, "–is the exact replica of mine. Even the Star of Seba and the ruby red gemstone match to the exact miniscule detail."

Cathal let the man's words sink in as he waited for the monarch to continue.

"Do you know what compromises the crimson gemstone in the center, General?" Cathal shook his head of midnight black hair. "It's a single drop of blood from the Guardian of Seba. The precious stone is forged so that it can take only *one* drop of it and *only* that of the true Keeper of the Portal. Any other's blood would simply evaporate from the pendant, it wouldn't hold. So, the question is, how is it possible that there are two identical keys to the Gateway, and how did Duna's grandmother come by one?"

"It could be any ordinary trinket that resembles yours."

"Absolutely. Except, I had already tested it. The necklace, without a doubt, opens the portal. Which leaves me with only one conclusion." He stepped close to Cathal, his unnerving stare piercing him. "There is another portal on our Continent, and Duna's grandmother had been its Guardian."

"That's not possible. I have spent millennia searching for a way to reach Polaris. I would have found it had another one existed."

"You searched for one that was artificially made. There are forces in nature that can act as vessels for intrinsic gateways to other realms." The King appraised him. "Lakes, forests, caves – all anyone has to do is have the proper item on himself that will act as a conductor or a speckle of blood from the chosen ones appointed to guard the portals, and they would be able to travel through it." A sorrowful expression colored his features. "It must be hard, to be away from your home for so long. To not be able to see your dear ones."

Cathal swallowed, pain lacing his heart as he remembered what he was forced to leave behind. "You are mistaken. I have no one that matches your description." Everyone that he had ever had a tiny inclination of affection for had betrayed him. They were nothing to him now.

The King made his way over to the terrace doorway, taking his time as if memorizing his surroundings. Passing through onto the open space, he disappeared into the darkness.

The General followed him out, inspecting the ancient man as he stood stoic, observing the star filled sky, his face a mask of calm and determination.

"I have lived through centuries of loss, despair, tragedy, and turmoil. There is nothing that can surprise me anymore. Not even my own son, who has become the very thing that I had feared he would turn into as he matured. He has always been ambitious, sometimes to his own detriment. But it had never deterred him from doing the righteous thing. From being an honorable male." He paused. "Something has changed in him lately. He is not himself. As if another being has entered his mind, controlling him and his actions. I fear the extent to which he is prepared to go to fulfill his need for absolute power."

"I will keep him under control, Lucan. You have my word."

The King smiled, his features turning soft as he gazed up at the heavens. "You have been the only constant in my long life. I would not be standing here if it wasn't for you. I don't believe that I have ever truly thanked you for saving my life on those plains, General."

"That's not necessary. I would do it all over again if I was faced with the same choice."

"That is why I must finally do what I should have done many centuries ago." Turning to Cathal, he opened up his robes, revealing a menacing sword with ancient runes engraved on it's hilt and a blade of the brightest silver metal that Cathal had ever laid eyes on.

Unsheathing it, the King cupped the edge of the sword with the palm of his hand, and gripping it tightly, pulled it over his bare flesh. Dark red blood pooled in his fist, dripping down his fingers, coloring the white stone beneath their feet.

The male kneeled down then, lifting in his arms the magnificent weapon now drenched with his life's essence, extending it towards the midnight sky. His head bowed down low, he bellowed for all the world to hear, "I, King Lucan of the Royal House of Raidon, leader of the people of the mortal Kingdom of Nissa and the one true Guardian of Seba, eternally pledge myself to you." Black smoke simmered in the air around him.

"Please, do not do this. You do not owe me anything."

He grinned, a satisfied little smirk gracing his aging face. "In this life and in the next, wherever Fate takes me, I forever bind myself to the Supreme Lord and Ruler of the Realm of the Dead, knowingly forsaking my right of passage into the Afterlife. May you take my soul into the Underworld upon my death to willingly oblige you until the end of time."

Shadows erupted around the King, enveloping him as he remained kneeling on the dolomite ground. Cathal watched, horrified, as they swarmed the male's body, entering every one of his pores and cavities. Like a violent typhoon they raged on, cocooning him until he was no longer visible to the mortal eye.

The General pressed his hand through the blackening storm, stepping through into the tempest. The King straightened, locking gazes with him, as despair and frustration overtook him. "What have you done, old man? You have doomed yourself to a half-life. Your soul will never know peace now, for as long as I exist."

"It was worth it, Holy Prince. There is no greater honor than to be your loyal servant in the heavenly Kingdom of Khalfani."

CHAPTER
32

Trekking through the dense jungle, her wrists bound in front of her, Duna cursed the day that she ever laid eyes on the Prince of Nissa. She should have left him and his two companions rotting on the cold ground all those months ago in the forests of Tyros.

"Keep moving, we've got a long way to go."

Swearing colorfully under her breath, Duna placed one foot in front of the other, trying with all her might to not cut her soles even more than was necessary. She already had an ugly gash on the bottom of her left limb. It was a miracle that she had any use of the organ at all.

"Don't make me put a leash on you, Duna."

"I bet you would enjoy that, wouldn't you? Except your precious princeling would whip you if you ever laid a single finger on me."

"Don't be so sure that he won't do that very same thing to you for your little show of rebellion."

Snorting, she limped along through the thick foliage. "I'd like to see him try."

Mikella shot her a stern look, disapproval flashing in her bright grey eyes. "Let me give you a piece of advice, woman to woman. You should keep your mouth shut more often, especially around Madir. He doesn't appreciate being talked back to."

"Well, it's a good thing then that I don't give a rat's ass about his preferences."

"You should, you'll be seeing him soon enough."

Over my dead body. "I'm never going back. I would rather rot in hell than ever let him touch me again."

Sighing, the female warrior trudged on. "You don't have much of a choice, Duna. There isn't a place on this Continent where you could hide. He would only hunt you down and drag you back to the palace."

She stopped dead in her tracks, foaming at the mouth. "Are you hearing yourself? I am not some wild beast that needs to be captured and locked up in a cage, to be whipped and tamed as my master seems fit."

"Oh, for fuck's sake, enough with the dramatics." Grabbing her by the elbow, Mikella dragged her along through the wilderness. "It is for your own good, Duna. He means you no harm. Please, don't make this any harder than it already is."

"You're all delusional. Besides, how did you know where to find me?"

"I followed you."

"How? I flew here on a bird's back. Last time I checked, you don't have any wings."

"Hilarious." Smirking ironically, she shot Duna a stern look. "I saw you leave with the snow harpies. It doesn't take a genius to figure out that you'd be heading for Navajo. After all, that is where the rest of your company is."

She rubbed her aching wrists as pain laced through her body. "So Madir doesn't know that I'm gone?" Rustling of leaves followed their light footsteps, making Duna suddenly very aware of their surroundings.

"He wrecked the whole palace when he found you missing. A few of the guards even lost their heads."

"What?" Shock washed over Duna at the blatant display of cruelty. "But it wasn't their fault! If anyone is to blame for the current situation it is him, Madir. Had he not treated me in such a disgusting way, I would never have felt the need to flee in the first place." She heard it again.

"Look, I'm not saying that I don't agree with you, but–"

"Shut up," hissing, Duna grabbed Mikella by the back of her shirt, pulling the woman closer to herself. A soft, muffled sound reached her ears from their left.

The female froze, her gaze going wide as she perused the area. "What is it?"

Shaking her head, Duna whispered in her ear, "I can't tell, the trees are too packed together. We need to stop moving, maybe the creature will leave us alone if it realizes that we aren't a threat to it."

"You're insane!" Mikella hissed back, not turning her face away from the tree line. "I refuse to be a meal for these wild beasts."

"You shouldn't have followed me all the way out here, then." A low moan came from in front of them. "Untie me. Now."

"Absolutely not! Do you think me stupid? You'll run away the first chance that you get."

"Mikella, untie me *right now* and give me a fucking dagger." They were running out of time. A second growling noise echoed from behind them. She retreated until their backs touched.

Both women stared as two massive saber-toothed spotted tigers emerged from behind the bushes. Each one was at least two and a half meters long from head to tail with their powerful shoulders reaching to the top of the women's heads. A pair of fifteen inch long upper canine teeth hung down from their jaws. Deadlier than a two edged blade, they came to an exceptionally sharp point at their ends.

"Dear gods, what the hell is that?" Panic seized Duna's chest as the mammoth cats inched toward them, their yellow eyes locked on their prey.

"They're the smilodon. An ancient apex predator that roamed these rainforests since the beginning of time."

Closer they crept, circling the two women. "Now would be a good time to unfuckingtie me, Mikella!" Fumbling with the knife, she barely managed to untie her before the two beasts pounced on them.

"Run!" Bolting for the trees, they charged through the dense jungle, the smilodon chasing them. Duna could hear their ragged growls behind her, breathing in her ear as she ran for her life. Leaves upon leaves of the packed trees blocked their way, lianas hanging from the canopies like desperate lifelines.

Hearts pounding erratically, they came upon a small clearing in the middle of the foliage. Spinning around, she realized that they were alone. The smilodon were nowhere to be found.

"Where did they go?" Mikella's eyes were wide with fear as she frantically searched their surroundings. "Here, take this." Reaching into her chest strap, she withdrew a seven inch long blade and threw it over to Duna.

All encompassing silence washed over the clearing. Everything went dead still, as if the very air was sucked out from around them, their labored breathing the only sound echoing through the jungle.

Come on, where are you?

All she saw was a pair of yellow irises before the smilodon was on top of her. It loomed over Duna, a bear inch away from her face as she lay beneath it, its two sharp canine teeth dripping with saliva as the creature bared its teeth to her.

They stared at each other, beast and man, their eyes locked in a battle for dominance. Growling, the smilodon slowly lowered its head, its gigantic snout a hair breadth away from Duna's nose.

She held her breath, her lungs straining from exertion, not daring to move, lest a single wrong motion set the animal into a wild frenzy.

Gods, please, help me. She whimpered. *Please, I beg you.*

The smilodon tilted its head then, as if confused, not breaking their eye contact. It sniffed her, inhaling her mortal scent deep into its airways. Suddenly, it whined, licking her face with its moist tongue.

Stunned, Duna could only lie there on the warm Baqarian ground as the creature smothered her with affection. It nudged her neck with its snout, being careful as to not cut her fragile skin with its sharp teeth.

"I don't understand. Why haven't you eaten me?" The smilodon grimaced as if repulsed. Biting into her nightgown, it gently pulled her into an upright position. It inclined its head, as if acknowledging her, and silently padded back into the jungle.

Violent thrashing sounds reached her from deep within the rainforest. Duna's head snapped around as a sudden, piercing cry blasted through the air. *Mikella.*

Bolting in the direction of the fighting, she shook from horror, her heart pounding with fear for what she would soon discover. *Please be alive.* She gripped her blade, her knuckles turning white as she ran.

Another terrifying shriek bellowed over the trees. Dread washed over her as she frantically scoured the area for the female warrior. "Where the fuck are you?!"

A blood curdling scream cut through the humid air right in front of her. She jolted to a halt, her limbs trembling from apprehension at the horrific sight before her eyes.

Mikella lay on the ground, her clothes torn to shreds as blood leaked from deep gashes in her two legs. Her arms and neck were covered in deep cuts, crimson liquid dripping down onto her face from a wound in her forehead.

The other beast was circling her, his deadly paws swinging at the woman as she attempted to crawl away to safety. It seemed amused with the human's feeble attempts, taunting her like a cat would play with a mouse.

Not thinking about what she was doing, Duna jumped in between them, turning the smilodon's attention away from the woman. It hissed at her, furious to have its toy taken away.

Duna lifted her dagger as she got into a fighting stance, her eyes burrowing into the beast, all fear gone as she channeled it into raw power. "Bring it on, kitty cat."

It lunged for her, hissing and shrieking as she nicked it with the tip of her blade. She swung at it again, the weapon barely missing the smilodon's left forelimb. The creature tried going around Duna, turning its maddening gaze on the unmoving Mikella.

Her attention on her companion, she didn't see it move. Roaring, it pounced on Duna once more. She went down. The beast dived for her, its mouth gaping wide open as it prepared to bury its scalpel like canines in her jugular.

In a flash of black fur, the smilodon was thrown back. It thrashed on the ground as a massive four-legged shadow of the darkest night loomed over it, its brilliant white teeth clamped tight around the smilodon's throat. Deep red blood pooled on the ground underneath the creature, its shrieks of agony echoing through the jungle. In a final cry of despair, the smilodon went still, the life drained out of it.

All froze as the ebony black creature turned its monstrous head towards Duna, blood dripping from his fangs. Blazing ruby red eyes collided with hers, shocking her into awareness.

Her breath caught. It was the dire wolf from the lake. The one that had observed her as she had bathed in the woods by Captain Moira's barracks.

"What are you doing here?" she murmured as she approached the menacing animal, all sense of self preservation forgotten.

The dire wolf turned his whole body then, and sitting down on his hind legs, watched her as she strolled over to his side.

She extended her open palm to the beast's snout, allowing him to sniff her. Instead, he licked her, cleaning up the grime and dried blood from her arms.

Tilting his giant head, the dire wolf snuggled under her neck, rubbing his soft fur against her exposed skin. Her fingers glided through his thick coat, caressing the glistening black strands as he purred from pleasure.

Duna laughed, her body desperate for some form of relief from the tension. Mikella groaned on the ground, apparently alive but unmoving.

"You don't happen to be a healer, too?" The dire wolf licked her face. "No, I guess not." She sighed. "What I am going to do with her? She needs to be treated."

As if understanding her words, her formidable companion stood up on all four haunches and throwing back his head, howled into the approaching night.

Low pitched sounds emanated from his throat, rising and falling as he extended each subsequent howl over the next one. It went on for a few minutes, Duna's skin crawling from the bone chilling sound.

A chorus of howls answered him in unison. On and on they went, making Duna very aware of her pathetic human nature.

All she needed now was a pack of wild beasts.

"What do we have here?" a deep, raspy voice cut through her thoughts. She bolted behind the dire wolf, her mind already labeling the animal as her protector. "No need to hide, little lady, we're not going to hurt you."

Slowly, her eyes appeared from behind the creature. They landed on a man with skin of the richest, most lush almond hue whose height of six feet put him at an advantage over her. He was flanked by four intimidating guards.

Brown black curls ended just under the male's ears and a neatly trimmed beard and mustache adorned his defined facial features. A single gold hoop was attached to a straight wide nose. Amber eyes and a square jaw with a slight indentation in its middle embellished his handsome face. He was a substantial male, with elegant yet impressive muscles. Turquoise and peacock blue robes decorated his regal stature. A gold turban and matching band went around his toned waist.

"Are we going to play hide and seek or are you going to come out from behind that beast of yours?"

Stepping out from behind the dire wolf, she straightened, apprehension flowing through her over her distressed appearance.

"What, on earth, happened to you?" The male made his way over to the two of them, his piercing gaze perusing her clothes. He appeared to be completely unfazed by the massive creature whose threatening stare was watching his every move. "Roc, did you do this?" The dire wolf growled. "No need to be so touchy."

Duna found her voice. "His name is Roc?"

"Yes, we are old friends, aren't we, wildling?" The astute male patted her furry companion on the shoulder.

"What do you mean?"

"Exactly what I said. We go way back, to a certain incident when I was merely a young boy and I had found him roaming in my jungles. Seems to be getting more emotional over the years, however. Must be in accord with that broody master of his."

"Are you implying that this – *thing* –" she motioned her hands at the terrifying animal, "–is someone's pet?"

His eyes of molten copper brightened with amusement. "You are a strange one, aren't you?" Apparently so. Shaking his head, the formidable male walked over to where Mikella was lying motionless on the ground. Crouching down beside her, he examined the female's wounds. "How long has she been unconscious?"

"Since before you found us. We were attacked by a smilodon."

"I thought so, the wounds match their style of attack. It's a miracle you're alive." He stood up, his opulent robes billowing around him. Turning to one of his guards, he shouted, "Get the healers!" The armed male rushed back through the thick foliage from where they had first appeared.

After a few moments, he returned with two women in tow. The pair was dressed in long, plain red robes, their hair tied back with colorful bandanas. A stretcher was being carried behind them by two of the guards. Rushing over to Mikella, they wasted no time inspecting her. After securing her to the stretcher, they disappeared into the trees.

It all passed so quickly that Duna failed to register what was happening until the sturdy male began to withdraw into the trees.

"Wait, where are you going? Where are they taking her?" Running after him, she almost ran into his broad chest when he turned towards her.

"Best keep up, little lady. The smilodon are always on the hunt."

"What about Roc?"

"What about him?"

"We can't just leave him here." Freezing in his tracks, the man doubled over from laughter. "Well, I'm glad you find me so amusing."

Wiping the moisture from his eyes, he straightened up, his voice rasping, "Apologies. I mean no offense." Clearing his throat, he circled her, his keen eyes roaming over her body. "You'll clean up nicely. Indeed, you will be an excellent addition to my collection. If your friend is as entertaining as you are, you will both be rewarded considerably."

"Collection?" He ignored her. She tried to catch up to him as they emerged on the other side of the tree line. "Collection of what–" loud trumpeting cut her words short, her voice sticking in her parched throat.

Five gigantic grey elephants stood before them, shaking their heads as they lifted their trunks to the sky. Their ivory tusks were coated with brass, giving them sharp points. On each one was an impressive type of cabin made of light wood, with white sheets draping over its four sides.

Three servants were lifting the stretcher housing Mikella to one such cabin, a couple of female healers aiding them from atop the majestic bull as they awaited their injured patient.

Her mouth gaping wide open, Duna could only stop and stare at the spectacular sight before her. She almost failed to notice the man from before climbing up onto the largest of the bulls.

"Wait!"

"Your companion will be taken care of, don't worry. Only the Kingdom's most gifted healers are permitted to practice in the royal hospice." He disappeared behind the cabin's luxurious curtains, leaving Duna alone and confused.

"Little lady," a servant called down to her from a smaller elephant down the line, "please, hurry. We must be on our way."

Without another word, she was escorted up onto the monumental animal. Glancing up, her breath caught. The entire rainforest was spread out before her, the magnificent greens blending in with the blazing colorful flora that haphazardly sprung up between the towering trees.

Lurching forward, the elephant began to move. "Where are we going?"

The servant turned to her, a deep frown on his boyish face. "Do you not know?" Confused, she shook her head. "We are returning to the Grand Palace. You are to become His Highness' royal concubine."

She threw her head back, roaring with amusement at the young man's preposterous remark. "I don't think so. Your prince will first have to catch me."

"But he already has, little lady. You are now a part of Crown Prince Faiz's personal harem."

All blood drained from her body as she let the information sink it. Her eyes slid to the massive bull elephant leading the group, and the regal male in the turquoise and peacock blue robes that sat facing her.

His robust arms spread wide on the backrest behind him, his amber eyes locked on her as he dipped his head at Duna, silently acknowledging his newly acquired property and the truth that they both knew all too well – she had just willingly walked into another gilded cage.

FORGOTTEN KINGDOM CHRONICLES
· BOOK TWO ·

THE STORMS OF FURY

ISABELLA KHALIDI

ACKNOWLEDGMENTS

I would like to thank my parents who let my younger self walk around with my head in a book, even when it became a health hazard. To my family, for putting up with my long nights and never-ending piles of papers. To myself – for never giving up, even when others doubted me.

And finally, I would like to thank you, the reader, for giving my book a chance. I hope that it filled you with joy and a sense of wonder for the breathtaking world that surrounds us.

ABOUT THE AUTHOR

Isabella Khalidi has travelled all over the world until finally settling down in a small town in Europe. She is finishing up her medical studies while simultaneously helping out in her local family owned shop. From an early age she had shown love for ancient lore and mythology, igniting her dream of one day becoming a successful author. *The Snows of Nissa* is her first novel, with the *Forgotten Kingdom Chronicles* as her debut adult fantasy series, with *The Storms of Fury, The Sands of Titans* and *The Plains of Wrath* as the sequels. She is also a participating author for an adult fairy tale retelling anthology, with her story Buried Souls (a steamy dark fantasy retelling of Goldilocks and the Three Bears) as part of Vol. 3 – Down in Grimm's Dungeon.

For more news and the latest information follow her on Instagram @isabellakhalidiauthor.

WORKS BY ISABELLA KHALIDI:

The Storms of Fury:
https://www.amazon.com/dp/B0C199S14T

The Sands of Titans:
https://www.amazon.com/gp/product/B0C19B1FPK

The Plains of Wrath:
https://www.amazon.com/gp/product/B0C198SRTL

Down in Grimm's Dungeon: Volume 3 of Fairy Tales Reloaded:
https://www.amazon.com/Down-Grimms-Dungeon-Fairy-Reloaded-ebook/dp/B0CB2RVPS7

Printed by Amazon Italia Logistica S.r.l.
Torrazza Piemonte (TO), Italy